The Repulse Bay

The Adventures of John Grey

Book Seven

Frederick A. Read

A *Guaranteed* Book

First Published in 2010 by
Guaranteed Books

an imprint of The Guaranteed Partnership
Po Box 12, Maesteg, Mid Glamorgan, South Wales, CF34 0XG, UK

ISBN 978 1 906864 17 0

Typeset by Christopher Teague

Printed and Bound in the UK by
CPI Antony Rowe, Eastbourne

www.theguaranteedpartnership.com

Chapters

Foreword

John Grey and his friends make a voyage across the Atlantic, transit the United States by train to join their ship waiting to take them across the Pacific.

This extensive journey, will take them to several of the sleepy islands in the South Pacific.

For them it isn't a yellow brick road to follow, but the dotted blue line across very lumpy waters of the 2 largest oceans in the world, to end up in the land of Oz.

The friends make one particular port of call within the story, which takes them back to the island of 'free love'.

Therefore, the intimacy shared between John and his lover will be portrayed not so much as 'porn' but hopefully in a 'tasteful' manner to put across the implications of what takes place and also what had taken place previously in Book 5.

CHAPTER I

Just Relax

"**Officers** Grey, Larter and Sinclair, to see Mr Whateley." John stated flatly as they stepped over the gangway of a neatly kept ship.

The Bosuns' mate on the gangway nodded his head, asked them to follow him.

During their way through the ship, Sinclair remarked on how the brass work shone and how highly polished the lino was that covered the steel decks.

"Looks like somebody is fond of the old spit and polish around here, probably ex 'Pusser'." Sinclair remarked, and was replied by the escorting sailor.

"This is Mr Whateley's personal HQ which has to be kept this way when we dock alongside. He's always meeting and hob-nobbing with the rich or influential people around the world. Although it surprises me why he should see the likes of three ordinary marine officers." he sniffed, arriving at a large ornately decorated wooden door.

"This is his office. Wait here until you're called in." the sailor said, knocking on the door and entering the compartment.

"What a palaver. Still at least we're dealing direct with the top man holding the same position as Belverley, Invergarron and the other goons." Larter whispered, as the sailor reappeared telling them to go in.

"Good afternoon Grey! I see you've brought your two friends with you, which is good. Come and sit a while." Whateley said pleasantly, standing up and indicated the seats where they were to sit.

"Good afternoon Mr Whately. It's good of you to see us." John acknowledged, as Whateley shook their hands before they sat down.

"The fact you three are here tells me you wish to take up my offer.

You will be pleased to know that I don't give them out lightly nor too often, mind you. I can read your response two ways, namely from my point of view I'm gaining three very good officers, your former boss Belverley has lost three, even though you were branded as trouble makers." Whateley smiled, sitting back down into his chair.

Four well-dressed men entered the compartment, with a steward behind them carrying a large tray of drinks.

Whateley introduced these men to John and his friends, as the steward placed the drinks tray onto a large highly polished table then left.

"Now that we're all here and been introduced, we can start formulating some sort of planned careers for all of you. We don't have to delve into the finer details nor the formalities of having you vetted etcetera, as we already know of your, shall we say, individual performances.

So what I intend doing, is to give you the basic outline of our company, what we're about which is different to Belverley and his outfit. In other words gentlemen, we know all about you but you now have this rare chance to know a little about our shipping company." Whateley announced civilly then went into various details about the hopes and aspirations of the company, to where the three of them would fit into the scheme of things.

When Whateley had finished, three of the other men stood up speaking about policies or ongoing plans that involved other places they owned around the world, and how each man or woman in the company had a specific job or target to achieve for the success of the company.

Whateley finally rounded off the meeting by wishing them good luck, hoping not only they, but also both he and his staff would benefit from the momentous decision they had made to join the company.

John, on behalf of his friends thanked Whateley and the others, as the steward arrived to usher them out of the office.

"So you're to join the company! You lot must be privileged or something to get to meet up in a full board meeting. The rest of us have only gone through the normal shipping office channels to sign on." the sailor grunted, leading them into the saloon.

"You will wait here until Mitchell comes back from the meeting you've just been in. He'll see to you from here on. There are several V.I.Ps in the saloon at the moment, that's why the bar is open, So feel free to partake in some liquid refreshments, there's a light buffet over in the corner if you get peckish, it's on the house, so to speak. Your baggage will be brought to you shortly once you've seen him." the sailor informed them then left them to mingle with the others.

"I've just spotted one of my senior radio officer pals standing by the bar. You two go get us a seat, whilst I get the drinks. I won't be long." Larter suggested and left them.

John and Sinclair sat down on some empty chairs at a table, enjoying a smoke whilst waiting for Larter to bring the drinks.

"This saloon is something else, John. Look at the pictures on the bulkheads, never mind the pictures, I mean just look at the place. It's so opulent it's almost like being on the *Queen Mary* it is." Sinclair whispered, looking slowly around the place.

John too was taking it all in, feeling suitably impressed by the richness of the place.

"You'd expect this on a floating HQ. Maybe that's what the *Brooklea* looked like during her heyday. Still, enjoy it while we can as I don't suppose we'll ever get to sail on her." John responded, as Larter came over with the drinks.

"Here you are gentlemen. Drinks all round. Now who's turn is it with the fags?" he asked cheerfully.

"Cheers Bruce! Managed to chat with your old pal?" John asked, drinking deeply from his whiskey glass.

"Yes, I was surprised to find Johnny Rae here, he must have seen Macaroni to be transferred over sooner than we were. He said we were lucky to get a personal interview with the board of governors, which means that we're in for some interesting times ahead. That Mitchell bloke apparently is their Chief scout, or head hunter if you like, so he'll be the one that will start us off and get us assigned to our first ship." Larter replied jovially.

"You've both been in other shipping companies before. So then, what should I expect that's totally different from the Lea line?" John asked with uncertainty.

"Different ships different cap tallies, was the Royals motto, but pretty much the same. If you have a happy ship, and by that I mean a good crew who get on well together, then you'll not want to leave it.

According to Johnny Rae, this company is at the beginning of a golden era for it, which means we've joined it at the right time. Plenty of paid shore time if you want it, providing you earn your pay whilst at sea, as what Mitchell pointed out to us." Sinclair replied, while Larter nodded his head in agreement.

"John! Relax and let it happen and just enjoy the moment of your triumph over Belverley." Larter assured.

"My turn for the wets. Same again?" Sinclair asked, making his way over to the bar.

The afternoon slipped by as the other occupants of the saloon came and went, until finally Mitchell arrived apologising for his delay.

Larter went to the bar and brought back a fresh drink each, before they got down to business.

"So, to recap. I'm a full 2nd Engineer, Andy is now a 3rd Deck Officer, Bruce has his next rank up and our pay starts as of now. All three of us are going to Glasgow to join a freighter bound for Nova Scotia." John recalled in a courteous manner.

"Correct, so all you've got to do now is come to my office in the morning and sign your company contracts. In the meanwhile, I suggest that you make yourselves known to the Store-man on board, get your uniforms sorted out, and anything else needs to be done before we sail tomorrow." Mitchell said pleasantly.

"We're sailing back on this lovely vessel?" Sinclair asked.

"No. We're going to Southampton. You'll be catching the

night ferry over, where you'll make your way to your ship."

"There you are Andy! You'll be able to show the bosun how to sail his wee ship." Larter said with a grin.

Mitchell saw the obvious close bond between them and the friendly banter they enjoyed, which made him smile.

"It appears that you get on well together. We always like to have a happy crew on our ships so we can work around you three for our mutual benefit. Any questions or are you happy with what's been said?" Mitchell asked

"I have several questions to ask of you Mr Mitchell, most of which can keep until tomorrow. However, there's one mundane item we haven't discussed yet." John said quietly.

Mitchell looked at them for a moment before he realised what it was.

"Oh yes, glad you mentioned it. Here is some subsistence money to tide you over for tonight. You can sign for it tomorrow. Once you've finished your drink and conducted your business, you will leave the ship until 0900 tomorrow." Mitchell said, handing over a brown envelope to each of them.

"Thank you for your hospitality Mr Mitchell. See you then." John said, and standing up to watch Mitchell leave the saloon.

"Well gentlemen. You heard what the man said, so it's back to Mam's home cooking again. But first, I want to go to say s'long to Happy Day and the others. Coming along?" John asked, finishing off his drink.

"Home cooking sounds great, but I'd advise against going back into Belverley's den again. Especially when he finds out we've defected to his arch rival." Sinclair advised.

"I don't care a shit about him. Just as long as we get the money they owe us from the *Inverlaggan* inquiry, in case you two have forgotten." Larter said bitterly.

"As a matter of fact Bruce, that's one of the questions I shall be putting to Mitchell when we see him tomorrow. Anyway, let's go. We'll leave our bags with the steward before we go ashore. No sense dragging them all over the place is there. We'll have a drink or two at the Black Man pub next to our bus stop. Just follow me." John concluded, as they trooped off the ship and into the cool evening air.

CHAPTER II

A New Outfit

"Morning Mr Mitchell! Here we are, at the appropriate hour. Now where do we sign?" John asked, when they strolled into a well-appointed office, where Mitchell was sitting in a high- backed leather chair, writing in a large ledger book.

"Hello Grey; gentlemen! Just a minute, I won't be long." Mitchell responded, looking over the top of his horn-rimmed glasses.

They stood quietly, and patiently for a while until Mitchell slammed the giant book shut dropping it down onto a deck beside him.

"Now then gentlemen, let me get my bag of bumf and my other book from my locker. It contains all the records of each person employed within the company, mine included." Mitchell said amiably, fetching an equally large book from the locker, opening it to the appropriate page.

"Here are the company contractual agreements, the rule books, your new company pay and records log book. Just sign the contracts then the register book alongside your name as entered. Once done, we can complete the formalities for travel to your first assignment." Mitchell announced, offering John his fountain pen to use.

When they had signed the register, they received a collection of company literature and other document, with explanations given as each piece was handed over to them.

"It's almost like Christmas, what with all these gifts, and that." Sinclair declared with amusement, watching their collection getting bigger.

"Now that you've got some indicative reading to get on with, you might as well have your new uniforms too." Mitchell said with a chuckle, as a steward came in giving them each a large brown package to open in front of Mitchell.

All three did so, they were impressed by the crispness and smartness of their new uniforms, but most of all, their new badges of office.

"How much is this going to cost us Mitchell?" Larter asked, refolding his new uniform back into its packaging.

"It's all free, as is all your transport between ships, or between home and ship. Just observe our rules then all will be well. On the other side of things, we have a higher standard of disciplinary code than any other shipping line, so be advised to mark my words well."

"Well that's fair enough Mitchell. Now for some of my questions which I mentioned yesterday." John said civilly, Mitchell nodding his head and sat down to listen.

John briefly explained about their role in saving people from the sinking of both the *Chantral* and the *Inverlaggan*, along with the government enquiry and its recommendations.[•]

He also told Mitchell that they had, so far, not been paid as per those recommendations, even though everybody else including Belverley and his board of ship owners had been. And now that they had left the company, how would they go about getting what's due to them.

"In other words Mitchell, when do we get our share of the pay out?" Larter asked quickly.

Mitchell listened carefully to them, nodded his head in understanding their questions.

"It appears from hearsay, your previous company has already drawn your share of the award, which should have been give to you at least some 6 months ago, as far as I can remember the facts. If we had been involved, you'd have had it paid directly from the ministry not via the company books. That is one thing I can assure you, because I am the paymaster and the Chief accountant for the entire shipping line, including other associated companies amongst

---

[•] See *Fresh Water*.

other things I deal with." Mitchell said with concern.

"We have taken years to build up this shipping line as you've been told about yesterday, we're on our way up. Our ships are modern, manned by a happy and efficient crew. This is because we are square and above-board with everybody, indeed is what we demand it off each man in the company. Having said that, the only thing I can suggest is to leave it with me to sort out. I give you my promise I'll come back to you when I'm satisfied with the answers to some of my own questions I shall be putting to them. I can't be fairer than that." he added solemnly, taking off his glasses and laying them onto his table.

"That's fair enough by us Mitchell. It will suffice for now, and look forward to your deliberations in due course. Now that's been dealt with, we're looking forward to a mutual prosperity." John stated with sincerity.

"Okay then gentlemen, if that's the lot, then I suggest you get some lunch. Make sure you call into the Pursers office to get your travel documents before you leave the ship. Have a good voyage, gentlemen. Now if you'll excuse me, I've got a mound of work to do before we sail. On your way out, will you kindly send the steward in." Mitchell said, sitting down again at his desk.

"We know the feeling well Mitchell, so you're not on your own, no matter what trade you're in." John replied with a slight nod of his head, as they left the cabin.

"That was a delicious lunch steward, my compliments to the chef!" Sinclair said expansively then gave a loud burp, making everybody from the other tables look at him in disgust.

"Oops! Pardon me gentlemen." he said, wiping his face with his serviette.

"Excuse my friend, he's a pig!" Larter apologised loudly to the other diners.

"Tut tut Andy! You must remember you're an officer now. None of your hairy-arsed routines around these quarters!" John said with a deadpan face, but gave Larter a sly wink, wagging his finger in Sinclair's face.

"Yes 3rd Mate Sinclair! Your turn to get the wets!" Larter said with an equally straight face, holding out his empty glass.

"3rd Mate? My my, doesn't that sound grand. Fancy me being a 3rd mate! Only now that you've mentioned it, it does sound grand and pompous. Mind you though, at one time I was only offered a lousy 4ths job" Sinclair said with an ear-to-ear grin.

"Never mind the rank, but I think we'll have to take you under our wing this time, for a change Andy. No good showing up the rest of us, besides we've got standards to maintain you know." John riposted.

"Yes Andy, we'll get rid of your bad habits, because we eat with knives and forks not ruddy marlin spikes and shovels." Larter added, when Sinclair came back with a tray of drinks.

"Oh no you won't!" Sinclair said with a frown.

"Oh yes we will!" John and Larter said in unison.

"Oh no you won't."

"Oh yes they will!" said a voice.

They looked to see who had joined in and were pleasantly surprised.

"Hello gentlemen, remember me?"

"Well flippin' heck! How the devil are you Crabbe, erm Colin? Yes Colin that's it! What are you doing aboard here?" Sinclair asked with surprise, standing up swiftly and grabbing Crabbe's hand, shaking it vigorously, as did John and Larter.

"As you can see, I'm now 2nd Mate Crabbe, and this ship is my open-ended contract for the past year now. How the hell are you all? Tell me about yourselves! The last time I saw you all was during the Board of enquiry." Crabbe said, gladly sitting down with these three very special shipmates.

"We've been here, there, and everywhere, now we've just joined this shipping line today. We're about to leave for our ship in Glasgow. The thing is Colin did you get your share of the insurance money? Because we certainly haven't." John responded.

"Yes, I got paid directly from the Ministry of Shipping and Transport. I got an immediate interim payment of £500, with a further £2,000 a little later. But you three should have had an interim of nearly a £1,000 each, with several thousands to follow, if my memory serves me correctly. It's all spent now that I'm married to Glenda, the blonde secretary to one of the scientists who was with us." Crabbe said happily.

"What that tasty piece with the long legs that goes right up to her bum before she gets a bit cheeky!" Sinclair whistled as he looked up to the deckhead in his memory recall.

"Yes, that's her." Crabbe said with an air of cockiness and chuckled at his own good fortune.

"Some people get all the luck!" Sinclair responded by patting Crabbe gently on his back.

"Well anyway, back to the here and now. We've had a guts full of Belverley, so we decided to join this line. We've asked that Mitchell bloke to look into our payout, so hopefully we too can enjoy a few beers out of it whilst on our travels." Larter said, offering cigarettes all round.

"Mitchell! He's our Chief accountant. He'd get blood out of a stone he would, so Belverley had better watch out. Good man Mitchell, you've no bother on that score. By the way, the ship you're joining is a new one that's just completed its acceptance trials. Mr Whateley tries to ensure his best officers get to know their ship during a period before the rest of the crew join it.

Anyway gentlemen, we've got about 5 minutes before all visitors must disembark. Maybe next time you see this ship, you'll come aboard and we'll have a few noggins together. I must go now, so take care and look me up some time. Glenda will be very pleased when I tell her I met you all today."

"The feelings mutual Colin! We look forward to a glass or two, including this reprobate of a 3rd mate." Larter said with a grin, pointing to Sinclair's sleeves.

"Well done Sinclair! You deserve that at least. Listen to your fellow officers to put you straight on etiquette, which this company thrives on, especially ashore in foreign waters." Crabbe said shaking all three friends by the hand once more, then left the saloon in a hurry.

"I don't know about you two, but I've got a distinct feeling we're in God's pocket now that we've joined this mob. Anyway, time for us to lift and shift to a more familiar place, namely the Glasgow ferry." Sinclair said, picking up his baggage and hjs newly acquired paper parcel.

"Once more into the breach dear friends!" John quipped, following Sinclair with Larter, over the gangway to walk along the docks to the waiting ferry.

"Remember Andy, you're an officer now, so no going and showing off to the Bosun of the ferry." Larter said with a frown, which John twigged onto.

"It might be a wee boat in a bathtub, but…!" John commenced to say.

"All right! I give in!" Sinclair sighed, marching over the gangway onto the ferryboat.

"We've got a few hours steaming to enjoy a decent pint accompanied by the odd dram or three. So I think it's your turn John." Sinclair added, arriving into the crowded saloon.

CHAPTER III

Habits

"Here we go again, gentlemen. Last one over buys the wets." Larter said swiftly, leading them over their new ship's gangway to where a fresh-faced 4th Deck Officer was standing.

"Morning gentlemen. Come to join us?" the 4th Mate asked.

Larter introduced them to the 4th, who, by explanation, directed them to go into the saloon where the Purser would be found.

"Ah yes! Three more officers to the good! Welcome to the *SS Maple Leaf.* Come to my office and we'll sign your articles, allocate your cabins, etc." the Purser said taking them through to his office.

"You three have been assigned for another ship, but as your first task within the company, you will be working your passage across to Nova Scotia, but will enjoy the luxury of staying in the passengers accommodation area. Normal ships protocol is in force, so the three of you will introduce yourselves to your respective departments. You are advised that as you have transferred to this line, your retainer fee from your last line will be deducted from your next wage packet. I shall do the necessary paperwork, now that I've stamped your Books. Lunch is at noon but we'll be sailing shortly afterwards, so get yourself organised and be ready for the Captain's briefing at 1400." the Purser announced, handing them the keys to their cabins.

They thanked the man then left to get to know, first and foremost where the saloon was, then to their cabins before venturing into their respective departments

John made his way down to the engine room to find it was spotlessly clean, but put it down to the newness of it.

"Morning Chief! I'm 2nd Engineer John Grey." John greeted,

meeting a man in white overalls, examining some dials and pieces of machinery.

"Hello 2nd! I'm Nick Baxter. Glad you arrived early, as we've got a slight problem with No 2 turbine. Go into the office over there and find the maker's book on it. It is a large blue book and probably on the desk the fetch it to me if you would." Baxter asked politely.

John arrived back and gave it to Baxter, who flicked through the pages to find what he was looking for.

"Ah, here it is. We've got to take a cowling off the back to tighten up a few bolts. Yes, that'll do it. See the diagram John?" he asked, pointing out to the picture and descriptive remarks.

"Just a few loose bolts holding a secondary machine is that all Nick? Just as well it wasn't a foreign object in with the blades." John responded, taking hold of a spanner and assisting Baxter with the repairs.

During this time, John was told of his role on board until they arrived in Halifax, but that was as far as Baxter was able to tell him. This left John with a feeling of curious uncertainty which needed satisfying, so once they were finished, he thanked Baxter for the info then left to see if one of his friends could shed some light onto it.

"Hello Bruce. The Chief Engineer doesn't seem to have any further plans for me much beyond arriving in Halifax. Any suggestions?" John asked on entering the radio office.

"Hello John. As the Purser told us, we're off at Halifax to join another ship, but which one I haven't got a clue. I can't find any signal nor correspondence on it, so there's nothing through as yet, but you can bet we'll know when we arrive the other side of that ruddy pond. Mind you, I wouldn't mind a leisurely trip through the big lakes, as there's some spectacular sights along the waterways." Larter said slowly, whilst manipulating his large transmitter.

"This is Ron Underwood, the ship's Senior Radio Officer." Larter announced, as a well-built man stepped into the compartment.

"Hello Sparks!" John greeted, with nodding in reply.

"We need a new crystal for that frequency, unless you can get the aerial stabilised, Bruce." Underwood said softly, dumping a pile of books onto a table, making Larter whistle.

"It looks as if we've got some light reading to do Ron." Larter said, picking up one of the thick books to read its title, before tossing it back onto the pile.

"Well that's one book we won't have to worry about, Ron. It's for the MF/HF Transceiver in the corner. It has the same internal workings as the old B40 except it has a new BFO to tune into, that's all. Mind you the new VHF transmitter of yours looks pretty neat. I expect the skipper will be using it more often than you, so it would be prudent if it was patched through to the bridge on a permanent basis."

"Yes, I'm putting in a local switch control so he can change channels when he needs to save me from doing so every time." Underwood agreed.

"Anyway, my 2nd operator, Chris Boyall, will keep his eye on it for me, as he'll be on the bridge during harbour movements and the like." he added.

John sat quietly for a while, watching the two radio officers busying themselves, before he announced it was time for an early lunch before the Captain's briefings.

"We'll see you there as we've got a lot of work to complete, as you can see." Larter said affably, so John left a radio shack, which seemed to be far superior to all the ones he had visited in the past.

'Bruce would love one of those to himself no doubt. All mod cons by the look of it.' he reflected, arriving back into the accommodation compartments.

"2nd Engineer Grey! I've put your loan bedding and clothing away for you." the steward stated politely, standing with his hand on his hip.

John looked at the man and at his body language, but thanked him before shutting his cabin door quickly behind him.

'Yes, Julian is definitely alive and well, if this steward is anything to go by. Still, as long as he doesn't try to lift my shirt, he'll do' John muttered, getting himself ready for lunch.

Lunch was a delicious repast before they settled down to enjoy an afternoon cigarette and a drink. John was chatting to Sinclair about their short voyage when a 3rd Engineer came up to him.

"Excuse me 2nd. I'm the outside Engineer, Williams, can you spare a moment?" Williams asked.

"Hello Williams, what can I do for you?"

"I've got an acting 5th Engineer under my charge who needs extra tuition, cum engine-room duties. Any chance of you looking after him for me?"

"If you mean treated with favour, then you've come to the wrong person. I will treat every engineer on board, up to the rank of 3rd equally and fairly. That is to say, neither favouritism nor teachers pet; just equal share of my time. If you cannot wear that, then you'll have to wait until the ship gets its permanent 2nd. Why have you asked, is he belonging to you or what?"

"Yes, he's my younger brother, Ken. I promised our mother I'd see him right."

"Just as long as he does what's required of him, then he'll have no problems. I will however, let you into a little pet hate of mine. I hate slovenly Engineers, especially their shoddy workmanship so I shall be keeping my beady eye on you lot." John said with a deadpan face, but an inward smile as he remembered 'Spanners' Jones from the *Inverlaggan.*

"Thank you anyway 2nd." Williams said cheerfully then left, but John called him back.

"Williams! You will give me a conducted tour around the ship prior to it leaving tonight, as part of your daily rounds."

Williams looked non-plussed at this order and asked the reason for it, then told John that he didn't conduct any.

"You will make it a new resolution as of now 3rd. Meet me on the poop deck at 1500, with a new log book, something to write with, to accompany your torch and as standard issue wheel spanner." John ordered, when Williams started to protest.

"If you feel hard done by, then you should take up your complaints with the Chief Engineer. Let me know what he says when you muster as stated. Oh, and by the way! I have another pet hate, and that's been kept waiting, so don't be adrift!" he said sternly then dismissed Williams with a wave of his hand.

"I heard that 2nd and rightly so!." Baxter said, arriving from behind John's chair.

"Glad you did Chief! I've always conducted rounds twice a day at sea, especially prior to entering or leaving harbour. Good habits are easy to pick up, it's the bad ones I find hard to shake off the juniors."

"Snap! So I'm glad I've met up with a like-minded Engineer. Pity you're leaving us, as I could do with someone I can rely on. Still, can't have everything, even though we've got a brand new ship to play around with."

"That's just it Chief. New ships have the habit of producing unexpected problems just when you don't need them at the time." Sinclair stated, placing a piece of frayed rope in front of them.

"Well our engines are okay as is the rest of the machinery, so it's up to you sailors to sort out the knots and splices, 3rd. By the looks of it, you've got to reeve a new length of fore deck cargo rigging." Baxter replied, peering closely at the frayed rope.

"That's the one!" Sinclair said with delight.

"See John. It's not only you who knows a few knots or two." he added with a chuckle.

"Well, must get my bumf ready for the Captains briefing. But I need to see you after you've done your rounds with the 3rd." Baxter said evenly then left them.

"Looks as if we're in for a week of fun and games then Andy. By the way, just who is the Captain? I've not met him yet."

"He's Robin Bird. Known as Dickey Bird, but I met him several years ago as a 4th Mate. Then he was called, the ROBBIN bastard, because he was caught pinching from the crews' lockers. He's got a few fingers missing as we chopped them off for him. But for all that, he is a brilliant seaman. His claim to fame is that when he was a 3rd mate, he grabbed hold of a heaving line attached to a tow rope, then jumped overboard and swam to a stricken ferry boat. Once he secured it to the ferry, he swam back again taking charge of the tow to bring the stricken ferry back to safety again. Got the George Medal for it he did. He doesn't remember me, but if he should come the old one two with me, then I'll soon jog his memory."

"Well whatever, Andy. Glad you're a friend of mine, as I certainly wouldn't like finding a severed dick head stuck on the end of my bunk when I woke up in the morning." John chuckled.

"No indeed, neither would I, to be honest." Sinclair said with a grin, as the stewards cleared away the lunch debris and tidied up in time for the two principle officers to arrive to deliver their pre-voyage briefing.

"This is probably your first time to witness one of these briefings, Andy. So just listen up and answer any questions that may be put to you. In the meantime, how about you getting the drinks before he arrives! Here comes Bruce, so I'll keep the seats."

Sinclair smiled at John, tugging his forelock.

"Yes Bwana! On my way Bwana!" he said then left to get their drinks.

"Welcome to the *SS Maple Leaf*," the Captain announced.

CHAPTER IV

A Horse Shoe

The *SS Maple Leaf* sailed down the Firth of Clyde, turned sharply to starboard and passed the rounded tip of the Mull of Kintyre, before turning hard to port and into the open Atlantic, for her very first swim in this unforgiving ocean.

John was in the engine room giving engineering instructions to the small group of junior Engineers, taking them around the various metal parts of the engine room.

Once he had finished, and detailed them off to do various tasks, it was his turn to take charge of the engine room whilst the Chief rested in the engine room office.

The ship was an oil burner with two large boiler rooms, which turn the water into steam. The steam gets heated up again to produce super heated steam, which is piped along to the turbines that eventually turn the propeller shaft. This type of propulsion is to make the ship commonly known as a steam turbine ship. If it was driven by diesel engines then it would be called a Motor Vessel, which were becoming more prevalent as the marine engines were going through their own evolution, just like the outside of it on the upper deck.

As a new freighter in its day, she has two arrays of derricks, both fore and aft, with a much slimmer mid-ships super structure, and a high bow and poop deck aft, compared to a general cargo ship. She is 550 feet long, 80 feet wide, and registered as a 30,000 tonner, which means she can carry up to 30,000 tons of cargo plus room for 10 passengers. Her normal cruising speed is 18 knots with a range of a good 15,000 miles without refuelling. She has almost a flat bottom, with a maximum draught of only 20feet, because she was built purely with the Great Lakes of Canada and its canal waterways in mind.

As with all flat-bottomed craft, they are prone to capsizing in medium to large waves that the oceans of the world are littered with even on a calm day. That is why they need to be weighed down to their maximum draught, to prevent such an accident, although the *Maple Leaf* was fitted with bilge keels instead of stabilisers to keep her steady.

John strolled along the upper deck taking in the fresh sea breezes making his way towards the saloon for his lunch.

"Hello Andy. I see there're twice as many cargo derricks on her, given the size for size of the *Inverlogie*." John greeted, meeting up with Sinclair who was sitting at a table.

"Yes John, not only does she handles well, the crew's quarters are of a much higher standard than any the Triple Crown can muster." Sinclair admitted.

"Well the engines are pretty much standard stuff, as is most of the machinery I've seen so far. Having said that they've got a new fridge system, which looks pretty much based on what I produced for the *Inverlogie*. Maybe Joe Tomlinson or Happy Day have some sort of hand in that, but who cares." John said, with a shrug of his shoulders.

"Come now John, it seems as if you're regretting joining this outfit. Me! I'm happy as a pig in shit,
so is Bruce, from what I see of him."

"Oh yes, and so am I Andy. Can't think why I joined the Lea line in the first place." John stated quickly, as a steward served him his lunch.

"And so say all of us! You'd be hard pressed to find another freight line as generous as this one. I was on the ruddy Cathays Steamship Company before joining this line, some five years ago now. As long as you prove your worth on board for what they're paying you for then you'll have a great time." the lisping steward remarked, overhearing John's last statement.

"We thank you for your inside knowledge steward, maybe you'll fill us in with other little gems during the trip. We were invited to join, which I suppose makes all the difference." John replied.

“Indeed it does, therefore you will be among the privileged few to join some of the other officers and men on board. I count myself lucky to be amongst them, and by the way, my name is Denzil Phillips, but as I'm your steward you can call me Daisy!” he bragged, leaving them to serve some more officers that had just arrived.

“We have a good four days steaming before we arrive, so perhaps it would be in all our interests to gain as much inside info as we can on this outfit. Who knows, it might be very handy one day. Although having said that, knowing Bruce he's probably already half way through the company rules and regulations book by now. Good to have a friend like him, what Andy?”

“What's what?” Larter enquired cheerfully having just arrived at their table.

“John was just saying we've got to the other side of the pond to suss out what this company is all about. He mentioned your legal brain and, shall we say, knack of finding out the nitty gritty from their rules and regulations.” Sinclair stated, moving around the table to give him more room.

“Ah yes. Ron Underwood lent me his ‘company bible’, which makes good reading so far. Anyway from what I have read, it looks as if we're in for a very profitable adventure with them, providing we prove our worth on board and do what we've been paid to do.” Larter admitted.

John and Sinclair exchanged looks of mild surprise when they heard Larter make almost the same statement as Phillips.

Larter looked at their faces and asked what he had said for them to be surprised.

Sinclair repeated nearly word for word what the steward said, which almost tallied exactly to what Larter had said.

“Oh well then. It proves I'm reading the right book then.” Larter quipped, and started to dine.

When the friends had finished their meals they went out on deck for some fresh sea air.

“Well at least the oggin is behaving itself this time around.”

Sinclair joked.

"Mind you we could do with the 'Mad Monk' on this occasion as we're destined to go further north right into the white giants back yard." Larter teased.

"Now don't start that again Bruce. I remember your flippin' Sargasso Sea wind up, which turned into a proper nightmare." John chided mildly.

Larter laughed when he was reminded of the incident.

"But then you were as green as the proverbial grass behind your lug-holes." Larter countered, receiving a gentle poke in the belly for it.

Sinclair had been told before about John's little wind up and attempted to tease him again.

"Hang on now! Is this get John week or what? Because I'm onto you two! I've got my beady eye on you two you know!" John laughed, mimicking his late Chief Engineer Jones.

"John, can you remember those bolts we tightened up the other day? The ones we had to use a torque spanner on?" Baxter asked, as John was about to go off watch.

"Yes Nick, why?"

"One of the stokers reported seeing one of them which must have sheared off, fortunately for us it dropped into the engine room bilges." he replied, holding out the offending bolt for John to look at.

"Better tell the Captain that we'll be dropping speed for a while, for it looks as if we've got to shut down that turbine Nick. I've seen this before on one of the new '*Bay*' line tankers I happened to be on at the time." John said urgently, then went on to explain what he perceived the problem to be, and how he had tackled it at the time.

"No wonder the bolts were bloody tight. They must have been American instead of British Standard Whitworth, left handed thread instead of right, to boot." Baxter nodded, and picking up the engine room phone spoke into it.

His reply was given by the ringing of the telegraph repeaters in the engine room, which jangled loudly as the speed orders were changed from full to half ahead.

"Right then John, get some suitable replacement bolts whilst I get the machine stripped down. We might as well check the turbo blades while we're at it, as they're not sounding very healthy."

"I'll send a stoker with them, and remain on watch until you're happy with it!"

"No John, I need you to help me with this" he said then calling the Chief stoker and Williams the 3rd Engineer over and briefed them as to what was happening.

"Williams, this will be a good workout with the problem I gave you to do. Do a good job and write it up in the proper manner, then submit it to me during your 'teach in' tomorrow." John advised, before they left to sort the wayward machine.

Both men worked systematically for several hours before they were satisfied to feel safe to engage the turbine back on again.

"We had to make those modifications else we'd end up with a blown turbine John. You alter the drawings accordingly whilst I make out the amendment report. When finished, both our names can be registered as a confirmation to what we did."

John looked at his watch, tapping it to show Baxter.

"I think we'd better relieve Robinson and the Chief stoker, or they'll think we've forgotten about them. Robinson is supposed to be on now but he's already completed one full watch whilst we've been here."

Baxter nodded in agreement wiping his hands clean on a nearby rag.

"You take his watch for him John, but I'll be down early for my next one to relieve you. See you in three hours. Try and get those plans done during your watch. Maybe you can give Leading stoker Phillips an hours practice at taking charge, but you'll observe him all that time." Baxter suggested.

"Sounds okay with me. See you later then!" John replied, as Baxter made his way up the vertical steel ladder, out of the boiler room.

John relieved Robinson who was glad to see him, but the Chief stoker opted to remain on watch so he could monitor Phillips.

"That's good of you Chief. I'll be in the office if you need me. But let's inform the bridge we're back in business. Stand by to obey telegraphs again!" John directed.

The *Maple Leaf* swam peacefully across the Northern Atlantic as if she had been doing it for years. The ocean must have taken a liking to her, as it never threw a tantrum or cast its mountainous seas against her. Not even the Hodgson giants came near to bother her, so she was looking for a peaceful maiden voyage after all. Except for the patch of ocean off the Newfoundland coast that is.

John had just come from the saloon, making his way up to the radio shack when he looked out to seaward.

"Bloody hell!" he shouted, racing into the bridge instead. He found with total surprise that it was Crabbe who was the officer on the bridge, but quickly explaining about his experiences on the *Brooklea,* expressed his concern about the large impenetrable cloud of sea fog billowing swiftly towards them.

Crabbe moved quickly out onto the bridge wing, to make his own assessment of the situation as John looked at the radar screen, which showed a large blank area on it.

"Bloody hell John! I knew to expect sea fog in these waters, but I didn't expect it to develop as quickly as that." Crabbe said, rushing to inform the Captain in his bridge cabin.

Bird came striding out of his cabin armed with his binoculars, starting to scan the area around the ship.

"Port 15. Steer 195. Unless we can skirt around it, then we'll have to get all non-essential crew on deck, get prepared for the worst " Bird stated emphatically.

"On second thoughts! 2nd Mate! Get all off watch crew on deck to provide several crash fenders over the starboard side as you can. 2nd Engineer, I don't know why you're on the bridge, but advise your men below we're going blind shortly for a while." he countered sharply.

'Here we go again. But thankfully there's no Trewarthy this time.' John sighed, carrying out his orders.

The ship started to run away from the blossoming cloud of thick fog, but was quickly caught and was enveloped in a grey misty shroud which finally engulfed her completely in its deadly clutches.

John whispered to the helmsman to tell his assistant to start writing down all that was happening on the bridge, logging all orders and who said what to whom.

Crabbe came back shortly reporting that 3rd Mate Sinclair was on deck taking charge, and that the First Mate was on his way.

"Right then 2nd Mate! I have the conn. Get yourself down below, gather a damage control team together then position yourself aft of the superstructure. 2nd Engineer, you team up with the 2nd mate but make sure the 3rd Engineer has his fire fighting equipment ready on deck, as we just might need it. Someone get me the senior Sparker." Bird directed, calmly.

Crabbe and John rushed down the companionway ladder getting their equipment and the men organised before reporting to the bridge they were ready.

"Well Colin, it has been a total surprise to find you on board here considering you were last seen on the HQ ship, but here we are back in action together again. Pass the sandwiches if you please." John said quietly, emphasising the word 'sand'.

Crabbe looked at John for a moment before he recognised the phrase, which started a private little conversation between them lasting seemingly for hours.

During this time the fog got thicker and was getting more difficult for the men to see each other even though they were standing next to each other. The foghorn was sounding its very low, forlorn message to tell any ship out there to beware of them.

"2nd Mate! It's me, Able Seaman Magness. Me and my mate can

hear swishing sounds on the starboard side, come and listen." Magness whispered, tugging at Crabbe's foul weather gear fiercely.

John followed them to listen for a little while, but could hear nothing.

"Colin! Fog has the habit of warping sound, so that it appears to come from one direction but is in fact coming from another. If my hunch is right then we'd better keep a sharp lookout for'ard and to port. Send a runner up to the bridge to inform the Captain, but tell him to report back to us on the foc'sle. C'mon, let's get there pronto." John said quickly, literally grabbing hold of some of his men, telling them to make their way forward, as fast as they could.

"You take the starboard side with your men Colin, and I'll take the port. You know the plan, so stick to it no matter what." John commanded, as the group of men rushed onto the for'ard cargo deck.

John found a bale of rags telling his men to roll them into bundles, attach them to heaving lines then light them and dangle them over the side, to try to illuminate the ships side, then running over to Crabbe telling him to do the same.

No sooner had he arrived back to his own group of men, when there was a loud noise coming almost right next to the ship.

"Stand by all fenders and crash mats, forward of No 2 derrick! John shouted, just as the bow of a small ship appeared out of the gloom.

The other vessel must have seen them because it veered sharply away, only scraping down the side of the *Maple Leaf*.

John heard the clanging of telegraphs, loud curses and other noises coming from the unknown vessel, before a voice, aided by a loud-hailer aided voice was heard, which also alerted Crabbe who raced over to join him.

"Sorry whoever you are. I'm the fishing vessel *Sara Lee* out of St Johns. Managed to see your flares. I'm in company of six other fishing vessels who should all be in line astern of me.

We're in a string of about 1 nautical mile, and I'm the lead boat!" the man shouted.

"Bloody hell Colin! Quick, get somebody onto the bow over onto the starboard side. If they're joined up like we were off the *Inverlaggan*, then we're probably in the middle of them as if inside a horse shoe." John shouted, and grabbing two sailors helped them bring their large crash fenders up onto the bow.

He met the 3rd Engineer on the other side and told him to get his men to fend off the oncoming fishing vessels.

John managed to locate Sinclair, who was already on the starboard side directing his men.

"Stand by for at least three fishing vessels Andy. They're all joined up just like we were off the *Inverlaggan*. We met the lead vessel on the port side, who managed to see our flares in time to avoid a full collision." he shouted.

The fishing vessels harness keeping them together got snared by the bows of the *Maple Leaf* so that they passed either side of her almost, colliding side on as they sandwiched her.

The *Maple Leaf's* crew grabbed heaving lines thrown to them by the fishermen, as each smaller vessel was secured alongside her, like a mother hen gathering up her chicks.

Once the smaller vessels were safe, their crews scrambled over the side and onto the *Maple Leaf*, to congregate on the for'ard cargo deck.

Crabbe went over to speak to them whilst John and Sinclair came up onto the bridge to tell the Captain what had happened.

"3rd mate, ask the 2nd mate to bring the skippers onto the bridge, but get their crewmen into the saloon. 2nd Engineer, check the ship for damage both internal and external, in case some of their net booms have pierced us. First Mate, get the cargo derricks operated to move the fishing vessels aft of the bridge. I want to be able to navigate my ship without any further obstructions." Bird ordered.

John went back on deck with Sinclair, asking him to stay with him whilst he checked for damage.

"Thank God they were small fishing vessels, not the big whale factory ships usually in abundance around these waters, John!" Sinclair stated, finding that the damage suffered was limited to the odd dent or paint scuffing.

"Then it's just as well I remembered a few lessons from the old *Brooklea.* I can remember that bloody nightmare like it was only yesterday, Andy!"

"I was on the bridge for the last one. Now I know what you must have gone through. Each time this sort of thing happens, it's always a different story in some way or another. Which means you can't use the same tactics on every one. Still, we managed to avert a hefty shipping repair bill, on this occasion. Not bad considering we're only on passage, John. What do you say about that?" Sinclair responded, helping John up off one of the fishing vessels.

"I don't mind playing the Good Samaritan Andy, it's just all the damn paperwork afterwards that gets to me. As this is probably your first action on deck so to speak, you'll be required to submit a lengthy report, mark my words."

"You seemed to forget John, it was me that had to write a tome as a report from the *Inverlaggan* saga. This will be a doddle in comparison."

"Oh sorry Andy. Yes, I'd forgotten about your 200 page report. I'll bet you had to pay a scribe to do it for you though, probably costing you a good crate of malted drinks, if I know you."

"Aye, that it did John! Anyway, I'm satisfied my end, if you are, then lets get out of this bloody stuff and get ourselves somewhere warm. No doubt the unexpected guests will give us a hand to sink a few drams, as if we ever needed it."

"You carry on Andy, I'll see you shortly, as I've got to check the 3rd Engineer is okay." John chuckled and the friends parted company.

"3rd Engineer! Williams!" John shouted, to be suddenly meet up with him and almost face to face. "Get your men stood down then return your equipment. Make sure all deck machinery is in good order before you secure." John ordered, appearing suddenly next to the man.

"Christ! You nearly gave me a heart attack appearing out of the fog all of a sudden." Williams gasped.

"Sorry about that, but did you get what I said?"

"Yes 2nd! I need to survey the ship for damage, but hopefully it won't take me too long."

"I've already conducted a damage control search of the ship and have found nothing to be concerned with. As I've done the search it'll be me to make out the report, so you can relax. However, if you feel the need to remain on deck, then make sure you've got a companion, in case you disappear over the side without being noticed. Especially in this bloody pea-souper."

"Thanks for the warning, but I think I'll take your offer and get to the saloon a.s.a.p." Williams said slowly then left.

CHAPTER V

Special Arrangements

The ship crawled along slowly through the thick fog in case she bumped into another bunch of fishermen who might wrap themselves around her like barnacles.

Bird had the fishing boats manned by their own crews again, then got them to string along behind him so he could tow them out of the area. This lasted for another day, before the fog bank suddenly disappeared almost as quickly as it arrived.

The life-line cum tow-line was slipped so the fishermen could make their own way while the ship made full speed toward her own destination, Halifax in Nova Scotia.

John was off watch when they entered harbour in daylight this time, allowing him to gaze around the place remembering the last time he was here.

"Looking for a run ashore this time John?" Sinclair asked, arriving next to him.

"If what you tell me is correct, then yes. But the red light district will be the last thing on my mind, as I would like to explore the place first. Providing of course we've got enough time on our hands before we join our new ship."

"I've been speaking to some of the sailors who have been in the line a while, who tells me that the line only brings their ships here for marshalling or despatching. Else we would have gone up the St Lawrence into the Great Lakes to join all the others."

"That sounds odd Andy. Still, let's hope the next ship is as good as this one. Anyway, we've got to report to the Pursers' office as soon as we dock. That being so, I'd better get my loose ends tied up here as three certain young Engineers will be in the lurch if I don't."

"Oh you mean it's because you were their instructor you've got to mark their homework so to speak?"

"Something like that Andy. It goes with the territory and all that.

See you in the saloon first before we go to the office." John said, waving to his friend then left.

"John, there you are!" Baxter exclaimed, meeting John in the doorway of his cabin

"I was on my way to see you Nick. What can I do for you?"

"I have a bag of stores, instruction books and other items for you to take with you to give to your new Chief when you meet up with him. I'll have it ready on the gangway for you. As for your reports on your charges whilst on board, I've rubber stamped them as well as your damage report. That being said, I have filled in my report on your own conduct, which is in this sealed envelope for you to give to your new Chief. You will also be given a report from the Captain, which will be handed to you in the Pursers office, whatever you do, don't open them. You will classify them as 'sealed orders' "Baxter advised him.

John was taken by surprise and asked point blank what the reports had to say, stating that he had a right to know.

"You can rest assured John all is in good order. You will soon learn this is the way things are done in this shipping line. Everybody has a record of achievement and conduct, which gets filled in after each voyage. The management then uses it to gauge whether promotion, or in some cases demotion, should be handed out to those who are in line for one. Acting 3rd Engineer being a prime example of getting promoted, but the 4th Engineer will get his cards. Get my drift?"

"Well if you say so Nick. I have no fear of what's been said about me that's for certain. Now if you're finished maybe you'll let me give you my last report." John countered, handing Baxter a large brown envelope, explaining the basic outline of its contents.

"Thank you John. As I said to you at the beginning of this voyage, it is good to meet a like-minded person. Again thanks for your help and I wish you luck on your new vessel." Baxter said with a smile shaking John's hand in farewell.

"Thank you for the ride Nick. Hope to see you again some time." John said with a mock salute, leaving Baxter's cabin to get to his own.

"Hello Daisy, I see you've got everything all packed for me, like as if you're glad to get rid of me or something." John said with a grin.

"Yes 2nd, and your two friends. I want an early finish so that I can get ashore earlier. Me and the chef have got, erm, special arrangements ashore, shall we say."

"You lucky sod! This is my second visit here yet still I get no run ashore. Any idea as to which ship I shall be joining? Can you see her in harbour?"

"There're two other ships of the line tied up ahead of us, but I can't see which one you'll be going on as those are going onto the lakes." Phillips replied when he finished looking out of the porthole

"The mystery thickens, steward. Never mind, the Purser is bound to know. Anyway, here's a £5 for your run ashore, as a thanks for your help during this voyage." John said, slipping his overalls off and packing them into an open holdall.

"I'll make sure you haven't overlooked anything before I leave, so off you go now and good luck." John said, waving the departing steward off.

"Afternoon gentlemen. First off I have to read out this statement from the Captain, then give you a sealed envelope you will treat as 'sealed orders' which you will hand in when you board your next ship." the Purser stated civilly, then read out the statement.

When finished, they looked at each other in quiet amazement for a moment before John spoke

"My, that was a bit of all right Andy. What do you say to that Bruce?" he whispered.

"What you have stated is exactly what we three do on board ship Purser. Pity Belverley didn't appreciate us as he should have. Maybe we can call it our calling card to the management, shall we say." Sinclair replied quickly, which was backed up by Larter.

"Well, at least you know rather than being tempted to open your envelopes. Speaking of envelopes gentlemen, I have some more to give you, starting with your pay packet, along with your special travel arrangements in it." the Purser said with a grin, handing each of them a thick white envelope.

Sinclair opened his and peeking inside to see what was what, got a big surprise.

"Bloody hell! Must have come up in the pools or whatever!" he exclaimed, pushing his nose into the money and breathing deeply.

"Ahh smell that! Nearly forgot what paper money looked like, Purser!" he quipped.

John and Larter merely slipped theirs into their coat pockets, and asked what other envelopes they were to get.

The Purser produced a large brown envelope, tipped its contents onto his table then explained what was what before gathering it all up then handing it to John.

"As you're the senior officer Grey, you will be in charge of your group. Any questions?" he asked politely.

"Only one Purser. What happens if we hit a snag, or need support? Who can we approach or get in contact with?" John asked.

"You have a list of people who you can contact in emergencies, but you'll be in the company of one of our management team some of the way at least. You will meet him ashore, as he's waiting for you even as we speak. I have a taxi coming to pick you up, so you'd best be on your way, so good luck to you."

"Yes, thanks Purser. Maybe we'll meet again someday." Sinclair said as the friends shook the Purser's hand, shutting his office door quietly as they left.

"Right then skipper, which way is it?" Larter grinned, looking at John.

John picked up his bag, handing it to Sinclair.

"Here Boy! Carry my luggage for me." John chuckled, pointing to the gold rings on his arm.

"Yes boss! Ah's a comin' boss! Yo sho is de man!" Sinclair said, pretending to be a black slave, which made them all laugh as they went over the gangway onto the stone quay to a waiting taxi.

"Where to Mac?" the taxi driver asked, flicking the dog end of his fag out of his cab.

"To the railway station if you please." John replied, as they settled down for the ride.

"This line certainly doesn't hang about do they. You've only just docked when I got the call to pick you up!" the driver stated as he drove along.

"We've only been in this line just over a week. Maybe we've just missed our ship because they're sending us by rail to catch up with it at its next port of call." Larter responded, looking at the wad of railway tickets John held in his hand.

The answer seemed to satisfy the curious taxi driver, who remained quiet until they arrived at the station.

The friends piled out of the vehicle dragging their baggage with them.

"How much is it?" John asked, delving into his pocket to pay the man.

"You don't pay me. You should have been given a chit of paper for me to sign, for me to hand it in." he informed them.

John flicked through the sheaf of tickets, the bits of paper until he found the one the driver had mentioned. He asked Larter for the use of his pen then signed the chit before handing it to the man.

"Cheers. Now all you've got to do is go through those big double doors and hand in your travel pass. Good luck men." the man said, tooting his car horn then drove off again.

They gathered up their baggage again walking quickly into the railway station then made their way over to what looked like the ticket office.

"I have a travel warrant for three. Please advise me which train and platform we will use." John asked the sullen faced man behind the window-pane of the ticket booth.

The man took the warrant, looked at it for a moment then issued John with yet another sheaf of tickets and bits of paper.

"Here you are Mr Grey. Here're all your tickets to New York. Your seat passes, meal vouchers, and luggage tags. Your train is standing at platform 4, due to leave in half an hour. Just board the train anywhere, where you'll be seen to by the carriage steward." he said offhandedly in a flat voice, pointing to the general direction they were to take.

"Thank you I'm sure." John said airily, turning to dish out the travel documents.

"Platform 4 he said. Let's go gentlemen. It makes a change to travel by rail than fly. Although it would have been quicker." John said, as they strode purposefully through the ticket barrier onto the platform.

"Bloody hell! Look where the engine is. You'd need a ruddy telescope to see it." Sinclair stated, stopping to look at the length of the train.

"Let's get on here." Larter suggested, and climbing up the wooden steps boarded the train.

A smartly dressed black man met them at the doorway asking to see their tickets.

John told him that the three of them were travelling as a party and had seats reserved for them, then produced their seat reservation tickets.

"Welcome to the Boston & Maine Railroad. This is the *President Wilson Express* train to New York. We shall be leaving in 20 minutes, so follow me to show you to your reserved seats." the big man said politely.

They were taken through some open seated carriages of the train to their sleeper cabin which was neat and well appointed, with ample space between the facing two-tiered bunks.

"You may leave your baggage in your compartment if you wish to sit with the rest of the passengers. The refreshment and diner cars for this part of the train is just one carriage behind you if you care for a refreshment, but wait until I give the announcement over the address system."

"How long will it take, erm, Basil?" John asked, spotting the telltale name-tag on the man's lapel.

"Usually 12 hours, but due to a railroad speed restriction on the Boston section we'll take a further 2 hours or so, give or take a few minutes. We're due New York Central 0700 Standard Time. Evening meals will be served from 1900, and early breakfast at 0600, be sure you're seated in the diner car by then. Oh, a word of caution! Make sure you lock your cabin door before you leave."

"Thanks for the tip Basil. Have a cigar on us for now." Sinclair chirped, stuffing a fat cigar into the steward's top pocket.

"Thank you sir. I'll definitely enjoy that one." he smiled, seeing the size of the cigar, then left to fuss around other passengers that had arrived.

"Well! Here we are again on the move. Better give you two your own travel documents in case we get split up or they somehow get lost in transit." John advised, passing them several pieces of paper and bits of cardboard.

"Who's this management body we're supposed to meet, does it say John?" Larter asked.

John scanned their instructions, before handing it over for the others to read.

"According to these, we'll be meeting him in New York, but nothing mentioned about a ship. Maybe you can suss it out Bruce." John added, for Larter to read it whilst Sinclair looked over his shoulder.

"So we've got a choo-choo ride to New York. Still, as long as the company is paying the tab, I don't give a monkeys." Sinclair said, handing out the cigarettes.

"It says here that a Mr Bell will meet us off the train as he's got further instructions for us from there on." Larter said after a while.

"Well something to go at least." John said absentmindedly, looking out the window to see the extensive railway system dwindle away, making way for the open countryside.

"Time for that drink gentlemen." John prompted.

The friends made their way along the train to the refreshment area then settled down for their usual travel session of liquid refreshments and to enjoy the train ride.

The train steamed swiftly through numerous towns and villages that were just names on sign posts you had to be quick to read as they flashed past them. Stopping for several minutes only at the list of stops as called out by the Chief conductor.

John had already read through the little booklet extolling the virtues of the railway company, taking great delight in reading about the powerful steam engines that were all named after American Presidents.

'So that's why they called this the Wilson Express. It's a 4 cylinder 4-6-2 the same as our LMS or GWR engines, although they take on more water and coal than ours' he muttered, watching several different engines pass by.

"I don't know about you two but I'm ready for some bunk time." Sinclair said with a yawn, standing ups slowly, lazily stretching himself.

"Yes, we've got an early start tomorrow. Maybe we'll be on board and out to sea long before we're wise. Better give the steward our breakfast order first!" Larter agreed, as they left the diner car to make their way back to their cabin.

"Morning gentlemen! Here's your breakfast order." the steward said airily, opening up the door compartment to serve the friends with their breakfast.

"Morning Basil! That food smells and looks good. How're we doing for time?" John asked, rubbing the sleep from his eyes.

"We've made good timing after all, so we'll arrive New York by 0630. You've got half an hour to eat and brush up. I'll be taking your tickets when you get off."

"You might as well have them now Basil!" Sinclair said handing the steward his ticket wrapped in $5 note.

"For your kids at home Basil, thanks for looking after us." he said with a smile, as the other two followed suit.

"I knew you English Limey sailors were A O.K." the steward beamed, pocketing his money.

"Scots Limey if you don't mind Basil!" Sinclair said, correcting the steward.

"Yes and I'm a Scouser Limey, and he's an Irishman." Larter added.

The steward just grinned, saying.

"Whatever, but you all look the same to me. Have a nice day!" then slipped out of their cabin.

"That's the first time in bloody years I've been called a bloody Limey." Larter grinned, looking at John's bemused face.

"Before you ask John, the Yanks call us Limeys due to the fact that during Nelson's days we drank lime juice to prevent getting scurvy. We call them Bloody Yanks, because they always have the habit of shooting us instead of the Jerries." Sinclair volunteered.

"Yes John. Every time we lined up against the Jerries, and as any Jerry P.oW would admit, when they fought us Tommies as they called us, they knew to duck every time we shot at them. Then when they shot at us Tommies we also knew to duck. But when the Bloody Yanks turned up and started shooting, then everybody had to bloody well duck. Hence the expression." Larter explained.

"The question never even crossed my mind, but thanks for the info!" John replied with pretend innocence, causing the other two to throw their smelly socks at him.

CHAPTER VI

All Change

The friends joined the stream of passengers getting off the train, and walked down the long platform to the end where several people were waiting.

Sinclair saw a man holding a small placard with their names on it, pointing him out to the others.

"Are you Bell?" John asked politely, as he approached the tall slender man dressed in a fur-lined coat.

"I'm He. Come over to the ticket office where we can talk without disturbance." Bell commanded gruffly.

"Christ, talk about out of the frying pan Bruce!" Sinclair said with annoyance, as they followed Bell to a less busy area away from the already crowded ticket office.

"I have train tickets for you three to Chicago. From there you'll be going to the port of Los Angeles where you will join the *Repulse Bay.* I was supposed to accompany you but I shall be flying there instead. Here are your travel documents etcetera, most importantly, some subsistence money to tide you over until you get on board. Here is the number of our shipping agent who you will phone when you get to Chicago. He will meet you to collect that bag of spares you've got, but will give you a smaller one to take to the *Repulse Bay.* Please accept my humble apologies for this change of plan, but it really is necessary for me to inform you of such for you to know exactly what is going on."

"If that is the case Mr Bell, then why the hell didn't you meet us in Chicago instead of coming all the way down here only for us to go all the way back up there for our train. Surely we could have had a direct ticket or something?" John asked indignantly.

"You have a genuine grievance to ask, but equally there are many reasons which I can speak about to explain this detour. The first being that the train you came down on belongs to just the one company which has the franchise to operate between that part of Canada and the United States. Secondly, you would have to get to Chicago to be able to transit the States from one coast to the other and on the same train. That is because the city of Chicago is the main terminal for all cross-country rail travel in the U.S, in any direction across the map you care to choose. Sufficient to say, what I have given you to enjoy your overland trip, should be enough for you to have a decent trip. As long as you don't get involved with any of the local characters or strange odd-bods that patrol the Yank railway, then you should be okay. Grey, you have your despatch instructions, use any means you feel necessary to complete your journey. If there is some sort of hold up, and I mean well over a 4hour period, then you have the necessary phone numbers to use in emergency. I really must go now as I've got a plane to catch. Good luck and I hope to see you the other end." Bell said slowly and deliberately before climbing into a waiting taxi to disappear into the thick of the traffic.

"That's what we used to call, 'You've got your hammock, kitbag and gasmask, so on yer bike! Don't call me just see the Regimental Travel Office (RTO) if in doubt." Sinclair said with annoyance.

John opened the new large brown envelope to examine its contents, waiting for his two friends to calm down from the very brief and dictatorial meeting they just had with an unknown person who came out of the blue, then simply disappeared again.

"We have our tickets and suchlike to take us up to Chicago, but there is this warrant that I must produce to get our travel arrangements from Chicago. The envelope states that there are $100 dollars each as subsistence allowance, also a couple of business cards for taxis' or hostels we may be forced to use should there be a problem whilst in transit. It also states that if we require any more travelling money, then we're to arrange it through the numbers listed on the brochure for whatever place we're nearest to at the time. He gave an example such as arriving in Chicago, Denver, Albuquerque, or even Laramie."

"Head them up! Roll them out! Yee Hah!" Sinclair shouted aloud, in a cowboy accent.

Larter laughed at the reference, but John was not amused, as he was trying to remember the information they needed to make a safe and successful journey the entire width of the United States.

Sinclair saw the look John gave, and struggled to master his boisterous nature, by saying.

"Okay big white Chief. Tonto and me will see your scalp remains on your 2nd Engineers head."

Larter started to chant and dance around them.

"Hiii Yiii Yii, Hiiii Yiii Yiii Yaah!" he chanted, waving his hands around John's face.

Sinclair chuckled at this parody, but was rudely interrupted by a man who looked the real thing.

"You takin' the buffalo chip out of me?" he asked menacingly, pulling out a large hunting knife.

Sinclair stopped his caper, grabbed hold of the hand that held the wicked looking knife the man was wielding, saying.

"There is no need for you to draw your war weapon, as we do not wish to offend your tribe whatever it is. We are but three travellers making our way across a strange land and wish to do so peacefully. It's just that our friend has a short rein to guide himself by."

The Indian looked intently into John's face, before turning round and gave his opinion.

"I can see he is a greenhorn with not much savvy. Nobody offends the Arapaho and lives, but I will forgive you this occasion." he stated, putting his large knife away then left, much to their relief.

"Now look what you've done! You nearly started another Indian uprising." Larter teased, but winked at Sinclair.

John simply sighed, grabbing his bags, walked towards the platform where their next train was waiting for them.

"We've got a further 14 hour journey ahead of us, so c'mon!" he said crossly

They walked for several minutes along the side of the train looking for the named carriage where they would find their reserved seats.

Again as they boarded, a tall, slender black man appeared at the carriage doorway, inviting them on to the train.

John made his introduction on behalf of the three of them, and after showing the man the tickets they were escorted to their seats first, then onto their sleeping quarters.

"We had to come down on the Boston and Maine RR express. During which time I happen to notice some of your engines and rolling stock. If that is the case, then why couldn't we change at say Bangor then across to Chicago, rather than coming all the way down here to catch one of your boys to take us back up again?" John asked civilly as the steward escorted them to their seats.

"We have diesel powered engines on this line, which need stronger rail roads. We also have a wider gauge than they have which means that we can travel faster. But the main reason is because they've got the only permit to cross the Canadian Border, this side of the Appalachian Mountains."

"I'm a Merchant Marine Engineer who understands the differences between motor engines and steam. But why the sudden change when steam is the most economic way of propulsion?" John asked, glimpsing a large and very powerful engine standing still and quiet at the end of the long train of carriages, whereas the hiss of steam escaping slowly from the live steam engine held everybody' gaze.

"Don't ask me, I'm only the carriage steward. Go and ask the Chief Engineer, he'll tell you all you want to know." he said with a shrug of his shoulders, then added.

"Here is your cabin. If you need to partake in liquid refreshments, then you've got to go down 5 carriages to the diner. Otherwise, I'm able to see to your needs, should you have a private party going on. If you need help to celebrate then just contact me with the cabin phone over there in the corner." holding out his hand for his expected tip.

Larter smiled at him, gave him a pat on the back, then ushered him out of the cabin door saying,

"Thank you for the info steward. Your room service won't be necessary but we'll call you if we need you."

"But but…!" he stuttered, still holding out his hand expecting his obligatory tip.

Larter chuckled when he saw the still outstretched hand, and slapped one of his large cigars into it, before shutting the man out of the cabin.

The muttered thank you was heard as the three friends began themselves for another long, seemingly unnecessary journey.
John took out the travel pack that Bell gave him, reading through the instructions first before passing them on to the others to read. Once they all had read them, John collected them up and put them back into the envelope.

"It looks as if we're on an extended rail trip that nobody else in this line has ever undertaken. Perhaps it's cheaper by train than by plane, who knows. But I for one would like to have at least one day off before we think of going straight on board." Larter stated.

"Yes, that's probably what Bell had in mind for him to fly over instead of accompanying us. He'll have at least one full clear day off before he has to report on board." Sinclair said almost absent-mindedly.

"That's exactly what grabbed me by the throat. We're the officers needed to man and sail the ship out of harbour. Yet here they are spending good money on a strap hanger just so he can have a company paid holiday." John said in disgust.

"Well never mind. Just as long as they're paying for it, we might as well enjoy the trip. I pinched a bottle of Bourbon from the last train, all we need now is some beer to go with it. Lets call it a special souvenir, Budweiser seems a good beer which goes well with it, so lets try it one more time. Who knows, we might just like it, certainly after a few full glasses of this whiskey of theirs." Larter said jovially, showing them his bottle.

***

The train eased gently out of the station and started to pick up speed for its headlong rush towards the northern city of Chicago. As it was still early the friends decided just to relax on their bunks, to let the train rock them to sleep, not caring about the scenery or the commotion created when the train stopped along its way.

John slipped in and out of sleep as if something was niggling at him. He peeped out of the window behind drawn blinds to see that it was jet black outside, and the train had stopped. He looked at his watch finding that it was only midday, decided to go and speak to the carriage steward.

"Why are we stopped in a tunnel steward?" John asked politely.

"This is the three mile Pittsburg tunnel, which has three sets of traffic lights for us to go through. It's on red so it means the train ahead of us is still on that section. It's probably a freight train which takes twice as long as us to clear a section." the steward said evenly, seemingly unconcerned.

"How long is our train in comparison?"

"We've only got 19 carriages but if it's a freight train then they'll probably have around the 40 mark. We don't have the large trains in our company compared with say the Union Pacific or the Santa Fe Railroads, some of their trains are 2 or even 3 miles long. In fact several rail-road companies have three maybe four double locos which haul their coal or iron ore trains that can be 3 miles long and can take up to twenty minutes to pass you. In fact the Canadian Pacific rail-road trains that haul their cereal wagons can be up to 5 miles long. We have six trains a day shuttle service on this run, and we normally allow about ten minutes for hold up in between each stop. Our Engineer has a mobile connection to the controller who sometimes re-routes us if there's too much of a delay. Most Railroad operators do the same, so maybe the train in front of us was re-routed onto our track to get onto this section before us." he explained, as the train started moving off again.

"As I've said, we've been held up so the Engineer will be pouring on the speed as soon as we're clear of the tunnel. Anyway, must get lunch on the go. See you in the diner." he added, but the sound of the engine's horn reverberating loudly down the tunnel drowned his voice.

John went back to the compartment, to find the other two drinking coffee and was offered a cup from the hot percolator.

"Here John, have some of this. The Yanks certainly know how to treat their passengers, this coffee is delicious." Larter said giving John his cup.

"Thanks Bruce. I've just been speaking to our steward. He tells me that lunch will be served in the diner soon. Judging by all the passengers, I suggest we get there early to find ourselves seats." John replied, gulping down his coffee.

"Sounds a good idea, I'm ruddy starving." Sinclair said rubbing his belly.

They made their way along the train to the large diner car where they saw their steward clearing some tables of the debris from someone else's lunch.

"Here you are gentlemen. All nice and clean! Here's a menu card, I'll be back for your order." he announced, handing them a large menu folder to read.

They enjoyed their overly large lunch swilled down by several bottles of the local beer, before deciding to stroll back to their compartment.

They met up with the steward again on their way who advised them to stay in their cabins until the train had left the next stop.

"When do we get to stretch our legs steward?" Sinclair asked

"We'll be changing Engineers and be adding another loco onto the train at Toledo. You have the chance of a five-minute stroll then. I shall be serving the evening meal shortly after Toledo."

"When do we arrive in Chicago? I ask this because we've got

a connection to make." John asked showing the steward his travel itinerary.

"We hope to arrive around midnight. That is the 3am Stopper train all the way to Denver. But if I were you I'd go for the 0800 L.A. Express, as it will reach LA long before that one. I have a cousin on it, so look out for him, he's the Chief steward."

"What would we do until then? Is there any place for us to stay or do we have to wait at the station?"

"You can stay in the great hall, take in a late movie or even a few hookers to warm you up. But as you're in mid-transit go see my cousin, as he can fix you up with a cabin straight away. Mind you, you'd have to put up with the noise of the cleaners, or the Engineers getting the trains shaped up."

"That sounds the better option. Anyway, see you later for supper." Larter said pleasantly, giving him another large cigar.

"Here, you enjoyed the last one, so enjoy one more for your troubles."

The steward held it to his nose, and sniffing deeply he sighed.

"You Limeys always like a good cigar. Klompen Kloggins did you say they were?"

"Yes, they're Dutch, much better than those crap Havana's." Sinclair said, blowing a large smoke ring towards him as they entered their cabin again.

"If we've got a few hours wait, we can phone through for some more money to get ourselves shacked up for a while. We could call it 'overnight expenses." Sinclair suggested, which Larter thought was a good idea.

"Now then gentlemen, you really must control your animal instincts, although we could do with a few more dollars in our wallet in case we don't get the chance at any of the other stops." John said, dodging the magazines and papers the other two were pelting him with.

CHAPTER VII

Down Mexico Way

The train arrived at its destination platform in the busy station of Chicago, allowing the friends stretch their legs once more after their 14 hour journey.

They walked through the ticket barrier and entered the great hall. Wall to wall vending machines were stacked up almost to the rafters, with stairs and walkways so the travelling public could get to and use them.

There were people milling about, people sitting around and eating, people trying to sleep, with the odd drunk wandering around cadging cigarettes or the money to buy another drink.

John looked up at the train departures to the long list of stops each train had to make.

He spotted the 0300 Denver train had over 40 stops in its list as far as Denver then saw the 0800 LA Express with only 14 stops to Denver, but a further 16 from there to Los Angeles.

"Look at that gentlemen! Only 30 stops between us and our ship!" John remarked sarcastically, pointing to the train information.

"It looks like we've got a bloody 8 hour wait before it leaves too." Larter moaned.

"Here's one person who's not hanging around this place. Once I've found a vending machine to get some food, I'm off to see that cousin of the stewards." Sinclair said grimly.

"We'll all do that Andy, but we're supposed to be meeting someone first. Then maybe we can get ourselves replenished with Yankee dough before we do anything else." John advised.

The tannoy was rattling out the names of destinations the next train was to take when it was interrupted by a message for John and his friends.

"Mr Grey and party are to go over to platform five waiting room." It said twice.

"That's us! Glad to be shot of this bloody sack, it weighs a flippin' ton, so it does." John said, starting to drag it across the not so clean marbled floor of the hall.

"Hello Grey! I'm Chief Engineer Harley. That bag is for me, but I've got one in exchange." Harley said, shaking John's hand, introducing himself to the other two.

John took the much smaller bag off Hartley, asking him a couple of questions, which Harley partially answered.

"Not sure myself Grey. Here're your new lot of instructions, how to find the *Repulse Bay* once you arrive at L.A etcetera. Don't forget, if you have any hold ups on the way report them from where you're stuck. I did your overland trip last year which was one hell of a trip. Mind you, I went alone, but at least you've got company. Well must go now, I've got a taxi waiting to get back to my ship. Take my tip and travel on the 0800 flyer, it is one lulu of a train in many senses of the word." Harley said, then waved them goodbye, dragging the heavy bag behind him.

"Well that's that. Now for item B on the list." John sighed as they walked along the rows of vending machines.

"By the look of it, you can buy anything from a nappy towel to the promise of a quick knee trembler from these things. Just feed the machine that's all!" Sinclair said, pointing out to see through door of a vending machine that had a list of telephone numbers of girls willing to warm you up.

"We'll get something to eat and drink then go see this steward." Sinclair said when they arrived at the section selling hot food and drinks.

They bought their food and drink then found a place quiet enough for them to enjoy it without being bothered or pestered by other equally hungry passengers.

The time seemed to drag by for them until John said he had had enough and wanted to go to see if they could board their train.

"The advertisement board states it's the 'Super Chief! The all Pullman train that will guarantee you three days of comfort as you glide through the natural beauty of several states, all the way to Los Angeles." Larter quoted, pointing to the large poster adorning the entrance gateway to the platform.

Walking down the side of the train that was in darkness, save for a few dim lights from the platform, they saw that the carriages looked to be something special.

"Yes, it's a Pullman alright, which means the engine must be something special too, John. Why don't you go down and have a good look at it while we try and find somebody." Larter suggested.

John carried on walking right to the front of the train taking some pleasurable minutes looking at the big steam engine being stoked up by the Engineers.

"Hello in the cab!" John called a couple of times before a grimy face appeared in the doorway of the footplate.

"You want somethin' Bub?" the Engineer drawled, spitting a great gob of tobacco juice at John's feet.

"I came here to ask you a couple of questions about this engine, not to be gobbed at." John snarled.

"Well why didn't you say so in the first place! What sort of questions do you want to know?"

"I'm a ship's Engineer and know steam engines, but this one seems something special. Any chance of coming on board to have a look round?"

"A ship's Engineer! In that case, come aboard." the Engineer said in a more amenable way.

John looked at the controls asking a few questions, which were given a swift reply to. Several questions later, the Engineer sounded a bit peeved, so John admitted he was a naturally curious person, but he didn't want to upset the man.

"Mind you, I've been driving this engine for almost 40 years now. This is one of the last runs it will make before we both get pensioned off. They're bringing in the new diesels complete with a new set of carriages and other rolling stock. They can keep them, there's nothing like this train in the whole world excepting of course for that Orient Express you Limeys run." the Engineer said glumly.

"We've got the same problem on ships. Oil burners replaced all the coal burner ships but they were still classed as a steam ship. Now they're slowly being replaced by diesels, what is known these days as progress." John said in commiserating with the man.

They had a few more minutes of conversation until Sinclair arrived saying they had found the Chief steward.

John thanked the Engineer for his time and left the footplate to join Sinclair.

"You should see the controls on that beauty, Andy. It will pull us along at a good 80 knots, and that's with all 25 carriages you see hitched up to it. No wonder the engine and its Engineer are called the Super Chief!" John enthused, walking swiftly towards an open carriage door, where a very large fat black man was standing holding it open.

"Nobody's allowed on board before 7.30, so get on board quickly." the steward whispered, shutting the door quietly behind him.

He led them through the sumptuous, well-appointed carriages until they came to the sleeping cars, where they were ushered quickly into an empty compartment.

"The lights will be switched on around seven, which is your cue to get yourselves out of here and into some seats further towards the back of the train. I'll check your tickets then." the steward said, then held out his shovel sized hand.

Larter, put two 1 dollar bills into his hand, as Sinclair gave him two packs of cigarettes.

These were greatly received by the man who promised them a 'special looking after' during their trip across the states, then sauntered off back into the darkness again.

"I'll bet he's got a few more people tucked away in these cabins, and I'll bet the company doesn't know of it. A couple of bucks and a carton of fags just for a few hours kip on a train that we've already got tickets for, is definitely a good scam he's pulling. Still, good luck to him, I say." Sinclair whispered, as they settled themselves down for a much needed sleep.

From the travel brochure found in the sleeper compartment stated it was a Mr Pullman who demanded that his trains would each be a mobile carriage fit for a King. He'd also designed the carriages, and gave lots of other facts and figures that the SANTA FE RAIL ROAD was proud of. The only thing that could perhaps spoil their enjoyment was the fact of yet another long train journey was ahead of them, of some 40 hours this time.

"Oh well gentlemen. We might as well change into some clean clobber, and have these seen to by the on board laundry." John stated, starting to unpack some of the extra clothes he had bought from the vending machines.

"I've noticed some of the carriages have a glass dome on top for passengers to go and look at the scenery. Might have a shufty at one later., and yes you're right John, we might as well enjoy our stay, perhaps we'll get the chance to meet up with some of the other passengers who're going all the way." Larter said, changing out of his formal suit and putting on some clean casual clothing.

All three decided to sit in one of the scenic carriages to read the local papers bought from the kiosk in the last carriage of the train.

The train steamed merrily through the vast open countryside stopping at its list of stations on the way. Despite all the changes of passengers the train was kept immaculate, with the passengers well looked after by the 'Harvey Girls' the Santa Fe RR was famous for.

"A man called Fred Harvey, got the catering contract for this line, so he recruited several hundred young women to work on his trains, providing the food and so on. Each girl was special but they kept getting married to men who lived all along the rail network, so he had to get more. These girls were named after him, hence the name 'the Harvey' girls. The Engineer is married to one of the first ones who got to the top as Chief chef." the steward informed them as he handed them their clean laundry.

"Sounds a good idea. Maybe you married one too ?" John asked innocently.

"Not allowed, not even today. Cos' dey's all white folks only." the steward grunted, as John slipped some money into his hand.

"Never mind, maybe one day when you lot get yourselves organised like us civilised Limeys, your sons and daughters will be free and able enjoy the same liberty." Larter said earnestly, to which the steward nodded in response.

"There's something in what you say, but keep it under your hat otherwise your opinions will be taken as insults by some of the passengers." he warned, then left the friends

"Speaking of which gentlemen. I've noticed several weapons openly displayed on board, but mostly hidden under jackets and the like. Maybe they're out to start another war, but the last person I saw toting a weapon in public was the Ulster Constabulary Sergeant in Dunmurry." John informed them.

"The Yanks have a powerful claim to weapons because of their past records as cowboys. I think it's called the 'Gun Lobby' who has ensured the God given right to pack a firearm. To protect against evil doers, I think the saying goes." Larter said, pretending to draw a gun from his hip and shoot it at the overhead light.

Well, maybe the steward has something after all. Don't want to get riddled with bullets do we. I mean, if we went swimming we'd sink like a sieve." Sinclair replied, making the other two smile at the very thought of water-spouts coming out of their bodies.

"So how does that square up to the fact the Yanks are all bible-thumpers of whatever religion, yet they can go around pacing guns to shoot at anybody they want?" John asked, which caused a look of amazement from the others for a moment

"Trust him to come up with yet another cock-a-mamie question, but damned if we know!" Larter chuckled, and flicked John around his head with a brochure he had in his hand.

* * *

"We've got a hold up ahead at Denver. If that's the case we'll go on the northerly route via Laramie and Salt Lake City for L.A. then end up in San Diego where our depot is." the steward informed the friends, placing yet another tray of drinks in front of them.

"Oh! How long is this expected hold up steward?" John asked with concern.

"Haven't a clue. Last time it was several hours."

"That means that we've got to phone our shipping agent. Our ship won't be able to sail until we get there."

"We normally split the train at Denver, so that any passengers going on the southern route to San Diego can go on that line. Usually via Albuquerque, Phoenix, Tuscon, Yuma, then Tijuana on to San Diego."

"Sounds like real cowboy country which we in Great Britain have been hearing about, what with all the cowboy films with the likes of Tom Mix, Randolf Scott, The Man from Laramie and the rest. Maybe the reasons why there are a lot of guns on this train. What's the difference in travel time?"

"If you have one of our big boys to take you over the big hump then it will take you four hours longer. But if you have one of our new diesels with double-decker carriages, which can travel faster than these, then you'll be in San Diego two hours earlier than the Super Chief going north. We won't know until we arrive at Denver what traction engine we'll be using."

"Well, whatever the route, I've still got to phone our agent. How long is it to Denver now?"

"Fort Morgan is our next stop so there's plenty of time yet. About 2 hours or so!" he said, looking at his fob watch.

"Maybe I can phone from there instead." John said hopefully but the steward shook his head.

"You'll have plenty of time to make your phone call at Denver, as it will take a good hour to get the new train organised. People normally use this stop and Albuquerque to stretch their legs, so you might as well join them." he said, leaving to serve other passengers.

* * *

Arriving at Denver, John made his call to their shipping agent, who instructed them to take the southern route to San Diego, where their ship would be waiting for them.

As they settled on their new train, the friends were not too pleased with the surly manner of their new steward. They didn't care very much because of the double-decker carriages where they could sit and watch the desert slide past them whilst enjoying a cool drink.

Yet again, the list of stops seemed daunting as John read them out to the other two.

"I wonder if we'll have time for a quick flutter in Las Vegas, before the train leaves. Maybe we'll get to see the home of this railway company, as it's supposed to be a nice place. Santa Fe that is." John said with interest, but got little response from his friends.

"What I'd like to know is, if they were three officers short, why, or at least how did they sail from LA to San Diego?" Sinclair asked gruffly

"What the agent had said was, one of the lines' ships was staying in LA for a week or so, and lent our ship the officers to get her there. It just means those officers will be sent back by train once we arrive on board. He also stated our ship has a change of route across the Pacific but wouldn't give any further details. Anyway, we've got a shorter journey now."

"A shorter journey he says. We will have travelled the best part of 3,200 miles with only about the last 100 of them chopped off." Sinclair sighed.

"Never mind Andy, once we've passed Albuquerque it's all down hill towards the seaside. Look we've only got another six inches left on the map to go!" Larter grinned, pointing to the places on the train guide map.

John looked out the window to see their train in a large curve as it rattled along the ribbon of rails. He counted fifteen carriages in front of him with a further ten behind him. There were two large, very powerful diesel locomotives at the front belching out black smoke, which John took to mean those engines were on full throttle. He was pleasantly surprised to see another train coming into the curve from the other end, which looked as if it was one big train that stretched for miles.

'*So that's one of the big boys' the Engineer was telling me about.*' John whispered quietly, seeing a massive steam engine with so many wheels on it, he needed to recount them over and over again.

'4-*8-8-4. Double heated and with a double extendable funnel. It looks just like two engines welded together.'* he enthused, watching the big steam engine pass them. It took the passing train a good twenty minutes to finally pass theirs and still on the big curved track.

"It's all right for you looking at the choo choo trains, we normal people have got to put up with empty spaces each side of the track." Sinclair said, yawning with boredom.

"We can always go below to the cinema and watch a few 'westerns' if you want." John replied.

"We're already in cowboy country John, all we need now is for a gang of Indians to come and attack the white mans' iron horse." Sinclair quipped

"Yea, or maybe a posse of good guys riding their horses daft, chasing some bank robbers. Or even wait until Butch Cassidy and his bloody sidekick the Sundance Kid to come to rob the train." Larter added.

"That's the spirit! Let's barricade ourselves in here in case the Commancheros come." John smiled.

"Better still, pretend we're out shooting those ruddy Arabs." he added.

"Never mind all that, the bar should be open again now. So get off your horse and let's go for another wet. I could do with looking at a block of ice now." Sinclair suggested, so they got up and went below to the dining car.

It was the following morning before they arrived into Albuquerque, where the train was to stop for a while whilst the passengers sorted themselves out either for going down Mexico way or to the beaches of California.

There was a strong Mexican flavour to the place as the people wandered about in gaily-coloured clothing, and very large brimmed hats. The friends even bought one each to wear as they strolled along the roadway next to the train.

"Just as well they've got very low steps to hop onto, as I wouldn't fancy trying to climb aboard when the train takes off." John observed then saw the telltale sign of the engine starting to rev up.

"Bloody hell! Quick, get on board as it's starting to move." John shouted, hopping onto the low steps, swiftly followed by the other two.

"That bloody steward told me we had a good half an hour stop. In fact it was only fifteen minutes. Wait 'till I get my hands on him." Sinclair snarled

When they arrived at their cabin, they found the steward rifling through their belongings, stuffing things into a brown paper bag.

As Sinclair was the first through the door, he kicked the steward's backside so hard that he seemed as if he was airborne. Larter grabbed the bag from the man, whilst John shut the door quietly behind him, then witnessed the steward being systematically beaten up, before they picked him up to take him to one of the carriage doorways.

"You have the honour of throwing this thieving bastard out, John. Besides he's not got a valid ticket!" Sinclair said, swiftly opening the carriage doorway.

The steward was pleading, begging them to stop, but John shook his head and pushed him off the train.

Another steward, who must have seen the body leave the train, pulled the emergency stop lever for the Engineer to stop the train. The screech of tortured metal on metal even reached their carriage, as the train juddered to a halt in a concertina fashion.

An Engineer came running back to demand what the problem

was, to be told that one of the stewards had fallen out probably checking that door lock was engaged properly.

The unconscious, badly cut and bruised man was carried on board, witnessed by most of the other passengers who were peering out of their windows.

"Clear away! Let me see him!" A tall well built man wearing a white Stetson on his head denoting he was somebody of authority, pushed his way towards the group who were trying to resuscitate the steward, giving a cursory examination to satisfy himself then said,

"He'll live, but we'll get an ambulance to meet the train at the next rail crossing to take him to hospital." he announced, then wandered over to John and his friends.

"My name is Special Agent Isted from the Santa Fe Rail Road Police. Maybe whoever did this should be commended for getting rid of this scum that has been giving the company a bad name. I've had him and his gang under surveillance for some time now, but we don't take kindly to passengers who take the law into their own hands all the same. So if you come across the men who were responsible, then tell them from me to keep a low profile until they get off. " he said quietly, tipping his hat to shade his eyes from the blazing sun, then gave them a knowing wink he sauntered off to somehow disappear amongst the crowd.

"Consider ourselves tipped off. Lets hope we don't meet any of the stewards sidekicks, or it'll be us ending up as jailbirds instead of those thieving bastards." Larter said quietly, as the friends returned their cabin, to tidy up to look as if nothing happened.

"Maybe that steward I saw, with the large dagger tucked into his belt who was hanging around with that bastard is one of them. Better keep an eye on him too." John said quietly, seeing the very man coming towards them.

"I'm Antonio, your new steward. Me make your journey a nice one, yes?" the man asked in a broad Mexican accent, holding out his hand expecting a tip.

"You get nothing until you earn it pal." Sinclair said, laughing at this man's barefaced cheek.

"Okay, I wait." he said with a shrug of his shoulders, barging past them.

Over the next several hours, each time the steward attended them he always had some minor accident. First it was accidentally spilling a full ashtray over Sinclair's lap, or slamming their beer onto the table too hard so that it splashed over them. Every time, he grinned profusely apologising for his clumsiness.

John and his friends knew they were being wound up, but kept their cool during each incident, resolving to get their own back but behave as the sheriff had said.

So they decided to prolong their drinking bouts, each taking turns ordering just one drink, or only ordering one meal, for the man to do a repeat performance with the other two. They kept him on the go well into the early mornings, and complaining about their cabin wasn't clean or tidy enough for them to stay in it. They made the steward's life a total misery, so much so all the other passengers were complaining to him that they were being neglected due to the three friends.

The train called at its obligatory stops before finally stopping at the end of the line, San Diego.

"Thanks for the ride steward. Remind us not to stop off at Albuquerque next time. For you not to take it too personally, my two Amigos and me have left you an appropriate farewell gift in our cabin. Make sure you don't spend it all at once. See you some time." Sinclair said with a big grin as they left the train and walked slowly to the terminal.

They didn't get far before they heard the shouting of cursing and swearing from the steward who jumped off the train and threw his so-called present at them. The large dollop of excrement in a brown paper bag they had left him, flew in a large arc and landed on to make it splatter all over an immaculately dressed man.

"You Dago son of a bitch! The man exploded, drawing a gun

from his coat pocket firing in the direction of the steward. Fortunately he missed, but it caused a panic among the rest of the passengers who cowered down to get out of the way of the bullets.

A policeman came running over, drawing his gun from his holster at the same time, and told the man to put his weapon away.

"The goddamn son of a bitch! Look what he threw at me! Either you arrest him for fouling private property or I'll shove my gun so far up his ass he'll have bullets for teeth." the irate man shouted.

The three friends were enjoying the moment, but kept walking without a backward glance, as they finally got through the ticket barrier.

"Now you know why the Yanks carry their guns around. To stop train stewards throwing shit all over them." Sinclair laughed, as they waited for a taxi to take them to the docks.

"What a way to end a six day journey. Let's hope for our sakes, the company sends us by air next time." John breathed, when he saw Bell coming to meet them.

CHAPTER VIII

Man Overboard

John looked at the very large tanker resting quietly at her berth as the taxi arrived alongside the gangway.

"Here we are gentlemen! Time to get your articles signed and my ship on its way." Bell said, reaching into a large holdall, placing a smart cap that had a gold braided band around its peak.

"No wonder you had to fly over. You must be our Captain then!" Sinclair observed.

"Just a relief Captain, but how astute of you 3rd Mate. Perhaps you three would fill me in on your trip overland, as we intend repeating that exercise the next time we need crew this side of the continent." Bell said with a grin, as they piled out of the taxi and climbed up the steep gangway.

"Welcome aboard the *Repulse Bay* gentlemen. Come to my office and sign your articles." Matthews the Purser greeted.

John and his two friends looked at their surroundings as they passed through to the office.

"We have a brand new ship and a good crew to sail her, now that we've got a relief Captain on board. Here is a brochure for you to read, it will inform you of what the company policies are governing officers and crew, both on board and ashore. It's your company employment rules or regulations, if you like. Just do your duties as you are paid to do then all will be well. If you have any queries or problems of a departmental nature, then see your head of department. Although, you Mr Larter will be the exception to that, in your case you refer directly to me. Grey, I'll have your travel instructions and other documentation now if you please, and of course, also the brown envelopes you were given you by your last Purser." Matthews said in a droning voice, as they handed over the required envelopes.

The Purser put his head through a small hatchway to speak to somebody for a moment, before the slight figure of a steward appeared who accompanied them to the accommodation area of the ship.

"Most officers and all the crew are normally living aft on board, but in this ship all officers will be accommodated in the main bridge superstructure. You will be required to attend all meals promptly and always in clean clothes, that includes all your watch-keeping Engineers. We have an excellent laundry room on board, which will take care of your needs, any charges will be added to your tally in the lounge bar." the steward announced, showing them to their respective cabins.

John stepped into the cabin to find it spacious and airy, with two portholes for him to look out of. His bunk was on top of a wooden chest of drawers with a small writing bureau next to it, which had a low-backed chair nestling under it. He noticed a small half-sized wardrobe beside another wooden locker, which on inspection, told him it was for his Engineering books and such like.

The deck was covered in dark blue carpeting matched the small blue curtains adorning the portholes.

He had a large deep basin that had an oval mirror with a small strip light fitting over the top of it. He noticed he had plenty of deck space between his bunk and the portholes, and the deck head was higher than he could reach up to.

"Very nice indeed. Let's hope the rest of the ship is the same"' He said softly to himself starting to make himself comfortable in his new home.

A man dressed in white overalls who entered his cabin followed a knock on his cabin door.

"Hello 2nd! Glad you made it then. I'm your Chief, Alan Hodgson." the Chief said introducing himself.

"John Grey. Recently off the *Maple Leaf* with Nick Baxter as my Chief." John responded, returning Hodgson's handshake.

"I was about to make my way down to the engine room to find you. Here is a bag I was asked to give you. Now that you're here, you might as well take a seat."

Hodgson sat down as invited then opening the bag and examined the contents which seemed to please him..

"Good. Just what I've been waiting for." he said, putting the contents back into its bag.

"I've come to speak to you about your duties on board, which you will find departs somewhat from what you've been used to before.

The *Repulse Bay* is one of the new breeds of multi-fuel tankers, in that she can carry up to four types of fuel. She is a Hong Kong built and registered ship, of some 65,000 tonnes fully laden. She is 700 feet long with a beam 110 feet wide and a laden draught of 40 feet. She has a double bottom but although she is what is termed a single hull, her skin is a full one inch and a quarter thick. We have twin diesel engines powering two propellers at a cruising speed of 20 knots. I said it was a new type of ship, because of the new twin funnels arranged side by side. she has a range of 20,000 miles without refuelling, and due to the extra evaps on board we can make as much fresh water as we like. We have a special boiler to provide the power to the capstans or other lifting gear because we cannot have electrical machinery to operate them. An electric motor may cause a spark that would ignite the fumes and gasses escaping from the tanks, whereas steam is an inert gas and does the job just as well. As for the rest of her make up, you will discover them from our Engineering drawings and the likes later.

Because we are a large tanker, we have two sets of Engineer Officers. One for our normal engine-room watches, with a smaller one just for the fuel tank management and cargo handling.

This will be your duty as the Tank Management 2nd Engineer, but you will have two junior Engineers plus a few stokers in your charge. You will not do any training, or any instructional duties save for those required by your two juniors. You will have a separate office next to mine and should you need to use the repair unit feel free to do so. As you're a qualified tool maker, plus a qualified fitter and turner, I will be requiring you to provide various handmade parts during sea transits, once you've got your department settled down into the transit routines. Any questions so far?"

John finished scribbling his notes on what Hodgson had told him, then posed a battery of questions that seemed to catch Hodgson unawares.

Hodgson answered each one then smiled when he said.

"Your employment profile did say you had an inquisitive mind, but I hadn't realised just how. I like a man who asks questions, because it shows his mind is on his job. What else do I have to know about you John?"

"I have the maxim whereby I make my reports on a regular basis, but relax them when requested so that I only report when there's something to report and not when there's not, if you get my drift."

"That will suit me fine. The less paperwork the bloody better. But if you find something that can be improved for the good of both the crew and or the ship, then this company runs a special suggestions scheme. If someone's name keeps cropping up, that merits a special mention, then the management board will be looking to promote that person. From what I understand it's how you and the other two officers came to join the company."

"What, no patent snatching or pinching other peoples ideas?"

"Anybody found doing that, will be immediately sacked. No, this company lets its employees do all the thinking. All they do is promote those ideas. Anyway must go now. Come to see me after lunch, as I'll give you a personal tour of the ship. You get the best from the best, and only your best will do, if you follow me." Hodgson concluded leaving the cabin with his bag.

'Now we're getting somewhere. But I'll still send my drawings to Fergus for safe keeping.' John thought.

"Hello 2$^{nd.}$ I'm Penrose your steward. My caboose is down the corridor if you need anything. If I'm not there, leave a note for me and I'll come back to you. I collect your laundry every other day at sea then as required in harbour. Give me your beer and fags requirements on a weekly basis for me to get them put into your cabin. You will find a post box in the saloon if you've got any mail to go. The stamps will be put on for you, and charged to your mess bill as normal. There is a double shower and bathroom almost opposite your cabin, with separate double heads next to it." Penrose informed him in a broad Birmingham accent, which John paid particular attention to, as he was unfamiliar with it

"Thanks for your info Penrose. In the meantime can you now direct me to the saloon."

"I'm going there myself, so follow me." Penrose stated, leading John along a passageway then up a flight of steps, which brought them directly into an open foyer type space with glass panelled doors to the saloon facing them.

"Should you want to go on deck, just go through any one of those double doors each side of the foyer." Penrose said, pointing to either side of him, as they entered the saloon.

Again John was surprised by the opulence of the place considering it was only a tanker, and said so.

"The whole ship is like this 2nd. Even us crew living aft have carpet on our decks. Anyway, if you're here for lunch you're a bit early. Suggest you go take a pew then enjoy an early pre-voyage drink." Penrose replied swiftly, rushing away to whatever errand he was on.

John went over to the bar and got himself a drink before choosing a seat for himself but with his friends in mind, should they find their way here.

He wasn't waiting long before Larter came with another officer who was introduced to him.

"John meet my 2nd Officer Kenny Brown who is also our radar operator genius amongst other things. You want to come and see our set-up, it's far superior to what the Triple Crown line can muster." Larter enthused, as they sat down and were served by a passing steward.

Brown had been on board the ship for one return trip across the Pacific already so was telling John and Larter what to expect, who was what or what to look out for

"It all sounds very interesting, and the daily routine will take care of the mind numbing dullness you mention. Still, it's a far better ship than any other we've sailed on." John said philosophically.

"I've yet to see the engine room, but my duties are still on deck" he added.

"Yes, and I'm to see you don't fall off it either, John." Sinclair quipped arriving, sitting down by them to enjoy his drink.

Sinclair nodded his head to Ken Brown as they were being introduced to him.

"The only way to get over the weather decks to the foc'sle then aft to the poop deck is by a central gantry walkway. There are two smaller catwalks running port and starboard side of the ship, but they're only for the access to all the tank top valves. You should see the size of the bloody anchors 'cause they'd make two of the old *Brooklea's*. Not only that, it's a long way down the side of the ship when she's running empty. A good 40 feet at least." Sinclair informed them.

"You would expect that from a ship this size. She's nothing but a diesel driven oil-well." John enthused.

A steward announcing that lunch was now ready to be served in the dining room interrupted their conversation.

John found his seat with his little name card sitting in front of his several items of cutlery.

"Would you look at all this! Two sets of cutlery just for one person and a fancy serviette next to a very clean drinking glass." Sinclair said in amazement.

"Mind your manners now Andy. Keep those elbows tucked in instead of trying to take off with them." Larter joked, sitting a few places down from Sinclair yet opposite John.

John saw that to his left was a place for another 2nd Engineer, with two 3rd Engineers to his right with four junior officers next to that. The Captain and Chief Engineer took up the top table.

Opposite him were the deck officers in order of rank going down to Larter and his junior officer, whereas the bottom table formed the rectangle had the Purser, the ships doctor and the ship's Stores Officer.

'At least the table is laid out in normal ships protocol.' John breathed as the other 2nd Engineer sat down.

"Hello Grey. I'm Dave Fagg, the 2nd for the engine room side." Fagg said, introducing himself.

"Presumably we have lunch with the Captain before he gives his pre-voyage speech?" John asked politely.

"Not in this ship. The Captain will have his lunch in his day cabin, then sail the ship out of port at the given time as per notice board. In case you've not had the chance to read this very important board which keeps everybody informed of what is going on, then I suggest that you do." Fagg growled

John shrugged his shoulders declining to respond to the sudden rudeness of the man, but turned to the 3rd Engineer sitting next to him.

"3rd! Have you got your department buttoned up for sailing yet?" John asked politely.

"Not quite, 2nd. Anyway, due to a hold up whilst we wait for a new officer to join, we're not due to sail until 1900." the 3rd replied affably.

John thanked the Engineer, smiling to himself at his clever ruse to find out when the ship did sail.

The *Repulse Bay* sailed slowly out of the harbour like a Leviathan as she dwarfed most of the pride of the American warships that were moored or at anchor seemingly anywhere and everywhere. The little tugs tooted farewell as they scampered back into their little haven, as with a big puff of smoke, the *Repulse Bay* ploughed her way out into the big wide ocean, that now dwarfed her.

Soon she took on a gentle swaying motion as she moved through the water, leaving a silver trail behind her to mark her passing.

John made his way for'ard from the bridge, reminding himself of the various valves, depth gauges or other important valves Hodgson had shown him. His standard sized wheel spanner he found was not of a sufficient size, so he sent a junior Engineer to fetch him something more suitable.

Fortunately it was a fine evening with a full moon casting its silver beams over them, creating the illusion the sea was like a mirror, when the junior Engineer found himself falling overboard.

John gave the alarm telling the other junior Engineer to keep his eyes on the victim, as the ship started to shudder violently in slowing herself down to a stop.

He saw a launch being lowered down its davits and noticed Sinclair was in the launch taking charge. By the time the ship had stopped it was several miles away from the hapless Engineer.

'Let's hope he's okay, as it's a big drop. In future I will insist on life jackets on and safety harnesses being worn whilst on these catwalks.' he quietly avowed.

John watched the junior Engineer being hauled back on board in a stretcher, and decided to go and see if he was alive at least.

"Broke his neck John. I told you it was a long way down. Even at 15 feet it would be like trying to go head first into a concrete wall. Just as well we weren't in ballast or it'd be nearly 40 feet. The Captain has radioed for a helicopter to pick him up to take him to hospital. He'll live but won't be able to laugh for a while in case his head falls off." Sinclair said with relief, giving the hapless Engineer a lighted cigarette to enjoy.

The helicopter duly arrived and took the casualty away before the ship went on her way again, as John was giving the Captain a verbal report on the incident. It was then he gave his suggestion of the wearing of lifejackets and lifelines, for Bell to nod his head in accepting the report and readily agreed on the suggestion.

"The next time you practice 'MAN OVERBOARD' Grey, make sure I get to know of it first. The 3rd mate happened to be on the bridge wing at the time to spot the man. Next time it happens, the poor bastard might not be so lucky." Bell hinted, then dismissed John.

John left the bridge and went back to his group of men, who were naturally concerned about one of their number.

"He'll live, but from now on, everybody is to wear a lifejacket and a safety harness whilst on these outboard catwalks. We'll continue this exercise tomorrow morning at 0900." John stated, waiting for the leading stoker to get the other stokers to understand.

'A big, beautiful ship like this and yet half the men can't speak the language' John thought following the rest of his men aft and into the main superstructure then dismissed them for the night.

On his way back to his cabin he met Hodgson coming out of his, and requested an explanation for this strange set-up.

"All British ships, including those registered in a British port, must be manned by British officers. The crew would be made up from the local entry seamen and stokers. In our case, we've got Hong Kong Chinese, but most of them can speak or understand basic English. Once we've educated enough of them in our ways of doing things, then they can man their own ships. The principle officers must be able to command in and speak the Queen's language. However that is still a long way off for what this company is trying to achieve. Sufficient to say, maybe one day, this ship will be manned by a 100% Hong Kong Chinese crew. Perish the thought on that one." Hodgson said.

"That makes sense then, because I came across such a ship, years ago now. Out of the 8 officers on board, only the Captain, the radio officer, and the Chief Engineer were British." John replied, remembering the ship he helped whilst in transit to the Falklands.

"Must have been a rogue company then, as ours will be the first to have such integration of officers and crew as I said. Anyway, from what I've heard, you're slowly getting rid of my staff. Was it Turner who fell overboard?"

"Yes. The stupid idiot was forever being told about his faulty footwear and his undone laces. He lost his footing, and tripped over his own laces. So I've suggested to the Captain that lifejackets and safety lines be worn on those outboard catwalks, to prevent any further loss of crew, British or Chinese" John sighed.

"Sounds okay to me. You've just opened your suggestions account with the company now, and that's what I like about bright thinkers. It saves me thinking for them, you know." Hodgson said with a grin.

"Must get on watch now. Perhaps you could come down to get yourself familiarised with the place, in case Dave Fagg can't make it. He suffers from Malaria and can be off duty for several days you know." he added glumly.

"If that is so, then it could easily have been him to fall overboard, and maybe is an explanation to the short fuse he showed me at the dining table during lunch."

"Thanks for telling me. That is a usual sign of another bout coming up. If you've finished with the tank inspection, then see me after supper. You might have to take over in a hurry."

"And here's me thinking I was on a two week Pacific cruise Alan." John teased.

Hodgson laughed at the idea shaking his head.

"A Pacific cruise, he says! Sorry to disillusion you and all that, but there's no room for extra passengers on this ship, John. I can vouch for that, and Bell will make certain of it anyway." he chortled.

"Oh well Alan, mustn't disappoint the boss must we. Anyway, I'll see you around 2100, once I've entered my figures and have them written up!" John confirmed with a grin.

"Yes, that'll do, see you later." Hodgson said, disappearing down the passageway.

It did not take John long to settle into a good Engineering routine, even though he had to double up in the engine room in pace of Fagg who was confined to the sick bay.

The crewmen were trying to find things to while away the lazy days in the balmy sunshine, whereas the few passengers on board were going stir-crazy, as they had nothing to do except do nothing.

The same two films kept to amuse the souls on board were shown almost daily, until everybody was an expert actor, taking on or speaking the parts of those on the screen. Fortunately the well-stocked saloon bar helped to pickle some of their brains enough not to notice how slowly the days were slipping by.

Until one day, a tropical storm found them and started to play around with them, which changed the routine, and had all the passengers staying in their cabins practising being seasick.

John was in the engine room about to come off the middle watch (midnight to 4 am), when his 3rd Engineer came looking for him.

"We've got a blown tank valve 2nd." he shouted over the noise of the big powerful diesels.

"Nothing we can do until the weather slackens off. Just make sure the heaters are switched off in that tank, as it will allow the fuel to solidify and choke off the outflow pipe." John shouted, pointing to the row of coloured lights on the tank control panel. John watched as the 3rd switched off the series of lights indicating the heaters were now off.

"Okay 3rd that should do it for now. Tell the electrical officer what you've done in case he gets a power surge in his grid system. Inform the duty officer on the bridge before you get turned in." John ordered, sending the 3rd away again.

Hodgson had come down early to relieve John to witness John's actions.

"Well done John. Suggest you get that valve fixed a.s.a.p. You might have to make a new valve cotter and a sleeve if we've run out of them. Those valves are sub spec making them prone to blowing even in a light breeze. If the tanks get too full beyond its safety level any movement of the ships expansion plates will force the contents out of the weakest point, which are the valves.

Weather permitting, try to get it sorted out during the forenoon watch, as Dave should be back to normal by then." he whispered in John's ear

John merely nodded his head, then after showing Hodgson the current state of the gauges and fuel consumption, he signed the engine room logbook, climbed up the vertical ladder, and out of the engine room.

'Problem one: How to ensure a correct level of tank capacity. Two: How to ensure the pressure relief valve operates before the cotter pin or the sleeve gets broken. Three: How to' John murmured, falling fast asleep on his bunk, despite the ship trying to roll him out of it because of the storm.

CHAPTER IX

A Birmingham Spanner

John was eating a leisurely breakfast of hot buttered toast and marmalade with relish, when Sinclair entered the dining room to join him.

"Morning John! This ship could do with your STAN when this storm goes away. Because the Bosun and his team have been up all night trying to keep the ship on course." Sinclair, informed him with a nod of his head.

"Why all night Andy? You must have been on the bridge to know."

"They had to steer by hand for several hours apparently, all through my watch anyway. It appears to be fixed now, so long as it doesn't break down again. Maybe you could sort it out?"

"Unless the 3rd asks for help then there's nothing I can do. Its the Chief's pigeon not mine, anyway, I've got a problem of my own to sort out once the weather gets a bit calmer."

"That's the fourth problem this ship has picked up since we've come aboard. You don't think it's jinxed do you?"

"No Andy. A new ship has a few teething problems from time to time."

"I was on a destroyer that seemed to be jinxed. It was always on a convoy getting hit by the big guns of the Eytie cruisers. Or running aground or getting hit by a torpedo in its bows and such like. Later on, another destroyer and us were the only warships to survive an aircraft and submarine attack from the Jerries when we were on our way to Malta. The aircraft carrier plus several of our big ships got sunk, as did most of the merchant ships. In fact only one ship got through on that occasion. That was a large tanker too but not quite as big as this one. Anyway I believe that we make our own luck as far as I'm concerned." Sinclair concluded when the steward arrived with his breakfast.

John listened to this story in silence, as it was one of several other ones that he and Larter had told him, thinking that he was glad they had survived that terrible time for him to meet up with them when he did. He finished off his breakfast but waited for a moment before leaving.

"Must be going now, but I'd appreciate a favour, say in about two hours. And that is to have a sea boat on stand-by just in case I lose some of my men again. I have to get two tank top valves fixed which means dangling under those outboard catwalks."

"I have no problem with that John, but you'd better see the Captain first. He's worse than Blayden when it comes to rule books and the like, yet he seems to have the expert skills of Trewarthy."

"Are you sure it's not his brother in disguise Andy? I mean we're talking about lynch mobs and all that." John quipped.

"No you're safe there John. Besides, no other shipping line would take him. He's too much up the arse of Belverley and Company for that."

"Thanks for cheering me up Andy. Maybe see you later." John said with a grin, then went to prepare his team to sort out the overnight problem the storm had given him.

"Right gather round men. I know the sea is still a bit heavy, but as we've got a job to do I want two volunteers to help me." John said over the noise of the occasional wave that splashed up right over the decks below their catwalks.

John waited for a response but got none, even trying to entice a couple of them to step forward, as the men looked nervously around them.

John asked one more time for two men to volunteer else he would detail two off, but still no takers not even the ones he eventually got detailed off, refused to obey his orders.

"Okay then. Everybody get back to their mess and stay there until we dock. That means you have no job nor have any further purpose on board this vessel. Your pay will be stopped as of now and for you to pay for all food and accommodation you have been enjoying for free. This will be your penalty for refusing to do a job you were taken on board to do. Now get below and I don't ever want to see you lot ever again." John shouted angrily, waving them back into the ships superstructure.

He remained where he was to give a close examination of the task to be done, paying no heed to the spray of the water that was drenching him. After several minutes he left the broken valve and went to see Hodgson in the engine room.

"I've had a mutiny on my hands Alan. The junior Engineer and the stokers refused to carry out my orders." John stated then went on to explain the situation, before telling Hodgson what he was intending to do.

"I'll see Ken Matthews the Purser to have their pay stopped, as they will be off loaded in the next port." Hodgson asserted, then went and got John a spare valve fitment.

"We've only got this one left, but you need to use that as a pattern to make more. We have the spare metal and lathes to do these types of repair, even to make new propeller. But you'll have to trade with the outside Engineer if you want him to help you." Hodgson advised.

"Thanks for the info Alan. I intend doing this work myself but I know a man who will help me any time of the day. Must get onto that tank now. I'll report back when the job is done." John replied, leaving the engine room with his vital bits of equipment.

"Ready when you are John. Lowering away now." Sinclair shouted, lowering John down onto the broken valve that was still spurting oil every time the ship dipped into the trough of another oncoming wave.

John stripped the broken parts off, giving the pre-arranged signals for Sinclair to send down the parts or tools he needed, just as an operating theatre assistant does when handing the surgeon his instruments by demand.

The operation took a long time due to the leaking oil and the sea spume, but Sinclair stood firm and holding onto his friend until John signalled that he could be hauled back up again.

"You've fixed the worst one John. Maybe the other one can wait until we're in calmer waters?" Sinclair asked with concern, observing that John was completely drenched to the skin, shivering with the cold.

Both men walked back along the catwalk heading to their cabins for a good hot bath and a hot drink to warm themselves up again.

"See you in the saloon later Andy. I've got to make another part for the other tank top. But as you said, it can wait until we're in calmer seas again." John suggested.

"I've got the afternoon watch John, but we'll definitely have a noggin together after supper." Sinclair grinned as they went their separate ways.

"Got one done with one to go Alan. Now where's the spare metal, as I'll be making a couple of the bastards before I go on deck again." John said, as he met up with Hodgson again.

"Well done John. There's no need for you to make them, as I've got the second 3rd Engineer to do it. When you've completed the repairs make sure your written report has any amendments or alterations you may have made. The spares I gave you were not the correct ones for the for'ard tanks, only for the aft tanks. That is to say, the ones aft of the bridge superstructure have a slightly different configuration and I do apologise for the mix up. I only discovered the mistake after I had checked the stores item number with the makers design specs." Hodgson admitted.

"No wonder I had to use a Birmingham spanner to force the pin and spider valve on. If it wasn't for the escaping oil acting as a lubricant, I'd never have got them on. Still, it will take weeks to get them off again, that's for sure." he said soothingly, putting his Chief at ease.

Hodgson just nodded his head in appreciation to John's calm acceptance of the mistake, then told him that as Dave Fagg was back to normal again, he could resume his duties again, even though he had no 'staff' to work with.

"I'm used to working alone. But I would appreciate the loan of the other 3rd Engineer from time to time."

"I'll arrange it as and when John. Come back after lunch as I'll have those parts ready for you. Don't forget to tell the Captain if in fact your deck officer friend hasn't already done so." Hodgson stated leaving John to conduct more inspections and machine monitoring.

'Cheers Alan, I nearly forgot that.' John muttered to himself as he made his way onto the bridge.

"2nd Engineer Grey reporting Captain." John said quietly, entering the quietness of the bridge, which was totally opposite to the noise of the main engines.

"Hello Grey! There's no need for you to report. I've been watching you and your progress from here. Both you and 3rd Mate Sinclair were brave men to do what you did., but I will not allow you to attempt such a feat again. You will wait until the weather is calm again before you even venture onto those outside catwalks. Both of you could have been swept overboard at any time, especially when those rogue waves kept hitting us right where Sinclair was standing." Bell chided but with softness in his voice.

John admitted that he intended to do just that, but that particular repair was an emergency that had to be done. He also informed Bell as to how he had intended to do the work in the first place, and the refusal by his team of workers to do their duty despite a direct order as given by him.

"Did they by damn! I will not have my officers treated in contempt that way, even though some of them deserve it. In the fighting navy that would be tantamount to mutiny, and I'll not have it on my nor any other of the line's ships. I'll see to it they'll have their pay stopped forthwith then get them off my ship in the next port." Bell hissed.

"Leave that with me and the Chief, we'll have that sorted for you." he added.

"I am capable of sorting them out through the departmental procedures Captain, but then I naturally bow to your power of command." John replied calmly.

Bell looked at John for a moment before answering.

"I've read your portfolio Grey which backs up your statement. You are proving to be a good Engineer who this company hopes to benefit from. However, kindly leave the company policy of discipline to those whose job it is to enforce it, namely your Captain. We'll say no more on that Grey, but thank you for coming to report. Your Chief will appreciate your report more than me, as my first interest is getting my ship and all who sail in her safely from one port to another, with the cargo coming a close second."

"Thanks for the lecture Captain, I'll bear that in mind." John said and went to leave the bridge.

"Before you go Grey, I need you to do me a favour, and that is to assist the outside Engineer in getting my steering gear fixed properly. The forecast is for fair weather for the rest of this leg of the voyage, so you'll have time to complete your work as well. Speak to your Chief about it first though." Bell appealed.

"Unless the 3rd Engineer specifically requests my help there's nothing I can do Captain. It's his domain not mine, and I don't think the Chief Engineer can intervene either. I will speak to the 3rd Engineer on your behalf though. I dare say if he does require my assistance, then I shall be the first to help him." John countered, and left the bridge with a backward glance to see Bell standing there, looking surprised and with his mouth agape.

The *Repulse Bay* had sailed almost 7,000 miles during which all her teething problems were finally ironed out, and the crew were feeling proud of themselves as they lounged on the upper deck and taking their well earned rest. The mutinous crewmen were banned from such luxuries as they were now kept in confinement well below decks.

John had helped the outside Engineer with his problem who

eventually became almost an indispensable member of the Engineering department, as he helped solve the various engineering problems. In so doing, he was having his portfolio marked accordingly, just as Hodgson had informed him when he first joined the ship.

The time was seemingly slack so John managed a few meetings with Larter in his Wireless office, and even a little get-together in the saloon when the opportunity arose.

"Brisbane is just the other side of the Great Barrier Reef about a hundred miles or so. When we get there, I'll be able to look up a couple of friends living near the Brisbane Cricket club. The 'Gabba' I think it's called." Sinclair said, enjoying a cool glass of beer.

"You seem to have relatives everywhere Andy. Not Like Bruce and me." John grinned.

"Listen to him. He's probably got a whole tribe waiting for him back in Maoi." Sinclair chuckled.

John smiled at the reference to TeLani, making a mental note to try to contact her to see how she was.

"You been to Aussie land before Bruce?" John asked.

"Yes. Up in Darwin and Perth, with the *Fernlea.* We came down from Singapore before ending up in Capetown." Larter said with a far-away look on his face, which John recognised as yet another 'nostalgia trip'.

"I went Sydney, Brisbane, Townsville to Port Moresby before arriving Singapore to end up in Colombo on the *Cloverlea*." Larter remarked.

"Yes, we both met up in that bar in Capetown we visited John." Sinclair said with a grin, as they began to reminisce about old times again.

"Whoa hold on! Don't I get a look in here." John protested feebly.

"No mate. You're still a youngster at this game." Larter said with a large grin, and tousled John's hair with a friendly gesture.

"Well, on account that you've joined the clan, you can get the wets in John." Sinclair quipped, holding out his empty glass.

The banter between them was flowing freely and had become a talking point with the passengers and the rest of the officers on board. For it was between three different departments who normally and by tradition, were stand-offish to each other.

CHAPTER X

Executive Decision

The *Repulse Bay* arrived in Moreton Bay during the early morning, which allowed the few passengers to disembark and the transfer of several thousand tons of fuel into the thirsty fuel bunkers that stood in rows like gigantic galvanised dustbins.

Moreton Bay was discovered by Captain Cook in 1770, but the land where the adjudged second largest capital in the world was built, is the beautiful city of Brisbane, and was attributed to a surveyor called Lt Oxley, who finally went on to become the Surveyor General of New south Wales. The original name for the new found settlement was Ed Englassie but was renamed in honour of Sir Thomas Brisbane who was their first Governor of New South Wales (N.S.W.) and the town as it was then got gazetted in 1834.

Since those heady days, Brisbane is known as the capital of the Sunshine State, some 18 miles up river from its namesake river mouth that pours into Moreton Bay. Its name is not surprising as it basks in an equability of climate, with a variety of natural delights all around in great abundance. The Great Barrier Reef, with the fabled Gold Coast that has several miles of sandy beach are only two of the too many to mention.

It was also a location for the state's new immigrant settlers, with some original buildings which can still be seen today as yet another attraction for the curious wanderer and tourist. Many were fortunate enough make a new beginning for themselves and live a totally new life from the old days. To pay a paltry sum of £10 just to take them from one end of the earth to the other, Great Britain to Australia, was better in comparison to those who first arrived as convicts between the reigns of King George II through to King George V[th] era. This then is the new temporary home of the ship and her crew.

* * *

John had supervised and completed the discharge that afternoon, even had the tanks flushed out ready for the next load, when he decided it was time to get ashore.

He was on his way to his cabin when Hodgson met him, asking him to come into his cabin for a discussion.

"John we've got a problem with one of our propellers that needs specialist handling. So the Captain has the go-ahead to take the ship upstream to the Deakins ship repair yard, at Kangaroo Point. We can't go much further than that, as there's a large steel bridge in our way. According to the map it's called the Storey Bridge. Once we get there, we'll be staying there for a couple of days. We've been offered a hotel room for our stay, at a place called the Hotel National, but the crew will be given accommodation in the immigrant compound that's next to the yard. We should be there in a couple of hours." Hodgson explained, taking off his not so white overalls.

"Oh well, might as well enjoy a free ride when I can. I expect the pubs will be shut by then anyway. I've been told they open 10 to 10 each day and shut Sundays, so just as well it's mid week then." John replied philosophically.

"In the meantime we've got some unfinished business with our mutineers. The Captain wanted them off the ship and stranded, but I've managed to persuade him otherwise. The proviso being that as it was your problem it is for you to make the final, shall we say, executive decision." Hodgson said with a frown.

"I've done all right without them so far, which means that they're extra to requirements, excess baggage and all that. Then again, we don't know what's in store for us after leaving Brisbane. Add to that, the next 'Tank' Engineer might not be so lucky as me. Nor dare I say, as professionally competent to carry out these duties. Therefore it comes down to a proper management decision as to whether the line can do without these so-called 'excess baggage' therefore less manpower per ship. Or to ensure that the post held for such an important job be at least a 2nd

Engineer such as myself." John said diplomatically.

Hodgson studied John's reply for a moment, then took out a blank form from his desk and put it onto the table.

"This is the great executive decision moment John. The Captain dictates that it will be only your decision and signature on the form and nobody else. Just put their names down and sign it that's all." Hodgson said ominously as he watched John very carefully.

"What happens if I refuse to sign it? What other outcome can this have?"

"If you don't sign it, it means that you are not Chief Engineer material. If you do, it means that you have dashed the careers of those perhaps up-and-coming Engineers of the future. Either way, you're in a cleft stick John. It's either your career or theirs, it's that simple."

John sighed, and began to write down the names, starting with the two 4th Engineers. When he had finished he signed the form and dated it before throwing it across the table.

"I got to where I am through hard work to merit my rank of 2nd Engineer. I don't take kindly to blackmail nor boardroom games such as leapfrogging or the back-stabbing. I know the worth of a man when I watch him or work alongside him." John growled, handing back Hodgson's pen.

Hodgson opened his locker, taking out a bottle of whiskey, poured a large measure into two glasses and gave him one.

"Welcome to the club John. You have just proved to me, now to the management team to which the Captain is part; that you are definitely suitable for further promotion. It might take a little while, but promoted you'll get, even if they forced you to become such a bastard to sack the lot of them. In this line, its 'dog-eat-dog', therefore you've got to become such a thick-skinned, hard nut bastard as the rest.

Me included, because that's how I learned to survive in this shipping company. That however, does not cramp your style or work ethics, which the management team encourages and endorses fully, believe it or not." Hodgson comforted, swigging down his drink.

"Thanks for the lesson. I hate being used in this way, as I would have preferred a different outcome, even though I don't have one right this minute. But I'm glad you know where I'm coming from, at least." John said ruefully, drinking the offered whiskey, then handing back the empty glass.

"I knew where you were at when we first met and that probably also goes for the management team. Which as it happens, will just help to ease you into the mainstream of thinking by the shipping company. However, it means that you're on your own now John.

Remember this lesson and learn well from it, because I'm telling you as a friend, not your enemy. See you ashore some time." Hodgson concluded, putting the form into a brown envelope, sealing it shut.

The ship was riding high 'unladen' to make it easily up the twisting river 'till it came to the steel barrier of the Storey Bridge.

There was a gang of men waiting to tie her up to her temporary berth with a crane to lower the gangway for the crew to get ashore.

John was watching the procedure when Sinclair arrived alongside him.

"I managed to contact my friend Jock Kerr and family. He said that they will be over in the morning to pick us up. In the meantime, I suggest we grab a few wets in the saloon as the bars ashore are now shut. Bruce will get the local radio over the tannoy for us to listen to, so we will have some idea as to what is on offer ashore. Coming?" Sinclair invited.

"That sounds a good idea. I've got a rather bitter taste in my mouth that needs washing away." John moaned.

"Well come on then, let's go!" Sinclair egged, so they grabbed their bags to return to the saloon.

When they entered the saloon there were a couple of strange

officers settling down with a drink yet in company with some of the ship's officers.

John looked at one person's back, staring at him for a moment before realising it was an officer he knew.

"Well if it isn't the old lead swinger Clarke." John said with delight, for the man to turn around and recognised him.

"Strewth, if it ain't me old Cobber John!" Clarke chirped, as they shook hands energetically in their earnest greeting of each other.

"What brings you down to Oz land then John?" he enthused. Before John answered, he re-introduced Sinclair, then Larter who also walked into the saloon.

"We're going to have a good time. I've got a mate who's got a tugboat upstream. We'll get him to take us around by sea to the Gold Coast, grab us a few feisty Sheilas and have a barbie on the beach." Clarke avowed, as they sat down to toast their renewed friendship.

The reunion lasted well into the early morning, before the steward decided it was time to shut the bar, and for everybody to get their heads down for a few hours to sleep it off.

"I've got a spare blanket and pillow so you can kip in my cabin, Aussie. C'mon you old dog, show us what an Aussie can do." John said quietly, helping the well-oiled man away to his cabin.

They woke to the sound of a radio commercial jingle for Cotties the great tasting lemonade, and the promise of a good bargain from Arunga's genuine Aussie souvenir shop.

Clarke got up off the floor, sluiced his face in some cold water before gargling some of it.

"Never mind the lemonade, lets get ashore and have us a real breakfast before we hit the town." He said with a grin.

"We'd better see Purser Matthews for some Aussie 'Mickey Mouse' money first and I've got to check into the National Hotel, Aussie, then perhaps take a look around the town, before we sail.

I don't want a repeat of Capetown and all that." John reminded him.

"Fair enough John. I'll take you over the short way, I've got a mate who's the skipper on one of the river ferries. He'll take us around the bend there under the bridge and drop us right by the place no worries."

"Come on then, I'll get Bruce out too, but Andy is going to meet up with his friends who live by the Gabba. Erm, Jock Kerr and family, I think he called them."

"Must be a new family in town. Still if they live right by the cricket ground, then he's got lots of bucks to spend, or at least, earning it to spend. We'll catch up with Andy later then." Clarke opined, walking swiftly across the gangway, through the small repair yard and down to a small pontoon, where he hailed a passing ferry launch on its way upstream.

John chuckled, as did Larter when they realised Clarke had just whistled for a boat ride just as you would hail a passing taxi.

"That's how it's done around here lads. Now lets get some tucker first shall we, I'm ruddy starving I could eat…."

"Yeah a scabby Roo!" Larter recalled.

"Cheez, he even remembers that too. Still, what can you expect from a man who can stand on a bloody great block of ice, raising a radio station several thousand miles away on his first shout." Clarke reposted•.

This made the three old ship-mates laugh, adding to the excitement of a good day ahead of them.

"Aussie, I meant to ask you, why is Kangaroo Point so called? Why is the river around the city just like the Thames and London. Why…?" John asked in quick succession.

Clarke looked at John, scratching his head.

"Bloody hell mate. Are you always full of questions? I thought you only saved them for other goliahs and not me."° he

---

• See *Ice Mountains.*

° A goliah is an Australian slang word used to describe a 'fool'.

scoffed but waded into the answers as the river craft sped its way up river into the heart of the city.

"Kangaroo point is where all the £10 pound a time immigrants land. They stay in the compound you saw for up to a month before they're slung off to make way for the next lot. It is their jumping off point, in Roo terms that is, for them to get a job and settle down to wherever they find a spot. Most do, but there's always the element of the whingers, commonly known as the 'Whinging Pom' who are less welcome than a nest of rattlesnakes.

The word POM is a reference to the mashed potatoes that was the diet of the immigrants instead of the real knobbly brown items called spuds." Clarke stated then carried on in his unmistakeable Aussie accent, which was both colourful and full of sayings that John and even Larter needed time to sort out what was meant.

"Let me tell you Cobbers what. Just keep with me an' all will be well." Clarke bargained, getting an unanimous yes from John and Larter.

The water taxi surged up river passing under several impressive bridges. To John, judging by what he saw, with river taxi's and ferries darting back and forth without a care in the world, it felt almost like watching the dodgems in a funfair.

"It seems that we're got caught in the rush hour Aussie, is there no rule of the road or seaway courtesy whatever Andy calls it?" John asked with concern as several ferry-boats came close to him, only just missing that would otherwise cause a collision.

"There is a strict rule of the river, as upheld by the Harbour master in the building next to that jetty over there. That particular jetty is more distinct from the all the others lining the river, because there's always a fast river patrol craft alongside to nab the speed merchants. My mate with the tug who we're about to meet, comes down stream twice a day regular as clockwork. He goes down on one allocated hour then comes back on another allocated hour. His route is right down the middle lane of the river and is restricted to a 5knot speed limit, unless it's in an emergency down at the docks. At least that is the rule. But unfortunately the skippers of the ferry-boats or the pleasure craft that you see nipping around, think they rule the river so see it their God given right to set off whenever they want to, never mind who's on the river." Clarke grumbled, just as their river taxi had to swerve to prevent a collision with another water taxi who had darted right out in front of them.

"See what I Mean?" Clarke said in disgust.

"This place sounds like Venice, then." Larter opined.

"Ain't that the truth mate." Clarke concluded as the water taxi arrived at a ferry landing stage.

Clarke thanked his friend as they stepped onto dry land again with John looking at a very prominent building, which seemed to tower over all the other high-rise buildings.

"That's the City Hall clock. Some 300 feet high, because most of the local politicians and councillors have got to see the time to come in from the outlying areas for them to clock in on time for their meetings. Also they need it to remind themselves they've got four faces on them just to keep their fiddling perks going" Clarke informed them.

"Anyway, this is the Eagle Street Wharf. Your hotel is just down the road from it on Adelaide Street. I'll give my mate a call from there before we go down river." he added, as they walked briskly towards their hotel.

When they arrived, they met up with some of the other officers and a few from other ships that were in harbour.

Larter met an old friend who wanted him to go up country to see the new radio station, but as he was in two minds he asked John if he minded.

"No, not all Bruce! Your trip to Mt Coot-Ha or however you pronounce it is your particular cup of tea. I've been promised a look over Aussie's tugboat, which you'd probably find just as boring as I would a radio set. Maybe we can meet up here later on, and have a wet then. Don't forget that Andy might be popping back later as well. If you see anybody looking for me, tell them I've gone walk about." John replied evenly, for Larter to nod in agreement then left them.

"It looks like it's just thee and me 3rd Engineer Clarke." John teased, when Clarke came back with two large jugs of ale.

"Oh well, that's more of the amber nectar for you. Here grab a load of this." Clarke beamed, giving John an overflowing jug.

"Cheers John. This is one schooner I've owed you from God knows when, mate. You're all right in my books, matey." Clarke declared, holding out his hand shaking John's in mutual respect.

John smiled at this unexpected and sudden exposure to Australian male bonding, which is a vital ritual between two good friends with a history of fellowship between them.

"I hope to have a look around this lovely city of yours, Aussie. Maybe we can all meet up here tonight to plan a sightseeing tour." John said hopefully.

"No worries mate! Aussie's got it all in hand. But hold fire, as I've got two beaut Sheilas for you tomeet. They should be on board my mate's tugboat. Them and about a dozen more just to make things a bit more even." Clarke bragged, drinking the last of this ale.

"I'll be back in a tick John. Here's a couple of dollars, get them in. Just ask for Clarke's special, but watch he gives you twenty cents change, if not then let me know, because he's a fiddlin' bastard" Clarke advised, before going over to a wall mounted phone.

John got his jugs of ale with the correct change then waited until Clarke came back from what he could see was an animated exchange of phone calls.

"Me mate's called me back to the tug, as we've got to move you down stream to the slip yard, which is about five miles away. Apparently your ship is too big for the dry dock, so it needs to be hauled up stern first onto the slipway to ship the new prop. When we're finished, we've got a meet up with the others for a long trip down to the white continent." Clarke said despondently.

"So that means, I can have a cruise on your tug but only as far as the slip yard? What about this other trip?" John asked non-plussed.

"Our tug is one of six chartered tugs that go south to bring back an iceberg to use as fresh water. We take about two weeks to get there and select a suitable berg, something on the same lines as the one we were on, then tow it north for about four weeks or so, to a desalination plant near Freemantle, where they convert it into drinking water. The cubic ton of ice water pays us but it's soul-destroying work when we see almost half of what we've been towing for weeks on end just melting away. What we really need is at least two ships of your size to come with us, so we could melt the ice down and have it piped on board, rather than see it disappear the way it does. In other words, instead of a million tons of ice water, we only get about half of it." Clarke moaned, slurping noisily with his ale.

John looked at Clarke, whilst mentally visualising the spectacle and the colossal undertaking of towing an ice mountain some two thousand miles, yet using only a half dozen tugs.

"So this tug you're Chief Engineer on, must be some powerful beast then Aussie. I'm looking forward to see your engines for a start." John stated cheerfully in an attempt to cheer his friend up.

"Not so much the engines, but the four synchronised propellers, John. Your ship has two ordinary props, bigger engines, but your gearing is much higher than ours. You're only pushing about 65,000 tons but we can tow or even push at least ten times that, plus of course we've also got the other five in harness towing the same weight ratio. Mind you, it's all in the length therefore the weight of the tow line that counts." Clarke bragged.

"Anyway, we've got ten minutes to get to the Customs ferry wharf, to join it." Clarke added, draining his glass.

John followed him to the wharf and boarded a small launch waiting to take them to the large tug chugging its way down the middle of the river.

They watched the tug come slowly alongside the launch for them to jump on board, and then make its way down stream.

"G'day Sport! Where's the skipper?" Clarke asked as he reached the fairly spacious bridge.

"He's below looking at some plans, Clarke. Just as well you got aboard, as your bloody stoker nearly had us going upstream instead of down. Maybe you'll teach him the difference of going ahead instead of astern." the seaman said sarcastically.

"Never mind my grease-monkey, keep your ruddy eye on the road will you!" Clarke riposted.

John had witnessed a typical encounter between the two Australians, which he decided was downright rude, but at least it was plain speaking.

John stood looking around the bridge, then at the busy river which was brimming with all sorts of craft that were both commercial and pleasure.

As the tug was rounding a bend to take them under the large steel archway of the Storey bridge a ferry boat full of passengers, came from seemingly out of nowhere, directly in front of the tug almost under her bows.

There was no time for the tug to stop and go astern or steer out of the way of this craft, which resulted in the ferry being rammed amidships, causing it to sink rapidly within seconds of the collision.

The helmsman cursed loudly at the skipper of the ferry as he wrestled with his steering wheel, stopping the tug only by grounding it on a mud bank just a few yards down from the accident.

The skipper of the tug was on deck issuing orders to the crew, as John joined in to help pick up some of the survivors of the ferry. The skipper managed to drag a few of the women and children out of the water and even the ferry-boat skipper whom he literally threw onto the deck like a freshly caught fish.

"You fuckin' stupid goliah! The ferry-boat skipper started to shout, before the tugboat skipper grabbed him by his lapels and dragged him right up off his feet.

"You mister, are responsible for this. You came right out in front of me, giving me no chance to stop. You should know that I'm due down this stretch of water, and you should have let me pass before you decided to cast off. I had right of way and you've caused me to ground the boat." the tugboat skipper screamed.

"You should have watched where you were going. You're the one at fault. And besides, by the smell of your breath you've been drinking, which is against the rules of pilotage in these waters." the ferry- boat skipper countered.

John managed to fish out several more survivors, each one blaming the tugboat for the collision despite what the tugboat skipper had said to the contrary.

There were other craft on the scene picking up survivors, until only floating dead were left to be picked up by the Customs cutter.

"That was an accident waiting to happen John. These ferry-boat skippers are like the pedestrians on a busy road. They step out into the road from between some parked cars right into the path of an oncoming vehicle. It happens so quick that a driver has no chance of stopping, nor any place to turn in case they bump into any oncoming vehicles. This is just like it, whereby these ferryboats, especially the cruise launches think they own the place and feel they can just cast off into mid-stream without regard to other river users.

Our skipper will now be facing a murder inquiry, probably to have his skippers licence torn up in the process. In the meantime, it looks as if our trip has been cancelled, and another tug will get the contract to dock your ship." Clarke said angrily, kicking the feet of one of the ferry-boat deck crewmen who happened to be sitting on deck nearby.

"If it means anything to you Aussie, I can put a word in for you to come on board for a spell and earn yourself a decent wage for a while. I should imagine that this board of enquiry will take a couple of months though, as you'll probably be required to stand trial as part of the crew."

"Don't forget you're on board too John, but I should imagine a written statement from you will suffice for you to get sailing again." Clarke said, reminding John of his own involvement.

"Yes, if Bruce or even Andy was here, they'd be able to pinpoint the fault straight away, and that being the careless ferryboat skipper was not looking where he was going nor observing the rules of the road, for him to get steam-rolled the way he was. He just got in the way of a faster moving craft so was not able to speed up to get out of the way. I mean, he must have cast off from that point several times already today to be fully aware of the regular traffic making their way up or down stream, so he should have waited until you had passed his point. It really doesn't matter if you were all drunk on board, because you were in the usual place at the usual time, same course and rate of knots. That would have been sufficient for anybody else to give way to you, and let you pass. It's the ferryboat skipper who's at fault and I shall be stating that, especially given that I've already witnessed such careless and cavalier attitude of boat handling by these ferrymen earlier on today. I shall be writing that, even though I am an Engineer not a qualified sailor like Andy or your helmsman." John avowed.

"When we get alongside the wharf, make sure you give your statement to the Harbourmaster before you get back to the hotel. Our tug will be going nowhere now for a while, neither will I, so maybe I'll see you later on, perhaps tomorrow morning. Remember, your ship is being towed downstream 5 miles to the slipway and will be there overnight, so give my regards to Andy and Bruce for me." Clarke said miserably, turning to and kicking the prone body of the ferry-boat skipper once more.

"You fuckin' blind bastard. You've just cost me a day out with me mates. I've got a good mind to throw you back into the water again to join the rest of the turds floating down river, you piece of Roo dung." Clarke said angrily, before his skipper grabbed hold of him and calmed him down.

The local TV and pressmen had somehow gathered in their numbers, forming a large crowd on the wharf, as the tug along with the remains of the ferryboat got tied up alongside.

John pushed his way through without hindrance, making his way back to the hotel where he managed to watch the scenes on the television screen hoisted way above the bar to prevent anybody tampering with it.

From the comments being made in the bar, John deduced that everybody seemed to be well qualified as sailors to be able to pass judgement on both vessels' crews, but coming heavily out in favour of the tug.

"Bloody 'river jay walking' the idiot was doing. Listen to him saying that the tugboat skipper and his crew were drunk and it was they that caused the collision. That tug goes up and down the river twice a day, regular as clockwork, yet that skipper off the ferry never knew it. He's a fuckin' liar of the first water he is, 'cause he's got a mate working on one of the other tugs that share the same work." one man said angrily, which several other drinkers vociferously agreed with.

John said nothing but drinking his beer, quietly slipped out of the bar and made his way to his room.

CHAPTER XI

Shacked Up

John was sitting in the lounge reading the local paper which depicted the dramatic scenes of yesterday splashed all over it, noting the comments being made by the 'know all' admirals such as those he had heard in the bar. But it was the expert thinking which placed the blame squarely onto the ferry-boat skipper, given that the tug had the right of way. The several deaths were as the result of the ferryboat skipper placing his craft into the path of an oncoming craft and that he did not take the precautions of visually checking to see the middle lanes were clear for him to enter them safely.

Yet it was the crew of the tugboat who had been cautioned for reckless navigation, and the families of the dead blame the drunken tugboat crew for not being able to stop their boat in time. The tugboat Captain had been remanded pending a full enquiry into the matter, whilst the ferryboat Captain was still allowed to work on another ferry.

'My statement was taken yet nobody took a blind bit of notice of it. Perhaps the fact I am an Engineer not a sailor has made them decide my statement was of no account. I'll speak to Bell about all this when I get on board again. See if I can get Clarke a berth on board for our next voyage, given that we're a couple of Engineers down.' John said quietly

"There you are, still talking to yourself I hear." Sinclair said with a grin, sitting next to John.

"Hello Andy. I was just commenting on this bloody fiasco on the river yesterday. Look at the papers. I was on board the tugboat with Aussie Clarke at the time, and I've given a statement into the local Harbourmaster and the local police." John responded, throwing the paper to Sinclair to read.

Sinclair read through the several articles whilst John got him a beer.

"My friend Jock's got shares in one of the local ferry

companies, says that the ferryboat skipper from that company is a bit of a show-boater. He likes to show off in front of his passengers, by trying to outpace other river craft around him. The tug was on its usual run, so the ferry should not have tried to cross his bow in an attempt to beat the tug down river. As far as I'm concerned, the ferry got run over through the stupidity of the ferryboat skipper in not looking where he was going, nor to see if anything was coming. You're supposed to look left and right and then left again before crossing the road, and on the river it's exactly the same thing. On top of that, his craft was probably overloaded for it not to respond as well had it have been much lighter, or the passengers not sitting down to make the craft stable whilst in the initial manoeuvre of taking off from the jetty. I wonder if the ferry skipper had a few snorters himself before leaving the jetty, because there was supposed to be some party-goers on board. For my money, it was the ferryboat skipper's fault for undue care and attention to river traffic requirements as laid down by the local harbour or river authority. Let's hope this will be a lesson to any future such happenings." Sinclair said at length, throwing the paper back to John.

"Anyway, I've come to see if you're fit for a quiet run ashore to see the local sights of this fair city. I've got a map of the area so we can go around by tram or the odd taxi if we want to." Sinclair added with enthusiasm.

"Why not Andy. Oh, and by the way, the ship was taken down stream to some dry dock, so we've got another couple of days ashore before we're required again. There's no message from the ship, so I can take it we're not needed for a while. Incidentally where's Bruce? I haven't seen him since we came ashore yesterday."

"I gave Bruce Jock's number in case he wanted to meet up. He phoned me yesterday evening saying that he's got himself lashed up with some Met office girl at the radio station. He must have something special in his trousers for him to pull every time we come ashore, no matter where we end up."

"C'mon now Andy. Let's not be too jealous. We've got a beautiful city to look around that will only cost us the bus fare. Poor Bruce might be dipping his hand into his pocket too often with his latest find, and probably come back on board stoney broke like he did last time." John rebuked mildly.

"Aye, s'pose your right again. Still, we'll have another wet before we go walk about, as the locals say."

"I've managed to pinch one of the Jackson tourist guides from the reception, we can use that to plan our trip." John said, taking out a folded pamphlet from his trousers pocket.

"Well then, what are we waiting for, lets get going. We turn to starboard when we get out of the hotel." Sinclair responded as they walked quickly out of the hotel and onto the bustling pavement of Adelaide Street heading towards the city hall to commence their tour of the city.

"Well that was a bit of cultural fun, John. Now let's get a few wets down our throat before the bloody bar shuts for the night!" Sinclair stated hoarsely, when the pair finally arrived back to their hotel again.

"There's a message for you Mr Grey, the receptionist stated as she handed John a sealed envelope.

John read the note then showed it to Sinclair who simply shrugged his shoulders and said.

"If he's allowed to sail again. The local constabulary will probably keep him ashore until the public enquiry has taken place over that sinking. Although I would have thought it would only concern the skipper and his deck crew, but not the engine room staff who are usually below when navigating any river or waterway."

"Glad you're with me Andy. I hope to get Aussie a trip on board for our next voyage out of here, as we're at least two Engineer officers short." John replied with relief.

John went to call the phone contact that was mentioned in the message.

* * *

"Come down to the hotel sometime this evening so we can get you booked in. I hope to see Alan Hodgson in the morning, so if you're around, I can introduce you to him and see what he says. Nothing promised though Aussie." John stated, concluding his little phone call, before joining Sinclair in the lounge for a well-earned beer.

"Aussie Clarke should be coming here soon, but the hotel is booked up, so he'll have to stay in my room overnight." John explained, telling Sinclair of the possible future arrangements.

"He can always use Bruce's room, seeing as he's already shacked up ashore. I'll get the keys for him." Sinclair answered and left his beer to get Larters room key.

"It's already been collected, which means that Bruce is already in residence, probably got his leg over right now the lucky bastard." Sinclair said in a fit of jealousy when he returned from the reception desk.

John laughed at Sinclair's momentary show of jealousy placating him with a large fat cigar and a large measure of whiskey.

"Best keep decorum Andy, in case of some tropical disease you could pick up from these places." John said, with a chuckle.

"Chance would be a fine thing, considering all the clinics I keep seeing dotted around the bloody place. Still at least there are plenty of real virgins around, even though I can't trap one just right now." Sinclair snorted, as Clarke came through the door with two very stunning young women one on each arm.

"Aussie, you golden bollocked bastard! Any chance of sharing?" Sinclair asked with jealousy, licking his lips at the sight of the two girls.

"Glad you could make it Aussie. Come and wet your whistle with a few of the Amber nectars." John greeted, when Clarke handed one of the girls over to Sinclair.

"Here you are Andy, she just simply adores Scotsmen especially when they're wearing their kilts. She likes to see if anything is worn under them." Clarke chuckled then introduced the girls.

"No Aussie. There's nothing worn under my kilt as any lucky girl will find out. It's all cocked and ready for firing." Sinclair said with a large grin, emphasising the word 'cock', before he planked the giggling female down gently onto his lap.

During the course of the evening, Sinclair disappeared with his new-found girlfriend, they came back later on, him having a big smirk on his face and her with a grin from ear to ear.

When they arrived, Sinclair started to explain his absence, whilst the two girls giggling and compared notes.

"They must be Fishermen's daughters judging by the measurements they've been showing with their hands." John said innocently, but knowing what the secret discussion the girls had was all about.

"Listen to him. Saint John of the Maoi Islands. The only man in the whole crew to screw the King's entire female relatives." Sinclair said rudely, but with a large grin on his face.[•]

"Tell us more John, or are you too shy to tell." Clarke's female friend asked sweetly.

Before John could answer, Larter and his new girlfriend joined them.

"Looks like poor John is the duty gooseberry. Let's get him lashed up, poor man." Larter suggested, then turned and whispered to his girlfriend.

Soon another girl appeared as if from nowhere, and sat next to John, indicating that she was his girl for the evening.

John scowled at this sudden arrangement, but soon mellowed his attitude as his 'company' was seemingly quite charming and pleasant to know, which to John had to be a pre-requisite before he even contemplated anything like Sinclair had just conducted.

The bar had shut but the friends adjourned to Larter's rented room, as it was the biggest with two extra beds to use up.

[•] See *A Beach Party*.

"Aussie, you can have my room as I'll stay here. We have to be down for breakfast by 0700 and I'm meeting up with Hodgson at 0800. So try and be around by 0800 in the reception." John instructed

"Right you are John. 0800 it is." Clarke said hastily, as he and his girlfriend rushed out of the cabin with one obvious thing on their minds.

The breakfast the following morning was a casual affair, as the four friends met up in the foyer, yet without the girls they were with the night before.

"That's how I like it. The Sheilas gone home to prepare for another night of snake charming, whilst we men get down to more serious drinking business." Clarke drawled, when they met up with Hodgson.

John introduced Clarke to Hodgson, giving Hodgson a brief profile of Clarke's background and his recent involvement with the tug. All of which was received with surprising ease, considering John was anticipating some sort of protest or rejection.

"You appear to come highly recommended by my 2nd Engineer, Clarke. We do have room for a good Engineer, but we'll have to clear it with the Captain, who is also part of the company management team. I should caution you that if all is okay, we can only take you on just the one trip from here. All subject to legal contracts and the like from your present skipper." Hodgson said, shaking Clarke's hand.

"That's fine by me Chief. I'll soon find my way back no worries." Clarke said affably.

"We're due out of dock some time today, then come back here for a few more, shall we say, alterations to the turbines. We've got a change of Captains who is hoping to sail tomorrow evening to load up for our next leg of the contract. For that, I'll need you on board when the ship arrives back in the Deakins' yard, John. Clarke here might as well join you for a 'preview' of his job. Get

Purser Matthews to sign his articles. Must go now, so see you then." Hodgson announced, leaving John and his friends.

"Now that's a better shape than the bloody Triple Crown line. Let's hope they're better payers as I could do with some extra bucks in my wallet." Clarke said softly, watching Hodgson walk swiftly to a waiting taxi.

"Well it seems that John has done you a big favour Aussie. Let's make certain you don't try to lynch this skipper or we'll all be up the bloody creek." Sinclair advised.

"Never mind that, Andy. Just where is your next voyage taking you?" Clarke replied swiftly.

"According to my schedule, we're due to pick a shipload of fuels and deliver them to at least 8 different places, ending up back here again. Incidentally John, according to my radio schedules, we're due to return to the Taraniti Archepelago. Thought you might want to get yourself prepared as I'm referring to extra special presents and all that." Larter stated, reading from a small diary that he produced from his top pocket.

"Thanks for telling me Bruce. Hope I can get a quick run ashore before we leave, or perhaps get something on one of the places we're visiting.

Clarke offered to help out which was gratefully accepted by John.

"Anyway, when we come back from our delivery round, we'll be loading up again to be on our way to Hong Kong. Subject to present company operations, that is." Larter added, putting his diary back into his pocket.

"I've met quite a few of the friendly people on the so-called friendly islands. Most of the Micronesains and Polynesians too, but Hong Kong is the place where all the action is. Yes! That'll do very nicely!" Clarke said excitedly, punching the air with his fist.

"It is obvious that the poor people of Hong Kong have met you before then, Aussie." Sinclair said with a grin.

"You'd better believe it. I know quite a few bar tenders with lots of lovely little slant eyed girls who really know how to please their men-folk." Clarke bragged.

"A typical Aussie. Only two things on their mind!" Larter chuckled.

"Up there for swallowing the amber nectar, down there for playing the didgeridoo!" Clarke quipped, pointing to his throat and then his crotch.

CHAPTER XII

Brass

"Here you are Aussie, this one's your cabin." John said when they arrived into the accommodation area.

Clarke stepped inside and took a look round, before he dumped his case onto the carpeted deck.

"Hmm! It'll just about do. I suppose I just might get used to it by the time we reach Hong Kong." Clarke stated in a typical Australian offhanded manner, yet secretly relishing the thought of living in it.

"Typical Aussie gratitude that is! Never satisfied." John said with mock horror.

Clarke chuckled, holding his arms out wide.

"Well, beggars can't be choosy I suppose, John. Anyway, lets get down to that donk shop of yours to see what I'm up against. Before we do John, what's this special preparation you've got to do. Some Sheila you've met and have put her up the spout? " Clarke asked, quickly donning a pair of overalls to get himself ready for his conducted tour.

"Something on that line yes. But as a matter of interest, were you here when the *Inverlogie* arrived for repairs, some eighteen months ago? Only I've not heard anything from the dockyard workers about it. Like as if she never arrived."

"Oh yes, I remember the *Inverlogie*. She had a complete one year refit as a Super Fridge freighter and collected her cargo up on her way back to Britain. That was nearly nine months ago now, so it just shows how time has flown. I've been down to the white continent and back three times since then. Their skipper had to be taken away to the funny farm, but the Engineer seemed decent enough, Blackmore I think his name was. Yes Blackmore, I met him only the once and he mentioned that he knew you. That was why I hoped you'd be on this ship even though I found out it wasn't a Bay ship from the Triple Crown line. Still, close enough to be perfect John." Clarke informed.

"Blackmore and I were on fridge trials on the *Inverlogie,* until we arrived at our destination port of Maoi I'ti. We had an extended stay due to the fact that the whole archipelago was hit by a mega tsunami leaving only the main atoll and half of two other islands standing. The rest was completely washed away, with most of the locals killed. We managed to survive it but the ship was so badly damaged, she had to be towed here by two of your big tugs. I'll tell you about it one day, but sufficient to say, that I met the local King and his family who took a shine to me. Hence the special presents to take there." John said quietly.

"What old King Phatt man and his robbing bastards? You met them? You must have a set of golden bollocks to survive that lot. Strewth mate, you'll need extra help and I know just the man to see. Afterwards, maybe I'll nip ashore to see one of the lads in the dockyard, who'll get what you want.

Be ready with a fist full of dollars though. In fact, better make that two fists, as Phattie is a bloody rich bastard who has expensive tastes, according to one of my mates who'd just come from there with a wrecked fishing boat."

"Well whatever Aussie, better stow this gum beating as you put it, and get our tour on the go." John concluded.

They went all over the ship, with John pointing out various machinery, valves and pipe-work that would be of particular interest, before they finally arrived back into the engine room where they met Hodgson, Fagg plus the rest of the officers and stokers gathered in a meeting.

"Good! Glad you've arrived. I can now finish my meeting." Hodgson said evenly, concluding his meeting with the department, before turning to John and Clarke.

"Clarke! Until I've sorted things out, you'll be doing engine room duties with 2nd Engineer Fagg here, who will see to your watch keeping and other requirements. As for you John, you'll get a junior Engineer plus a couple of stokers assigned to you, as you'll need them on this leg of the voyage. I've looked at your diagrams, reports etcetera concerning the tanks, and will be taking them up once we finally get back to Hong Kong. But for now, you'll have to do things the hard way just as they are now." Hodgson instructed, then left them.

"See you later Aussie, but remember what I've said. Big ships with big routines and all that." John said quietly, then left the engine room.

John was now able to read between the lines from what had been spoken or promised him, he knew he was totally on his own, which meant that he now had nobody in tow to look after or having to nursemaid somebody as he did earlier.

'Maybe I can get some decent work done now, and set up my next project. At least I don't have to belong to the 'Sandeman's' gang of cloak and dagger merchants.' John muttered to himself, as he strolled back down the stairway into his corridor leading to his cabin.

"Aussie, you won't be required whilst we're going down stream for fuelling and storing. See if you can find that mate of yours who had the wrecked fishing boat and ask him to come on board to see me. But first, go to see the foundry man and tell him to give you two finished brass wheel valve assemblies for a ten-inch wheel valve. Be quick about it Aussie, you've got about one hour to meet up again.

"On my way John. I know where you'll be docking, so I'll see you then." Clarke replied, swiftly removing his overalls then raced ashore just as the gangway was about to be removed.

John watched him race into the foundry building just as Hodgson arrived next to him.

"What's Clarke doing ashore John?" Hodgson asked abruptly.

"I sent him ashore to get me two ten inch wheel valve assemblies, as we've run out. I have to convert the tank valves on the after tanks from steel to brass, due to the highly inflammable fuel we're taking on board. Here is my loading schedule and the tank usage." John replied softly then took out a crisp piece of paper from his inside tunic pocket.

Hodgson looked at it for a moment then nodded.

"It is good you're pretty well switched on how to load up a ship. I had forgotten just how dangerous the loading of aviation fuel (Avgas) can be. Once we've taken the fuels on board, the Captain wants to have a pre-voyage conflab. We're one of the biggest tankers in the world down this part of the hemisphere at the moment about to take it into coral reef territory, maybe that's why."

"I've an idea of where we're going, but I should imagine we shouldn't have many places with docking problems, or at least deep water anchorage."

"I've been around a few of them and yes you're correct there. But I'm a bit sceptical dodging around the archipelagos with our deep draught all the same." Hodgson admitted.

"Speaking of which, Alan. Can you give me a discharge tariff, so I can work out the internal balance tank differentials?"

"We won't know that until Sparks has got all his fuel requirement signals. In the meanwhile, all we can do is load to capacity on all four fuels. We can carry the equivalent of two maybe three tankers worth in one go, so it'll be a very highly profitable voyage. Providing of course we don't get stuck on some infernal reef slap-bang in the middle of nowhere."

The two Engineers stood for a while watching the scenery slip by as the ship moved slowly down stream and towards their fuelling point.

"Must go now. But in case I don't have the chance to see you before the Captain's spiel, I won't be taking on any fuel until I get those valves fitted. I need to load all three fuels in one intake, so as to keep the ship on a stress free loading and to maintain a decent trim." John concluded, and was given a knowing grunt from Hodgson, before he left.

"Here're your valves John. A mite heavy to put in your back pocket they are, and here's my mate I was telling you about." Clarke said, handing over the heavy brass equipment, introducing his friend.

"What's the problem Blue?" the friend asked, shaking John's hand as a greeting.

"I understand that you've come back from a disastrous trip to the wrecked Taraniti archipelago. I know about that because I was there when it got wrecked with a 300foot tidal wave." John commenced, then telling him briefly about the beach party then asked him what he wanted to know.

"Bloody hell mate. So you're the Iceman! The Phatman and his tribe have a stone carving of you, which they adorn with Leis every so often. Yes, there are lots of little Indians running around, and from what I've counted there're about five of them who belong to Phatties daughters. If you're the one responsible, then I'll take my ruddy hat off to you especially if you managed all that in just one party. You must have one like a stirrup pump." he said with gusto and seemingly impressed.

Clarke looked at John non-plussed not quite taking in what was disclosed.

"Do you mean to tell me that you stuffed all the Kings women then carried on as if nothing happened?" Clarke asked in amazement.

John said nothing, merely stood looking at the two men.

"Then my friend, I know just what you can take. Lets see now." the friend said stroking his chin, looking skyward as if to visualise what he intended to do.

"If you give me say $40, I'll fix you up like a Joey in his mum's pouch!" he said after a little while.

"I haven't got any more Aussie dollars, but I can give you some Sterling. Quick, come to my cabin and get it." John urged, rushing off towards the accommodation area.

When they arrived, John went to his wardrobe and got out his wallet.

"Here's £20 Sterling, that should be sufficient to get a couple more for the mums with enough to get you a few wets for your dusty warbler." John smiled, handing over the money.

Clarke just smiled at John's reference to his friend's warbler, as the man smelt the money before he pocketed it.

"Ta mate! That'll do very nicely. C'mon Clarkie! Shake a leg, we've got some very expensive shopping to do down at the old Dog and Duck." he cooed, and turned to leave.

"You're on your own mate as I've got to sort out our 2nd here, 'cause he's no use with brass spanners and the like." Clarke replied, shaking his head.

"No worries mate. Leave it all to me, I know exactly what to get. See you both later." the friend said, slipping silently out of the cabin.

"But he's going straight to the Dog and Duck!" John said with disquiet.

Clarke chuckled telling him the name was used for a place all fishermen visit to get their special presents for their Sheilas back home.

"Gift wrapped and all guaranteed. Anyway Cobber! Let's get these bloody brass things shipped or we'll never get loaded. I'm on my way to Hong Kong you know." Clarke said with a big smile, grabbing the heavy sack with the wheel fitments.

John led the way to the after tank deck to convert the valves with Clarke's assistance.

"That's the female ends ready. Get all the male nozzles checked for'ard then get ready for the switch on, Aussie. Let me know, face to face as opposed to signal or shout." John directed.

Clarke came back ten minutes later to tell John that all was ready.

"All tank top valves open and connected up. Vent hatches open. No smoking lights switched on, and the hazard flag is flying. I've got 2 stokers on each tank standing by as fire watchers."

"Well done Aussie! I've checked the pump valves and load gauges, so get ashore to see the pump supervisors. Start with the two Avgas pumps for No4 tank. Give me ten minutes before you open the two FFO pumps for No 1 tank. Then in another ten minutes open up the two Avgas pumps for No 3 tank. After that ten minutes, start up the two diesel pumps for No 2 tank. Then another ten minutes for the single pump for our own refuelling. I calculate that we'll take about 10 hours before we complete the loading. I make it 1645 local time Aussie, what about you? Tell them to start at exactly 1700, and by your watch not theirs. Okay on all that?"

"1645? Right, I've set mine to that. So its ten minutes between each fuel pump being switched on. Start 1700." Clarke repeated back before he went swiftly along the short concrete fuelling jetty to the pump house.

When Clarke came back he informed John that the pump supervisor had shown him an automatic switch off mechanism, which stops pumping once the required amount has been reached.

"Something to do with the tank depth-gauge and the flow-meter regulator being coupled up to a timing device."

"Sounds pretty much what I saw at the Panama pumping station. We can relax for a while now Aussie, so if you want to take a few hours off, now's your chance. Go and see what your pal is doing with my money." John encouraged with a big smile.

"That sounds a bit alright! I'll be back around 2359 to give you a break if you want, no sweat."

"Fair enough Aussie. See you back on board, with my presents mind you." John agreed, as Clarke left John to observe the fuelling taking place.

He wandered up around the catwalks, checking the valves, also checking all the types of depth and fuel gauges that he hoped he would one day get rid of.

'A proper multi-fuel tanker would have split tanks with multi internal separation bulkheads. Fore to aft instead of beam to beam. Filters on each intake pipe, A pressure gauge that would tell me when the tank was full to the correct level, to make the pump switch off. A double hull with a sub pressure pump to keep the fuel from leaking from an accidental puncture hole in the ships' side.' he mused then decided to stop for a breather.

"Hello John. Everything okay?" Hodgson asked, appearing alongside John.

"All going well! I've borrowed Clarke to help me get the set up as I wanted. I've let him ashore now but he'll be back to relieve me at midnight." John admitted.

"That's fine by me John. As a matter of fact, I've got a good mind to swap him over with the new outside Engineer who came on board just before we left the Deakins yard. We've got a good rig on this ship and the pump-station ashore is first class, so what we'll be doing is testing out the discharge systems of the ports we're visiting. Have you seen the pump-station ashore?"

"No Alan, but I would like to. Maybe when Clarke comes back I'll have a look."

"You'll be lucky. The supervisors will be knocking off soon, once our tanks are half full. If you want a look, I'm doing nothing, so why not go now." Hodgson suggested.

"If you're sure Alan, then I'll be glad to. It will help me with my own project anyway." John said, then strolled ashore to the pump-house.

When he came back he told Hodgson that the set up was more advanced than he thought, and instead of a calculated 10 hour load, it would be done in 8. Which meant that the Captain would be able to sail on an earlier tide than expected.

"That is good news, but the Captain will be sticking to his planned sailing time anyway. However, it will give the rest of us a little more time to get organised. Such as our own supplies, the deck cargo still has to arrive, the tons of mail and the passengers. Besides, the pilots don't like being called out too early in the morning, let alone the big tugs who are needed to shift us from here."

"That's another thing I've got my mind on Alan, which can wait until we're out to sea again. I have some other item that I had hoped to discuss with you during our voyage across. Maybe if you're in the mood right now I can roll the gist of it past you." Hodgson looked down at his empty pipe then up at the NO SMOKING' signs that were illuminated all around the ship.

"Might as well John, as we've got a long time before we can smoke again." Hodgson sighed, stowing his pipe back into his top pocket.

John took it slowly, going through the critical points as he described STAN, stopping only to answer any immediate questions that were offered.

"Sounds interesting to me. I've heard of something similar from another Chief Engineer, a friend of mine on another shipping line. STAN did you say! Okay then, John. We haven't got all the parts this side of sailing, but if you submit a parts list to the Storeman at Deakins yard, then we'll get it fitted up for our trip to Hong Kong. I'll speak to the Captain about getting the authorisation to fit the ship, but in the meantime have a design plan drawn up for me to look at."

"The design is already in the patent stage, so there will be no need to draw up another. Sufficient to say that as it was myself who invented it, as the inventor I have no need of an engineering drawing."

Hodgson looked amazed at this discovery, and was quick to congratulate John.

"In that case, John I will take it as read that we're about to be graced with your invention before we know it." Hodgson added.

"As it happens Alan, my two friends, Larter and Sinclair already know of my design. Therefore all you've got to do is ask them if it works or not. Sufficient to say that it has been tested thoroughly on two ships already." John said quietly but proudly.

"Can't wait to see it John. Leave it with me to broach it with the Captain, but he'll want to see it for himself too. Anyway, must get ashore to have a smoke, before I get turned in. See you later, if not, then at the Captain's spiel scheduled for 0800 tomorrow. See you!" Hodgson concluded, then brought out his pipe again then strolled off the ship towards an empty jetty where others were sitting having their smoke in safety.

CHAPTER XIII

Coloured Crew

"**Good** morning gentlemen! My name is Captain Denton, your new Captain. From my predecessor's notes it seems that we've had a good loading during the night and we're almost ready for sea." Denton commenced as he produced a large map of the western Pacific.

"As you can see from the red pencil mark, that is our route around all the islands that I have circled.

I need not remind you of the dangers and hazards that we will face going in or around these islands, especially as we've got a very large ship to move around, let alone our very deep draught. Once we've left Fiji and the Tonga islands that is where our fun begins. Therefore, I shall be requiring a special echo-sounder watch mounted on the bridge. Each watch officer will make himself fully acquainted with this new device, as it will be our only reliable source of keeping sufficient water under our keel. Because we have the capacity of at least two ordinary tankers, we shall be offloading at each port of call, and at their maximum holding capacity. I have the discharge tariff for the Engineer responsible for the discharging. Once our last customer has been seen to, then we can head back here in ballast for you to get the tanks cleaned and ready for the next delivery. I expect to return here in about 9 weeks from now. The Purser will be carrying various amounts of local currency to use during our stops, but Sterling will be used at any other time. Although we will be visiting British Territory or Protectorate or even Sovereign states, you will be required to comply with the local Customs, Medical and Local laws of the place. We will be moving passengers in between the various islands, so again, I expect proper decorum from my officers and crewmen. We sail in two hours. Have a good voyage!" Denton concluded, gathering up his documents leaving quietly with Hodgson tagging along behind him.

"Looks like we've got an excursion around the Melanesian and Polynesian worlds of the Pacific islands. People would give their eye-teeth to be able to visit all those lovely tropical islands." Larter whispered, for the First Mate to make his small declaration.

"Once you've seen one tropical island, you've seen them all, Bruce." Sinclair declared, which seemed to be a mutual consensus of opinion.

"From the map, it seems that Taraniti is our outermost point before we boomerang back here. If the skipper decides to chance his luck through the Barrier Reef then at least we should be in ballast, then we should be able to float over it." John said, recalling the red pencil marks on the charts.

"I've been to a couple of those places before, during my time in the Royal Navy. There was muck and bullets, blood and guts flying everywhere, so hope the place has been cleaned up by now." Sinclair said glumly, showing them once again, the scars on his legs that were his favourite 'battle scars'.

"Well, wherever we go, we're in for a nice time. Plenty of local beer to sup and a few rabbits to bring home for old time sakes." John responded in a more cheerful manner.

"Listen to him! He'll be like the Pied Piper once we get to Maoi I'ti. He'd better have a crate of 'rabbits' to dish out there or he'll be next in the ruddy pot." Larter joked.

John smiled meekly, agreeing with all that was said, so as not to let on that he'd got a cabin full already, by courtesy of Clarke's old shipmate.

The meeting had finished so everybody drifted off to their own part of ship in readiness to sail away into the blue yonder.

John was given his discharge tariff that had arrival and sailing times of each place they were to visit.

'Norfolk Island, Fiji. Tonga, Tokelau, Tarawa, Tuvalu, Tarnaiti, Ocean, Nauru. It looks like a tourist guide to the Pacific Islands.' John breathed, returning to his little office in the engine room.

When he arrived, there were two 4th and one 5th Engineers waiting patiently for him.

"Yes, what can I do for you gentlemen?" John asked politely.

"The Chief has assigned us to your work detail. I'm 4th Green, this is 4th Black, and 5th White over there." Green stated, introducing them to him.*

John asked them to come into the office and started to quiz them on their trade knowledge asking to see their project books to assess their worth to him.

After a little while he gave them their books and bits of papers back again, then taking off his clean uniform donned a pair of overalls.

"I shall be instructing you in all things pertaining to my duties on board. I will expect top performances from you both. I'll expect you to get yourselves dirty from head to foot whenever the job calls for it. I'll also expect you to provide suitable and precise reports with drawings of what I have instructed you on. When I need you to do a job or report to me no matter what time day or night I'll still expect you to turn up. If either of you don't ask questions to relevant problems that we find then I will deem it as you're not interested in doing the job in the first place. I don't want any namby- pambys nor slackers in my team. So if I find that you do not keep up or not do as requested, then you will be referred back to the Chief. For that to happen, you will consider as being 'in the shit' with demotion being the prospect. Do I make myself clear?" John warned gruffly.

The juniors looked at each other wide-eyed, and then at John.

"Do I make myself clear?" John insisted.

"Yes 2nd!" they whispered, giving John a worried look.

Clarke was passing his office and poked his head in through the open door.

"Hello 2nd! Getting the troops lined up?" Clarke mused.

"Morning 3rd! Did you get your swap after, or are you still on engine watch-keeping?" John responded with a smile.

"Nah mate! But if there's a chance those young buckaroos

want a cushy time in the engine room instead of the real hard graft on deck and in stormy seas, let's know." Clarke said, giving John a sly wink.

John looked at the two very nervous junior Engineers who nodded their heads vigorously at Clarke's suggestion, but bowed their heads as if to accept their fate.

"How do you feel about it Green? How about you Black, and you White?" John taunted.

"We just want to become Engineers and learn our engines first, 2nd. Maybe we can swap with the 3rd?" Green stated, looking hopefully at John then at Clarke.

"It appears that both of you should not have been let out of the Engineering College so soon. 3rd Engineer Clarke was just like you two, once. I taught him all he knew, now just look at him. Top Cluck of the chicken run, aren't you Aussie!" John maintained, giving Clarke a smile.

"Yep! Best 2nd Engineer instructor I've come across. But he really does need total focus and commitment from his men, I can certainly vouch for that, that is why my hands are so chapped and full of hard skin." Clarke responded cheerfully, showing them his hands.

Hodgson, who was entering his own little office, noticed the little gathering, so joined in to see what was going on.

"Hello Chief, glad you came along. I've got a particular manpower situation that needs your specific attention as Chief of the ship, to make the final decision thereof." John greeted, then went on to explain the small situation that occurred.

"Well that's fine by me 2nd. I get three men instead of one. I've been given these juniors as extras for, shall we say, training purposes. I understand your need for a qualified Engineer as your assistant, so I've no objections if Clarke wishes to be that man." Hodgson stated civilly, much to the great relief of the junior Engineers.

Hodgson took out his pipe and commenced to smoke it whilst making his decision. After a little while but through a big cloud of smoke, he nodded his head at the proposals.

"One on condition though, 2nd. If I need Clarke to augment the engine room watch-keeping from time to time, you will release him for those duties. I will let you know in advance of such times, naturally."

"Well, that's settled then Chief. I've been trained up by the 2nd here anyway, so I know his modus operandi, so to speak." Clarke drawled.

"Thank you for your deliberations Chief. I might still need the odd stoker or two now and again, but would reciprocate in the same manner by pre-arrangements." John responded evenly

"Very well 2nd! So be it." Hodgson concluded, then turned to the junior Engineers and directed them to their first assignments.

"Glad you came Aussie as I needed somebody reliable. Those three were of the same ilk as the ones I had sacked from the previous voyage. I would have licked them into shape, had they the guts to take me on. But again, I don't want namby-pambys fobbed onto me, nor am I willing to wet-nurse all the waifs and strays the line seems to give me."

"Glad to be of service, mate!" Clarke interjected.

"Whereas you, Aussie Clarke, are a disgrace to our uniform and a bum as well. A good one at that mind you, but still an Aussie ball and chain merchant." John finished, as he grinned at Clarke's impish smile.

"You an' me made a good team on the *Inverary*, John, glad to be with you again." Clarke said as he held out his hand and shook John's in friendship.

"You did a good job last night, which Hodgson knew about. That's why he was more than happy to team us up. Yes Aussie, welcome aboard. Now let's get our department ready for sea." John concluded, as both men started to wade into their tasks.

The *Repulse Bay* sailed majestically out of Moreton Bay heading down the Coral Sea towards their first stop, Norfolk Island.

The sea was calm and the sky a uniform blue as the ship

steamed her steady 18 knots through these waters. As she was low in the water, due to her enormous 65,000 tons of liquid cargo that was destined for several thirsty ships and aeroplanes who visited the islands where she was going to stop.

"We'll get this last flap valve secured before we go for lunch Aussie. Afterwards, we'll sort out the paperwork before we secure for the day." John advised, as the two men clambered over the tank decks.

"This step ladder needs a weld to secure one of its feet John. It will give way if somebody was to step on it during a drop of roughers." Clarke informed, pointing to the small ladder they had just used.

"Make a note of it on the rounds log, Aussie. Time for lunch as my stomach thinks my throat is cut." "Lead on! By the time we get washed and changed, lunch will probably have all been scoffed by then."

"Exactly my dear Antipodean friend. Don't forget your ball and chain!" John joked as the two men hurried to their cabins to get themselves into 'suitable attire' for their meal as they would not be allowed into the dining hall until they were.

"Right then 3rd! Let's go and meet our public. You're buying the beers this time around." John said as the two men entered into the saloon taking their allocated places at the officers table.

"What will you have 2nd, roast pork or chicken dinner? What about you 3rd?" Penrose asked with a dead-pan face.

"I'll have a nice whale steak with a dozen eggs sunny side up!" Clarke joked, but got a mean stare from the po-faced steward.

"Roast pork for me, and I'll have the tropical fruit salad for afters, please." John replied civilly, kicking Clarke's shin to induce him to behave.

"Ow, that hurt. I'll have the same as the 2nd." Clarke said swiftly, rubbing his shin.

"Behave Aussie, we're not in the Triple Crown line now. All officers must show decorum, remember?" John whispered.

"No worries John. I'll get the beers whilst we're waiting."

Clarke said and getting up, moved over to the bar.

Larter arrived at the table, so John called over to Clarke to get another beer, which he acknowledged with a nod of his head.

"Hello John! Been busy lately? Only you normally come to visit us around the time we sail." Larter asked.

"Yes Bruce, I've got Aussie in my team, which means that we can get things done quicker and easier now compared with our last voyage."

"Then you'll have plenty of time to spend lazing around getting your suntan topped up again. I'm the opposite as Kenny Brown was sent onto another ship, so I'm on my own for a while. That means I've got a lot less time to sit around." Larter said glumly.

"Well never mind Bruce. We'll come and keep you company. Mind you, I'm hoping to get STAN installed either during this trip or on the next one up to Hong Kong. "

"Sounds good John. Don't forget to let Andy know, as he's been taking advanced navigation training, which the Captain seems very red hot on. Next to Joe Tomlinson, including maybe your old friend Trewarthy, he's pretty good, at least from what I can gather."

"Just as well, considering we've got a good 50 foot draught under us and we're on our way to those friendly islands that's surrounded with lumps of coral with even the odd volcano to deal with."

"Speaking of which. Clarkie is supposed to know some of these waters, what with all the fishing and whaling he's done." Larter replied, as Clarke arrived with the beers, closely followed by the steward with their lunches.

"Just in time, Bruce. Here's an aperitif to get your belly ready for what we're about to receive." Clarke said as he bowed his head in a mock attempt at saying 'grace'.

Clarke looked at the jumbled up mess on his plate, then told the steward to take it right back to the pigs, as it was only fit for them anyway.

Brown, the Chief steward came swiftly over and asked Clarke in a whisper what the problem was.

"Listen here mate. If that's the way you serve the food in this joint then you can ruddy well stuff it. Ain't you heard of presentation and making the food look good even if it tastes like ruddy swill?" Clarke replied vehemently.

Brown looked at the food served up, stating that there was nothing wrong with it. That it was a well cooked, well-balanced meal, full of vitamins.

"Yea Yea! But it might as well be pigswill. I mean, look at the state of it! Where on the plate can I find some meat? Is it under the pile of cabbage and mashed pom? What vat of gravy did you run off to swamp the rest? Look at the ruddy clakker•, it's just a lump of soggy dough! I mean, come on Brown. Where is your so-called professional pride that the rest of us has to show?" Clarke snarled.

Fortunately it was the slot for officers only to dine, as the rest of the officers also started to complain noisily about their food, and he manner in which it was served.

When the First Mate came in to take his lunch, it was he who took up the complaints.

He looked at what the problem was, deciding that yes, the officers had a genuine grievance, which made Brown threaten to resign there and then.

Somebody sent for Matthews, who came to examine for himself what was described as a waste of valuable food which could not be replaced on account that the groceries on board were to cater for the whole voyage.

He stated that the chefs and stewards were to brush up on both their food preparations and food service immediately, as he would examine each one of them to see who would be sacked for causing this problem.

• Clakker is a slang word to describe thick and hard pastry.

He reasoned the fact that if the officers were served in such fashion then so would the passengers. That would mean a large drop in future passenger numbers if the word got round the catering fraternity in the other shipping lines. In the meantime, the officers were asked to eat what was given them this time so as not to waste the food.

As Clarke was the main instigator Matthews and the First Mate reasoned with him until he agreed to do so, but only if he could have a few extra beers to help wash the swill down.

Matthews knew he was in a cleft stick on that, and gave into the demand by giving permission for all the officers to have a couple of beers, on the house, but only for this one meal. It would be back to normal at supper time.

Once the furore died down and everybody got back to eating their food again, things went back to the normal tranquillity of a ship swimming peacefully through calmer waters than the storm in the proverbial tea-cup on board.

CHAPTER XIV

A Greased Palm

The ship was nearing her first port of call, which had John and even Denton nervous, because although they had a deep water harbour, the on-shore facilities were not expected to be up to their requirements.

"I have the tank discharge pumps primed and ready for unloading Captain. But insofar as your sailing time is concerned, then it will all be down to the capability of the dockside." John stated, as he spoke to the Captain on the bridge.

"Yes, thank you 2nd. If your discharge tariff is correct then we shall be about 2 hours alongside the oiling jetty before we move alongside the quayside of the harbour. Kindly let me know when you've finished, as my schedule here is pretty tight." Denton disclosed.

"Aye aye Captain!" John responded then left the bridge.

"C'mon Aussie, we're on parade in about two hours when we dock. Let's get our monitoring equipment set up and the tank tops ready." John stated, and both Engineers got themselves ready for their first act in a long play.

Norfolk Island which is about 850 miles Southeast of Brisbane, was among most of the Pacific Islands that were discovered by the famous Captain Cook in the 1700's.

In the early 1800's for a short time it was a penal colony used by Britain. It was also a settlement first was set up by the infamous HMS *Bounty* mutineers who left for their own special islands of Pitcairn. It is under the Australian protection and has a large military installation on its 13 square mile land.

"Here we are Aussie. Get the tank top vents opened up, then the connectors lined up whilst I go see what their shore facilities are like. Back in about half an hour. Any problems give me a shout at the pump-station." John directed.

"No worries John, although I will need an extra pair of hand for the Avgas." Clarke shouted back.

"I'll be back before then. We won't discharge until all the pump connectors are on line." John responded, then went over the gangway onto the pencil slim fuelling jetty and ashore to see the pump supervisor.

"Morning!" John greeted, meeting a scruffily dressed portly man coming out of a small building next to the maze of pipes which led to the massive mushroom shaped fuel tanks.

"Morning! My tariff says that you have 2,500tons of Avgas plus 1,000 tons of FFO and diesel, but I can only single-pipe them. I can transfer the fuel in 1 hour per each fuel if that's okay." the man stated.

"Three hours!" John reflected, scratching his head in thought.

"Tell you what. If you've got the shore-lines connected up, then whilst you're transferring the Avgas, I can get the diesel done at the same time. The FFO can be cross-pumped once your Avgas lines have been cleared. We can do it in about 2 hours, so what do you say?" John explained but giving a question to round it off.

It was the scruffy man's turn to think for a moment before he made his own comment.

"I'm paid for the 3 hours of the discharge, which means that if I do it in two, not only will I lose out on one hour's pay, but the unions will be down on me like a ton of bricks considering that we're on a go slow strike anyway."

"Strike? Who said anything about a strike! I have three petrochemicals to discharge within two hours before we supposed to move to the harbour and discharge our other cargo and passengers. If your union wishes to hold passengers to ransom for your strike cause then I suggest you get your boss to speak to our Captain." John said vehemently.

"Don't get on to me admiral, I'm only protecting my job. If you want to connect our shore facilities to your ship borne equipment to speed up with the transfer then I will not stop you.

But I will only transfer whatever fuel you want on the single line for one hour at a time." the man stated meaningfully throwing a set of keys to John.

John caught the keys and looked at them for a moment as if to decide which key fitted in which lock.

The man saw the puzzled look John gave as he examined the bunch of keys.

"The square key with the red tally on it is for the diesel. The blue one is for the FFO. The three diamond shaped keys are for each start up motors of their pumps, and the three round headed keys are for the stop valves when you've finished. We have a special screw down non-return flap valve that needs to be operated once you've completed your transfer. Also, there's a panic button on each suction valve head in case of a spillage or mishap. Ordinarily and only if you're up to the job, it should take you about one hour between the two of them. Should you cause a spillage, then you will have the honour of cleaning it up. I can provide fire cover for the Avgas, but you'd better have your own crew to cover the other transfers. Remember one thing though. Should you be approached by one of the union bretheren then you will tell them that it's you that's transferring the fuel and not me. If all goes well then just think of us poor buggers on a go-slow strike. All donations gratefully received." the man said glumly, holding out his dirty cap.

"I thank you for your honesty. We will get the transfer over as quick as we can. When we have done so, we shall make sure your, shall we say favourite charity, will be duly rewarded." John replied softly and diplomatically, so as not to get the man into trouble nor incur the wrath of the strike happy unions.

The triple fuel transfer took just over an hour to complete, during which John had time to see the Captain and explain what the situation was ashore, allowing the Captain to offer some sort of remuneration to the pump supervisor.

"Here's $10, a bottle of whiskey and a carton of cigarettes. Tel him that we've got several such stops to visit and that is all we can spare each stop." Denton said with a smile.

John looked at the offering, scratching his head.

"Do you meant to tell me that we've got to bribe our way around the world. Is that all this transfer is worth Captain? Considering that we're shipping the best part of a million pounds worth of petroleum on board?"

"You'd better believe it 2nd. It's what is called, greasing the palm, to ease the process of getting on with business. It's happening a mile a minute in the high finance and business circles of the world. We're but small cogs in that big wheel. Unions are a different kettle of fish, therefore that's all I'm prepared to donate, if that's the word. Any problems other than that Grey, I'll let you deal with." Denton said with a frown.

"Thank you Captain. I've got the picture, and I'll deal with it as I see fit." John said, gathering up the offerings and leaving the Captain's cabin.

"All pumps switched off, valves cleaned and cleared, including the hoses. Vent hatches shut down, discharge details logged, John!" Clarke reported cheerfully, so John could go on his way over to see the scruffy man.

"Thanks Aussie. Before you wrap up for the day, make sure the hazard warnings have been cleared off the board. See you in the lounge afterwards." John said, and went over the gangway with his 'offerings'

"Here you are matey! Here's the donation to your favourite charity." John greeted as he walked into the dingy pump room office.

The man took the money, which was instantly pocketed, then held up the bottle of whiskey to examine its potential taste.

"The missus will get the money for her housekeeping, but this little beauty will be wrestling with my tonsils for a while. I haven't had a decent bottle of Dimple in years." the man said with gratitude.

"And this is a little something from me and on behalf of my fellow Engineer who helped me get our transfer done." John added, handing the man a carton of Gold Leaf cigarettes and a box of five cigars.

The man looked at the second offering, then sighed.

"Thanks for the gesture mate, but I'm a pipe tobacco man. Still, the cigars will go down a treat. The problem is that, as you'll appreciate, there's a smoking ban around this depot."

"Well never mind. You'll be able to flog the fags ashore for whatever pipe smokes you want. But the cigars are, shall we say, a lot better than the average one you can buy in the shops. Anyway, I must go now, and it was nice to meet you. Take care!" John said politely, bidding the man farewell.

"Yeah! Thanks for everything. Hope to see you again sometime!" the man shouted back as John made his way back on board, to catch up with Clarke.

"How did the handshake go John?" Clarke asked with concern.

"Went like a dream. If we ever get this way again and that gaffer is still on shift, then we are, as you might say, in a Joeys' pocket. Anyway, being as it's your turn, lets get a few wets down our throats before the Purser starts to shut shop on the proverbial beer well." John enthused.

"Geez, I might 'ave known I was teamed up with a ruddy guzzler, especially a ruddy Irish Pom at that!" Clarke protested, but with a large grin on is face, as they both went into the saloon for their well-earned drink.

CHAPTER XV

The Real World

The *Repulse Bay* sailed again out of the harbour turning hard to port for her next leg of her swim through the world of coral islands. Her next stop would be the second of such a voyage, which would be some three days sailing, to the thriving islands of Fiji.

"John, we're about to dock in the deep water fuelling jetty in the Southern basin of Suva Suva.

This discharge should be as per schedule, but it means it probably be a dirty one. Suggest you get some sort of oil spillage measure organised, for fear of pollution and other menaces. We don't have any spare foam or other coagulants to contain any spillages, so I would recommend you apply your brain onto it, just in case." Hodgson stated, showing John the harbour installations to match other certain relevant details on the diagram.

John looked at the very detailed map, for a little while, before he handed it back.

"It seems perfectly straight forward to me Alan. It just means we discharge at three quarters the going rate. Maybe if you speak to the Captain to prepare him for an expected delay, then all will be just fine. The thing is, is that my team can do the job as required, but are always subject to delays unknown to me, therefore I am unable to counteract these imbalances in the discharges."

Hodgson looked at John for a moment, thinking over the deep responsive answer John had given, before he decided to reply.

"It is your duty to ensure all discharges are conducted as per schedule. If you find a specific problem, job wise, then it will be up to you to sort things out. If however, the problem lies ashore, then you will be required to seek either my help or that of the

Captain. Since you've already done this on our last drop, then you will know what is required of us. We are merely sailors doing a service for the local politicians, and as such if we bugger it up it's us who will carry the can and get sacked, whereas they will merely offer an extra dinner bash to smooth things over so everything returns to normal again." Hodgson replied with a look of disgust.

"I understand where you're coming from Alan. At the end of the day, for my part, I shall make the decisions on my departmental performances, rightly or wrongly. I would expect that you and the Captain support my decisions. Speaking of which, I wish to register my disgust in having to pay our way with back-handers, as I believe most fervently, that what our jobs entail, means that we're doing a genuine job to warrant our existence on board. Coupled to the fact that each transfer is made for the good of the local economy, eventually to become the good of our Gracious Commonwealth."

"Yes John, something like that. But it still takes the odd shirt-lifting or palm-greasing, to make things work even in the modern world of trade and economics. This by the way is the real world, and not a fairy-tale rub of some bloody magic lamp." Hodgson stated philosophically.

"I don't deal in politics Alan, but privately I agree whole heartedly with everything you've said, especially when it comes to the bloody strikes and the like."

"Yes, I agree. Anyway, enough of putting the world to rights, what brought all this on?"

"Glad you asked! It's just that every time I meet a strike situation, it's always a Union movement who is always joined at the hip to the Labour government, no matter where you travel around the world. It's a pity we can't forget the bretheren of the Labour Union movement, even better still, to ban the bastards so we get on with our jobs without having to pay back-handers just to get on." John said in exasperation

"How the hell did we get into this subject John, which is a no-no, especially when you're on the move around the world. Maybe it's only now you've been able to get this off your chest and I am glad you've decided to get yourself sorted out, because we've got several ports of call to make. All of which could be a potential face-off just like Norfolk. Just to put yourself squarely in the 'Rembrandt' (picture). You are only a simple marine officer doing his job in supplying these islanders with their shopping list, that's all. Outside that, then you'll either go mad, or the MI5 people will be coming to lock you up in some padded cell for the rest of your natural life. I've nearly been there myself John, so take it from me, just lay off the politics on board but especially ashore." Hodgson concluded, taking John's discharge notes from him.

"Whatever Alan. I still maintain until my dying day that it will be a Labour government who will betray our country and sell us all down the river just like Judas did to Jesus. As for me, I hope to become a first-rate Engineer like you, with enough money to take me away from the fate that is due to befall our ancient homeland. There's no such thing as democracy in the labour movement, they don't even know what the word means, because they'll kill it stone dead! But then it would not matter if I was a woofter sidekick of a Labour Prime Minister, as I along with all the other greedy, self aggrandising MP's would've already feathered my nest and would just bend over for the next golden rivet to fix me up, never mind the soap. Nobody will convince me otherwise, as my friend Andy Sinclair has the appropriate maxim, which states that 'The hand of the man that tosses the Captain is the one that rules the ship'. The slightest denial to it would mean it was true, so you can ignore the names such as being called a homophobe. In fact Alan, if someone is a shirt-lifter or even called the new name of gay, what would they rename the famous painting of the Laughing Cavalier or is it the Gay Cavalier? Oh look! I've just been given a peerage job via the back door (or is it via my back passage) by my sausage friend the Prime-Minister and now I feel quite gay today. Oh! And by the way, here's a few billion quid more extra for the next forthcoming Presidency nomination to add to the billions my 'cocky' friend had already given, allegedly, to buy his. From then on you can just call me 'Lord of the Hairy Rings' for us both to shaft the proletariat!" John said vehemently, but left to perform his duties.

"There you are again John! Inciting racial, homophobic and anti-continental feelings among the poor crew of this multi cultural shipping line that happens to own a very large ship that is manned by the various coloured sailors the world has to offer." Clarke said with mock effrontery.

"Coloured? As in Brown, Green, Black, White even Grey, or just the plain run of the mill black men and Asians? 'What a load of Roo shit Bluey' to quote one of your own sayings. I tell you what mate, it gets right up my bloody nose having to give back-handers to people to do a job when they're paid to do it in the first place." John snorted.•

"Welcome to the real world John. Without those brown envelopes, vertical handshakes, playing leapfrog or whatever, not much will be done or be achieved in the world today. It helps the business world go round, without that we'd be still alongside the harbour wall of Brisbane. Mind you though, it's only the politicians that can claim it all on their expense sheets to get away with it. The rest of us get means tested for anything we wish to keep in our pockets and get shafted by any snooty pen pusher employed by the knob-jockeys and their arse bandits ashore." Clarke commiserated.

"Anyway enough of this crap, lets get back to business. We've got a fair discharge in Suva to conduct, so let's make sure our pumps and valves are on line." John said ruefully, as both men went onto the weather deck.

• For the benefit of all you 'PC' readers: This is the true meaning of having a 'coloured' crew.

CHAPTER XVI

Out of Order

Fiji was discovered by Abel Tasman, who had the island of Tasmania named after him in the 16th century, but was explored by Captain Bligh of the HMS *Bounty* fame, in the 1790's, when it became a British colony.

The native inhabitants are the frizzy haired Melanesians and the long-haired Polynesian. This mixture was added to by British slave traders who brought people from India to work the sugar plantations, who eventually rose up to become free thus to form the middle class shopkeepers or other local businesses.

It has over 300 islands with many extinct volcanoes creating coral reefs that fringe the islands, but it is strategically placed to become the crossroads of the Western Pacific, between the Antipodeans and the Americas.

Suva is its capital over some 500,000 souls, boasting several major industries such as gold mining, sugar refining, coconut products and forestry. Therefore a well-appointed deep-water harbour was provided to help the increasing larger fleet of ships from the trading nations who visit this part of the world.

"We have treble the tonnage for offloading since the last one, but we still need the same sequence of discharge, Aussie. I'll make sure the valves on the jetty are in good shape before we tell the pumping station to start up." John advised, and clambering down the steep gangway, making his way to the slim fuelling jetty which ran parallel with a much wider main jetty that the ship was secured alongside to.

"Hello the pump-house!" John called, entering a building that was a forbidding concrete construction, yet was roomy and very cool compared with the hot sunshine outside.

A large brown skinned, giant sized man wearing a gaily coloured shirt with matching shorts, appeared from behind a large row of levers and valves.

"Morning, I'm Engineer Grey off the *Repulse Bay*. I'm ready for the discharge as per your manifest." John greeted cordially.

"Morning Grey, I'm Sinha the pump- room supervisor." the man responded with matching civility, as he took the paperwork off John and looked at it.

"Your discharge papers are slightly out of order. I ordered an extra 500 tons of all three products some days ago, probably just before you sailed. I see you have a discharge at Tuvalu. That will be impossible as their tanks have just been dismantled and are in the process of being rebuilt. I suggest that you have a word with your Captain about this, as there're only two other places which can take the extra, and we're one of them." Sinha advised, handing back the discharge papers.

"Yes, I think that would be wise, but in the meantime we'll get the discharge started up as per my paperwork. The extras can be sorted during that time. Ready when you are." John responded.

"We have twin turbo powered suction pumps that can draw up all three lines in about 2 hours. We have a switch off point that I shall set for your original amount, but we can take all you've got on board."

"I doubt if your combined storage tanks have that capacity as we're carrying a good 62,000 tons of the stuff. Anyway, I'll signal my deck Engineer now to commence the load." John replied quietly, while Sinha looked in amazement at John when he mentioned the tonnage.

Going up a set of steps Sinha, looked out through a large window towards the ship. He came back to tell John that he hadn't realised just how big the ship was, and how wrong he was with his assumptions.

"We're one of the biggest tankers in this end of world. If things go on as they, are then by the time this ship is ready for the scrap yard, it will be just a rowing boat compared with the ones of the future." John stated as he left to signal Clarke.

'If I have anything to do with it, at least double the size. There would have to be very deep-water loading and discharge berths for the ships, probably

dredged, or a very long fuelling jetty out to sea to connect the ship up to. Must remember to put that in my notes' John muttered as Clarke returned his signal.

"Right Sinha, I'm off now to see about this discrepancy. See you in about two hours then" John shouted over the loud hum of the powerful pumps.

Sinha simply waved his answer and carried on with his job of pump attendance.

John found the Captain was in his day cabin talking to another sea Captain, but diplomatically explained his intrusion into their meeting.

"Tell them we can give them the extra 500 tons, but that will be all. I'll need company guidance as to the Tuvalu discharge though." Denton instructed, but was interrupted by the other Captain.

"Tonga, Taraniti and Nauru have brand new storage facilities. If it was me, I'd discharge it at Taraniti as it's the furthest out. Especially the avgas, as they've got a brand new airport and air service which will be taking all the big Trans Pacific jets. I know this because my brother-in-law is a pilot with the Cathay Pacific Airlines."

Denton looked at the discharge figures and made a mental calculation before making his decision.

"We'll do just that. Okay 2nd amend the figures for Taraniti accordingly, then give them to Larter for his next transmission. That will give us time to see if our management team will agree with it."

"Aye aye Captain." John replied obediently and left the two men to talk again.

'Let's hope I can get ashore after this. I don't want to spend all my time pratting around when there's a whole new world ashore for me to explore.' John whispered, as he left the bridge.

"That's just why I have been looking for you." Larter said quickly, catching John by surprise.

"Hello Bruce didn't see you! That's kind of you, but I've got some work for you to see to." John said handing Larter the amended discharge figures as ordered by Denton.

Larter looked at them scratching the side of his nose.

"Thanks John. I'll phone them when we get ashore. I can't transmit whilst you're still offloading anyway. How long will you be, only Andy and I are waiting for you in the saloon?"

"About another hour. You carry on ashore with Andy as I'll be along with Aussie later, but where will we meet?"

"Just go out of the main gate that's by the Harbour master's watch tower, then turn left down the avenue. When you come to the Lone Palm Court hotel, turn right and down the main high street towards the post office. You'll see the Moonbeam Hotel almost opposite it, which has a fairly large wooden veranda. Just a few doors away from it, you'll find a bar called The Outrigger. That's where we'll be. You can walk it in about ten minutes, but grab a pony and trap, it'll only cost you a few bob and you'll be able to see the place much better." Larter advised, stuffing the piece of paper into his immaculate Hodgson tropical shirt.

"Aussie's been here before so I'll tell him the Outrigger bar. Mind you I want to pick up a few rabbits here before we return on board again tonight.

"Why tonight? We can stay ashore until tomorrow night, at least that's what our schedule says. Anyway, see you there." Larter concluded, then smiled, leaving John to go back to his duties.

CHAPTER XVII

The Gamble

"Here we are. My, hasn't this place changed since I was here last. There's more brick and mortar buildings around now than the usual timber huts. I see Woolies are still in business, and the local Fern Leaf grocery store has grown twice its size. When we get a chance, we'll go down the local quarter and get some decent rabbits at half the price they're charging the poor ruddy tourists." Clarke explained, as they jumped down from the pony drawn carriage.

"Here ye are beaut! A quid for yer troubles. Keep the change!" Clarke drawled, as the man taking his money, waved to them before he turned his trap around and trotted off.

"A quid just for that short journey Aussie? That's a bit extravagant coming from you?" John said in mild sarcasm.

"Nah mate! It's just that the bastard remembered me, as I owed it to him from my last visit here. Now that we're quits he can come to fetch us back again by way of the local jungle bunnies bar I know of." Clarke said cockily, leading John in through the batwing doors of the wooden building, into a world of mayhem of sailors busy swilling their beers then pinching the bottoms of the waitresses who were struggling to keep up with the thirsty demands.

John stood for a moment looking around, before he heard Sinclair call him from a far corner of the very large room.

"There you two are. I heard you more than saw you, as the smoke is that thick." John said cheerfully, with Clarke following closely behind carrying two overflowing flagons of beer.

"Here John, grab a fist of flavour. It's got Nelson's blood in it to get you up to speed with the others." Clarke said with a beaming smile, handing John his beer.

"Where have all these sailors come from? Only I counted several bars and hotels on the way here and there are only four ships in harbour." John asked with a smile that was enlarged with the froth of his beer that was all around his mouth.

John's friends laughed at his new appearance before a waitress came over, wiping his face clean with her more than ample bosom. His look of surprise at this impromptu courtesy made them laugh all the more.

"You buy Juicy Lucy a drink sailor boy?" the waitress asked in a low husky voice.

John nodded meekly and started to put his hand into his pocket when a large unkempt sailor came over, dragged her away from him, saying.

"C'mon big girl. Let's you and me make lots of waves in that bathtub upstairs." which made the girl giggle lewdly and start to grope his privates.

"C'mon then big boy!" she challenged, so he picked her up and put her over his shoulder, carrying her up the rickety stairs to disappear through a curtained doorway at the top.

"Now that's what happens to naughty boys, John. I'll bet he'll be on board in the morning with the galloping guns, and a mouth like an Arab's jockstrap. That juicy Lucy is one hell of a slapper, who can satisfy at least ten men in as many minutes. She's the top slapper here next to her old boot of a mother in the other corner. She's the one with plukes on the end of her nose that would upstage even Ayers rock." Clarke said with a grin, finishing off his drink with a loud burp.

"Right let's get a Yorkshire going, say five quid each?" Larter suggested.

"Yes, but only beer, fags, big eats and a bed for the night!" Sinclair amended to which everybody was in agreement.

"Anybody else who joins us will cough up too. Any horizontal capers then you pay your own!" Clarke added, putting his money into the pot, which was greeted with a laugh as a collective agreement.

"First off though let's have some fun, so I'll start the ball rolling. I've come prepared for a special event. Let's get a challenge going with A Yard of Ale contest. A quid to enter, winner takes all. What do you say lads?" Sinclair said, producing his large glass from a hessian sack that he held all the time.

"Sounds good to me. We'll take on bets, just to spice it up a bit. I'll be the bookie, to make sure nobody cheats unfairly." Clarke offered.

"That sounds a great idea. What we've got to do is get them in the mood, is start them practising on full flagons, first. That way we can size up the competition to offer odds on some of the better ones. We don't want our own champion to find that there's a better drinker in the tavern than he is, now do we." John added.

"Yes Andy. You're going to have to pretend you've already got a good skin full, but slow yourself down a mite to make it look like a fair challenge. That way you will be able to suss out your rivals. With a bit of luck most of them will have had more than enough to drink anyway, or at least be 'airlocked' enough to quit. Remember Capetown when one of the Geordies nearly came up to your time." Larter advised.

"John you get up onto a table to make the challenge. Then Aussie will get a few tables removed so that we can have an open arena to see that all the contestants are drinking, not pouring it into someone else's' flagon. You will act as MC and conduct the challenge. Don't forget to place a bet on someone who looks like coming close to Andy." Larter added, as the friends prepared themselves.

"We have a shipmate who will challenge any man to a yard of ale drinking contest. It's a quid to enter, winner takes all, and gets all his beer paid for. If any man thinks he's up to it, then come into the arena and start practising first. The fastest man to drink the yard of ale non-stop, which is two and a half pints, will win. If any of you can drink two and a half pints in 12 seconds then you're on to a winner. Bets can only be taken from those who are not taking part in the drinking. Any takers?" John challenged in a very loud voice that hushed the room for a moment, before there was a scramble to the swiftly arranged 'arena'.

"Right then gentlemen, pay your entrance fee then get yourselves all warmed up first. You need to get your swallowing right, and your throats loosened up into a good slurping mood. To get warmed up, you'll need two quart flagons of ale. Once you've done that and everybody is ready, I will put you under starters orders to time you all fairly. First off, you need to have a practice run with your first flagon, as your second flagon will be used as your timed run and the knock-out round to sort out the men from the boys. During that round, anybody who spills even a gob full, or stops to take a breath, or pukes up will be out." John announced to the many challengers, which was almost half the sailors in the room.

Once the men returned from the bar, John had them drink their beer as quick as they could. Clarke and John took the timing of each man whilst Sinclair and Larter stopped those who broke the competition rules.

At the end of the trial there were only seven men left, with each of them around the 12 second mark.

John told every man his time, which was greeted with claps and cheers from his friends, whilst Clarke marked the men's times on a board giving betting odds to see who would win. This was greeted with great interest as the scene was set for Sinclair to enter into the ring.

"It appears that we have a challenger to the winner. Is there anybody else who wishes to challenge these contestants?" John baited, for two more men to step forward with Sinclair.

"Aye, I reckon I can beat 12 seconds." the three of them boasted, before giving Clarke their money.

"Then you will have to go through the same as the others. Just to prove that you can do the qualifying time instead of bragging about it." John dictated, which drew a roar of approval from the other contestants.

Sinclair swigged his flagon to produce eleven seconds, which was matched by the other two.

John had the men lined up in order of timing, with Sinclair

second to last, then each man took up the yard of ale glass and was timed. By the time that eliminator was over, there were only three men left including Sinclair. The betting became the more furious as more and more men latched onto the big gamble of the night. The other two men had several friends egging them on, so not to make it seem a fix, Clarke suggested that he'd place Sinclair third favourite asking if anybody wanted to help him win. There were very few takers to that suggestion which meant that Sinclair was left in peace but with Larter in attendance. Clarke, in fact, had achieved the ultimate hustlers aim, by getting them all to do exactly what he wanted them to do.

John had the three finalists take their turn at the glass for their last attempt with a new time of ten seconds, adjudged by most in the bar as almost impossible.

The first man was disqualified as he tipped most of the ale all over himself, the second one finished in ten seconds dead, with all eyes on Sinclair to see if he could beat that fabulous time.

Everybody took the count, which stopped at eight, as Sinclair took the glass from his lips, tipping it upside down to show there was nothing left in it. There was total silence for a moment before a hugh roar of congratulations erupted and everybody, even the losers came to shake his hand.

"Best yard of ale drinker in the Southern Hemisphere." they all said in tribute to Sinclair, who was stuffing his pockets with his winnings.

As a gesture of goodwill, Sinclair told the barman to give each contestant who was still capable of swallowing, a flagon of ale, he would pay for it. This was accepted as a generous and popular payback by all those who nearly won if it wasn't for the myriad of excuses they offered for the rest of the night.

The night wore on until the bar was almost empty save for the friends and a few latecomers.

"Oh well then gentlemen. I've paid out those who bet on Andy, but we've got enough for our hotel cabins for the night, and still have ten quid each." Clarke said with a twinkle in his eye, doling out their winnings.

"You ran a close thing though Andy. Just as well you stayed your hand at the last second otherwise we would have been lynched if they thought we staged it all in the first place." Larter said quietly, nursing yet another drink.

"Yes, I'd been watched by a couple of them, so decided to make a decent run of it. I could have really done it in seven seconds, but didn't do else the game really would have been up. They came over to me afterwards telling me that it really was a close thing, giving me the benefit of the doubt. My biggest worry was that one of the earlier contestants who got disqualified, was my nearest rival in Capetown the first time around. He didn't recognise me but I certainly did him, that was why I waited for the second round." Sinclair admitted

"Well, time to get turned in, but I've no idea which hotel we'll use. I fancy we've got a good run ashore in the morning." John said with a stifled yawn.

"The Moonbeam is a class hotel, let's go there. Even the Bounty Bar just down the road takes lodgers. You can get a piece of the horizontal action if you're willing to share with one of their Sheilas." Clarke suggested.

"The Moonbeam sounds just right. At least they're bound to have empty cabins not booked up, unlike the Bounty Bar. Besides, that place is guaranteed to give you the galloping guns and a swift trip to the Rose cottage, if my memory serves me correctly." Larter stated, which was agreed unanimously by the other three.

John was up and about early while his friends were still sleeping, so decided to take a stroll down the sparsely populated streets enjoying the cool of the fresh morning air.

He found a newspaper shop and spotted a three-day-old British newspaper, which he purchased, but noticed the headlines of the local daily so purchased that too.

"That will be three shillings for the British one and three

pence for the local, please." the shopkeeper asked, as John fished out his money.

"Here you are. I hope your local papers are truthful, not like the lies that get printed in ours." John commented as he paid up.

"Yes, they are. My Brother-in-law is the assistant editor." the shopkeeper replied as John left the shop only to nearly bump into a local policeman who was wearing a Hodgson shirt with three red stripes on each arm, and a long skirt with little triangles of cloth running along the bottom hem. A large truncheon was in the black belt around his waist, and a big pair of hobnailed boots that belied his matchstick legs.

"Morning officer. Lovely morning for a stroll." John said politely to the man, receiving only got a grunt and a smile in return before marching off down the road.

He passed a shop window that was full of adverts for holidays, with the logos of different Air and shipping Lines logos attached to bargains tempting the would-be holiday-maker.

'Thank goodness I've got a job where the company pays me to go to those places. It would cost a fortune to do so otherwise. Perks of the trade, shall we say.' John mused, arriving back to his hotel rousing his sleepy friends.

"C'mon you lot, up and at em! Show a leg. Time for breakfast before we go sightseeing." John shouted, moving around the room, making as much noise as he could.

"What time is it? I've got to collect the mail." Larter asked sleepily as he almost fell out of his bed.

"It's 0730, and breakfast finishes at 0800. I'll go to get us a table. See you lot in five minutes." John announced, then left the room and making his way to the dining room.

"Morning sir. Are you taking breakfast?" the immaculately dressed waiter asked politely as John found a suitable table.

"Yes. I have three friends who will be joining me very shortly. I will order for all of us, to save your time, if that's okay?" John responded with his own question.

"Glad to be of service, sir." the waiter replied, jotting down onto his note pad what John ordered, then left in a hurry to comply with the demand.

"That was decent of you to order our favourite breakfasts John. Let's have a smoke and a coffee to round it off." Sinclair said then gave one of his now infamous burps, which drew ribald remarks from the rest of his friends.

"Now that we're all in one piece again, so to speak. Let's go and have a decent rabbit run ashore. No doubt Bruce will keep us informed of the time as we're all due back on board by 1400." John suggested, looking at his watch to confirm the time.

"Yes, we've got the usual pre-voyage meeting with the Captain, but I've also got the mail to collect. Let's go and spend some of the winnings courtesy of the rest of the sailors, who, no doubt have already sailed ruing the moment they met our Andy." Larter quipped, joining the rest of them to laugh at the previous night's events.

"Maybe you've got a last chance to purchase something for all those nippers you're supposed to have sired, John. Better make them good ones, as they will need to be passed down the generations if you're not around to replace them." Sinclair hinted.

"Yes John, what are you going to do when we arrive at Maoi I'ti? I mean according to the head count and what's been totted up, you're down for at least five of the nippers who're starting to run around the place." Clarke added, which started a ribbing session from them, and all against John.

John smiled at his bantering friends and stated.

"Whatever the consequences of my night at that Beach Party, and according to our ex Captain Joe Tomlinson whom we all know as a good friend, nothing will be expected from me considering that I am, and I quote, 'like the evening breeze, soft and gentle', unquote. Therefore if I should only visit the place just once more in my own lifetime, let alone that of the offspring that I have sired, my name will always be written down I'll always be known by as the Iceman, even though my loins were like the volcano and full of fire." John said quietly, with a wistful look on his face.

"Strewth mate! That's exactly what I was told only last year. Hey Cobbers! If we're due to visit that place again, then we're in for another good night. Courtesy of volcano dick here!" Clarke exclaimed, putting his arm around John's shoulder, hugging him in a gesture of close friendship.

"Well, be that as it may gentlemen. We've still got the whole Melanesian area to visit before that, and enter into the so-called friendly ocean called the Pacific." Larter reminded them as they left the dining table.

CHAPTER XVIII

Island Hopping

The *Repulse Bay* sailed quietly out of the modern harbour of Suva, for her marathon swim around the coral islands of the Western Pacific. From Tonga to the Samoan Islands, to Tokelau, Tarawa, right out to Taraniti then onto the Ocean and Nauru Islands and back to Australia via the Solomon Islands, playing follow my leader to all the dolphins who came to play with her.

Whilst each place warrants a decent mention as per tradition in each of John's visit, and as the voyage covers several thousands of miles, it will be in a small statement to each place, if only to chronicle those visits by John and his ship. This is not to deny all those lovely places, but merely to keep within the overall picture of John Grey's life at sea, and to keep within the confines of this book as he sails onwards on board his ship.

"Okay Aussie! That's the last hatch battened down until the next discharge. I'll go and report to the Captain, whilst you get the hazard lights switched off and the stokers stood down. When you've done that, I need to see your copy of the discharge figures along with the other items I'm expecting you to keep." John instructed, as he went to make his report.

"No worries John! I've got it all sussed and almost ready for your report anyway." Clarke responded

"Thanks Aussie!" John replied, leaving Clarke to supervise the last of the chores until they arrived into port again.

Although the *Repulse Bay* is a tanker, it nevertheless carries mail, a few passengers, plus a certain amount of freight as deck cargo, for delivery to the inhabitants of the groups of islands it was scheduled to visit.

"2nd, I need a word with you concerning our delivery figures!" Denton demanded, during John's brief conversation with Sinclair.

"Certainly Captain. What is it you're concerned with?" John

responded civilly.

"We appear to have offloaded several hundred tons too much from all four tanks. If this is repeated before we offload the deck cargo at Taraniti, then we'll be too top heavy. If we meet a tropical storm then we're in queer-street and no messing. Is there any way you can redress the balance from underneath, so to speak?" Denton asked with a deep frown on his face as he circled some figures on a cargo-loading sheet.

"The only way I can think of doing that is if the ship had some sort of compensatory filling system, so that when the oil or diesel gets offloaded it is replaced by water, a sort of second fill if you like. My stabiliser tank is empty and only gets topped up when there's a shift of balance from one side tank to the other. As you know it prevents the ship from keeling over from port to starboard during transfers." John stated, drawing a few sketches to illustrate his point.

Denton scratched his head, tapping his pencil agitatedly on John's drawings.

"Thanks 2nd. It seems that it's a seamanship problem now, unless you are able to transfer some from one tank into the other to fill it up again?"

"Yes we can, but only after Tonga has taken her discharge. We can ask them to transfer the FFO for us to save time. When done, I'll ask the engine room to fill with seawater to maintain the see-saw balance. In fact, that could be done to all the tanks once we've completed our run at Nauru, if you so desire."

"No that won't be necessary, as once you've cleaned the tanks and vented them, we return in ballast. We're supposed to be a tanker not a ruddy general freighter, after all." Denton grumbled, nodding his head to John, which was the signal that he was being dismissed.

John made his way out of the very roomy bridge then into the radio office where Larter was tuning one of his transmitters.

"Hello Fingers! Haven't you cracked that safe yet?" John joked, and sitting down helped himself to one of Larter's cigarettes.

"The stupid idiots only sent me the wrong crystals, now I've got a headache trying to match my transmitter frequency to the aerials." Larter moaned, shortly after he finally completed his task.

"What brings you to this humble place anyway John?"

"Come to see just where our voyages were taking us, on that magic map of yours. How long is it to Taraniti?"

"We're offloading in Tonga. Tuvalu is off as far as you're concerned, although we're going there with mail and medical supplies. Kiribati has been scrubbed. We have a drop at Tokelau and Tarawa, so I reckon on being alongside Maoi I'ti in about 18 days. According to my schedule, we're due for a two day stay there until the next freighter arrives from Singapore. Which believe it or not, is the old *Constantlea.* She's just left and should arrive the same time as us. Whilst we're at it, here's a new brochure of the place, you'll hardly recognise it, see for yourself." Larter stated, throwing some coloured brochures towards John.

John looked through the brochures, making noises of surprises as he turned each page, before giving them back again.

"You're right enough there Bruce. It looks a positively healthy and wealthy place now with all the new land and those new high-rise buildings. I see they must have rescued some of the old docks and turning the water between Ilani and Maoi I'ti into their new harbour. That new airport is looking swish too. I wonder where they got the vegetation to replant it all again though?"

"It says in the brochure, that our King Phatty splashed out some of his gold to have the place rebuilt and done out. It must have been a major reconstruction site after we left. The volcano is still performing its usual act, which means it has plenty of rich soil dumped onto the islands adding to the guano off the Wianii Island we sheltered behind."

John nodded his head in agreement as his mind was instantly transported back in time. He shuddered at the memory of the horrendous and awesome sight of a 300 foot tidal wave trying to tear down an island mountain to get to and wreak havoc on the ships who were sheltering behind it.

"We had a bloody close shave that time Bruce. Any news of that bloody Mulani whatever it was called that caused the wave?"

"It's only a couple of pieces of rock sticking out of the ocean now, with a lighthouse and a small weather station stuck on the top of them."

"Shame about the pink lagoon though Bruce. Still, the beach they've created from the destroyed airstrip they tried to build earlier looks pretty inviting. Maybe they'll get round to replacing a few more sandy coves around the islands again. It could be a marvellous place for holidays."

"Not to mention the skinny dipping and the all night orgies on the beach, John!" Larter teased, for John to throw a signal pad at him in response.

"Yes, well I've got prepared for all that. Just so long as I'm not expected to give a repeat performance. I mean, Queen Phatty nearly broke both my legs when she planked her arse on me. Just as well there was plenty of sand under me. Anyway Bruce I must go now as I've got a small shift down the engine room to see to. See you at lunch time maybe!"

"That's a promise, because one of the passengers has been getting birthday telegrams all bloody morning. From what the Purser says, he's a very rich goldmine owner making the journey from Fiji to Tonga, which means there's bound to be a beer or three in it for us officers." Larter said cheerfully as John left the office.

"Aussie, we've got a possible tank transfer at Tonga, once we've completed their discharge. We've got a ballast pump out of action which the outside Engineer hasn't had time to fix yet. I'm telling you these things, as we are forced to make our own repairs. The Captain's got a weight balance problem in that we're very much top-heavy for his liking. So we'll need the pump for when we compensate the weight of the oil transfer from that tank. Get the necessary tools mustered then meet me on deck aft of the bridge, I'm off to see the Chief."

"No worries John. Could do with a bit of real engineers action instead of acting like a ruddy milk monitor in a junior school."

"We'll do it after lunch, so see you then Aussie. Better bring along the manufacturers book as I've not seen that type before."

"I have John, and they're a piece of cake. Even a lowly acting 5th could repair one of them."

John smiled at Clarke's eternal cheeky responses.

"This will be your shout then 3rd Engineer. You have the chance to instruct the instructor for once." he said, dismissing Clarke to get on with some paperwork.

"Hello Alan, can you spare me a moment?" John asked politely when he poked his head into Hodgson's office.

"Sure John, what's the problem?"

"The Captain has informed me that we're discharging too much, which suggests to me that there may be dodgy flow-meters in use ashore. I've checked our tanks and flow-meter gauges and they're okay. The discrepancy is only about100tons on each fuel and on each discharge, but if we're to reach the other end, then we won't have enough to supply them with. I should like to think on dodgy flow-meters rather than think 'grand fiddling' going on. I mean, for every tanker discharge, it appears there is an amount of fuel being creamed off for racketeering purposes." John explained, as he showed the amended fuel figures.

Hodgson looked at them for a moment then reaching into one of his store lockers, got out a fuel gauge and examined it, before commenting.

"This and the other one are brand new gauges John. On your next discharge of avgas and diesel, make sure it is fitted onto the pump first. I say those two, especially the avgas, because they are the more lucrative fuels to siphon off. It is much lighter but more volatile than the rest, selling at double the price to the airlines than FFO does to shipping lines. You will bring the replaced one on board for to have it examined before we do 'blow the whistle' so to speak."

"Thanks. Maybe we can get gauges made just for each specific fuel as opposed to relying on memory to reset them. Anyway, I have a more important item for you, one I need to roll past you to see that I'm on the right track." John replied, then went on to his diagrams and sketches which could help the Captain with his top-heavy load problem. It took him several minutes giving the basic rudiments of his ideas and suggestions before Hodgson started to get the picture.

"Sounds good to me John, but you'll need a secondary ballast pump to do all that. You would also need a lighter or barge to catch the spillage once your first filling is near completion, because once your subsequent filling has come through there will be oil by the ton floating around the place. Okay at sea as the slick can be dispersed by the ocean, but in a confined harbour space, it would be very messy, let alone polluting the harbour for ages."

"Once the colour changes, and only oil is coming through then we shut it down. Maybe a ton at the most as opposed to the hundreds of tons jettisoned out at sea when the tanks are washed through. Mind you we can only do it with the FFO and the diesel, Alan."

"Water in the fuel is a nasty business at the best of times John. What do you suggest to remedy that?"

"The fuel and water mix gets poured down through a tundish, leading to a fuel separator. The drawing I suggest is a vertical helix that will create a vortex spinning the oil to the side-walls by the centrifugal action, as it's lighter than water, which then gets forced through pipes leading to the ready-use fuel tanks. FFO or in our case diesel, it doesn't matter. That will then leave any water to drop down to an outlet pipe, then be subsequently discharged outboard. It would be on the same principle of providing fuel for the ship, but could also be adapted to providing water free fuel going ashore as long as there's a good suction pump and discharge pipe on tap. On the face of it, it would solve the so-called 'missing' fuel, because the flow-meter would be taking the water / fuel mix in one go." John said at length.

Hodgson stood for a moment reflecting on what John had told him, then said he could not try it out until such machinery was available on board. He suggested that John should get his sketches and drawings sorted out ready for inspection by the management team when they reach Hong Kong.

"We have the capability due to the tank separators in each main tank, but the tank transfer can still go ahead Alan?"

"Yes, providing the outside Engineer has got the deck ballast pumps seen to."

"As my 3rd would say, No worries Chief! We've got it lined up for repair after lunch today. Well that's it Alan, if there's anything you need to tell me or I should know of?"

"Yes John. Those bloody junior Engineers you swapped me with are three out-and-out misfits who shouldn't have left the Engineering college. I've got them swabbing the ruddy decks and helping out the grease monkeys. Remind me not to swap with you again." Hodgson moaned, as the subjects of his ridicule came strolling past the office.

"Funny you should say that Alan, because that was exactly what I told them in the beginning. To think that you might have been like them at one time." John smiled, teased Hodgson, who flicked two fingers up at John's remark.

"Must go now Alan. You know where to find me. I'll give the outside Engineer the good news, to save you the bother." John concluded, climbing up the vertical ladder then out of the engine room.

CHAPTER XIX

A Small Job

The sun was an orange ball drying up the morning mist floating above the smooth waters of the ocean, as the *Repulse Bay* reached the Pacific's 'Friendly Islands' both in name and the nature of its people. It was the start of another balmy tropical day in an area of 160 mostly uninhabited islands, but those that are, belong to a Kingdom of Polynesians, which we know as Tonga.

She arrived alongside the new harbour wall to off load a large mountain of mail and other items the islanders needed, before she had to move to the new fuelling depot further down the coast.

John was standing on one of the for'ard catwalks with Clarke, looking at the beauty of the islands.

"It seems there's an abundance of fruit-bearing palm trees around here Aussie." John opined, offering Clarke a cigarette.

"Yes, mostly coconut products like oil and copra, water melons, and bananas. You mentioned the *Inverlogie* being equipped for long-haul fruit cargo. Well this is where she started her voyage back home again. She took several thousand tons of the stuff off here, Tuvalu, and several other places before going through the Panama again. The Triple Crown line has the franchise for that route, but rely heavily upon this line for its fuel and the like. They have four ships making the round trip, but so far none has gone as far west as the Philippine archipelago nor Malaya and Singapore, which is where this line comes into the equation, especially for the fruit and the meat cargo from Oz and Kiwi land."

"Apart from sailing the entire length of the Atlantic a couple of times, I haven't made such a long haul as that, have you?"

"Up to Japan and back, then across to Capetown to meet your lot on the *Inverary*, John. But I've never got to Europe nor

Yankee land. I'm quite happy floating around these places, because the wild life is just great, let alone the local Sheilas."

"Each to his own I suppose, Aussie." John sighed, observing the passengers leave the ship, only to be replaced by a few more.

They stood for a while taking it all in before Sinclair came along the catwalk and spoke to them.

"That's the Tongatapu Island John. The collection of buildings you see is Nuku Alofa, Tonga's capital. It doesn't look much but those buildings would withstand any cyclone these places are famous for." he stated knowingly.

"Yes Andy. See that building over there on the stilts? Well that is where you will find the Flying Angel club. Clean sheets, clean women, good grub, but best of all, lovely cold beer that would rot the teeth of a crocodile." Clarke drawled, as he started to point out some of the buildings, which seemed to be playing hide and seek among the ubiquitous palm trees.

"Well it looks as if that's all we're going to get from this place, but I saw Bruce nipping ashore, the lucky Scouser." John responded.

"We're moving down to the new fuelling jetty soon. Maybe we can have a quick run ashore to stretch our legs before we sail again." Sinclair opined.

"Must be nice to be a Deck Officer on these ruddy things John. We're the ones who do all the work around here." Clarke teased, giving John a wink.

Sinclair knew it was a wind up and chuckled.

"Oh shucks! Now you've got me all embarrassed. Still never mind, it's about time you Engineers earned your living. I mean it's us sailors who make sure you get to see all these lovely places." he said with a grin, which started up a small bout of inter-departmental banter.

"Well anyway. We mustn't keep our deck officer any longer. He's got a ship to row, row, down the stream, and merrily too, because life's just a scream for them." John concluded, as Sinclair left.

"Speaking of which Aussie. Before we make our discharge, I need you to do a small job. I have a brass flow-meter for the Avgas and diesel pipelines for you to make a change over with the ones ashore. Once you've done that, bring both of them back to me. If you have a problem with those people, tell them it's the new safety regulation brass gauge and all you're doing is swapping one for one. Then it's the usual routine. We've got the same amount of transfer as Fiji, but we've got the ballast pump to back up their suction pumps. Our tank tops must all be open fully else we'll be sucked to collapsing point. Once that is done, then I'll see the Captain over the cargo transfers I spoke to you about earlier."

Clarke knew there was something behind John's request and asked him what the real reason was.

John explained what he thought was the problem with the discharge figures and how he was hoping to prove himself correct.

"Standard trading practice in these waters John. It's live and let live, if you like. That's how these people survive, John. By trading and bartering their bunches of bananas and coconuts for the fuel we bring, plus all the other things that we take for granted, yet for them lots of things are still new."

"Be that as it may Aussie, try telling that to the last poor sod at the end of the line, when we've not got enough to give them. It would be like the Purser only giving you half a voyages wage, just because the Captain and the other officers got paid out first."

"I'd bloody skin the bastard alive I would." Clarke responded vehemently at John's suggestion.

"Exactly, Aussie." John sighed with relief that Clarke had got the meaning of what he was trying to do.

"Fair do's John. I'll get them swapped no problem." Clarke conceded, as they started preparing for their next fuel discharge.

"Here you are John. They were like lambs when I told them what you said. Now let's get this shift over with, I'm starting to get rather peckish again." Clarke announced, when he arrived back on board with the replaced flow-meters.

"I've got everything lined up for you. Now it's my turn to make myself noticed. Time now is 1030, so give me ten minutes to start up at 1045. Two hours should do it this time, but I'll be back for when we start up our own pumps." John said civilly, putting the two valves into a sack.

"Here, put these somewhere safe and out of prying eyes. We don't want them disappearing ashore for somebody else's beer fund." he concluded, and left Clarke to go and see the pump-room supervisor.

"Morning the pump-room!" John called out to a seemingly empty wooden building that housed the powerful pumps.

"Morning, can I help?" A small skinny man asked as he appeared from behind one of the large fuel valves.

"Morning! My name is 2nd Engineer Grey. I've come over to check our discharge figures with you!" John said cheerfully.

"Pleased to meet you Grey, I'm Shepherd the pump supervisor. Here is our schedule. It should only take about three hours." Shepherd greeted, handing the schedule over for John to see.

"I need a quicker transfer Shepherd, as I've got to make a load shift when the discharge is finished." John stated, then went on to explain what he required.

"No problem. I'll commence pumping now but give me a further ten minutes to open the other pipelines. You can start your pumps when I give you the signal." Shepherd agreed, starting up his powerful machinery.

John went back on board again and waited for the signal, which was soon given.

"Right then Aussie, let them rip!" John ordered, as their ballast pumps started to assist the shore pumps in the discharge.

"I'll do the first hour Aussie, so off you go and stretch your legs a while." John encouraged, which was swiftly taken up by Clarke.

"I'll get these gauges stowed first then bring you a cool drink before I go." Clarke responded quickly, walking swiftly away.

"Right then Aussie. After lunch, here's what we'll be doing for a couple of hours. Drain tank 1aft with the FFO into tank1 for'ard then fill the empty tank 1 aft with water to three quarters full. We will do the same procedure for tank 2 with the diesel. Then drain all of tank 3 with the avgas into tank 4 to top it up, then refill tank 3 with water to three quarters full. Once we have more or less stabilised the ship and the Captain happy with it, he'll sail out. We'll have to complete the water fill whilst at sea, that's all"

Clarke swore under his breath, but John got the gist of what he said, and merely commiserated with him, as they finished off the discharge routine.

"Let's get scrubbed up for lunch John, I'm starting to feel rather peckish."

"I've just remembered something that Bruce mentioned. Something about a few wets on offer from one of our paying guests." John said with a smile, instinctly knowing what sort of response Clarke would offer.

"Now that's more like it. Me old warbler needs cooling down after all the ruddy fumes we've inhaled these last couple of hours. C'mon 2nd, lets shake a leg so we won't disappoint our well-wisher." Clarke breezed, leading the way back to their cabins to get cleaned up.

"Not so fast Aussie, we've got a couple of hours grafting to do before I can report to the Captain. Mustn't get legless in the meantime, must we!" John teased, which was received with a two's up sign from Clarke. Ordinarily John would not have tolerated that gesture from any other junior officer, but to him Clarke was not just another junior officer, so accepted it with a knowing grin.

"Tank transfers completed, and am taking on water for weight distribution. Should complete the task in about another four hours, Captain." John reported.

"Well done 2nd. I'll put to sea whilst you're doing that. How much tonnage are you taking on?"

"Three quarters of the total discharge weight so far Captain, which is 12,000 tons to be precise. Once we've discharged at Tokelau and Tarawa I can give you a further 4,000 tons. Taraniti will take about three quarters of what's left, but then after that it will be strictly academic, I presume."

"Indeed 2nd. You've got me out of a dilemma so I'm thanking you for it. Make it 'job and finish' for you until next time." Denton said with delight, dismissing John with a nod of his head.

"First Mate, get the gangway lifted off and the de-berthing party organised. Get the 3rd mate to stand by to receive the tugs. Bosun, tell the engine room to obey telegraphs. Let's get going, we're late already." Denton ordered to his bridge staff, as John left the bridge.

He rejoined Clarke for a quiet smoke on the lifeboat deck taking the chance of looking around at the place he visited but didn't get to see.

"It's like that sometimes John. Pity really because you Poms are Northern Hemisphere sailors and sometimes don't get the chance to revisit these places ever again. But then it would be the same as us south of the equator going up your way and all that." Clarke commiserated.

"Still, at least you get the chance to see the fruits of your wild oats before you do get back. Most men would duck out of that daunting experience, John." he added.

"S'pose you're right Aussie. Just a bag of old cards and photos would be all most of us get to feed our memories on, of all these places we had visited during our life." John said philosophically, stubbing the last of his cigarette out.

"Strewth mate, put a sock in it will ya! I'll be blubberin' in me amber nectar next. C'mon, lets finish off this job so we can relax." Clarke urged.

"Tell you what. If you take the for'ard pump and I'll take the aft pump, and I'll be in the saloon afore ye!" Clarke started to sing.

John pretended to cringe at hearing Clarke sing, then smiled as they completed their refilling task.

Once more the ship sailed majestically through the calm waters of what was named the peaceful ocean, on her way to another idyllic location that most people would never get the chance to know about let alone visit!"

During the next couple of days it was literally balmy breezes, warm sun and cold drinks, mostly of the alcoholic type, that the souls on the ship enjoyed, as she swam lazily towards Tuvalu.

"Hello John, enjoying the cruise?" Sinclair asked, arriving and sitting down next to John.

"Hello Andy. Yes, not bad. Any idea what the score is on Tuvalu?"

"We can't go too near the place due to our draught, but we're going to meet a small ship who'll take off their mail and medical supplies."

"But we're supposed to have made a discharge there. How was that going to be managed? Lighters or something?"

"We're due to lay off the island in the morning. Best get yourself up onto the passengers boat deck and see from there. Bruce will be seeing to the mail, so ask him to get you a postcard and a few stamps from the place. At least, that's what I do when I can't get ashore. I have a whole drawer full of them at home, as you know."

"Now that is a good idea Andy."

"What's a good idea?" Larter asked as he too joined them.

"I was suggesting to John that he should start up a little postcard collection of all these places we can't get ashore on. Being as you're the Postie, you could fix him up with one or two, and the stamps to go with them. I mean, Tuvalu is just as famous for its postage stamps as the Christmas Islands and even the Pitcairns. See what you can do for him, Bruce."

"I'm not going ashore, just handing over the mail. But I can always radio them to bring me some cards and stamps when they come out to meet us. I believe two or three packets of cigarettes would be the right exchange. Leave it up to me John, you can owe me the fags later." Larter stated, sipping his iced drink.

"Tuvalu has excellent fishing waters, second to none, as the islands are surrounded by shallow lagoons. You like your fishing, John. S'pose you'll try your hand whilst we're transferring the medical supplies?" Sinclair asked.

"Not this time Andy. I think I'll grab a spare pair of binoculars and have a scan of the islands, as you've rightly suggested. Anyway, we're a bit high out of the water for my line, as it's only a short reel I've brought."

"One of the stokers I just saw, joined a few heaving lines together, then putting some raw meat onto a boat hook that's tied to the lines throws it overboard. I've seen him land a good-sized shark with it. They love shark meat, and even make shirts out of its skin, too." Sinclair said off-handedly.

"Yes, I saw something like that this morning. No wonder they were babbling away like rock apes." John replied with a nod.

"Well gentlemen, must go and get some paper work done now before supper. I've already seen the movie twice so I think I'll have a quiet night in for a change." John announced.

"And here's me thinking of calling for you to accompany me on a night out on the tiles. Silly me!" Larter joked.

"He's washing his hair again. Watch Julian doesn't come and perm it for you John." Sinclair called as John left the saloon.

CHAPTER XX

Old Codger

John looked around the small collection of islands, which made up the atoll of Tuvalu.

He marvelled at the lush vegetation of these very low lying islands, that seemed to be like emeralds dropped into a sea of jade, with almond shaped lagoons between them.

He watched a small ship steam slowly towards them with a small flotilla of out-rigger fishing-boats scurrying along to keep up with it. Soon the steamer was alongside, taking its cargo on board, while the fishermen arrived all around the ship to bargain with the crew. On offer seemed to be several large lobsters, crabs, fish, and items made from bamboo, in exchange for cigarettes, soap or anything else the crewman had that was attractive enough to complete the barter.

Soon the scene was disturbed as the small steamer tooted her horn, cast off and made her way back to the small collection of buildings that appeared to be the focal point to these people.

"Here you are John. Four different postcards with a few famous Tuvalu stamps on each of them." Larter announced, arriving onto the boat deck to go into his radio office.

"Cheers Bruce. What's the damage?"

"40 Woodbines, and a marlin spike in its leather sheath."

"A ruddy marlin spike Bruce! Where on earth did you get one of them, or need I ask?" John asked in amazement.

"Saw one loafing on the boat deck just before I brought the mail over to the steamer." Larter whispered, pointing to a puzzled sailor, who was looking around the lifeboats for something he had apparently mislaid.

John turned around to see the sailor, then grinned from ear to ear.

"Why you old codger Bruce. I'd better keep schtum then. I'll give you the cigarettes at lunch time." John replied quietly, stuffing his postcards quickly into his overalls pocket.

"Tricks of the trade didn't you know John." Larter said with an equally large grin, as they parted company.

Yet again the *Repulse Bay* left one idyll place for another some two days sailing from it, and yet again the ocean was benign and gentle with them.

John was in the radio office looking at the map to see the two important lines on the chart, which indicated the equator and the International Dateline. He had already experienced the capers of 'crossing the line' of the equator, but wondered aloud if there would be a similar caper for the date line.

"None except that we get to put the clocks back 12 hours, as of midday tomorrow. Mind you, Aussie will have 2 birthdays in the same day as we pass from 12 hours ahead to 12 behind. It can be very confusing, that's why in my trade we always deal in GMT or ZULU time, to make things even." Larter explained.

"I was going to say that because I couldn't remember anything specific when we crossed it coming over from the States. We cross the dateline tomorrow, so Aussie might get himself legless twice in one ay? Thanks for the warning, Bruce. Mind you though, he's not required for any duties until we reach Tokelau, which, judging by your chart will be around 7 the morning after. No wonder he likes coming on these voyages at this time of year, the crafty sod. He gets two birthdays for the price of one."

"Speaking of which. We've got the chef to make him a cake, but instead of candles he'll get bottle tops on it. Each bottle top will be one beer for him to drink, and he must drink them all in one sitting. But just for you to know, it's Stubbies beer, which comes in much smaller bottles than our half pint bottles. So in effect, he will get about 12 pints. We've also got him a large cigar that one of the sailors made from several smaller ones. We've been careful that no wacky bakky has gone into it else the Captain will go mad. He doesn't mind the booze but draws the line on drugs and the like. It will be your responsibility to look after him during his party, and to clean up after him if he's been sick or whatever. On that though you should be okay, because we've already seen him in action."

"Also, he'll have that large card we've all signed. I'll get him lined up around dinner-time, so then he can have the rest of the night sleeping it off. He's supposed to cover the last dog-watch in the engine room as a favour owed, but I'll do it for him I suppose. Could do with a swift couple of hours down there just to keep my hand in."

"That's shipmates for you John. Can't do anything with them nor get anything done without them."

"Says he, as if he's on board all on his own. Anyway, must leave you to your gizmos Bruce, as I've got gizmos of my own to tweak from time to time." John teased, and left the radio office.

Clarke's birthday went well for him, before John eventually turned him in some hours later with help from Sinclair.

"He can certainly wobble his warbler, as he puts it. Didn't know he could sing as good as that, though." John admitted.

"Yes, he certainly is a live wire character. He started to get a bit shirty with the First Mate though, but glad you managed to cool him down. Still a good afternoon's one man show it has been after all." Sinclair said with a grin, leaving Clarke sleeping on his bunk.

"I've got his shift to do now, so I'll catch up with the rest of you later Andy. Thanks for the hand with Aussie." John said gratefully, shutting Clarke's cabin door quietly behind them.

"Yes John, it's good of you to cover for him. That was the condition the Captain stipulated, else he would not have authorised Aussie's drinking session in the first place. Penrose will look after him until he wakes up again."

"You'd do the same Andy." John replied softly then left Sinclair to go down into the engine room for Clarke's shift.

"Okay then Alan, I'm your relief for this watch, as Clarke is otherwise engaged. Birthday and all that!" John explained, arriving noisily onto the inspection platform.

"Hello John. Glad you turned up because I've made a report on those rogue flow-meter gauges you brought on board. It seems as if somebody has discovered that if you put a shim in between the neck and the calibration ring, you'll get extra gallons added on per ton of liquid. The thicker the shim the more gallons you get. In this case, it's a single 'thou', which will allow five gallons per ton flowed past the meter. Not enough to warrant a major investigation if it was just a one-off discharge, but it means that as we're doing a multi-drop with multi fuels, the person at the end of the delivery line will be short on their supply. Now this is where the naughty bit comes in, as it will involve people such as the fraud squad, Interpol and the like." Hodgson explained, showing John one of the gauges.

John looked carefully at the modified gauge for a moment.

"We need these as evidence Alan. But as we're out of further replacement gauges, the only thing I can suggest is to check each flow gauge before we discharge. If the gauge is correct then okay, but if I find on inspection that it's not, then I'll have to stop the discharge at a time when the so-called extra was being taken off. That is to say, and as an example, about 100tons short of the delivery manifest. You will be given a written report on each gauge inspection that I find tampered with, and the name of the pump supervisor in charge of that discharge. It is simple enough, as each gauge has its own makers mark or special serial number, look." John stated, showing Hodgson a secret place where the makers name and serial number was to be found.

Hodgson looked at the name and the series of numbers then nodded his head in agreement.

"Well, bloody hell John! So that's where the recognition marks are kept. I'll bet not many other Engineers know where to find it either." Hodgson said in amazement, suitably impressed with John's keen eye for detail.

"We're due for a discharge in the morning, so I'll start off with that one. In the meantime Alan, I've got a shift to see to. Who is my Chief stoker and who is my relief?"

"That will be Brian Sandon, but your relief will be Dave Fagg plus those 3 idiots. Before I go, keep an eye on the fuel quality, as it seems to be inferior to what we're dishing out, therefore the engines are drinking more." Hodgson stated, before he wiped his hands on a clean rag and left the engine room.

CHAPTER XXI

An Outing

"All vents opened, hazard and warning signs up." Clarke commenced, stating his pre- discharge report to John.

"Okay then just one more thing to do now, which is for me to check the gauges shore-side, Aussie. When I give you the signal, do the same routine as Fiji." John said, acknowledging the report then went over the small gangway and along the thin fuelling pier to the pump-house.

John made his inspection then signalled to Clarke to commence discharge, before making his way back on board.

"Right then Aussie. Take yourself ashore to get us some rabbits. You've got 2 hours to report back." John ordered.

"Anything specific or just the run of the mill tourist tat?" Clarke asked politely.

"Some cigarettes off that freighter ahead of us would be nice, but I'll leave it up to you for the rest. I'll be on the foc'sle when you come back."

"Cheers John. I like going walkabout here. There's plenty of old wartime souvenirs to be had, buckshee too. See you later mate!" Clarke said gratefully, and went swiftly ashore, seemingly to disappear among the traditional forest of palm trees.

John sat on the foc'sle having a quiet smoke and looking at the scenery with the binoculars he had borrowed off Sinclair.

'*So this is Tokelau. No wonder the Japs put up a fight to stay on these small islands. You can still see the wrecks of the landing crafts our boys used to evict them, and the holes in the ground that were probably Jap gun emplacements. This must have been another of the Japs* R&R *just like Tuvalu. Plenty of small islands with plenty of fruit palms and by the looks of it plenty of good shallow fishing grounds. The little harbour seems to be kept nice and clear, for these ships to be able to anchor in. Just as well our fuelling jetty keeps us off the corals or we'd make a right mess of their beach.*' John mused, and managing to spot a small flying boat making silver streaks across the blue ocean as it landed in the water and stopped by one of the other little islands in the small atoll.

John looked at the half concealed fuel tanks ashore, guessing that they must have been belonged to the Japs at one time.

"I bet there is a good trade in inter-island flight. Imagine coming here for a fortnight's holiday. It would take you ages just to get round them all. Lovely by air too I shouldn't wonder." Sinclair pondered as he arrived onto the foc'sle with two large mugs of tea, giving gave one to John.

"Cheers Andy!" John said, taking his mug.

"I was just thinking. The war is over by a good dozen years or so, yet this place still has some scars left." John added.

"Yes. The Anzacs re-captured all these islands including the Tuvalu archipelago, whilst the Yanks went west towards the Philippines. The Japs had this earmarked for a hidden base camp, because the islands are scattered over a good 400mile area. They were trying to build up their forces in readiness to invade the Hawaiis. Truk and Tarawa were already set up, but when the Yanks caught up with them there was wholesale slaughter. Especially at Truk. There were more Jap ships sunk in one day in that natural lagoon than any other sea battle ever fought in these waters so far out in the Pacific. The facts have it, that it was a good 75 ships got sunk within a couple of hours, and all by a couple of Yank aircraft squadrons. The Japs certainly had a pasting that day. In fact the entire island got beat up pretty badly as well because the Japs had several bomber squadrons with a full army ashore ready to do their dirty work. The Anzacs had an outing here too mind you." Sinclair stated knowingly, pointing out to some half-covered wreck stranded on a coral reef not far from the ship.

"If what you say is fact, then Mother Nature has been kind to the islands by helping to bring back the vegetation again. If you've seen the new brochures on Maoi I'ti as I have, then Mother Nature can be proud of herself. Man always seems to have the uncanny knack of spoiling all the nice things in life, especially when he is intent on destroying all before him. Maybe that is the curse of man, Andy." John sighed, scanning around the place once more with the binoculars.

"Especially when you've got some lovely lagoons for fishing, but discover there's at least several hundred tons of unexploded bombs or other ordnance lying around just waiting for some poor soul to pick it only to get blown to pieces. Most of these Pacific Islands who were invaded by the Japs then subsequently re-taken back by our Allied troops, will take several more years, but sadly some never will recover from the onslaught of modern warfare." Sinclair agreed.

"Bruce tells me that we're due for a couple of days on Maoi I'ti. Let's hope we don't run into more of the same as we had last time, Andy." John stated hopefully.

"Life has certainly moved on in that place since our visit, John. There's no need for you to worry about being first in the cooking pot, you mark my words. Anyway, must dash now to get prepared for sailing again. How much longer will it take to complete your discharge?"

"About another half hour. I haven't seen Aussie come back yet, so let's hope he comes back in one piece."

Sinclair looked through the binoculars to scan the terrain where the so-called capital of Tokelau was situated.

"Can't see him, but knowing him, he'll be along very soon with a few of his so called 'sheilas' after him." Sinclair chuckled, then handed the glasses back.

"Well, really must dash now. See you in the saloon later." Sinclair added, as he left John alone on the foc'sle.

John finished the discharge routine single-handedly, but was waiting until he saw Clarke coming back on board before he reported to the Captain.

Sinclair came down off the bridge then made his way along the after catwalks to where he saw John standing looking at the collection of buildings ashore, through his binoculars.

"Where the hell is Aussie, John? The Captain knows you've completed your discharge and whilst he's waiting for your report, he's also waiting for the high tide for us to move off." Sinclair asked.

"I'll report to the Captain when Aussie comes back. Only then can I officially state that the discharge is complete. You already know that Andy, so what's the problem?" John responded with a question of his own.

"Ah, so that's it! Aussie's not back yet, and the Captain doesn't know he's ashore. Let's hope he gets on board without Denton seeing him, or he's in dead trouble. He's got about half an hour before the gangway is taken off then another quarter of an hour before high tide, John." Sinclair said anxiously.

"Go back and tell Denton the reason why I haven't reported the completion of the discharge, is that I'm waiting for the shore-side discharge figure they haven't made up yet. Tell him that I may be forced to go ashore to get them myself but in time for the high tide." John replied evenly, tapping his wrist-watch.

"Between you and me, not even Bruce is back off shore. Which means, and I suspect, that they're together. The outside Engineer is on deck somewhere. Find him quickly to tell him to test the ship's horn, in shall we say, a robust manner, which should remind our friends ashore that we're waiting for them, pronto. Tell the Engineer to make one short toot followed by two long toots then another short one again. He is to do that again five seconds later, and make sure it must be done on full steam. They will hear the letter 'P' in morse code, which according to Bruce, means Peter, or, the ship is about to sail."
Sinclair nodded his head repeating the instruction before he left John in a rush.

John heard the signal blasting across the peaceful waters, looking through his binoculars to see if the two wayward sailors were on their way.

He didn't have to wait very long before he saw them running towards the jetty, with their arms full of parcels or other items that they were dropping, only to stop so as to go back to pick them up again.

John decided at that moment to go ashore to the pump-house to create a diversion, so that they would get back on board without any undue awkward questions.

"Bruce, you'd better make out that those parcels were airmail for the crew, that just landed from the seaplane. Aussie, get yourself back into overalls again then wait for me on the after catwalk. I'm going for the discharge figures as my excuse to cover you." John said loudly as they rushed past him.

"Cheers John. See you at lunch." Larter gasped, but Clarke merely nodded his acknowledgement to his orders.

John came back brandishing a piece of paper to show the watchful eyes on the bridge that he had got what he went for. As soon as he stepped off the gangway, it was lifted off the deck, for the ship to float away from her temporary home.

"My apologies for the delay Captain. It's just that I had to tally the shore figures with those on board.

From what you will see, you will discover the discrepancies which have been highlighted since we left Brisbane." John announced, arriving onto the bridge and handed over the pieces of paperwork.

Denton looked at the schedule and all the numbers, which were ringed in red pencil.

"You certainly have discovered a massive scam, 2nd. No doubt our management team will thank you for that, but I dare say you'll be given the proverbial 'BLACK SPOT' from those involved in the scam, when they find out it was you who blew the whistle on them." Denton opined, but kept looking at the radar screen then at his chart.

"We have just one more discharge before we get to Taraniti, but it seems that the weather might be against us. Can you give me some extra weight below water level?" Denton asked.

"No Captain. I need Taraniti to give me a chance to do that." Denton frowned, scratched his head, doing some of his mental arithmetic.

"Oh well, we'll just have to manage." he muttered, then issued a series of orders to his bridge team.

"We can always top up the fresh water tanks, and raise the level of the sewage bilges. That would give you about an extra 200 tons, Captain." John offered.

"200 tons should just about do it 2nd. My inclinometer might like that. Mind you, let's hope the Plimsoll line is up to the mark if we do meet the nasty typhoon heading our way. Okay 2nd, ask the Chief to do just that. We can always pump the sewage bilges out after we leave Taraniti." Denton responded in a more cheerful manner.

"Aye aye Captain. Nothing else to report." John concluded, for Denton to dismiss him off the bridge.

"What the hell happened to you Bruce?" John asked, on entering the radio cabin.

"Hello John. Aussie and I got involved with a bloody thieving git of a Dutch Auctioneer, and his two toady sidekicks. Aussie spotted they were systematically fleecing the other sailors who were trying to buy rabbits to take on board, took extreme exception to it. What you saw, was us carrying what we managed to grab off those bastards before the others decided to get some of the action. Last I seen of those thieving gits, they were being frog-marched away by a bunch of hairy arsed Sumo Wrestler type of men that were the local constabulary. As there was nobody to look after the stuff, and as I've just said, we had the first pick before the rest dived in who cleaned the place out."

"So that's what happens ashore when my back is turned. I can't take you anywhere Larter." John teased, picking up a cardboard box shaking it.

"Nothing in the damn thing except straw and a handful of camel turds made into pellets. Mind you though, the pellets turn out to be pure cannabis resin. Maybe that's why the unopened boxes cost £2 a time. The box with the so-called 'China pot' is nothing but a bloody clay plant pot with some paint daubed over it. And so the story goes on. In fact, what we've grabbed is a load of crap with a capital K. Just as well Aussie managed to grab all our money back off those thieving swines before the Indians took them away." Larter moaned.

"At least you've got something to barter with now Bruce. Maybe that resin will come in handy when we hit Hong Kong, if what Aussie's been telling us is true?"

"Oh yes, he's spot on there, John. Drugs are a big thing in China, including the rest of the Orient, so long as the customs men don't get a whiff of it or we'll all be in the cooler before we can spit."

"I'd better warn Aussie to lay off the stuff, and just spend the money."

"He gave all the parcels to me keeping the money until we got back on board. So we've decided to get you and Andy together then share what there is amongst us."

"That explains why I met him empty-handed. Glad he did that, because if the Captain saw him coming on board all loaded up almost as we were ready to cast off, having no permission to be ashore anyway, it would have spelt real trouble for him, let alone me."

"Maybe that was his way of showing his gratitude to you for covering his watch for him last night."

"Well, we've got a day's visit to Tarawa, so I'll get the run ashore this time. No sense trying to make lightening strike twice on the same spot, Bruce. Anyway, I've come to see you about this typhoon that the Captain is on about."

"Nothing to worry about John. It's just a local tropical storm, which brew up in these waters during this time of the year. As long as we're well away to seaward from these islands, then we've got no problem. This ship can handle itself in those seas but not in restricted waters of corals or near low lying islands."

"Well thanks for that Bruce. Must go and see if Aussie is still with us, in case he's already had a taste of that camel shit." John said, and leaving the radio cabin went below to his own cabin.

***

"C'mon Aussie, shake a leg, we've got some tank maintenance to do." John said aloud, on entering Clarke's darkened cabin.

Clarke raised his head and with bleary eye asked John for a drink, for John to give him a large glass of water.

Clarke took a swig from the glass then spat it out all over the cabin floor.

"Geez John! You trying to poison me or what?" he shouted throwing the glass onto the deck, where it shattered and lay where it landed.

"Tut-tut Aussie! Now look what you've done. Penrose won't be very pleased to find that you've gone and ruined the brand new carpet. Besides it's time for us to get our department back into shape again. On top of that you're due for a couple of hours down the engine room." John admonished, dragging the bedclothes from Clarke.

"Tell you what John. Give me another couple of hours to get rid of this ruddy headache and I'll even loop the ruddy loop for you." Clarke moaned, holding his head in his hands.

"I didn't mind you sloping off ashore, providing that you came back in a decent manner. Now it appears that you've been on the camel shit already by the looks of you Aussie. I'm normally pretty easy-going, but if anybody in my team gets affected by drugs or whatever causing him to be unfit for duty, then I'll come down on him like a ton of bricks. Consider this your first and last warning Aussie. Now get yourself together and muster on the foc'sle in half an hour. I'll get Penrose to bring you a large cup of black coffee." John said with irritation, leaving the cabin to see Penrose.

"Penrose, would you be kind enough to make sure 3rd Engineer Clarke is out of his cabin in about 20 minutes, bring him a large black coffee to drink down. He needs something to line himself up into something like a proper 3rd Engineer." John asked, when he popped his head into Penrose's little caboose.

Penrose was sitting, all crunched up in a large easy chair, babbling and chanting to himself, making John suspicious as to his state, let alone the strange smell coming from his cabin. He made a quick investigation of what he saw, and realised that Penrose was spaced out from the effects of cannabis resin, which he found scattered all over the little table. He realised it was a lost cause to try and revive the steward so left him, doubling back to see to Clarke and get him almost human again before the First Mate conducted his daily 'ROUNDS' of the ship.

"Hello John! Time up already? Sorry and all that, but that dope must be the real thing, compared with what's being pushed ashore. I've stowed it away tidy so nobody can find it easily. I'm nearly ready, just give me time to put my strides on." Clarke said as he slowly but surely put his working gear on, getting ready to perform his duties.

"Right then Aussie, now that you're with me albeit only in body, we'll commence our tour of duty. We'll start on the upper deck for'ard, which will get you some fresh air down into your lungs again. Bring your extra-long wheel spanner with you." John said firmly.

"That sounds good John, but do me a favour will you? Next time you come to shake me, don't ever give me a glass of plain water again, as it's bad for the kidneys let alone my morale." Clarke said, finishing the last of what looked like a stale bottle of beer.

"Aussie, you're a good Engineer, so why spoil it for yourself by taking this load of crap, and I'm referring to that camel shit you brought on board. I was hoping to find you a better man than all of this. You know my policies concerning dope and the like, so I'll give you fifteen minutes to pull yourself together before I stop making allowances for you. We may be old friends and all that, but our job comes first!" John stated, leaving Clarke's cabin to knock Hodgson's cabin door.

"Hello John, what can I do for you?" came the jovial response from Hodgson, who was reading one of his ship's drawings.

"Alan, I have a specific problem with the last discharge figures. Correct me if I'm wrong, but I think as we're 'upside down' so to speak, then we should be much heavier than we thought. Take a look at our figures, to see what I mean. Especially as we're about to head into a tropical storm." John responded automatically, and explained his theory on the matter. Hodgson looked at the figures, scratching his head whilst he pondered on his answer.

With a flourish of his pipe-laden hand that was like a blazing inferno, Hodgson explained the technical anomalies of the figures telling John not to worry.

"Besides, once we get past Tarawa and take on more water to compensate the cargo shift, we shall be okay. It just means we'll sway a little more than usual until the storm blows itself away." Hodgson concluded with a big smile.

"Thanks for confirming my own theory on the subject, and for your time Alan. I'm off onto the upper deck now to complete my departmental checks." John confided, then left Hodgson who had returned to reading his drawings.

CHAPTER XXII

The Lifebuoy Ghost

For the first time since leaving Brisbane, the ship sailed into troubled waters that had her rolling like a drunken sailor, which in normal circumstances would not have affected her.

"Just as well we completed our deck inspection or we'd be swept overboard." Clarke shouted above the noise of the storm and the crashing of the waves as they first slapped against the ship then washed the deck to disappear over the other side.

The bows were digging deeply into the huge swell, and in doing so causing a cascade of water, which burst across the catwalks of the forward tanks, stripping yet a few more layers of paint off the metalwork.

"This is no place to stand around Aussie, better make your way below." John replied, shoving Clarke roughly through a small watertight hatchway, just managing to get himself inside with the hatch shut before another wave cast itself against it.

"Get to the bridge to make the report Aussie, I'll be along in a moment when I've secured this hatchway. Don't want the whole Pacific trying to get through it now do we." John demanded, as Clarke acknowledged his order and left.

"How is it out there, John?" Sinclair asked, climbing up and out from a lower deck hatchway.

"Pretty rough Andy. Judging by your foul weather gear and your Mae West, you're about to find out." John replied, observing Sinclair's apparel.

"We've got some deck cargo just aft of the bows, that's somehow worked loose. Maybe the lashings need re-applying, but unless we secure it, the whole bloody lot will be lost." Sinclair shouted.

"We found a loose wire from that area and have re-lashed it as best we could. We're no good with knots and splices Andy, but we did our best."

"Better go and sort it out or the skipper will have my guts for garters, storm or no ruddy storm."

"In that case, I'll come with you." John replied quickly, donning his life jacket again.

"No that's okay, I've got Leading Seaman Doug Hughes with two sailors to help me."

John looked at the two sailors who were almost puking up with each heave or lurch of the ship.

"It's just you and me Andy, or you won't get out of this hatch, that's the deal." John said defiantly, leaning against the exit hatch to prevent Sinclair from going through it.

Sinclair who towered above John could have easily moved him aside, but merely shook his head slowly to agree to John's terms.

They were two very close friends who had shared many a dangerous moment together, and both knew this was yet another job needed to be done with a trusted friend rather than with someone unknown to them.

"Hughes! You'll be sentry on this doorway, to make sure nobody comes after us. You two men better get below." Sinclair ordered, then turning to John, gave him a stout piece of rope with larger metal clips on each end.

"Here John, clip one onto your harness. When we get onto the middle catwalk, clag the other one onto the running rail. Just pull the lanyard as you go along. But whatever you do, don't unhitch it or you'll be washed overboard as sure as God made smalley apples. The 'Lifebuoy Ghost' won't be able to see you either. Sinclair explained, getting their safety harness and the life-lines organised.

Sinclair listened to the waves for a while, which kept thumping against the hatch door.

"Ready then John? When I say go, just shut the hatch after you."

Sinclair gauged his moment and shouted go, then opening the hatch stepped onto the catwalk, with John following closely behind.

They were met by the next wave that sloshed itself noisily over the ship's deck, momentarily buffeting them, as if to show just who was the master.

Sinclair waved his arm for John to follow him, and ran along the catwalk towards the relative shelter of the bow section, which was built much higher out of the water than the main deck.

John pointed to the steel rope that he them fastened to, but Sinclair pointed to the reason why they were there in the first place.

Sinclair grabbed one end of a broken line and rejoining it to the other end showing John where it was to be re-tied to, whilst he did the same to yet another broken line.

John had completed his little task to find Sinclair was struggling to make the next broken lines meet up so that he could rejoin them. He saw that Sinclair had unhooked his safety line, using it as a strop to make the connection, before managing to make good the securing line.

John was greatly alarmed at seeing this, so quickly felt for and removed his trousers belt, which was under his overalls, under his foul weather gear. He tied one end to his safety harness then made a secure loop onto the catwalk handrail with the other end. Sinclair held his thumb up to indicate that all was well so they could get back into the ship again.

As Sinclair climbed back onto the catwalk, John grabbed hold of him, swiftly transferring his own safety harness onto Sinclair, just as a rogue wave literally crashed right down on top of them, flattening them to the grille of the catwalk, before it flowed angrily overboard again. They managed to get to their feet and started moving, all the while being lashed by the cascading water that raised itself up to tower over the ship. Several times they were knocked off their feet by the wind and water, but eventually they managed to get back to the safety of the hatchway again.

"Hughes, help get this crap off us, then get Engineer Grey back to his cabin." Sinclair ordered breathlessly amid a fit of coughing.

"John, I've to make my report to the Captain. Best get a good shower, so I'll see you in the saloon later." Sinclair wheezed, helping Brazier to strip John down to his very soggy underpants and socks.

John nodded his head meekly, carrying his sodden clothing to stagger towards his cabin.

"Well done Hughes. When you've escorted the 2nd Engineer to his cabin, get hold of a padlock then lock this upper deck hatchway. When done so, report it locked to the Bosun for him to have the key." Sinclair said hoarsely, wringing his clothes out before putting them back on to make his report.

"3rd Mate reporting." Sinclair announced, standing next to and clinging onto the ship's binnacle, then delivered his report to an astonished Captain.

"Well done 3rd Mate. You and Hughes have saved some very valuable cargo. The upper deck is off limits to all personnel, except in emergency and the 'Life-buoy Ghost' (sentry) aft. Get yourself a good shower and a hot meal from the galley. You can stay off watch for the rest of the day and I'll call you when needed." Denton said gratefully.

"Actually Captain it wasn't Hughes who assisted me, it was 2nd Engineer Grey. Maybe, and I suspect that's why he had 3rd Engineer Clarke make their own reports." Sinclair said sleepily, as fatigue began taking its toll on him.

Denton was taken by surprise with that piece of information, and admitted that it was indeed Clarke who made the proper report.

"Very well 3rd Mate, you can go now. I shall have a word with Grey soon enough about this." Denton concluded, scribbling a notation into the bridge logbook.

"Remember Captain, both the for'ard deck hatchways have been padlocked shut." Sinclair stated, leaving the bridge to make his weary way to his cabin.

The tropical storm had finished playing with the *Repulse Bay*, as she neared her next port of call. The morning air was calm and the placid water belied its earlier temper as a long string of equally exotic islands appeared over the horizon.

The *Repulse Bay* had skirted around another long group of the Ellice Island archipelago during her fight against the tropical storm, and had arrived at Tarawa, the main island of the Gilbert Islands archipelago.

"See John! I told you that this place is still suffering from being liberated from the Japs. You can still see the war debris that Mother Nature is trying to disguise." Clarke stated, pointing to various eyesores marring the beauty of these tropical islands.

"Was it your boys who re-took the place, Aussie?"

"Aye that we did. The little bastards got evicted but it cost us plenty in the process. Still, it's back to where it belongs, and I hope to show you the sights once we've finished our discharge."

"Glad you said that, 3rd. Only this time you will confine yourself to the grass skirts of the local sheilas, not the ruddy grass that you started smoking back at Tokelau."

"Fair enough mate. Anyway, do you want me to check the gauges ashore again or what?"

"Yes, but make doubly sure on the avgas before you set the discharge timer off. We should be about two hours before we can secure. You can stay ashore until then, but remember what I've said."

"On my way John." Clarke breathed, ambling ashore to the now familiar huts made from bamboo and palm trees, which constituted as the pump houses.

"Ship secured from discharge, Captain. Do you want me to adjust the trim?" John asked, making his report to Denton in his day cabin.

"No that's okay 2nd. Due to the storm, we've been delayed a good 12 hours. Which means that we've got to curtail our stay here and press on to Taraniti. If you want a quick run ashore, you've got literally 30 minutes worth, before I get the tugs to get us off this bloody fuelling jetty. Mind you, the Postie has a good taste in souvenir hunting. He said he will be bringing a few souvenirs back with him, so maybe you'll be able to purchase something from him." Denton replied, sipping a large fruit cocktail.

"That sounds about right Captain. How long to Taraniti?"

"With luck, we should be alongside Maoi I'ti in a little over 2 days providing we don't meet another storm. At least we're guaranteed a couple of days ashore this time. If you've finished your report, I have a subject that has come to my attention which I want cleared up before we arrive Taraniti." Denton said, changing his mood from being a mild-mannered man into one full of wrath and gloom.

"Now then 2nd, I have been told by the 3rd mate you assisted him on deck with a highly perilous, dangerous task which only he volunteered for. His duty as the For'ard Deck Officer means that he and his crew deal with any deck cargo not secured for foul weather. That goes with the territory, if you like. Nobody asked you or called upon you to help him, also, if things had gone wrong, I would have been down a second officer and an engine room one at that. How do you suppose I would go about explaining to the management team, let alone your next of kin, your loss of life whilst on deck during a storm when it was not part of your remit as tank Engineer?" Denton ranted.

John looked out of the cabin porthole at the blue cloudless sky, which was the backdrop to the lush green tropical island that surrounded the ship.

'I could be ashore now stretching my legs for a while, taking in the unforgettable sights of these lovely islands'. He mused, as he stood there listening yet not listening to Denton, who continued to rant and rave. He went on about the ship and the crew being lazy, slovenly, not worth their pay. Of how useless his officers were, of how the company was treating him, and how he should have been the Captain of one of the cruise liners out of Sydney, instead of acting like a delivery boy. His tirade went on for several more

minutes, before John managed to bring himself to listen to what else Denton had to say.

"According to the Captain's log which records all major incidents on board, this is the second time you and 3rd Mate Sinclair performed such a hairy-arsed stroke on this ship since joining it in San Diego. Do you two have some sort of death wish or what? What is it with you two, or is that too personal a question which, I find abhorrent behaviour, to know about?" Denton asked with obscene gestures, but got no further.

John strode across the cabin floor, pushing the much bigger, bulkier body of Denton back so roughly that he stumbled to land heavily into his big armchair.

"You stop right there Captain and listen to me very carefully before I do something I might regret, you ungrateful bastard!" John snarled, thrusting his face right up against Denton's face.

"3rd Mate Sinclair, Radio Officer Larter and I, and to a certain extent 3rd Engineer Clarke, are long time shipmates. We have been invited to join this shipping line for, shall we say, performance par excellence. Sinclair, Larter and I have saved many a ship from sinking, many a passenger from perishing on the skeleton coast of Africa, and the last time we were in these waters, saved an entire island of people from the aftermath of a 300 foot mega tsunami. When we get to Taraniti, you will discover just what sort of shipmates we are. I helped my trusted friend out of a dangerous situation, only doing exactly what he would have done for me.

We owe each other our lives, and we're a small band of brothers if you like. So forget the crap about shirt-lifting or any other innuendoes you might harbour in that bird-brain of yours. And whilst I'm on the subject Captain, not only have I've saved your bacon but also this ship, thanks only to your own crass stupidity of allowing her to be too top heavy. Even a decent acting 3rd Engineer let alone a qualified Deck officer could have told you how and why the ship got to that state. Now that I have said all this, maybe you as Captain will start showing some respect to some of the officers who are here to help you sail your ship all the way to Timbuktu and back if you had to.

I've sailed with some real Captains during my career, but you're just a jumped up cabin boy compared to them, so don't come the bloody old salt with me. Think of what I've just told you before you start telling stories in your logbook, Captain. Now if you'll excuse me, I have some work to do before I can sit on my arse quaffing funny drinks." John raged, then stormed out of the cabin leaving Denton totally bemused and shocked at what had just happened to him.

John met Penrose who was coming towards him, who stopped him asking if Denton was okay and what was the fracas all about.

"What's the matter with Denton? Not getting enough vertical hand-shakes or what?" John growled.

"From where I was standing and by what I heard, you certainly read him the riot act. But you really shouldn't have pushed him the way you did. He could put you on a disciplinary charge then have you beached at our next port of call. Sufficient to tell you, he's already marked your card as a trouble-maker. Mind you, if what you've said is true, then you'll not hear another word out of place from him. It's about time somebody stood up to him because he'd been such a pain in the arse ever since he came on board. Nothing seemed to satisfy him and his mood swings are getting more and more common, just ask the sailors about that. Let's hope he gets taken off when we get back to Brisbane." Penrose confided.

"It was his fault to insinuate I was a shirt-lifter. No offence to any or all such people on board, but just as long as they don't try it on me that's all." John concluded, then left the steward to his duties.

"Glad you came back early Aussie. Hope you had a good run ashore. We've only got half-an- hour to get ourselves buttoned up, ready for sailing again." was John's greeting when Clarke sauntered over the gangway wearing a few flower garlands around his neck and a grass skirt around his waist.

"Hello John! Got myself re-acquainted with the local sheilas again. I've brought you a bottle of the local moonshine which will guarantee a good night's kip if ever you need one." Clarke greeted him cheerfully, holding out a bottle of liquid that seemed of dubious quality.

"Thanks Aussie, I'll have it later if you don't mind. I've collected the figures from ashore which, surprise of surprises, match up with ours. I'll leave you to correlate the figures onto our chart once we've sailed. Which incidentally is in about 20 minutes. Get the remaining hatches of the after tanks shut down before then." John ordered, and leaving the gangway going for'ard to seek out Sinclair.

"Hello John! Come for'ard to see our handy-work?" Sinclair asked, putting extra securing straps to the deck cargo.

"No Andy, I've come to tell you about my altercation with the Captain." John responded, then explained all that had happened, and what Penrose had said.

"You certainly know how to pick a fight with a ship's Captain, John. Fortunately or unfortunately, depending on which side of the coin you look at, but I'd say you're consistent at least. Penrose is correct with what he says about Denton, in that he's a classic Jekyll and Hyde character.

According to Bruce, we've only got 3 more weeks at sea with Denton in charge, as he's due to be relieved when we get back to Brisbane. His card has been marked by the so-called management team, so I don't suppose he'll have the cheek to mark yours over that incident." Sinclair assured John, who thanked him for his remark.

"Did you get ashore this time Andy, I know Bruce did."

"Yes, we met up in the Toc H club just down from the local eatery. We saw Aussie performing with the local natives and guessed that you were still on board."

"Somebody's got to look after the ship Bruce. I'd like to have gone ashore as it is the third time I've missed out." John said ruefully.

"Never mind, we've got two full days ashore in our next stop, so you know what that means." Sinclair enthused.

"Not really Andy." John teased, but smiled at his friend.

"Flippin' heck, listen to him. A picture of innocence, I don't think." Larter quipped as he joined them.

"Hello Bruce. Hope you've brought me a couple of smalley rabbits this time, as it's getting that I can't get into my cabin with them all." John joked, and had his hair ruffled by Sinclair for his trouble.

"He's just told me about his recent performance with Denton." Sinclair stated, then related exactly what John had told him.

Larter's reply was almost word for word to what Sinclair had said, making John feel much better.

"Anyway, must be away and get my radio flashed up. See you both after tea." Larter called then left them.

"Yes, and I must get ready to receive the tugs John. Catch up with you later with Bruce." Sinclair stated, leaving John standing on the centre catwalk.

'Oh to be the outside Engineer again, to be able to stand on the foc'sle and look around the place as we enter or leave the harbour.' he whispered to himself, before he too left the upper deck and went into the bowels of the ship.

"John, come into my office will you." Hodgson directed more that requested.

"Hello Alan, yes certainly. What is it I can do for you?" John replied civilly, stepping into the engine room office.

"It's Dave Fagg. He's got another bout of malaria, which seems to be worse than the last time. Doc Caughey has him confined to the sick bay, which means that I need you to cover for him." He started to explain when the ship's doctor entered the cabin.

"I'm afraid he's got it really bad this time Chief, and really needs to be flown home a.s.a.p. I've emphasised this in my report to the Captain, but he's quite unmoved by the man's plight. The only thing I can suggest that he remains in the sick bay until I can get him more or less back into shape again to return to some duties on board, albeit light ones at that. It's the best I can do for you." Caughey stated then left the cabin as quickly as he entered it.

"There you have it. Which means I'll need you again and for Clarke to cover your sea duties during this leg of the voyage until we get to Taraniti. Once we've got alongside you can resume your tank duties again." Hodgson said sombrely.

"If what the Doc says, how long do you think he'll be out this time? Can't we get a relief 2nd Engineer flown out and waiting for us when we arrive? Can't you get a 3rd Engineer to cover him? It's just that I'm asked to do double duties on board yet again and not getting paid for it. I know Clarke is a good Engineer but not sufficiently qualified to take over my duties as the Tank Officer, which means that I will be required to fill my normal role on top of Faggs." John asked.

"The Captain has stated that he won't be asking for a relief 2nd Engineer, pointing out that it would be too costly to fly one to meet us only to return back with the ship within the fortnight again. He's right of course, but then he's not thinking about the welfare of his existing officers. The thing is, I need a 2nd Engineer, like for like, as a 3rd would not be qualified enough to relieve me of my duties should anything happen to me during the voyage. Mind you, I have to admit that I suspect his decision was made as the result of the altercation you had with him earlier on, and before you say anything, he told me all about it. I must be seen to uphold the authority of the Captain, even though I personally disagree with what he has decided."

John looked concerned at the revelation of being spoken about.

"I'll bet he didn't tell you what really happened Alan. I have a witness who Denton doesn't know about, who witnessed the entire scene. I shall not go into the realms of that again, sufficient to tell you that I will do these duties but under protest. You will get my full co-operation and my professional best, as you'd expect. I must inform you now that as soon as we've completed our discharge on Taraniti, I shall be living ashore until such times as we set sail again. You have my word on that Alan."

"That's fine by me John. I shall take over the instructional duties just as long as you maintain the standards required by our juniors when on watch. Is that a deal?" Hodgson asked softly.

"Yes, that will help Alan. Make it so then. When is my first shift?"

"Our watches are 1 watch in 3. You'll commence by taking the 1st watch then the forenoon. Same routine as before, except that if you're needed for tank duties whilst on watch, you will get relieved for the duration. But you must return to the engine room on completion. I shall have the watch roster up on the notice board for you to observe." Hodgson explained.

"Right then Alan. Might as well get myself up top and off duty until then." John agreed, and left the noisy engine room.

"What's the matter John, you look as if you've lost a shilling and found thruppence?" Larter asked, sitting down next to him in the saloon.

"Fagg's in the sick bay 'till god knows when, so I've got to cover for him again. Denton won't bother to get a relief for him whilst we're in Taraniti on account that it would cost too much just for the sake of the couple of weeks left on this voyage.

The Chief told me that Denton had a word with him concerning my face off with him, and he reckons that I'm being got at in this way. The thing is, I'm looking forward to stepping ashore in Taraniti again as it's my first run ashore since leaving Fiji, apart from anything else that is." John explained with a crest fallen expression.

"Sorry to hear that John, but you must have expected some sort of backlash for accosting the Captain on his own ship, and all that. Don't you worry about not getting ashore, as I shall be contacting Taraniti to let them know who we are, what we're doing and will be arranging shore facilities for the ship and the crew. That also includes what is called Diplomatic Pratique, which means that the local departments such as the health, customs, and even members of the government will be requested to come on board and be welcomed by our Captain, on behalf of his officers and crew. If by any chance our names get mentioned, yours in particular, then we'll be getting the red carpet treatment just like Captain Tomlinson got on the *Inverlogie,* whether Denton likes it or not.

Now that my dear friend, means that you will be taken off the ship and be lashed up in King Phatty's palace for the duration of our stay. Which also means that if Denton protested against it, or brings you back on board for some obscure reason, then he will be responsible for an unholy diplomatic row between here and Whitehall, let alone the bad press created for the shipping company.

Best keep a low profile until we get there John, and as I've just said, let Andy and me sort you out." Larter comforted.

"Well if you're sure Bruce, then so be it. Mind you, it would be nice to find out who is responsible for what. I won't be responsible for the fruits of the so-called 50 year old virgins that you and Andy had a bash at, mind you." John chuckled, remembering that magic night.

"That's the spirit John. Now how's about a fresh glass around here." Larter smiled, holding out his empty beer glass.

John started his first watch down in the engine room, making certain that all he was responsible for was as it should be, before he managed to enjoy the rest of his watches. He had one small problem to deal with considering the complexity of marine engine, which was due to the low pressure of the lubricating oil.

'*Had to change over tanks and get the oil filters cleaned.*' He wrote in the engine room logbook.

"Morning John, I'm your relief now. We're about two hours

off Taraniti, if you want to get yourself organised." Hodgson announced, arriving onto the inspection platform of the engine room.

"Hello Alan. No problems to report, it's all in the hand over log." John replied, showing Hodgson his write up in the log, which Hodgson scanned quickly, then nodded his approval.

"I'm off now Alan. See you ashore some time. If you ever get to the Kite flyers club, say hello to the Met Office boys for me." John said pleasantly, taking off his dirty overalls.

"You've been here before John?" Hodgson asked in surprise.

"Sort of Alan, its a long story soon to be revealed once you get ashore. Must go and get my own troops organised now." John responded with a smile and left the engine room.

"There you are Aussie, thought I would find you skiving." John greeted, surprising Clarke who was having a quiet smoke under the for'ard central catwalk.

"Jeez John, don't keep doing that." Clarke blurted, quickly stubbing his cigarette out onto the deck.

"Just as well we're on the FFO tank and not on the avgas tank, 3rd Engineer." John chided mildly, kicking the offending article overboard.

"We've got about two hours before we tie up alongside the fuel storage jetty, we shall be discharging three quarters of the remaining fuels. I'm not sure of the pump facility ashore as it has been changed since I was here last, but you can bet it will take us a good 6 hours to complete the discharge.

Once we've finished with the discharge, the ship will be moving over to the main harbour for docking alongside to transfer the deck cargo and the like. During that particular time Aussie, you will be in charge of the proceedings, as I will more than likely be required elsewhere, by what Bruce has been telling me." John explained.

"Fair enough Cobber! No doubt I'll see you ashore at some point, you lucky bastard." Clarke drawled.

"Nothing of the kind Aussie, it's just that whilst you've

enjoyed the runs ashore in all the other places I was on board doing the duty. Now it's my turn don't you think. The Captain will be hard pressed to get me back on board much before we sail again that's for certain. I'm telling you this now Aussie, as you'll be the one in the firing line if anything needs to be done."

"Thanks for the warning, but not even that idiot Denton will have any hope in finding me, once I get ashore and meet the local sheilas. I've just got me another new wife ashore here, seeing as my last one was lost during the great flood, you know. Their problem now is that there're not enough mums to go around the orphans, and that's why my mate in Brisbane got you a load of toys to bring with you. I've got almost as much as you in a spare caboose, so their Christmas will be coming pretty early this year. Why do you think I volunteered to come on this ruddy floating petrol tank, it certainly wasn't for the grub nor the ruddy pay." Clarke bragged, making John gasp in surprise.

"Oh well Aussie. Seeing as that has put things into perspective, I needn't worry any more about being cast as the scoundrel of the seas." John muttered.

"You? No mate, you're only one in a long line of sailors who got the works from the local female population." Clarke said with conviction, watching the realization of what he said, flicker across John's face.

"Anyway, Aussie. We've just got time to get ourselves sorted before we start up again. See you in about an hour. Usual routine." John concluded, then left to go to his cabin, to sort out his own affairs.

CHAPTER XXIII

Return to Me

The large bulk of the *Repulse Bay* came to a gentle halt then was pushed sideways to its allocated berth by the little harbour tugs that were in attendance. The harbour was a new one, built by using the salvaged remains of the old one to speed up the rebirth of an atoll, which was almost wiped away by a mega tsunami. This natural catastrophe was caused by a high sided volcano destroying itself by its massive explosion, which created a 280foot high, 400 yard wide wave, measured from the front to the back of the wave, and travelling at the speed of nearly 400mph. The force of which wiped away most of the lower lying islands and dumping their remains onto the main atoll of Maoi'I'ti. So instead of a garland of tropical islands that surrounded a lagoon, it was now a collection of peaks or flat coral reefs arranged in a semicircle, with the old lagoon filled in with the debris from the outlying islands. The Taraniti archipelago with the twin islands of the Maoi and Maoi I'ti Atoll as its capital was now called Taraniti Atoll, to remember most of the islanders who lost their lives on that terrible day.

"Here you are John. You had better put these on" Larter suggested, giving John a large brown paper parcel, with a label attached to it.

"What is it Bruce?" John asked, reading the label on the parcel.

"Just you put them on and follow me, John. The gangway is ready for placing, but you need to be ready to receive our hosts when they arrive. Look here they come." Larter replied, pointing to the approaching welcoming party.

John looked at the reception committee and immediately remembered how it was the last time he was here. Especially when Joe Tomlinson walked ashore in his ermine robes and regalia of a Lord.

He tore open the parcel to find it contained the very same robes that Tomlinson had worn, with a sealed letter attached to them, which he opened and read:

'Dear John Grey. If you are reading this letter and are examining the contents of this parcel, then I will assume you are about to become part of the ceremonial welcome that was only accorded to a very few men before me, and now you. You will conduct yourself according to the Naval Officers code, and render yourself to the furtherance of good relations between the Kingdom of Taraniti and our gracious Monarch. Both of us share a unique experience, which has been recorded in the annals of the Kingdom of Taraniti. You will however, need to be seen to be wise and just, when it comes to making judgements on the affairs of state. In other words, diplomacy is the key essence required.

One last thing and as my successor in these things, I cal tell you that you will be informed of what is required of you by the Priestess, if not, then certainly by the Queen herself. These you must do without thought, or personal objections, the reasons will become clear as the events finally unravel and reveal themselves to you.

Do well my friend for indeed both our names will be called into question otherwise. Present this to the King and tell him it is from me. That should make your acceptance much easier for you.

When you return from Taraniti, I would request that you write to me and let me know how things are.

I look forward to be meeting up with you again.

Good luck John!

Regards Joe Tomlinson."

"Bloody hell Bruce! It looks as if I'm going to be the proverbial sacrificial lamb again. I've already got a cabin full of rabbits for those young ladies I was forced to go with, but if I continue, then I'll require more than this vessel to carry them all in. Here, read it for yourself" John said in bewilderment and handing the letter over

"Serves you right on becoming known as the Iceman, John.

On top of that, it appears that not only will you look like a Lord you'll live like one whilst we're here. The down side I should imagine, is that you might be required to give a repeat performance of your last act whilst here last time. You lucky sod." Larter teased, then read the personal letter quickly.

"When will I ever get a quiet run ashore Bruce? So far on this voyage I've visited plenty of marvellous fishing grounds, but I've never even got my fly wet." John moaned.

"Never mind John, at least you're on shall we say, 'Government Duty', which attracts loads of freebees especially when there's females involved. By the time you're finished your flies will definitely be wet to the point of drowning." Larter commiserated.

John watched the gangway being lowered as the melodious welcome from the islanders was performed. He looked intently through the lines of topless dancing girls, managed to locate TeLani with her sisters, who were surrounding the large chair King Phatt was being carried upon.

He made his way to the gangway and started to go over but was rudely called back by Denton.

"Since when have you been Captain of this vessel, Grey? I get ashore first, besides it's my duty to welcome our hosts, not yours." Denton shouted with sarcasm.

King Phatt along his equally large wife stepped off their ornamental chairs striding over to the gangway to await Denton arrival, then saw John instead.

Denton went to shake the hand of Phatt, but the King held his ornamental ivory baton out fending Denton off, before pointing to John who was waiting to cross the gangway.

John put his ermine robe on and his coronet with the help of Larter, then strode with an air of majesty down the gangway to meet the monarchs, with Denton gasping with the shock of seeing an Engineer wearing a Lord's regalia.

"It is good that you return to us Iceman John Grey. Come,

we've got some celebrations to make." King Phatt said, waving his baton as he beckoned John to join him, then turned to address Denton.

"You are the Captain of this very large ship. You will see to it that Engineer John Grey is released from all duties until you sail again, yes? If you need anything for your crew, speak to my Chief advisor whom you'll find in my castle up there." Phatt insisted, pointing up to the castle behind him.

"John Grey, your return will be a happy one for my daughters." Phatt greeted, first shaking his hand then giving him a bear hug, which when finished left John gasping for air.

Queen Phatty gave him a huge hug then clapped her hands, which summoned the garland bearers to come to him.

Each girl put a garland around his neck then stepped aside for TeLani and her sisters to greet him.

TeLani smiled through her tears as she approached him to place her garland on him.

"You return to me and my sisters John Grey. Look! I still have your lucky charm around my neck." TeLani whispered, smiling joyously through her tears as she placed her garland around his neck.

"I have come to see if you are well, but I leave in two days time." John replied softly, kissing her tear stained cheeks, before repeating the same ritual with her other sisters.

"Iceman John Grey has proved himself a man even though he is still looking rather thin. For he has fathered several children, who he must see when we arrive in the castle." Queen Phatty announced.

"Your Majesty. I bear gifts for the children of your daughters, although I fear not enough for each child in your Kingdom. They are on the ship awaiting to be brought ashore by my two faithful friends who were with me during the big flood." John responded, which was received by a big smile from Phatty.

"I also bear greetings from my friend Joe Tomlinson and have brought a humble gift for your royal majesty." John stated, holding out a large brown package for Phatt to take.

Phatt looked at the parcel with surprise, but took it to open it there and then.

It was a very large half sleeved silk shirt with bright colours as the background to the royal crest of King Phatt's heraldry.

He held it up and looked at it admiringly, before taking off his ceremonial garlands and his heavy chains of gold, to put it on. It fitted perfectly, much to John's relief.

Phatt looked admiringly at it, whilst Queen Fatty examined the material.

"I have such material for your good self and your daughters, your majesty. You will be able to make lots of pretty dresses out of it." John informed her.

"Today will be a holiday. Come John Grey, we go now to the castle. Bring your friends with you." Phatt announced in a booming voice.

John turned around beckoning Larter and Sinclair to join him, which they did in double quick time.

The welcome party moved along sedately in front, with John and his two friends being carried in chairs just like Phatts', only they were not so ornate.

John managed to catch a last glimpse of a totally confused and angry Captain.

"It looks as if Denton has been upstaged for once, Andy. I warned him of such an event when we arrived, but it was obvious he didn't believe me." John said quietly so as not to be overheard.

"You'll be getting a roasting when you get back on board again, I'll bet. That is of course if you survive the next beach party." Larter opined.

"I've worked hard on this leg of the voyage, and as far as I'm concerned, I'm entitled to the time off, especially with the Chief's blessing." John responded, as TeLani and her sisters walked each side of his chair

They arrived into the castle, which was overlooking the new harbour. John caught a glimpse of the new shape of the island, realising Mother Nature had worked hard to heal the wounds and scars of the mega tsunami that had wiped away so much of the archipelago.

John and his two friends were escorted into the central hall of the castle, which was really a large cavern carved out of the island. Phatt saw John looking around pointing to various features that were not there on his last visit.

"We still have some of the machinery and the water pipes you fixed up John Grey. Our clean water lake is good again, but we need you to make the water fresh again. You do this for us?" Phatt stated more than requested.

"My friends and I will fix those things for you before we go in two days time, your majesty."

"You speak as wisely as friend Joe Tomlinson. But first you must meet the fruits of your loins." Phatt replied, clapping his hands to command his daughters and the servants.

"Daughters, bring your children here for John Grey to witness." he commanded, for the women to hurry away in obedience.

"Now is the time to get the presents out gentlemen." John whispered, as TeLani and her two sisters came back into the room.

TeLani held a little child in each hand and walking them towards him, sat them down in front of him. She had a twin girl and boy. Her two sisters did the same in quick succession, until John was looking down at a little row of faces. John was amazed at how every one of them looked almost identical even though one pair was mixed twins, one was set of twin boys, with a single girl from the different mothers who were sisters.

"Bloody hell John, twins run in the family or what? I wonder what we got from the stork?" Larter whispered as four more young women came into the large room and placed their babies at the feet of Larter and Sinclair.

Larter and Sinclair looked astonished to see the young women standing behind a row of little children who were all looking up at the three friends with happy smiles on their faces.

"Bloody hell! We've started another tribe all by ourselves!" Larter whispered but smiled back at the sea of faces.

"You'd better believe it dear friend! But what happens next will depend on whether we get away without paying child maintenance or such like." John whispered, still in awe at the result of his past visit to the islands.

"So between us three, we've produced 4 girls and 5 boys. That should keep the tribe going for another generation. Just as well they live all the way out here and not back home or we'd be in the nick for adultery, under-aged sex, cruelty to children and other related crimes." Sinclair responded.

King and Queen Phatt came over to witness what John had brought for their daughters and their babies.

John gave TeLani and her sisters a necklace each, but TeLani's necklace was the one Helena had given him. He showed her the locket with his picture in it, telling her that the other side would be for her picture. Each sister hugged him and kissed him as they looked at each other's necklaces.

John then bent down and gave each baby a soft toy, telling their mothers that they were called teddy bears. He made sure there were pink ribbons around the toys for the little girls, and blue ribbons for the little boys.

He then opened a huge sack and took out two large rocking horses. He picked up TeLani's mixed twins and placing them onto the back of one of the horses, rocked it gently. Explaining to the sisters that it was an animal called a horse, he gave them each a picture of a horse and its rider. He then gave Phatty her two large bolts of coloured silks and cotton.

Phatt looked in amazement but with extreme pleasure written on his face, seeing all the gifts that were being bestowed on the babies, which John had sired.

"I think you two had better take over. Leave the last sack for me." John whispered to his two friends.

Sinclair and Larter then carried out a similar little ceremony to each mother and child, which were attributed to them. Again each gift was received joyously with much pride being shown by the King and his Queen. When the two friends had finished they stood next to John, who was looking closely at the resemblance of between him and his babies.

Phatty looked at the remaining large sack then at John, asking what it was for.

John opened it, took out all the presents explaining they were for the orphans of the island, the 'motherless children'.

"You and your friends have honoured my family and my Kingdom with your kindness and generosity, John Grey. Come, we have a surprise for you." Phatt decreed, beckoning John and his friends to follow him. They were escorted through a passage, and up some steps that were also carved out of the mountain, then out into the open air Looking around they saw a large, magnificent, well-stocked garden with its own fountain and ornamental statues dotted around the place.

Passing through an archway of flowers leading to a quiet secluded garden filled with flagrance from a kaleidoscope of coloured flowers blooming everywhere. Songbirds sang to them as they walked along a path of white marble flagstones that led them into a patio with had carved figurines surrounding a gushing fountain. There were other statuettes around the place but John spotted a small area with several life-sized statues standing in a semi-circle.

John gasped in amazement as he saw a statue of himself, with his name carved in the plinth, and the caption, "'The Ice Man' John Grey".

"This was made in your memory John Grey. You can place it anywhere on the island you wish, or leave it here for all my visitors to see. Your friend Joe Tommyson had his placed at the entrance of the new harbour docks, as the old one had been destroyed." Phatt informed him.

Larter and Sinclair examined the pink marble statue, discovered that the pink lustre was caused by thousands of little pieces of gold inlaid to the marble so it sparkled in the sunlight, then to John marvelling at the great likeness and the finest detail of it.

"Better than a portrait John. Whoever did this must have been a master sculptor who kept a beady eye on you during your stay last time. According to the grapevine, this one will eventually be replaced by something similar to Michael Angelo's statue of David. Anyway from the looks of it, that statue must weigh a few tons and be worth a ruddy fortune with all the gold in it." Larter said approvingly.

"My gratitude to you, your majesty." John said pleasantly bowing to the King.

"The three airmen have a statue as well, but they have been put on the place above the Met office where they finally landed." TeLani informed them, as the entourage followed the King around the place.

"Now for something to eat. Come!" Phatt invited, as John and his friends followed the King back to the large hallway where the babies and their mothers were still playing with the toys.

Phatty waddled over, placed a hand on John's shoulder holding him while she whispered into his ear. John looked surprised, then gave a smile, but shook his head slowly.

"I will only serve your daughter TeLani again if you wish your Majesty, but as I told you last time when I left your islands, I cannot foretell whether I shall ever be back again. It is only with great fortune that I am able to visit to see the fruits of my loins, but it would be unfair to leave a child without a gift from the one who sired it."

"You speak with much wisdom just like your friend Joe Tommyson. I will make sure that in future, all babies will get a gift when they are delivered safely from the womb. As an Easterner from the great divide, your only concern with babies is in the making of them. It is for the women to nourish and look after the babies, from the time they are born to the time they leave the family house."

"I acknowledge your customs your majesty, and offer my support to your cause of rebuilding your tribal Kingdom. But what of the other tribes that may have perished, have they no women needing the seed of man?"

"There are only two main tribes left, and yes there are a few women left from them who have no man to give them the seeds of life."

"If your Majesty wishes to re-generate these tribes again, then probably only the 'Easterners' among us will be of use to you, but I have no doubt they will be only too glad to help them. I tell you this as most of our crew are from the Oriental tribes. However your Majesty, if TeLani wishes to have more babies then it is up to her to ask, not by royal command."

"It is my duty to see that all child bearing women in the Kingdom get a real mans seed to fertilise them. It is their duty to prove to me that they were given it, which is why we watch them to see they are given enough seed for them to bear a child. As you and your friends have proved you are real men, then you will be left alone to seed with the same women as when you were here last time. TeLani and her sisters will only be doing their duty, but I have to see that the rest of the women get a real man who can make her smile."

John knew this gargantuan woman out-gunned him, so he conceded to her royal demands telling her he was at TeLani's service.

The feast was held on the pink sandy slope of the wrecked aircraft landing strip, which was supposed to be built on a coral reef originally at the entrance of a very shallow lagoon.

The island's lush vegetation had regenerated itself enough to hide the scars of the oceans wrath, while palms that spread along the beach, waved gently in the tropical breeze.

The big lagoon that once raced these lovely islands had been filled in by the destruction of outlying coral reefs and low-lying islands. King Phatt had reclaimed the small lagoon, which was now the play area for both the islanders and the tourists that he hoped would flock to his islands. Even the friendly volcano had helped out by spraying rich deposits of black soil over the twin peaks of Maoi. Due to the atoll being so close to the equator, it was always hot and humid, which meant there was plenty of rain to help nurture the new plant shoots.

John, Bruce and Andy sat on the 'privileged' carpet next to Phatt and his Queen, whilst the other officers and crew of the *Repulse Bay* sat in a semicircle in front of them. There was plenty to eat and drink, especially the iced beers, which was a necessity at any decent barbeque. Whilst the sailors made merry, what few local tribesmen there were, were made to wait on them.

Soon the evening came upon them, with everybody feasting by the light of the large bonfires that were lit all around the campsite.

"This is when it starts getting interesting, gentlemen." John whispered to his friends, then explained the ritual, which was about to befall him first before them.

"Talk about a live floor show John! Even the famous Ah Fuk Yeu bar in the Wan Kin district of Kowloon would be knocked sideways if that's the case." Clarke joked on being told of the imminent ceremony that John was about to endure for Queen and country.

This time it was TeLani who acted as the Chief taster for John, with her other sisters performing the remainder of the ceremony. Once the initial ceremony was finished for Queen Phatty to give her approval, it was the turn of the other officers and the crew to play their part.

John spoke quietly and with tenderness to TeLani, during his performance of extra duties, in privacy and well away from the rest of the lovers of the night.

"Your babies will ensure your after-life, dear TeLani. I cannot know if when I may return, but may your Gods keep you and your children safe. Maybe one day when your children have all grown up you will tell them of me, and how I belong to the other side of the great divide." he said gently, smiling as he whispered her name into her ear, then put a flower behind her ear.

"TeLani, I will remember you above all others." He whispered when they finished their love-making.

"I was only 14 summer seasons old for you to be my first man. Now I am 4 summer seasons older you will be my last, as I am destined to become the 'Princess Royal', which makes me next in line to take over the Queen's crown. Your seed is sweet and as good as you have been kind to me and to my babies, who will grow up to become fine people of the islands. For me to be delivered and blessed with a twin boy and girl is a good omen, and a sign from our Gods that our peoples will live and prosper. This visit will be your last one to these islands, so as you are destined not to return then it will be only right for you to know of their names, especially the one which I shall deliver by the end of the next winter. I tell you of them as I will tell them of you. The two you have seen are the girl TeLani Telah named after me, the boy TeLani John after you. The one that will grow in my womb after you have gone will be called TeLani May, just in case when I'm Queen, you come back during this month she has been named after. My sisters have each named their children in a similar way, and share my good fortune that you have been their seed giver too. One of their sons will eventually become our King, but this time it will only be me, as my sisters will be given to your two friends to seed them." TeLani whispered, holding him close to her.

The gongs and drums sounded out calling the lovers of the night to return to the campfire and for King Phatt to declare the party over.

Phatty padded over the soft sand greeting John when he and TeLani appeared from among the throng of night lovers.

"It is good your seed will swim inside TeLani again John Grey. Now you must rest in your quarters at the castle, for on tomorrows dawn, you will do your mans work of making our waters fresh again." she said with gusto, giving John a hug with her huge arms, almost squashing him flat.

"Your majesty is kind to offer me quarters. Maybe TeLani will keep me company during that time as is the custom of my people?" John asked whilst gasping for breath.

"You sleep alone John Grey as TeLani and her sisters will be returning to their own quarters where no man is allowed. You will be allowed to see them after you have done your duty to the King. Now you and your two friends must join us in our dance back to the castle, but all your other friends from the ship will not be required. Tell them of this then join the parade again." she commanded sternly.

John merely bowed his head then asked Larter and Sinclair to tell the others to go back to the ship or some hostel, as only they were allowed to join him to stay at the castle.

Sinclair and Larter went around the officers and crew telling them of the procedure, who were most agreeable with the arrangements, all except Denton.

"How is it that you get to stay in the castle and not me, the ship's Captain, Grey?" Denton asked with rampant jealousy.

"I told you in your cabin Captain, what the score on this atoll was, but you obviously did not believe me. Sinclair, Larter, and Clarke to a certain extent, are distinguished guests of the King while I happen to be the Chief Guest of Honour. We're all under the royal protection of the King whilst we're visiting the place, but only we four gets the special treatment. If anything should happen to us ashore by known ships' perpetrators, then there will be one holy diplomatic row for you to sort out. See you sometime before we sail Captain, for I have a few jobs to sort out from the last time I was here. And by the way, kindly see that 3rd Engineer Clarke is sent to the castle at about 0700, with my bag of tools and the brown box which is in my office." John breathed, leaving Denton bemused, muttering profusely to himself.

CHAPTER XXIV

A Man's Job

John was woken up by one of the sisters, who silently ushered him to a large chamber, which he discovered was the bathroom, and found other girls waiting for him. There they stripped him naked, and holding his hands, led him into the warm waters of a large sunken bath, where they washed him, massaging his weary body with oils and lotions. Certain parts of his body got extra attention from each of them in turn while the sight of girls' naked bodies around him started to do their magic on him. John did not speak nor did the sisters, until TeLani entered the bath chamber who asked him to stand up.

He rose slowly out of the water as if in a trance, watching the equally naked TeLani come towards him with a very large white, gold-laced towel.

The sisters started to quietly giggle at John's obvious state of arousal taking turns to rub his manhood gently to see if it was real, but he paid them no heed, walking towards this beautiful young woman who was his lover only a few short hours ago.

The sisters came out of the bath and placing their hands on various parts of his body, started to hum softly but melodiously, whilst TeLani knelt down before him and commenced to pleasure him orally.

John felt relaxed, allowing TeLani to use his body but keeping his mind active as if to prolong the exquisite attentions he was getting.

'Maybe she's doing her Chief taster duties again, let's hope I can hold on a little longer than last time. Now what was that shim measurement that was added to those dodgy valves? One thou per hundred tons?' John though, but realising he had no chance against the special techniques these island women had in making a man cast his seed quicker than any other women in the world, he merely relaxed and within moments succumbed to the attentions of his attentive

lover. Only after TeLani felt and tasted that John had completely spent his seed, did she stand up to dry him with the large towel.

The sisters dressed him in a fresh tropical uniform, which astonishing him considering how creased and grubby it was when he saw it last.

"There you are John Grey, all ready for the King's work. Now you can join the King for your morning meal, before the tribal Chiefs visit him in his chamber." TeLani said with a smile, hugging him then kissed each side of his face as was their usual custom.

"Thank you dear TeLani. Maybe I can return your attentions before the night is over. Return the flavour as we say over the great divide." John whispered, which was received with a smile and a nod.

"You still have my sisters to see to John Grey, but as I do understand your custom of only one lover, it will be your two friends who to see to them. If the Queen allows another reunion, then work well today to build up your strength again." She replied before she and her sisters somehow disappeared through the billowing clouds of steam.

"Welcome John Grey, come and sit with me. Your friends are already here." Phatt boomed, pointing to Larter and Sinclair who were sitting at the end of a very long table that seemed to groan with the weight of all the food stacked high upon it.

John smiled and dutifully bowed to the King, nodding to his two friends in acknowledgement as he sat down next to the King. Queen Phatty, TeLani and her sisters filed in through another doorway taking their places at the table, followed by the tribal Chiefs, then the men John took as the Kings' men at court.

John was invited to tuck in, starting with a large slice of watermelon frosted with coconut flakes. He remembered what Joe Tomlinson had told him, so he ate what the King ate, only much less of a portion. His friends watched him closely taking his lead in what to eat, and in what order.

Phatt asked John a few questions about his trip home and how he came to come return to Taraniti. That, with a few somewhat educated questions on the state of the islands plumbing and other such mechanical items, making John smile by the almost correct hypothesis of the problems at hand.

He replied slowly and simply to guide Phatt through each answer, and was pleased that Phatt understood what he was describing or telling him.

This pleased Phatt who stated that he definitely liked John, and could almost understand why he, John, became his Iceman instead of that stupid person called Moore.

John had almost forgotten the man's name, so was impressed by the almost total recall of names or the events Phatt possessed.

Phatt clapped his hands loudly, which summoned the servants to clear the table, which wasn't much considering the vast quantities of food that had been consumed. John smiled at the meagre remains, yet wondering just how much of the food mountain ended up in his belly.

"Now then John Grey, the sun has risen from its sleep and the time has come for you to perform your mans duties. Come, show me what it is you will be doing." Phatt commanded, standing up, then burped long and loudly only to fart even louder before waddling towards the exit doorway.

"I have summoned my assistant, Engineer Clarke to meet me here with my tools your majesty." John advised.

"Ah yes, the Australian, Clarke. He has dined at my table a couple of times as his reward in seeding some of the women with babies from other lost tribes. If he's your assistant then I'll have him sent to you. In the meantime your friends can have the freedom of the island, but they must not return to the castle again until you have completed your work. They, like you, have a very important duty to perform later."

"Unfortunately your Majesty, I am in need of their expertise too. I request that they remain with me until my duties have been done." John asked boldly.

Phatt looked ominously down at John for a moment before he responded.

"I am unaccustomed to be argued with John Grey." He thundered

"Your boldness is noted. You will be afforded any person or equipment available to you. The Queen will see to your nourishment and other needs, but you will come and see me when you have finished, as I have some matters of state to see to." Phatt decreed, then strode out of the chamber with his retinue following meekly behind him.

John mustered his team of men with all the tools needed to do the several jobs, and had them follow him through the service tunnels which were flooded the last time John saw them.

He had the local men clean and clear up each cavern, putting some of his stokers to clean, grease, or make good several rusty valves and pipe-work, whilst he examined some of the salvaged machinery he judged to be of working order.

"Right then Bruce! Aussie will show you how to open and shut some of these gate valves. Andy, I need you to get one of those sacks then get it filled with grit. Engineer Brown, you start priming these pumps just like you would do on board. Engineer Green, you've had time spent in the motor room, so get those fuse boxes checked out. If the fuses are blown then find a suitable length of copper and make straps to bridge the gaps. I also need to isolate the caverns from the main fresh-water supply pipe, the one with the blue stripe around the flanges of the valves." John ordered, going from cavern to cavern.

They arrived in the cavern housing the water purification plant to find it was rusting but still usable.

"Only needs a few pounds of grease plus some oil in the engine, that's all. None of you will have met one of these beasts before, as it's one of my own inventions to meet the immediate needs of the islanders. The only thing I find is that they forgot to look after it by feeding it with oil from time to time. Aussie, see if you can get it flashed up, whilst I see to the main feeder tanks." John said cheerfully.

"Andy, take two men up that tunnel over there. It will take you to some spiral steps leading up to the top of the natural funnel of the rock. Check the reservoir you see there has a good head of water. Clear any debris in the sump but be very careful nobody falls into it or they'll drown, as it's a good 300 feet deep when full. Take one of the field telephones with you to keep in contact with Bruce. Bruce, I need you to tell me if all is okay from Andy, before I start opening the sluice valves and working the pumps.

Leading Stoker Banks, you will go over to those feeder tanks and check they are spotlessly clean. Take a flexible hose with you to connect up to the white-flanged steam pipe to flush it clean. 5th Engineer Green, I need you stand by the main gravity valve and get ready to operate it when I give you a shout." John ordered.

Each person departed to do their bidding, which left John to inspect various pieces of equipment which he had put in place last time around, to ensure a good water supply to the inhabitants of the honeycombed islands.

"John, Andy reports there is some water in the well, but it only covers the mud and rotten vegetation which seems to have bunged up the works. He says it would take days to excavate the sump, although the water seems to be going down anyway." Larter reported what was said over the field telephone.

John acknowledged the message then asked Sinclair to retrace his steps to see if he could find any walls of rock with water seeping from anywhere.

Sinclair re-appeared some half hour later reporting he found an area of rock which literally wept water, so much so a small stream had formed at the foot of the rock wall yet seemed to drain away down some holes underneath where they stood.

This was a clue for John, who decided to go look for himself, so Sinclair showed him the area he had discovered.

"So that's it. The water seeping through the mud from the natural funnel is being contaminated, is being gravity fed through the water system. The acid taste from the fresh-water must be coming from a natural water basin. Not only that Andy, I don't know if you remember our visit to an underground cave with all the fresh water and the clean air we breathed? Those holes the fresh-water is draining into must be the source of the caves fresh water. Where there's fresh-water flowing, there's also fresh air. That must be the oxygen supply to the cave." John exclaimed with delight.

Sinclair scratched his head for a moment, then remembered the occasion agreed with John.

"So if we find some sort of underground chamber which feeds that massive cathedral like cavern then we've got a new source of fresh-water for the islanders. If so, all we've got to do is siphon off some of the water and feed it into the system then we've cracked it." John shouted with glee, suddenly discovering the answer to his problem and his prime objective to his work.

"Andy! Have your men search very carefully to find out where the drain holes leads to. You trace these drains then make me a small drawing of it all. I'm going back to the main cavern to get the place decontaminated before we figure out a way to tap into these new water courses." John directed, rushing down the steep stairway back into the main cavern where the rest of the workers were waiting for him.

"Right men listen up!" he said, breathing heavily from his exertions.

" Banks, Have you finished cleaning out the header tank?"

"All clean and ready 2nd!"

"Okay, get your men to disconnect the main discharge pipe from the tank. You will then flush the pipes with the hot water from the hot mains as I've shown you. Green, you will screw down and block off the original water source, so that nobody can reopen the valve again. Aussie, I need you to help Brown to flush through some miles of water pipes. So get the pump flashed up on full pressure and get it on line. If we've been lucky enough to isolate all the unused outlets, then it should only take about an hour for the entire system to be sanitized from all the muck and contamination that's got into the system. Bruce, contact the castle and all the other main areas of distribution then tell them to open all their fresh-water taps wide, but stand well away from them.

Explain that it will take a good two hours to decontaminate the pipes and there'll be lots of debris and suchlike that will be spat out from them. Once they see clean water coming out of their taps or pipes, then they can turn them off, so the system can be fully primed again." John directed almost breathlessly, as his excitement grew at the prospect of finally curing the sickness and other water-borne ailments of the islanders let alone making their water sweet again.

The header tank was as big as two Olympic sized swimming pools, but it was scrubbed and hosed clean, then John laid a thick bed of grit with some layers of the volcanoes own ingredients of Blumstone and grit as his own special concoction to make the water sweet again.

Sinclair came back with his drawings which John analysed, discovering that all they had to do was extend one section of pipe, knock a hole through the weeping wall, and all the fresh-water was theirs just to tap off.

By the time the reports came through that all the taps and pipes were showing clean fresh-water again, John was ready to have the header tank filled up with new water.

"Nature will gravity feed the water into the tank, but the pump will push it through the system. All the islanders have to do now is to clean out the tank and reline it to purify the water." John explained to the men who had gathered to see their work nearly coming to a successful end.

They had worked hard and long on their tasks, not noticing the time slipping away. Apart from short stops for food, ongoing progress reports or even for a toilet, it was late in the following evening before they completed their mammoth tasks.

"Bruce, phone the castle and invite our Phatt friend come along to see for himself what we've achieved here." John requested, inviting all the workers to taste the end product, pure fresh water.

King Phatt arrived with his Queen Phatty with all the rest of his retinue, and was taken by John on a conducted tour of the caverns. He explained what he found, what was done, finally ending with the King and his followers sampling the life giving nectar of the island.

"You have done a man's job John Grey. My people will be grateful for the work you and your men have done. Maybe tomorrow you will fix our ice cavern in time for the next shipload of groceries, which is due sometime later on in the morning. Your friends and your workers can return to their homes now to feast and be merry then and join you again later, but for now, you will escort me back to the castle for our own feast. Come John Grey, TeLani awaits for your bath as you stink like a rotten Gapo fish." Phatt commanded, clapping his hands to dismiss everybody.

"Bruce! Find out when the ship is due then phone me. Give me about 4 hours before you, Andy and Aussie meet me up at the castle again. Bring me back a spare set of tropicals, and tell Aussie to see the Chief to release the spare A.C.U, plus a few bottles of Freon, for him to bring them with him" John whispered, preparing to leave.

"As good as done John. See you later than the others as I've got to meet up with the *Constantlea* Sparker first off. If she's on time then she should be arriving in about 6 hours or so, which will probably take most of tomorrow for her to unload. We're due to sail ourselves in the morning mind you, but if you can persuade old Phatt to keep us here until the day after, then Denton would be forced to concede it. See you then." Larter whispered back, bowing to the passing monarchs.

CHAPTER XXV

Seeds

John had his bath with TeLani this time, with her sisters in attendance. His evening attire was not his usual uniform but a loose fitting silk shirt with a long flowing sarong that had a sash around his midriff to hold the sarong in place.

John strolled around the castle grounds with TeLani, arriving into the courtyard with the old cast-iron cannons poking out of the ramparts.

John stood looking down over the panoramic view of the island below him, and saw the dramatic change the islanders had achieved since the Armageddon that befell the atoll. It was a moonlight night, but he managed to witness the incoming flight of an aircraft, which glided down to land gently onto the new runway that once was the large lagoon, previously used only by sea-planes. He watched the plane taxi back along the runway, stopping at the very new air terminal which was once the original Harbourmaster's building to the now defunct and filled in docks. He saw coloured lights that were switched on all around the islands, which highlighted the hotels and other places of importance, and was even able to trace the illuminated palm-lined avenues and streets that seemed to parcel the dark patches into little squares.

TeLani pointed out the various new buildings replacing the ones that got destroyed. She also pointed out the dark areas along the length of the islands were the caverns of the people who perished in the flood, saying that some of them were being occupied by some of the exiled islanders who were returning to help the place live again. One particular place she picked out was the little cove where John and his friends had had their 'au natural' swimming session, and where she first saw John.

"What happened to the three airmen from the Met Office?" John asked gently, cradling TeLani in his arms, who on taking hold of his hands, placed them onto her flower-adorned breasts.

"The Met Office airmen were sent home but never returned. It is still used by the Met Office but it is used more by the Scientific teams who seem to come back every year. They have their monument there as I told you earlier, dear John Grey. The anniversary of the day the big wave came comes during the next season. We mourn the dead in the morning then celebrate during the afternoon for the survivors. My Father's name of Joe Tomlinson, you as the father to my two babies, and those three airmen are mentioned during the celebration ceremony. It will be my duty to keep all your names said in our chant of history, with the names as written in the cavern of the Priestess.

All islanders are required to come to offer prayers and gifts in their memory. But the greatest gifts come from the seed of the menfolk that we women of the islands nourish to give our deliverance when the time comes.

For it is only when we reap the harvest of those seeds from off-islanders who visit our shores that keeps our island nation from extinction, as we womenfolk cannot deliver male children from our own menfolk. We have our children when young because our menfolk never live beyond 50 winters nor we womenfolk beyond 55 summers." TeLani explained solemnly.

"Your nation is not alone in your quest to remain in the folklore of time. There are many places with peoples in far-away beyond where I come from, who are much less in numbers that yours, and even some that have passed into the bygones of memories. As long as your people live on these islands there will always be off-islanders like me to come to visit you, for they will come in the airplanes, or by ship. All I ask of you TeLani, is to be happy and enjoy your children as it's the way of the world." John whispered tenderly, comforting her in a moment of sadness. He held her tightly for a few moments whilst looking around at the visible rebirth of a nation, then explained to her how people lived in his nation, of the cold weather, of why he was here on her Island nation.

TeLani listened quietly but posed some questions during his narration, which John replied as simply as he could for her. When he had finished, TeLani thanked him for telling her about his world across the great divide, hoping fortune would smile upon him as it had done for her in having him as the father of her babies.

John gave her a lingering kiss, which left her breathless, as she snuggled in his arms that seemed to protect her from the big bad world way beyond her shores.

A loud gong echoed loudly through the castle, which TeLani explained meant it was time for feasting again. She led him swiftly towards the large richly adorned cavern where everybody was sitting waiting to gorge themselves sick from the ever growing mountain of food being piled upon the very stout table.

"Come John Grey, you eat now!" Phatt commanded, pointing to an empty seat next to him.

John bowed his head and thanked Phatt for his kindness, before he commenced the mammoth task of trying to keep up with the eating habits of his hosts. He found his appetite was not half as large as Phatt nor the rest of his courtiers, but ate something from each course which was more than a number of people who were sitting at the table managed. The wine flowed as did the soft music played by the court minstrels, making John feel a touch of sadness as he thought of TeLani and what she had said about the mortality of her people.

John chatted politely and with great diplomacy with Phatt but especially with Phatty, discussing the bright new future the island was facing. He asked a few pertinent questions making some of the courtiers gasp in amazement that he dared to ask the King such direct questions.

Phatt smiled at John's boldness and put it down to the strange breeding of off-Islanders, but explained his answers to him. Even Phatty smiled at John's boldness, declaring that he was worthy of being called the father of her Daughters children.

The feasting seemed to go on for an eternity before Phatt clapped his hands declaring the feast over, and for John to take his leave to retire.

"I shall have your Ice cavern ready to receive your groceries off the *Constantlea,* by noon tomorrow." John responded, bowing his head to the departing monarchs.

TeLani and her sisters came around him then led him to another cavern, which was dimly lit but warm and smelling of sweet scented flowers. He saw a large pool in one corner of the cavern glowing in a creamy white light, which John took to be the same water that came from the special cave under the old causeway. In the opposite corner, was a seating area cordoned off by flimsy curtains and an ornamental table with baskets of fruit and goblets of wine on it. As his eyes became accustomed to the dimness, he saw there were several half naked girls waiting to serve these royal princesses.

John was taken by the hand and asked to sit on one of the chaise lounges as TeLani clapped her hands to summon the servants. Within moments the sisters re-appeared with the children who started to sing gently to him, whilst the servants plied him with yet more food and drink. He played a short while with each child before the servants took it away

'I could just about get used to this way of life. No wonder Phatt is as fat as he is if Phatty was the one who saw to his needs. If I'm being treated like a sacrificial lamb, this is definitely some sort of ceremony that's being performed. Still, no prying eyes this time, hopefully." John mused, feeling the wine start to take its effect on him.

He felt as if he was being manipulated and had no control of his body, lying spread-eagled on the luxurious bed, which somehow held him captured by his hands and feet.

He saw TeLani's young, voluptuous body towering over him as she impaled herself on him, for him to release his seed almost casually into her, several exquisite moments later and for her to give a triumphant orgasmic gasp of her own as if to seal their moments of ecstasy. It must have been the wine that allowed his body to be able to react to the onslaught of constant sexual demands from his female captor. For when they decided to call an interlude, John was still feeling as if he was only just starting on his own sexual release. Fortunately for him it was the sign of sheer fatigue that rescued him as he slipped mercifully into a deep sleep, for his sexual tormentors to leave him to his slumbers.

When he woke again he found TeLani lying beside him, she rose up leading him to the pool where the water was warm and scented, and where her sisters were waiting who took their turns in bathing him, until he was gently led out of the pool into the middle of the room where TeLani dried and dressed him once more.

"You have performed well dear John Grey. My sisters and I made certain that your body was not over taxed to ensure you shall not suffer from the excesses of what we women demanded off you last night. Now we must go and have our morning feast John. Then you must do your mans' job as you promised my other father, the King. You will be summoned later on by my Mother who is the Chief Priestess, to speak with her before you will be allowed to return to your ship. Before that comes to pass, you will have one more time to ravish me as you did on our first beach party. And before you say a word to disagree, it is the Queen who will take the ceremonial duty this time to see that your seed will be spilt over me."

"But I am only one man TeLani. If my seed is demanded from my body too many times in such a short time then I will not be able to perform my mans duty, as you put it. Maybe it is because you demand your menfolk to perform too often in such a short while, they have not got the amount of seeds left inside them needed to produce babies." John responded solemnly, as he began to feel the after-effects of too much sexual activity in such a short time.

"Perhaps what you say is true John Grey, but I can only be guided by your seed which I smell, taste and feel inside me. Maybe our Priestess will decide on that when she performs your last seed ceremony, which will be during my own ceremony called

Kiria Ma'ana of becoming a Princess like our Queen did. You should understand John Grey, you have become one of our chant legends who is among us yet still alive. For when you leave these islands, our Priestess will decree that you will only be allowed to return when you belong to the spirit world."

"I have been already informed of such things, and if that is your islands' belief then who am I to contradict such teachings. But you will find, first your mother then yourself and now your children are not of the same blood as your forefathers and matriarchs. For I predict you will live much longer than even your 60th winter, for you to become the great mother to the babies all your children will bear for you. You will tell this to your sisters, as they are to live as you will be doing." John replied TeLani put her arms around John's neck, drew his face down and kissed him then left with tears running down her cheeks.

John sighed wearily, following her into the great banqueting cavern, ready to devour everything put before him.

CHAPTER XXVI

Rehearsals

Mr Lewis, the King's Store man came over to speak to John, and after renewing their acquaintances, told John about the several thousand tons of food he was to see to making sure that none got wasted.

"I can only do my best Mr Lewis, as I cannot predict the performance of the machinery. By the looks of it, it is the original set I installed last time, so apart from a few alterations it can only perform in the same way. I shall need the services of at least two more Engineers to assist me. Kindly ask for the 3rd Engineer off the freighter and 3rd Engineer Clarke off my ship. They must be brought to meet me here in this cavern where I shall start my work." John announced, looking around the cathedral sized cavern, and at some of the machinery.

"So be it John Grey. I will return within the hour." Lewis responded, then strode away.

Whilst John was waiting for his helpers, he managed to sort out the modifications, which were new to him, even improving them to make the machinery more efficient and operable.

"Hello John, just guess who we've got to show us what to do!" Clarke greeted, arriving with another Engineer.

"Hello Ken! How the devil are you? I see you managed to make 3rd after all." John said with pride seeing Morris the Welsh Engineer stride up to shake his hand.

"Hello John. It's great to see you again. It looks like old times what with this ball-and-chain merchant and us together again." Morris greeted with elation, as his voice echoed around the empty cavern.

The three Engineers stood for a while talking about old times until they were interrupted by Lewis.

"It appears you are good friends who have met on a distant shore, but I must remind you that you have an important job to do.

There is several thousand tons of food about to come your way in case you've forgotten." Lewis appealed.

"You are not to worry Mr Lewis, I have two very able Engineers with me. We are almost ready for your first load, just make sure it's the tinned goods first, with the frozen stuff last." John announced, leading the two junior Engineers towards the area where they had to work.

"We have a problem of under cooling due to the pumps not working correctly. All we've got to do is clean them, then use a couple of gas bottles through the system to kick start the freeze cycle." John stated, instructing them on what had to be done. Soon all 3 Engineers were working swiftly and methodically through the fridge system until at last they met up again feeling satisfied all seemed well.

"The proof will be in the gas release. Stand by that valve over there then open it when I have counted to 3, Ken. Aussie, you time it from the valve opening to the last puff of gas from the bottle." John ordered, peering at a row of gauges.

"1-2-3! Open the valve. Aussie, it should take about 10 minutes for the entire system to be full of the gas, providing the bottles were full. If not then let me know immediately. Ken, come over here to keep an eye on the last gauge. When the temp gets to 10 let me know. I'm going round the system to make sure there are no leaks in the micro-bore pipes. Any problems from the console then for God sake let me know." John directed.

"Bottle finished! All gauges at set temps! No problems from the console." the 2 Engineers reported as John traced the main refrigerant pipes to check for leaks, but found none.

"Ken! There's a large valve in the corner by the main fridge unit, crack it open to let out some of the coolant gas. Count 30 seconds before you turn if off again. Aussie, you'll find a temp gauge strapped to the console. Take it and go around the cavern to make sure the temperature starts to dip below the zero mark." John guided, disconnecting the empty gas bottles to replace them with fresh ones.

Soon the place became very cold and misty with freezing fog starting to billow around the place. John switched on a second set of lights, which seemed to glow in the swirling mist, then called the two Engineers back over to him.

He explained what was to happen next to despatch them to their next tasks as he regulated the temperature control panels. Lewis was brought by Morris to look for himself who stated with elation that he was pleased with the work they had done.

"I shall have the first load arriving in about 5 minutes. You can leave the rest to me now." Lewis beamed with a warm smile even though he was rubbing his arms to warm the rest of his body up.

John thanked Lewis before suggesting to his 2 helpers it was now time to go up on top into the warm sunshine again.

When they arrived at the surface and walked into the bright sunshine again they were greeted by Hodgson, who explained that all 3 were needed back on board ship and why.

"I have other duties to perform for the King, which only I can complete Alan. Unless you are prepared to wait and all that." John states flatly.

"Hey 2nd! No worries! We can do all that Chief no sweat, as we've been trained by the 2nd here." Clarke drawled, while Morris nodded in agreement at their attempt to help John.

"Be that as it may, but the Captain wants to see you anyway John. He's most concerned about how much longer he'll be been kept waiting to sail and all that." Hodgson informed him.

"It is not up to me to dictate when we sail Alan. For a start, it will take a good 10 hours for the freighter to off load her cargo safely within the storage caverns. I have to make sure the temperature levels are maintained and stable before the King will even contemplate letting us go. The reasoning there is because I built the refrigeration units using my own designs, and now as I've returned to these islands it is up to me to see they are functioning properly before I leave again. If something goes wrong during my stay here, the King will expect me to fix it before I sail off into the wild blue yonder.

Denton has been put into a diplomatic cleft stick, catch 22, or any other phrase you care to use, but at the end of the day, the company management team will naturally side with the King on this one, forcing Denton to grin and bear it a little while longer. Besides, if we've got to refuel the *Constantlea,* then it will make visiting one of the two islands left out of the question. Remember the dodgy gauges we came across? Well that should give you another clue. Anyway, I'm expected back at the castle to give the King and his cronies my report. King Phatt might look a big, simple tub of lard, but he's no fool, and understands a lot more about what I've done than Denton gives him credit for. Maybe a quick radio message to HQ would clear things up and get Denton off the hook for once." John declared, as Hodgson merely nodded in agreement to what he was being told.

"That's fair enough for me John, and I'll tell Denton just what you've said. Probably the lads on board will appreciate your delay if they were to enjoy another day ashore." Hodgson conceded, starting to leave.

"Before you go, how is Dave Fagg getting along?" John asked politely.

"He's pulling through but won't be back on his feet much before we reach Brisbane again. Having said that, I'm seriously thinking of having him flown out of here on the next plane to get him to a proper hospital. The Doc and the Purser have agreed to arrange it, either way it looks as if you've got the cover duty again."

"It comes with the territory Alan. Now, I give you two very good 3rd Engineers to conduct your refuelling. Must go now." John concluded, waving to the departing Engineers.

"See you ashore some time." Morris shouted then disappeared out of view.

John arrived back at the castle to find Lewis was already there, speaking to Phatt in an animated fashion.

Phatt saw John coming towards him and greeted him jovially.

"Lewis here tells me that you have repaired my fridge and all is now well with the caverns, is that true John Grey?" he asked with a big smile.

John confirmed it was true but he still needed to monitor it for a while before he could be satisfied with it. This was greeted with much back- slapping and hand shaking from Phatt, and much to the relief of Lewis, who managed to slink away before Phatt had a chance to spot he was missing.

"You will be my guest of honour tonight, and will receive the blessings of our Priestess later. For now you may take your leave to prepare for the occasion." Phatt stated amiably, dismissing John then turning to his councillors, summoned them to follow him.

John found he was quickly surrounded by maid-servants who gently ushered him to his quarters then served him with food and wine.

'All this princely attention is fine, but I'll be glad to get back to sea again, if only to regain my strength.' John muttered, then lazed on a richly decorated chaise lounge listening to the soft music of the minstrels who appeared as if by magic.

He ate some fruit and drank some wine whilst watching a small group of girls dressed in diaphanous veils who danced slowly and erotically for him.

'This must be the prelude to what TeLani was telling me about. I need a good shower or bath first though as I'm starting to smell from all those refrigerant gasses, let alone being in a bath of sweat.' He muttered, starting to feel the wine take effect on his brain and the erotica taking effect on his loins.

'Yes, they certainly know how to get a man set up for the sacrificial altar. But where are TeLani and her sisters?" he added, standing to make his way towards the cavern which he knew was the bathroom.

He finished his toilet and was washing his hands when he was surrounded again by the dancers now company with TeLani and her sisters. She approached him and taking his hands, placed them gently onto her naked breasts for him to fondle whilst she put her arms around his neck then whispered into his ear.

"You and I will now be prepared for the Kiria Ma'ana ceremony and feast, John. You must not be alarmed at what will happen now or during the ceremony, but be very happy for me, as this is my big ceremony of initiation to become our 'Princess Royal.' As you have been the one chosen as my seed giver, it has been decreed that you will have a chance to see the children before my mother and the Priestess summons you to the banquet, because you will not be permitted to see them ever again. It is also decreed that this will be your last night in the castle for tomorrow you sail your ship away. For tomorrow you will be part of our chant history and just like your friend Joe Tommyson, you will never be allowed to return to these islands again. You will be bathed with me as I have told you, but you will not see me until you perform the final sacrificial ceremony after your banquet. I will ask you to eat and drink well John Grey, for I need to have as much seed as you can give me if I am to become our next Island's Queen."

"But what of my other friends, Bruce Larter, Andy Sinclair and Aussie Clarke? Don't they deserve the same ceremony as I?" John asked huskily, as she caressed his manhood.

"Bruce and Andy as you call them have already had their last seed ceremony. Clarke will be having his with his Islander wives and their families tonight. Only Clarke will be allowed back to the islands because he is one of our Islander menfolk who was selected to leave the islands to learn about the world before he comes home again. None of our menfolk are allowed to take part in any Kiria seed ceremony, and only by the decree of the Priestess will any off-Islanders be allowed the privilege to perform such an important ceremony as you and I are about to go through."

"Yes, but why am I selected as the sacrificial seed giver?"

"I have already told you, you have become part of our chant folklore to have a statue made in your image which is normally reserved for our King or any off-Islander menfolk who help our people through the times of great perils. It is only such menfolk get to seed the King s daughters no matter how many he has at the time."

"TeLani! I consent to become your sacrificial seed giver but I am only one man. Your sisters will have to wait until last for me to be at my best to serve you, but as you've already got two children from my seed then why must you demand more?"

"We womenfolk of these islands must have all our children delivered before our 22nd winter. That will give us time to live with them and for them to have children before we leave the island on our pyres around the time of our 55th summer. I have but 4 winters left before I become secluded with my Priestess Mother, who had Joe Tommyson's sacrificial seed for her own Kiria Ma'ana." she said with pride.

John looked into TeLani's dark brown eyes seeing a sparkle in them much brighter than any of the candles lighting up the room.

"Then dear TeLani, so shall it be." he whispered, kissing her on both cheeks, then nape of her neck, her shoulder, the base of her throat, down through the valley of her breasts, before he knelt down and kissed each inch of her young breasts, ending by gently kissing each of her nipples and caressing her in such a way she was starting to breathe very heavily.

She moaned softly at John's attention to her body then stepped away from him.

"You make my body light with fire John Grey which no man has done before. I am destined to fullfil the ritual of Kiria Ma'ana, when you will be required to scatter your seed several times inside and over my body. But I shall demand my right to enjoy a proper union between man and woman. I have told the Queen about our first time but she demanded a proper ceremony. Now it is my time to love you then and for you leave our shores in the knowledge that you have fulfilled the dream of all our Priestesses. My sisters will try to encourage your flow of seed, but only I will reap the rewards.

It is intended that my sisters will prepare you for my Kiria Ma'ana when I shall first taste, then receive your seed inside and over my body once more, and for me to remember it for all time. From then on I will never be allowed to taste or feel the seed of a man inside me ever again.

For your Ma'ana or sacrificial seed splashing over my body and my future celibacy will be honouring both of us, and our custom of adding to the historical chant for our people. Now just let my sisters prepare us, for the time is getting near."

John was asked to sit on a chair and given more food and wine to enjoy, as the maid servants danced in front of him, managing to show every curve and intimate places of their bodies to him, before dancing away almost in a sequence dancing formation.

'If this was in Blighty, I would definitely be locked up even just thinking about all this. But as it's part of the local custom, then who am I to complain, and who to, especially as its Queen Phatty who instructs them all? I might as well enjoy it, after all I have been tutored by dear Helena. Hope she understood my giving TeLani her locket as TeLani really needs the luck now more than me.' John sighed drinking his wine, taking in the most erotic display of female flesh that he would probably never see again, apart from his encounters with the sisters of and ultimately with TeLani.

The dancers had disappeared only to be replaced by the similarly attired TeLani and her sisters.

As they approached him they giggled and whispered amongst themselves, leaving John bemused as to what was going to happen next. He knew of the bathing session, and has been told what was to happen, but he was still not ready to stand up and be counted.

'Stand up and be counted, no less. Lets' hope they put a little bit more in that wine of theirs or I'll be ending up like a punctured balloon' he whispered to himself, feeling the sisters strip him totally naked then usher him to the foam covered bath, whilst Telani looked on.

He was given yet more wine to drink and fruit to eat before he was taken into the waist deep water, which radiated warmth and smelled like a fresh bouquet of flowers.

'Here we go, and there's nothing I can do to stop it. I do this for my Queen and country, let alone theirs. Let's hope they remember I have a repeat performance later on today. Mustn't disappoint Phatty let alone dear TeLani.' he whispered, resigning himself to what was about to happen to him.

John was almost in a trance as the sisters bathed him, and generally massaged him but mostly on his naughty bits to satisfy their own particular fantasy

"I am but a mere man who happened to help save your nation to survive. If the fruit of my loins which you have delivered some time past survive for many a winter, then I will be well pleased for you all. I have told TeLani of your future, so take heed of what she tells you." John whispered to them before he hugged and kissed the sisters one by one, making them sit down and weep into the very large towels they were holding.

John looked at the weeping sisters but was too weak to hug or comfort them again, so he merely sighed saying.

"TeLani, I have shown you what it is like between a man and woman on my side of the divide. We give ourselves to each other, not to be taken by force as your sisters demand of me. Sowing the seeds of love is a very special tender moment, which should not be violated. So if you remember what I've said every time you look at your children, then you will know I will always be with you, even if just in the shadows of your mind."

John went over to TeLani and kissing her and wished her luck, but she seemed to be in some sort of a trance which told him he was not going to get any reply from her until afterwards

When the sisters finished weeping, they undressed TeLani then started to administer some sort of ritual with her body.

John was mildly alarmed at seeing TeLani being completely shaved of body hair from head to toe, before the sisters turned then gently shaved all his off but from the neck down. When the sisters had finished oiling their bodies, they were dried off then dressed in long white flowing robes making John look like a roman senator.

The massage with the oils on his body made John feel like a new man again and he saw a happy smile on TeLani's face as she was taken away by the sisters, while he was escorted to the banquet.

CHAPTER XXVII

Kiria Ma'ana

"Come John Grey! Come and sit by my table." Phatt commanded when John entered the main banqueting hall.

John merely nodded courteously, placing himself next to Phatt as directed, where he was served with his usual extremely large golden goblet of wine.

Phatty whispered into Phatt's ear for a moment before he turned to John and announced in a booming voice.

"It appears that you have quietened all my daughters and that a chant legend blesses us with such glory. I bid you a peaceful long swim from these islands." Phatt toasted, raising his equally large golden goblet, urging John to drain his in one go.

'Wish Andy was here to challenge him with his yard of ale.' John mused, managing to complete the first challenge of the meal.

"My grocer Lewis has told me that all is well now in the ice cavern. He also tells me of the near Islander by the name of Clarke was helping out. He is one of our prodigal sons who has returned to these islands once more, and will be the only one of you off Islanders to do so. He has taken several wives from the lost tribe of Olaia, which was wiped away in the great wave.

They have delivered several of his children to help bring the tribe back from the fires of Mulani, and will be rewarded with a tribal funeral once he has finished his last big swim.

My daughters will always know you as the Iceman by the islanders, but as the Seed Giver. I have seen the children you have given them and have been told by my Queen they will grow to be healthy Taranitians. For this John Grey, as King of these islands I will always be grateful to you, and will inform your own Queen from the East of your services, but not of the services to my daughters mind you." Phatt boomed, giving a crafty wink when he mentioned John's service to his daughters.

"I am sure your Majesty will declare in good faith the truth of what was done during my visits. However, I agree with your reticence in referring the latter, in case our Queen may take offence at having one of her subjects impregnating young or underage girls. This would fall below the moral standards bequeathed to us by the late Queen Victoria."

Phatt's eyes lit up at the mention of Queen Victoria and asked him how he met her and when.

John took his time to explain the history of British monarchy since the Victorian era, which was greeted with a nod of recognition from Phatt.

"I knew of your monarch's history as told by my Chancellor. I made the great swim to meet your new Queen and found her very attractive but a bit too skinny for my liking. Now if she had been like my dear wife Phatty then your Queen would be handsome enough for me to grunt with her." Phatt said with a big smile.

"How kind of your majesty to mention my Queen, although as a common man in her realm I have not yet met her. Been too busy at sea on my ships you see."

Phatt looked at the comparatively diminutive figure of John for a moment then gave a huge smile followed by a large belly laugh.

"Hah! You sound just like your friend Joe Tommyson." Phatt exclaimed.

"I shall miss him very much John Grey, as I will do you when you leave. You have been told of our custom so understand why." he added sombrely, before he smiled again and ordered the food to be brought in.

The feast went with gusto as per normal, with plenty of belching and farting around the table. The food was being consumed with almost obscene swiftness, as were the large carafes of wines helping to wash it all down.

During the feasting, John was delighted to find his friends Sinclair, Larter and Clarke had also been invited to dip their noses into the proverbial trough.

He waved to them then asked Phatt to let them join his side of the table, which was granted with a nod and a smile as Phatt noisily devoured yet another leg of ham

"Glad you 3 could make it, I was beginning to wonder if you lot had sailed without me." John whispered into Larter's ear.

"What? Leave you to eat and shag yourself to death on this island of free love? No way my dear John." Larter responded.

"I understand you've got your final ceremony to perform John. If I was you, I'd get myself some of the special wine they dish out or you'll never make the distance." Clarke said quietly, pushing a cup of wine towards John.

"Yes, we had ours this morning John. That dark red wine in front of you is the stuff, which will save your mind from blowing, let alone anything else. Better get as much down you as you can. Phatty over there is already sizing you up for the kill, even as we speak." Sinclair opined, sliding his goblet over to John to drink.

John looked at his 3 friends and told them the sisters of TeLani, who were going to perform the last of his ceremonies in front of Phatty and the rest of the people around the table, had already drained him from an earlier ceremony.

"Just you get a gut full of the wine John, and let nature take care of the rest. We will be here to watch you do not fall foul of their axeman sitting in the corner over there. He chops your dangly bits off if you don't perform enough to please the Priestess never mind TeLani, as she will be in charge of the whole thing. Quenie will be keeping a close watch, and I mean a very close watch on all the nitty gritty that goes on. Almost as if she is getting it not the girl." Clarke advised.

.John started to drink all the wine he was given, as if to protect himself from the threatening looks being given by the big, burly man in the corner with a huge machete he was honing.

"But what I can't understand is why me? I mean I did nothing remotely like a miracle as they have deemed me to have performed, not once but three times. All I did was my job I was paid for, which all of you would have done anyway. It's nice to have the limelight for a while, but they seem to have latched onto me like leeches as if to suck my juices dry. Especially when the girls involved are only young teenagers, and would be enough to have me locked up for a very long time" John said quietly, feeling the effects of the wine.

"What you must understand John, is that the Priestess was at the same age as TeLani, when the young sea Captain Joe Tomlinson arrived on these islands. She is the mother of TeLani, all her sisters and her two brothers, will be next in line to become heirs to the throne and the like on these islands. Once the girls became of age to have kids, they need to have an off-Islander worthy enough to impregnate them and produce the next line of succession. TeLani as the youngest of the girls is being tutored to become Queenie's successor. Her oldest son will become the next King, then in turn so will the oldest boy child that you have given the sisters.

In other words Cobber, you've been shagging the arse off all Tomlinson's daughters so that the lineage of the King can be maintained. That is one hell of a privilege believe you me, especially as I have been doing the same to one of the lesser tribal Chief's daughters. The real snag if you wish to look on it that way, is once you've performed this special ceremony, you will no longer be allowed to step ashore here ever again. I'm the lucky one between us because I am able to come and go as I please, and able to keep tabs on the raising of the kids my missus had dropped for me. So just you enjoy the occasion John even though you will not be able to control your own body." Clarke explained, tipping a small vial of powder into John's drink, then giving it to him to sup.

"I've slipped a special powder into your drink to help you perform. You will not be able to control your body functions, nor will you be able to speak, but you will feel each pleasure administered to you. The Priestess will give both of you special drinks with this powder in them just to help the both of you through the ceremony. It just means that you'll feel a bit drawn and bloody tired afterwards. This is her big night and will at times be a bit painful if not totally exhausting for her let alone you. It will take about three sessions to complete the Kiria Ma'ana ceremony. Kiria is when you will be required to penetrate all three of her orifices, then afterwards have a break for the tribal chants and more feasting, then for the Ma'ana when you will be induced to splash your seed all over her body. But the Priestess will take special care of you both making sure you don't suffer any ill effects. TeLani will be just as doped up as you to help her own body cope with her side of it all. Oh and by the way, you'll feel a bit tender around your old boy and never mind the teeth marks you'll find, as they'll disappear after a few days as will the emptiness you'll also feel.

I tell you this John, because all the women of high rank have been taught how to extract a man's essence whenever she wants and not just when he can give it. So if you see or think that the river of seed streaming out of you is just a one off then you'd better think again. All you'll be able to do is just watch and enjoy the moments. It is the custom for the privileged off-islanders to stay here to witness this very special ceremony, but we'll see no harm will come to you. As I've said, just lie back and enjoy the ride John, and good luck." Clarke informed him, as Larter and Sinclair patted his back wishing him luck too.

Phatt clapped his hands as his customary signal to clear away any food that was left, and for everybody to accompany him to the ceremonial chamber. This was the place where John would be offered to the high Priestess to perform the very sacred, solemn ritual of the seed scattering offering.

'Aussie was right. I can see everything but I can't feel anything, nor it seems can I speak. It seem I'm at the mercy of the Priestess, and I hope that TeLani will not blame me if I don't perform as they expect. I told her I am just one man.' he thought, as he was taken to a large marble plinth adorned in white and gold silks which was placed in the middle of the room.

The Priestess was dressed in white diaphanous robes, dancing and humming to background music being played by a small band of musicians.

John was gently led to stand near the end of the plinth, serving as the sacrificial altar, by a few naked girls, whilst Telani's sisters escorted her into the room.

When TeLani stopped at the other end of the plinth, the Priestess gave a small speech in her native tongue before she clapped her hands, which was the signal for the sisters and the maid-servants to strip both TeLani and John naked.

The Priestess stood between the two of them and beckoned them to move towards each other, then her assistants gently helped them simultaneously onto the plinth.

John was left to stand whilst TeLani knelt down in front of him.

'She looks as if she's in a trance-like state as me. Lets' hope that bloody wine works,' John thought because he couldn't even whisper let alone speak.

TeLani performed oral sex on John, which represented his first orifice penetration whilst the Priestess watched John's body language closely during all three penetrations to announce each time he succeeded with his delivery of seed. As each penetration was completed, there was much clapping from Phatt and Phatty, whilst the Priestess hummed and chanted her sacred songs.

Once the three were completed, both of them were helped down off the plinth, they were given a goblet of wine to drink whilst their bodies were bathed by the young girl attendants and TeLani's sisters.

The two participants were given some more food and wine to consume whilst listening to soft music being played for them. The Priestess was performing her ritual dances, singing her praises of TeLani and her seed giver, just as if it was some sort of interlude.

This went on for a while until the Priestess stopped her singing and dancing to clap her hands to indicate the Ma'ana was the next but most crucial part of the ceremony.

John's Ma'ana was to cast his seed over TeLani's body, starting with her face down to her breasts then her stomach ending up over her unprotected vulva.

He was slowly and gently milked until he splashed his seed all over her face. This was his first Ma'ana offering with 3 more to go.

'Aussie wasn't kidding! Bloody hell where did all that come from. I hope it stops or she'll get drowned, as it looks like a ruddy hosepipe. Maybe if what comes next is what I think it is then there should be none left. Let's hope you're right, Aussie.' John thought.

John was given a little respite in between each performance, as TeLani had his seed massaged into her body by her sisters whilst the Priestess danced, singing her repertoire of rituals.

Before he had time to complete the last one, John was starting to sweat profusely needing to be towelled dry by the sisters, this was treated as a natural pause in the proceedings.

Whilst he was given a goblet of the special brew, TeLani was being massaged with sweet smelling oils to keep her body moist in the hot yet dry atmosphere

'Oh well, one more to go before I can go home. But it would be nice to have some say in this fun. I really would like to enjoy TeLani's body as a man and woman should, not with this public display of fornication. Let's hope that I performed well for your big night, as I sure as hell can't go through all this as an encore' John managed to whisper as if the wine was no longer taking effect on him.

The Priestess, Queen Phatty and all the other female assistants gathered round him so that they could watch very closely the moment of John's final release.

He felt his heart pounding, while his ears felt as if they were burning up by the time he had finished delivering what seemed to be a lot more than from his first time. Again the performance was greeted with loud cheers and claps from everybody who witnessed the final act of seed scattering.

TeLani had the seed massaged into that part of her body

whilst John was helped to his feet. When TeLani was finished with her body massage she crawled over to him, kissed then licked his manhood gently before she stood up raising her hands above her head in some sort of triumphant gesture, whilst John slumped onto the plinth like a deflated balloon.

The sisters took John down from the plinth and dressing him, waited with him until TeLani was attended to. He saw that TeLani was annointed with oils again by the Priestess, before she was dressed in fine silk robes then taken over to stand by John.

Phatty clapped and whooped with joy as she came over pronouncing the ceremony a success and John Grey's seed was a bountiful harvest, which would ensure the tribe would flourish and prosper.

"Let me rest for a little while dear TeLani. Then what about a special private session for one last time?" John managed to whisper coherently as he was now used to the special concoction of wine he had been plied with over the last couple of hours of the ceremony.

"The Priestess has given permission for you to ravish me in private, but you must leave immediately afterwards as I have new duties to perform." she replied, still in the same trance-like state.

"Well let's hope I can perform as well then as I have done these last hours. Anyway, how did we do? I should hate for you to be cast down for my poor performance?"

"Your seed was still as sweet last as it was first, and you were able to splash much more than even the Priestess had expected from you. She has told me I have been blessed and I will become a good Princess thanks to your generous supply of seed, which I was able to wash my body in.

Now come and show me how you perform on your side of the great divide." She said with a smile, leading him out of the room away from the gathered crowd.

"Our bodies have been truly worn past the limits of seed sharing, now its time for you to bathe and have your breakfast before you leave the castle. Go now John Grey, before my sisters find you still in my bed." TeLani whispered, and leaning over him gave his manhood a slow teasing caress, which responded almost immediately under her magical touch.

"Must I go now TeLani? Can I see you before I sail away?" John whispered sleepily.

"Yes John, but you must go now. I will bid you goodbye for the last time before you leave on your ship. You have your friends waiting for you at the breakfast table, do not keep them waiting as they too must leave very soon." TeLani answered, beckoning the young maidservants into the room ordered them to bathe him gently then get him to the breakfast table.

"See you later then TeLani, but I'd much rather stay here and be your man for ever." John said sadly, as the girls giggled when they saw his naked manhood swaying between his legs.

He was bathed and dressed in his newly laundered tropical uniform then led to the dining room where Phatt and his gang were already gorging themselves from the now ubiquitous mountain of food.

"John Grey, come and sit with me." Phatt demanded, to which John meekly obliged, given that he didn't seem to have the strength to protest otherwise.

"You performed as well as TeLani's father who is my good friend Joe Tommyson. My Queen says that it will be a good omen for our tribe and for the future of the people of these islands. I shall tell your Queen about your ceremony, so when the time comes to renew the blood of my people she will send somebody like you. Now eat before you leave for your ship, as it will be sailing before the sun is on high." Phatt boomed, shoving a whole cooked chicken in front of him.

John looked around the room and was pleased to see his friends already tucking into their food, as he waved to them in greeting.

They cheered him holding up their goblets in a silent toast to him, as he returned the gesture.

"How did the refuelling go Aussie?" John asked over the din

of the noisy diners, trying to try re-focus his mind again.

"No problems mate. Morris and me completed it in record time, as if we'd being doing it for years. Not a drop spilt anywhere. Which is more than I can say about your splash session last night. I told you, you'd think you had a hosepipe instead of a dick, didn't I?"

"Yes Aussie, you were right, and yes I'm feeling like a busted balloon. I'll be glad to get to sea to have a few days rest, but I wish I could return again."

"Then you must be a glutton for punishment. Why do you think I only come back every year or so, and even then for only a few days like this time around? Nah mate, it would take all the biggest dicks in the world between your legs to stay longer and to stand to what you've been through. Be thankful for small mercies and dick lesser demanding women from now on." Clarke countered.

Smiling and nodding at this crude remark, John took it as sound advice while he continued satisfying his grumbling belly.

It wasn't long before Phatt gave the command to clear the table, and for John and his friends to leave the castle.

John thanked Phatt for his hospitality turning to leave, but Phatt stopped him and giving him a parcel demanded he opened it.

Opening the package, John found the coronet wrapped in the ermine robes he had worn when coming ashore. It also contained a large gold chain and medallion.

"Thank you, your majesty. When I get back to my own islands I shall present this chain and medal to my Queen and tell her it is a gift from one royal throne to another. But I feel that the robe and crown should belong in your keeping until you find another chosen off-Islander to scatter his seed on your womenfolk. For it should be only he will wear it just as my friend Joe Tomlinson and I have done." John stated quietly and diplomatically, to which Phatt beamed with pleasure on hearing it.

"You have spoken well John Grey, and I shall see that the robe will be passed on just as you have said. Now go and tell your Captain I shall call upon him before he sails." he commanded.

John bowed his head in acknowledgement then led his friends out of the castle and down to the docks.

He saw the ship was riding high out of the water and dwarfing the *Constantlea* who was berthed opposite it.

"Looks like we're almost home and dry now Aussie. Have we no deck cargo to take back, or is that now the exclusive perks of the *Constantlea*, Andy?" John asked, making small talk to his now silent friends.

"We've only got a few hundred empty fuel barrels to take back that's all. I've made certain they're all lashed down tidy this time." Sinclair responded.

"You lot had better carry on, as I've got the mail to collect from the air terminal." Larter stated, leaving them.

"Better go with him Andy, just in case he needs a hand. We two Engineers have some small jobs to attend to before we sail." John suggested. Sinclair agreed, leaving the two Engineers to walk back over the gangway and onto the *Repulse Bay*.

CHAPTER XXVIII

Unforgettable

John, along with his friends were standing shore side of the gangway when they heard the music and singing of the advancing throng of farewell wishers. Phatt and Phatty were carried aloft behind the singers and dancers, as usual, until they stopped several yards away from the ship.

Denton came strutting down the gangway with the First Mate to receive the farewell accolade from Phatt, but was ignored in favour of John and his two close friends.

"We come to bid you goodbye John Grey." Phatt announced loudly, as Phatty clapped her hands, which prompted TeLani, her sisters plus the mothers of the children which Larter and Sinclair were responsible for.

John was the first to receive his farewell garlands from each sister as they kissed him who weeping openly, stepped away from him for TeLani to be the last to see him.

She wore a white and blue silk garment trimmed in gold that disguised her shaven head, but the clothing came from around her back covering her lower torso, thus leaving her magnificent youthful breasts exposed but tantalisingly covered by layers of flower garlands.

"You have come after all dear TeLani. You will always remember me each time you look at your children. I wish you joy in the deliverance of our last child. You will make a beautiful Queen and may your Gods keep you safe. It is your custom we shall never meet nor have any contact with each other again, but my friend Clarke will know where to find me if you wish it that I should come back to you." John said slowly, waiting for her to come to him. She looked radiant with a wistful smile upon her face but did not move towards him, merely nodded her head gently.

John gazed almost in awe of this girl who was the epitome of beauty as she just stood there looking on with aloofness.

John Grey, you have pleased my Gods by endowing me with your Ma'ana ceremony, which means I shall become a powerful Queen. For me to have a successor, just as I am to my mother, the man must be of tribal speak and of folk chanting as you have become in the eyes of our King and of our people. If our tribal tradition cannot find a suitable seed giver by the time my last-born daughter has reached her fourteen winters like I did, then you will be summoned to attend my temple once more. This is what happened to your friend Joe Tommyson, but I ask only this of you dear John, that you be happy for me and my tribe while you live your own life on your side of the great divide. May your long swim be a safe one."

ohn stood quite still as if in a trance, not knowing if he should hold her once more, but he remembering his last farewell from these islands merely returned her nod with one of his own.

So be it TeLani, you will always be my own Princess. You have the locket of my last lover who is deceased, but who still looks over me. It will protect you from evil as it had done for me. I cannot give you anything more than I have already, and hope you will also look after me as Helena has done." John said quietly and slowly for her to hear and understand.

I know of Helena, she has visited me several times before and during your two stays here. She is happy for me, as she was not able to give you children of her own which you both had wished for. She tells me of the *Fatal Encounter* in which only your ship survived, and how it was you who rescued her from certain death. She also told me of your *Ice Mountain,* of her tragic death on a bridge over a river, and of how others were tormented by the perpetrators of such a crime. She has asked me to tell you she is happy now, but you should never forget her even though you give your seed to others."

ohn felt a cold shiver run down his spine, despite the sultry tropical warmth.

How is she able to know of these things, when I have never mentioned them to her in the first place. Maybe that is why she will become a powerful Princess, who seems to have the gift of clairvoyancy.' he thought.

This will be my last meeting with you John, but I will reveal this to you. Your dear Helena and I are now as one, but you will meet another woman in your new world who will also bear you several more children as I have done. All we ask of you is to remember both Helena and now me. You must promise that you will tell her of us, of how we loved you, and of the children that you have given me." TeLani replied as if in the same trance-like state John was in. They were two lovers, the major players in this scene, yet both at arms length exchanging their farewells.

s she somehow emerged from her trance, she walked forward placing her garland of flowers around his neck.

Farewell dear John Grey!" she whispered, then stepped back before John could respond to her.

During this time, John felt his tears slip slowly down his cheeks, and promised her that both their wishes would be done. He did not move only marvelled at the exquisitely beautiful young woman who was being surrounded by her sisters and her helpers, and now lost to him forever.

Phatt and Phatty made their final speeches to John and his friends just as they had when they last left the islands, while John responded as diplomatically as he could for and on behalf of his friends.

Denton was finally brought before Phatt to be given a garland of flowers, by Phatty.

"We thank you for bringing John Grey back to us, Captain. He is now one of our history chant gods but our customs dictate that he will no longer be allowed back to these islands as long as I and my King are still alive. We have made our great swim to see the new Queen of your islands, and have full diplomatic papers with her ministers. So you will see to it that John Grey arrives safely back into the bosom of his own people.

John Grey has now served his purpose on the islands and you are free to go, Captain Denton. Have a safe swim back in your ship, and we hope you will come back again soon." she announced, as she gave Denton a bear like hug with loud sloppy kisses on each cheek.

"Thank you, your majesty. My officers and crew thank you for your wonderful hospitality and for letting us share your islands for a few days. I will see that John Grey never returns, but I look forward to renewing our royal friendships on a day only our Gods can decide. We bid you all farewell." Denton said, gasping for breath from his encounter with Phatty.

Phatt clapped his hands for the last time, which was the signal for the farewell party to leave.

John watched the now weeping TeLani and her sisters leave, as the procession started to enter one of the tunnels leading to the castle. He waved to them, listening to their music until they went out of sight even though they never turned around to wave back.

It was the deafening silence that brought the ships crew back to reality again, for them to prepare the ship to get under way again.

"First Mate, we sail in two hours. Have the officers meet me in the saloon in half an hour. In the meantime get the decks cleared, the on shore lines and umbilical cord disconnected, then remove the gangway." Denton ordered sharply, striding back across the gangway.

John took a moment to stand at the top of the gangway surveying the new dock facility, and at the colourful array of flowers attempting to hide the scars of that dreadful day.

He saw somebody running towards the ship just as the gangway was being lifted off, and ordered the crane operator for it be lowered again, as he recognised that it was Clarke making his way back.

He raced up the steep slope of the gangway, jumped down off it landing at John's feet.

"3rd Engineer Clarke mustering for duty." he said with a big smile then got up and dusted himself down.

"I won't ask where you've been, but glad you made it 3rd. Now get yourself into the saloon as the Captain wants a word with us." John said with as straight a face as he could.

"What? In the shit are we? Strewth, a man can't have a decent run ashore around here no more." Clarke moaned, then saw the smile on John's face and relaxed.

"You're getting as bad as me now 2nd. Anyway, glad you seem to be recovering from your symbolic ritual just as your Kiria Ma'ana last night was one hell of a ritual. You and TeLani seemed to have hit it off for it to be so successful, and I'm glad again for you. I've just had my last 'Gland shake' with all of my womenfolk that's why I am late getting back on board. I'm totally knackered now so its just as well I am glad you were still on deck or I'd be marooned here for at least another month until the next Triple Crown or one of our ocean going tugs arrived here."

"Apparently dear Aussie, from what I've been told, it goes with your territory. Maybe you'd be better staying on the island to help look after the machinery for Phatt and his gang. Still, we've got a ship to see to and you've got a ruddy great enquiry to attend when we get back to Brisbane." John concluded, then both Engineers walked swiftly to the saloon.

"Good morning gentlemen. Due to our delay here in Taraniti and other circumstances, we do not have the time, nor have we enough cargo to satisfy the remainder of our customers. Instead they will be visited by one of our other large tankers, the *Shatin Heights*. The management team has been informed of our successful in more ways than one, visit ashore here, so they have decided our pay packets will not be affected providing that we get back to Brisbane on time. Therefore, I have told them we shall be returning directly to Brisbane, making a quick pit stop at the Ocean Islands where the rest of our cargo will be discharged. If all goes well, we should be back in Brisbane in about two weeks. Well done everybody, that is all." Denton stated which concluded the short meeting.

"2nd Engineer Grey, I want a word with you in my bridge cabin. Meet me there in ten minutes." Denton ordered, as he was leaving the saloon.

John nodded in acknowledgement of his order and strolled out of the saloon with Clarke.

"I think he wants the latest tank dip readings Aussie, go get them for me." John whispered.

"On my way John!" Clarke muttered as he departed in haste.

"What's the latest buzz on the weather Bruce?" John asked when Larter arrived next to him.

"Clear weather for a few days, but there's a dirty great big typhoon coming our way, so let's hope we are secured alongside at Ocean." Larter informed offering him a cigarette, but begging a light in return.

John lit Larter's cigarette then gave him the lighter, getting a surprised look from him.

"TeLani gave me it this morning during breakfast saying it was found in the banqueting hall last night." John said with a chuckle. Putting the lighter into his pocket Larter smiled and looked down at his smaller friend.

"I remember telling you the first time we met John, about losing my lighter. That certainly seems a lifetime away." he said with a far away look.

"Yes Bruce, I remember it well when I was just a rookie Engineer. Maybe a little older but no longer a rookie, what!"

"More like a nookie Engineer. I'll bet this is one place where one, or maybe three more women in our lives will be unforgettable. TeLani is certainly one hell of a good looker John that was obvious even from where I was sitting. How you both managed to survive the ceremony I'll never know. I mean she took everything you literally threw at her, and seemed to beg for more. Me and Andy have been banned from the place for a good ten years or so, but as I've just said, it will always be an unforgettable time in our lives which will be indelibly carved into our memories forever."

"Yes Bruce, you can say that again. Probably Andy will agree with us when I have the chance to speak with him. Must go see what our illustrious Captain wants off me. Let's hope it's not one of those what Aussie calls, a 'gland shake'." John replied with a smile.

"Call by sometime and we'll have a chat. I'll see if Andy can make it too, so see you later!" Larter said, leaving John to go meet up with Denton.

John knocked Denton cabin door and was asked to enter but quickly pulled the door to again as he saw Clarke rushing towards him, who threw a bundle of papers at him.

"Here's what you asked for. I've had to re-check some of them just in case. Good luck!" Clarke whispered as John entered the cabin.

"You called for me Captain?" John asked politely.

"Morning Grey! Yes, two things! First, I have to inform you that it was fortunate you were on board for our visit to Taraniti. Not only does it turn out you're, shall we say, the flavour of the year, needed to shag your way through all the Kings daughters, (which is no mean feat I might add), but you've also managed to increase the credibility of our company standing with the local government. By that I mean, due to your Engineering expertise, your knowledge of the local infrastructure and their failing fridge systems, you were able to fix them. Our company has been rewarded by the King and his so-called Chief grocer, we have now got the franchise to provide all fuels and lubricants to the government, and also to set up a new aircraft refuelling depot at the other end of the island. You can take it from me, in what seemed to be your deliberate attempt to delay my sailing and discharge schedule, you were in for one big heap of trouble. For you to know, it turns out entirely the opposite, as I am instructed to make a suitably worded entry into your personnel file, which I'm also instructed must reflect your distinction in getting this plum contract from no less a person than King Phatt and his government. I am quite happy to do so, which will put an end to the spat we had when we arrived at Taraniti."

"The way I see it Captain whether you like it or not, it's a matter of 'I told you so'. I told you what would happen Captain, but you simply did not believe me because I was an outsider and in your eyes, a jumped up oily rag. Maybe in future when somebody else tells you something you find hard to swallow, you'll remember my name and Taraniti. As far as I'm concerned Captain, the matter is now closed. Now, if what I think the second item you wish to discuss is, I have the figures here with me." John asserted, holding out the tank capacity figures.

"Yes it is 2nd, let me see them." Denton snarled as he realised what John had said was the truth of the matter.

John handed the roll of papers over for Denton to unfold on the top of his table.

"Hmm! It seems that not only the *Constantlea* was more thirsty than we thought, but there appears to be more missing fuels than was initially bargained for." Denton muttered, but in a more pleasant manner, pouring over the long list of figures.

"I calculate a loss of 500 tons of fuel for two of them which was discharged over and above what was allocated for each customer, Captain. But what's intriguing me is the curve shown on the chart for the shortage seems to be more significant since we left Fiji, especially the FFO. The FFO figures show an overall loss of over 1,000 on its' own. " John opined.

Denton examined the curve John had shown him, but it seemed to John as if Denton did not grasp the inference of what his figures were showing.

"That looks about right. Which means that the company has lost the best part of £100,000 of revenue, which will take some clever lawyer or an accountant a long time to claw it all back." He stated, as if to draw a line under the cargo deficiency.

John stood for a moment before making his response.

"At least our last discharge will only take us a couple of hours this time. I can have the tanks cleaned and ready for use before we arrive back in Brisbane, that way we will have a quicker turn round to wherever our next delivery round takes us."

"According to the weather forecasts, we're due for a tropical storm during our passage to Ocean islands. We'd riding too high out of the water and at the mercy of the winds as well as the high waves. So if you can give me a low profile in the water, then we'll stand a better chance of getting through in one piece, 2nd."

"I can only load water into the empty tanks Captain, because we've not got a universal fuel separator to top up the other tanks with the fuels."

"What's one of them 2nd? I've been on tankers before, but never heard of that."

"A common piece of machinery used in the engine rooms which needs adapting for deck usage, Captain. That as they say, is being worked upon."

"Very well 2nd. That's all for now, but before you go, you will be allowed extra rations both liquid and food wise, until we arrive back into Brisbane. King Phatt has given me the stores to do this, but as normal, some of it gets shared among the rest of the crew."

John looked at Denton for a moment then smiled.

"Well that's all right Captain. When King Phatt has a snack, it would be at least a 10 course meal to us. I've seen his banquet table literally collapse under the weight of the food and wine. I don't mind sharing my victuals with my shipmates Captain so enjoy it with me. No doubt the Purser will be glad of a few less stores to worry about until we reach Brisbane again." John said leaving the cabin with Denton mumbling his gratitude.

CHAPTER XXIX

Kindred Spirit

John waited on the main for'ard catwalk until the deck crew completed their harbour duties, then watched the ship reverse herself out of the harbour with her fog horns blasting merrily away. Soon when Denton had judged he'd reversed far enough, he turned his ship around and pointed her to the new course she would carve out of the deep blue ocean.

John walked aft to the poop deck and watched the islands disappear into the tropical haze until he could no longer see Taraniti any more. He felt very sad and bereft at leaving, knowing that he would never return to those shores again.

He started to light up yet another cigarette when he felt a warm tingling glow which seemed to go from the top of his head, right down to his toes, and especially around his genitals. A faint breeze blew onto his face, like the soft kiss a lover would give, making him feel alive and happy again.

The breeze carried a faint melodious sound with it, but John fancied it must have been the wind strumming the rope holding down the deck cargo. But it was his name the wind seemed to whisper, and the warm feeling got so much warmer he felt a wholesome well-being that seemed to course all through his body.

Maybe it was just hazy shadows, but he was convinced he saw even for a brief moment, Helena standing before him and smiling, then TeLani and her children joining her in the same space. John stood quite still, with tears streaming down his face, but managed to wave and smile to them before their apparitions slowly faded away into the tropical mists.

John stood for a while longer, basking in this delicious warm tingling feeling, until it also disappeared into nothingness again. He wiped away his tears with the cuffs of his overalls and turned to go for'ard again when he bumped into Clarke.

"Sorry Aussie, couldn't see you. Must have had some soot in my eyes." John lied.

"No John. I've been standing right behind you watching you in case you fell overboard. You seemed to be wanting to climb the flagpole dangling over the stern, but I know exactly what you were going through, so I made certain you turned back instead of jumping overboard." Clarke said softly, and putting an arm around him led him to safety.

John looked at Clarke but could not speak to answer him until several moments later.

"I feel as if I've left my soul there, and have been visited by the spirits of their gods." John croaked, still trying to get hold of his faculties.

"I saw and felt what you saw John, because I have been visited in the same way as you every time I leave the islands. You can take it from me John you will have no worries to bother you during your exile from the islands. Your last girl, erm, Helena I think her name was, seemed to be happy for you when she met up with your TeLani. For it means that by you giving TeLani a few kids, you have made Helena feel whole again. At least that is what I've been told about my own experiences by some wise old Abbo just this side of the Black Stump. Seems to me you've got it made in their world, but it will be up to you to honour your pact with them, whatever it is, for you to survive a long life in this world." Clarke said comfortingly.

"A few kids? But I only know of the twins!" John gasped.

"Let's put it this way. I don't know if you counted the children Helena and TeLani had sitting beside them, but I counted 4. Two boys and two girls, all like peas in a pod they were."

"So that means TeLani will have another set of twins then."

"No John. One child was much older than TeLani's three. I would suggest maybe Helena was carrying a child when she was killed. That child just may have been yours, but you will only know when they visit you again. But as for when, I cannot tell you, sufficient to say, it's like a bloody nightmare not knowing what has come from whom. I mean, imagine if all the dicks that splashed inside your sheila, for them all to drop out nine months later, who would be the rightful father?"

"Maybe you Aussies have the right attitude, but that is one hell of a problem even to think about. All I know is I was Helena's first and her last lover before she got killed. I was the first and now am the last lover of TeLani, so between the three of us there're two children for definite, with what seems as two more in some sort of spiritual existence somewhere. As long as the girls are happy then that is all that matters to me. I might just be able to sleep well at nights now you've told me the score." John replied philosophically.

"When I first met you, I knew we were destined to meet up again. My first Taranitian wife predicted what happened to the island would happen, but I put it down to pillow talk. And she said you would be a prominent figure in saving the islanders from even more troubles, which also turned out to be true. So you see John, life down under does have is' advantages, ball and chain included."

John smiled at Clarke's self-effacing remarks, feeling much better in himself when Clarke revealed those very intimate secrets which only the two of them seemed to have shared, despite the close friendships between himself, Larter and Sinclair

"Thank you for your moral support and shall we say, kindred spirit Aussie, I will never forget this moment." John replied sincerely.

"Hah! No worries dear 2nd. It's my payback for all the times you looked after my back. Now let's return to business before we flash up the old waterworks." Clarke remarked brazenly.

John grinned at Clarke's indomitable spirit and led the way back to the saloon.

The *Repulse Bay* surged her way through the deep blue waters of the Pacific, feeling as light as a feather as she skipped over the rhythmic breathing of the ocean when each swell kissed her bows. This was the time when the flying fish and dolphins took their turns to happily play tag with her as she thrummed her propellers when she met the next ocean swell.

It was a glorious new morning for John to be found sitting on the foc'sle smoking a well-earned cigarette as were some of the crew.

"We know it's lovely up here, but when are you going to finish off ventilating the tanks 2nd? " a sailor asked, flicking his butt over the side.

John watched the butt arc over the side of the ship to see it land almost next to the ship. He also noticed a slight wisp of fuel coming from where the cigarette butt would have landed had the ship being alongside and totally motionless.

He stood up, looking over the side of the ship for a long while, before asking two sailors to look at the place he was pointing to, and then to comment on what they saw.

"Just white water from our bow wave going down the side 2nd" they said in unison, but John continued to look closely at what he was formulating in his mind.

"Thank you for your help!" he said quickly walking down the outboard catwalk towards the stern of the ship, until he reached the stern flagpole holding the 'Red Duster' over the stern to let the world know it was a British owned ship.

He saw the 'Lifebuoy Ghost' sitting on a high-legged stool, whose job it was to lookout for anybody having the misfortune to fall overboard. It was his duty to throw a lifebuoy tied to a very long length of heaving line over the side to the unfortunate person, and to raise the alarm for the Captain to stop the ship to recover the man overboard.

"Excuse me mate, but I need you to look over first the starboard side, then the port side of the ship to see if you can find any tell-tale signs of a fuel leakage. It might just be a wisp of oil or whatever which will glisten like a rainbow in the wake of the ship." John explained, going over to the port side to look.

"No 2nd! Nothing shown, except for white water." the sentry shouted after a little while.

John detected a tell-tale ribbon of multi-coloured water telling him that there was a fuel leak coming from the ship and whilst it wasn't much, he decided it was enough for a further investigation.

"Thank you mate. It appears we've sprung a fuel leak port side, probably forward of the bridge. Please come over here to confirm what I mean." John ordered, so the man came over to see what John was pointing to.

"Yes 2nd, now you've mentioned it, you're right. I've noticed that for quite a while now especially after leaving each port. It is much more now than in the beginning, but I just put it down to you Engineers doing whatever you do to clean out the tanks, or whatever." the sailor opined.

"You obviously take turns of duty to spend your watch here. When was the first time you noticed this, shall we say, discolouring of the water?"

The sailor thought for a while before answering.

"Come to think of it, my oppo pointed it out to me when he told me not to flick my fag ends over that side, ever since we left Tonga. Said something about not being allowed to smoke when the tanks were being vented or whatever."

John thanked the sailor and went quickly towards the engine room to have a word with Hodgson.

"Chief, can I have a word?" John asked politely, meeting up with Hodgson in the engine room office.

"Hello John, what can I do for you?" came the responding civil reply.

"I have just discovered a fuel leak coming from the port side for'ard tanks. Judging by the discolouring feature of the water, it looks as if it's from the FFO tanks." John stated, pointing to a ships hull diagram, which was on top of a pile of other Engineering drawings.

He grabbed the diagram and studied it for a moment, before searching through other drawings to find what he was looking for.

"We've got a riveted hull but seam welded decks. Is this part of the Engineering experiments this ship is undergoing, or is it as designed?"

Hodgson took the drawings from John and looked at them as if pondering over just what John was asking.

"Yes John. A very good design don't you think! What is it you've discovered apart from the odd leak?"

"Unless we get to look over the side of the ship's hull to see what is what, I am not prepared to offer anything more than the fact we've been losing fuel since say Tonga, which would knock our fuel valve theory into a cocked hat."

"We're due into Ocean Island soon, perhaps we can look at the problem then. I'm not prepared to ask the skipper to slow down or stop the ship, on the request of a 2nd Engineer no matter who he is." Hodgson said gruffly.

"Fair enough with me! It's just that I need to calculate the flow of leakage in order to amend my fuel figures as submitted to the Captain." John said, shrugging his shoulders.

"Once we tie up alongside we'll both have a look-see, John. That's the best I can do for now!" Hodgson stated with less hostility.

"Whatever Chief, it's not my oil." John replied flatly and left the cabin without a second glance.

'*Now to re-appraise those bloody figures! Must get Aussie onto it.*' he mused, then went to seek out Clarke.

CHAPTER XXX

Dip Sticks

Neptune and the Gods of thunder and lightning must have smiled on the *Repulse Bay* during her transit to the sad looking Ocean Island. For when she arrived alongside the makeshift fuelling jetty, they started to make life very miserable for all concerned as they threw everything they could at her and all those still occupying the island.

For this was no ordinary peaceful, tranquil island of the so-called 'peaceful waters', but was being systematically ripped apart and taken away for the minerals the island was created from. Maybe the helpers of Mother Nature were trying to tell the destructive animals called man, it was time to leave the island in peace and not take it piece by piece.

"We've just got the FFO and the last of the diesel to offload, Aussie. Get ashore to start up the pumps, I'll see to the tank tops." John shouted into Clarke's ear, trying to shelter under one of the catwalks from the howling winds and the lashing rain.

"I'll take my flashlight to signal to you when I start up. 3 short red flashes followed by 3 short white ones. I'll do that until you signal back with 3 long white ones." Clarke responded, holding up his torch to demonstrate what he was looking for.

John nodded his head in acknowledgement, flashing 3 long white flashes with his torch, before Clarke disappeared into the storm.

The wind was buffeting the high-sided ship against the flimsy wooden fuelling jetty, which was starting to buckle and crumble under the heavy pounding it was getting.

John looked intently over to where he could just make out the pump-house, managing to see Clarke's reply signal

John remembered some of the morse code that Larter taught him, so started to tell Clarke to stay ashore as the jetty was getting unsafe to cross. As he could not remember enough to warn of the danger, he raced along the deck up into the wireless office to tell Larter what he had spotted and that Clarke needed to be told, but he wasn't up to the flashing light business.

Larter followed John quickly down to the makeshift gangway to signal the alarm instead.

"Let's hope Aussie can understand the Aldis Signal lamp John, or he'll be in deep shit if he tries to cross the wrecked jetty." Larter shouted into John's ear.

To their amazement, Clarke responded to the signalling.

"Intend to remain ashore until the transfer is completed. Besides, I found a well stocked fridge that needs liberating and samples taken before returning."

Larter spoke out the words Clarke sent, which made them both laugh at Clarke's cheeky reply.

"Bruce, tell him I'll shut off the valves this end once I've taken a tank depth sounding. Will get something organised to assist you getting back on board."

Larter sent the signal and got the reply before John was satisfied Clarke was safe and well.

"Thanks for your help Bruce. Lets hope this weather abates for a while as we're getting pretty roughed up on both side." John shouted.

"How long will the transfer take John? Only we're in for one hell of a long day stuck alongside this place, otherwise."

"About 2 hours. But I need to inspect the ships side, port side for'ard, as we've seemed to have sprung a leak."

"Sprung a leak? If we're not off this jetty then we'll get more than a bloody leak John. I'd better go and speak to Andy about getting some crash fenders over the side. See you later John." Larter responded quickly, before leaving John to his lonely vigil of watching the discharges taking place.

John was busily taking tank depth soundings, shutting off each discharge valve as it finished draining. The hollow sucking noise from the tanks was almost as loud as the roaring winds, telling him that each tank was as empty as it possibly could be, save for the few tons left, which the suction pump could not reach down to.

'Right! The transfer valves are now disconnected and the tank tops opened for ventilation. All I've got to do now is signal Aussie and tell him to shut down the pumps.' John muttered.

He went over to the now almost ruined fuel jetty then signalled Clarke to return on board.

Sinclair had arrived with some sailors who were busy putting crash barriers between the ship and the jetty.

"Andy! Do you know how deep the water is alongside?" John shouted.

"I think it's about 6 fathoms out to about 2 sea miles, then it's nearly 1000 fathoms."

"We're too high out of the water now, even the propellers are showing. If we can stop the ship from being blown against this bloody jetty all the time, we could save her from further damage."

"What have you got in mind, or need I ask?"

"I need you to help me get Aussie off the island, then for the Captain to get the vessel slipped offshore if only a few cables off the jetty."

"The jetty has had it now so all we can do is to throw Clarke a heaving line to haul him inboard."

John saw Clarke had tried to climb over the damaged jetty but was stuck almost in the middle of nowhere, fortunately for him, the jetty was in the lee of the ship, so he was temporarily safe from the ravages of the winds.

Sinclair saw Clarke and threw a heaving line towards him but the winds kept blowing it away each time.

John went over to the decks' fire fighting locker then started to connect up some hose reels, before giving it to Sinclair.

"Here Andy! I've tied one end around the catwalk stanchion. If you throw the other end to Aussie, he can use it to climb back on board."

"Good idea!" Sinclair shouted, throwing the end of the reel towards Clarke.

Clarke managing to see it coming, ducking it to avoid the heavy brass connector that was on the end, grabbing it he started to haul himself slowly but surely towards several waiting hands that grabbed him and dumped him unceremoniously onto the deck.

"Engineer Clarke I presume?" Sinclair asked with a grin.

"Strewth mate! You nearly knocked my head off with that bloody brass bit on the end of the hose. Just as well I had room to duck before I was turned into a duck and fell into the oggin to swim aboard."

Sinclair smiled telling him it was John's idea, then turned to the sailors to retrieve the hoses and get them stowed back into its locker.

"Glad you're back Aussie. Now we've got some real work to do. Andy, a word if you please." John asked.

"Will you go and tell the Captain that if he lays the ship off a few cables, we can save her from further damage by getting the tanks loaded up to sink us onto the seabed and in so doing lower our profile against these winds. We could remain at anchor there until the weather abates for us to move off, but I need to know sooner than later, so Aussie and me will get the ballast pumps and other pumps running."

"Good idea John. On my way." Sinclair responded, leaving in a hurry.

"Right Aussie. Get the 3rd Engineer to help you with the porta-pumps, and have all the fire hoses connected up to the after tanks for loading up. We can use the main ballast pump to load up the for'ard ones. Should take us about 4 hours with luck. I'm off to see the Chief, but I'll see you back here in about half an hour." John instructed.

"Alan! There's about 5 tons of diesel left in each of the tanks, so if you can get it siphoned off and put into your own supply, I can start loading the tanks up with seawater to give the ship a lower profile in this storm." John stated, explaining what he was planning, and what Sinclair was telling Denton.

"Sounds good to me John. I'll get a team of stokers up on deck to help out." Hodgson agreed, then got his engine room crew on standby for the short move off the jetty.

"I'll tell you when to stop pumping Alan, but it will take about 4 hours or so, perhaps less if we've got a few more punctures in the ships side from that jetty."

John climbed up the vertical ladder out of the warmth of the engine room onto the gale swept decks again, where he met Sinclair talking to Clarke.

"The Captain agrees with your plan, and is getting us stood off half a sea mile from the island. He says he doesn't want his hull ripped open whilst on the seabed, so you're only to load up to the 25foot mark. You can start loading as soon as you like, but no higher than that." Sinclair informed.

"Thanks Andy! You will need one of your sailors to keep a close eye on the ships depth gauge mind you, I need him to tell me when we reach that mark." John replied before turning to speak to Clarke. "Right you heard the man Aussie, lets do it. Have a few reliable stokers armed with one of the old fashioned dip sticks and make sure it gets marked to the 7,000 ton level per tank. That way we can keep our own eye on the required depth the Captain wants."

Denton had the ship moved and anchored just off shore where John had it sunk almost to the seabed. The ships de-berthing party stood in awe watching as she struggled to get clear before she started to sink slowly in front of them. It caused alarm to those watching, but when they saw that the ship was now anchored they left the ship to the mercy of the storm.

"On the 25 foot mark 2nd!" a sailor shouted, arriving to where John and Clarke were standing.

"Thank you." John replied, before turning to one of the

stokers and ordered him to go tell the engine room to stop pumping.

"Get the pumps switched off Aussie, and have the stokers return the equipment before they get between decks. I'm going up onto the bridge to see Denton, so I'll see you in the saloon in about 1 hour." John ordered, before leaving Clarke to his duties.

"Captain. Have stopped all pumping as we've reached the 25 foot mark." John stated giving his report to Denton.

"Thank you 2nd! It certainly has made the difference. I would have taken us lower, but I don't want too many high waves coming over us. I managed to find a soft area of seabed so it's all down to the anchors now." Denton responded with a grateful smile.

They spoke briefly about the weather, wondering how long they would need to remain before getting under way again. Denton spoke of the successful voyage so far and how each man on board would be getting a bonus payment, providing they arrived back in one piece.

"Well, one thing is for sure Captain. We've got a few extra dents in the ships side and an unsighted leak from the port FFO tank. If our management team wants this ship to sail on another such run, then she will need some dockyard time to get sorted out."

"Leak on the FFO tank? That's news to me 2nd! When did that happen?" Denton asked with surprise.

"From initial investigations, apparently since Tonga. But then we've just left a wrecked fuel jetty, which no doubt has made a few more dents in our side. I had reported this leak to the Chief, as I was concerned with the cargo figures and the lack of fuel so to speak."

"We'll get this sorted once we're got back into Brisbane. The ship is due to return to its own ship builders yard in Hong Kong anyway, so maybe Brisbane will just patch us up until then."

"Hong Kong? That should be interesting Captain. Due for modifications or what?"

"Yes 2nd! The *Repulse* and her two other sister ships were, shall we say, specially designed. Unfortunately there are more than the usual teething problems with this one, so it's back to the drawing board so to speak."

"Now that's where I'd like to get my teeth into." John opined, but let the matter drop, as the conversation seemed to be at an end.

"You may go now 2nd. We'll be here for another day or so. So enjoy your time off when you can." Denton stated, dismissing John with a wave of his hand.

The ship had settled herself with her bows pointing out into the storms and to the vast wastes of the ocean. This meant she was having a less torrid time than when she was riding high with her entire length exposed to the strong winds when tied up alongside the remains of the wrecked jetty. The waves were getting less angry with her, apart from the odd big one washing over the decks as if to seek out some hole to make her sink right to the bottom. They were wasting their time because this ship had certain Engineers who made sure nothing else would happen to her, so she could just ride out the storm safely anchored to the seabed.

"Maybe we can get some tucker down us now, John!" Clarke drawled, meeting up with John in the saloon.

"Might as well Aussie. We can relax now until the man upstairs stops his huffing and puffing, the Chief has stood down the engine room crew, which means we're off watch until somebody presses the start button again." John agreed amiably.

"Hello John, Aussie." Larter greeted when he too arrived into the saloon.

"Well hello stranger! What's the buzz on the weather front?" John replied with a smile.

"Tropical storm force 8 but lessening to force 6 by nightfall."

"Night fall? And here's me thinking that it was night time already." Clarke chipped in.

“That’s what becomes of living upside down under the world dear boy.” Larter teased.

“Yeah! Well maybe we’re just having a bad day then.” Clarke responded, starting a short spell of banter between them, which was broken up by the arrival of the much-awaited food.

Clarke sharpened his knife with his fork and made a wisecrack, which making them all laugh, set the tone for the rest of the meal.

CHAPTER XXXI

A Black Sausage

The *Repulse Bay* took a few days to arrive safely back into Moreton Bay, where John had her tanks pumped right out, so she could sail upriver to get herself fixed up again.

"We're riding so high it almost feels that we're skidding along on the surface, John."

"Yes, Bruce. We need as much water under our keel as possible to reach that ship repair unit, or we'll never get under the bridge let alone turn the corner. So let's hope we've got the tide with us or we'll run aground."

Larter hauled one long black sphere up to the top of his signal halyards, before hoisting up other internationally recognized signals informing other craft who they were and what was required.

John looked at the coloured display for a moment then asked what the signals meant.

"It tells everybody on the river, er, for those that can read the international signal code that is, we are limited to manoeuvre as we're restricted to and governed by our length and draught. In other words, we need the midstream part of the river and have priority over any of the smaller vessels deciding to come into it, therefore we have the right of way. Unless you're a rookie coxswain who hasn't got those internationally recognisable flags as per Harbour Masters specific instructions, then he should not have proceeded until the channel has been cleared of river traffic. International signals etcetera is definitely in force around here."

"Yes John, you're getting the hang of it. Soon I'll be able to employ you as my Signalman if you keep on." Larter grinned, ruffling John's hair for him.

"No hope there dear Bruce. Got enough on my own plate as it is. Speaking of which, have you seen Aussie loafing around?" John said, smoothing his hair back into place.

"Yes, he's on the foc'sle now."

"We'd better get him to speak to us before we get ashore. You know he's got one of those accident inquiry board meetings tomorrow. Must try and stop him getting ashore in case he does something stupid, just like he did down in Port Stanley."

Larter looked up at his signals for a moment, then back to John.

"Yes, he certainly stirred the shit up good and proper. I'm with you later on when I've shut down my radio watch. I'll see you in the saloon in about half an hour. That should give the tugs time to get us alongside the repair yard."

"See you there Bruce and don't forget to bring Andy." John responded then left in a hurry to catch up with Clarke.

"All finished Aussie?" John asked, sauntering up to him.

"All done John. I see some of the smaller tugs have come down stream to meet us. Maybe it's got something to do with that ruddy thing looking like an Abbo's dick hanging over us on the yard arm." Clarke replied, pointing pointed up to the signal.

"Probably! According to Bruce, a vessel must display those if they need the deep channels to sail in. Something to do with the vessel constrained by its own draught. Lesser vessels of shallower draught must give way. I don't know about the others though, probably a secret signal from Bruce to some female ashore."

Clarke laughed at the idea but looked thoughtfully at the long black canvas bag for a while before he grabbed John by the shoulder, which surprised and hurt him.

"That's it John! That's bloody well it! You're a genius didn't I tell you. You bloody beaut!" Clarke said almost deliriously.

John rubbed his shoulder asking him angrily what the hell was wrong with him.

"Don't you see John? Our tug is an ocean going tug therefore having a deep draught to match. We need to keep midstream to transit the upper reaches of the river until we pass the Deakins repair yard this side of the Storey Bridge. We normally make the transit when the tide is at just up over the half, but on the day of the collision, we were slightly late in reaching that point, and even then we were almost scraping the river-bed at that point. We had to remain mid stream else we'd run aground good and proper, until the full tide came back in again some 8 hours later. Our tug is the only one with the clearance to come up as far as the Victoria Bridge, which means we could not be mistaken for anybody else. Everybody knows our transit times so everybody tries to stay clear until we pass, including that bastard on the ferryboat. Just wait until I get to see my mates, I'll tell them about this, because it's bound to make the difference to them of being found guilty to manslaughter and going free.

If that bastard gets off with a slapped wrist and my mates get banged up then he can look out." Clarke finished with a cold, deadly menace in his voice.

"Yes Aussie, I'm sure you're right, but unless you control that Antipodean anger of yours you'll end up getting a lot more than you got down in the Falklands." John said quietly.

Clarke looked at John for a moment then managed to regain his composure.

"Yes, that was some stitch up just like this one is going to be. Sorry about your shoulder John, I didn't mean to." Clarke whispered, his voice faltering as he recalled the incident.

"Well Aussie. Lets put this aside until this evening, as we've got some serious number crunching to do before we hand our figures over for the management teams inspection in the morning. You and me will be meeting up with Bruce and Andy later on in the saloon. So we'll get a plan of action sorted out to help you win the day." John coaxed.

"Besides, what will your wives back in Taraniti think if you mess this one up?" he added.

"Yeah John! That sounds like a bloody good idea. We'll have a council of war meeting first before I go ashore to beat the living daylights out of the bastard." Clarke resolved, meekly following John off the for'ard tank tops and back to their little office in the engine room.

* * *

"John. I've had a message from the skipper off one of the tugs escorting us up river. It appears we have two big dents, roughly to where you suspected, plus a few others what the jetty did to us. There is water leaking from three seams of popped rivets where the plates have been stoved in, along with a series of small puncture holes the size of a golf ball in the others." Hodgson announced when John followed closely behind by Clarke, arrived down into the engine room office.

John grabbed the hull structure diagrams from the top of the usual pile of technical drawings and studied it.

"Aussie, has the yard got any hot riveters in their midst, or are they all welders?" John asked almost offhandedly to Clarke who was standing next to him.

"Yes, all bloody good welders John, but I'm the only Engineer with riveting experiences around these parts. Nearest one would be down at the big naval dockyard in Sydney. Even then it's only what I picked up the *Inverary*."

"In that case Chief. It will appear that Deakins will just have to patch weld us up until we get to Hong Kong. Look at where the plates have been damaged. Right down two transverse ribs and along part of two longitudinals. Just as well the ship's hull is a good inch and a quarter thick or we'd be like a veritable colander." John offered, handing the drawing to Hodgson for him to look at.

"Just what I diagnosed. We'll have to make a double strength patch over those areas if we're getting a full load to take with us. By the way, here're the outline details for our next voyage." Hodgson replied, handing John the outline manifesto of the next cargo load.

John looked at it with Clarke peering over his shoulder.

"60,000 tons of AVGAS for Hong Kong, Chief? We'd have to collect that further up the coast, probably from Townsville or Rockhampton. At least we'll be able to fly up there with all that aircraft fuel on board." Clarke said with surprise.

"The only fly in that ointment is if Deakins can fix the cross member ribs as well. If not then we'll be either stuck here or be sent to Hong Kong in ballast. Either way, it'll cost the company plenty in lost revenue." John opined, which made the other two Engineers nod in agreement.

"Be that as it may. We've still got a week here in Brisbane before we sail out again. In the meantime I need you both to produce your discharge figures including the final tallies before the accountant arrives in the morning." Hodgson informed his officers.

"That's just what we've come to do Alan. I shall need you to rubber-stamp our figures when we finish, as there will be certain mismatches with them due to the dodgy valves and the timing of the leakage from the for'ard FFO tank."

"That's fine by me. Oh! And before you go. Clarke, you're to remain on board and in full sight of the 2nd Engineer here, until the management team have arrived in the morning. You might just be required to offer your services to them as an acting 2nd Engineer to cover manpower shortages. So stick around if you want to get your promotion." Hodgson added almost as an afterthought.

John turned to Clarke and slapped his back gently.

"There you go Aussie. Promotion for services performed above and beyond your call of duty, as Andy would say." he said amiably.

"But that's blackmail Chief! You know I only signed on for this one trip. Besides I've got a board of inquiry to attend sometime tomorrow." Clarke said with exasperation.

"Precisely! That's why we need to make sure that when you do attend, you'll be able to show them you know exactly what you'll be talking about, instead of an almost beached 3rd rate Engineer bumming his way around the oceans." Hodgson said sternly.

Clarke went to stand cheek by jowl with Hodgson, but was prevented by John's quick intervention.

"Now let's not get too excited about your promotion. Thank the nice Chief and let's get our work done before we wet our rusty warblers." John said soothingly, standing between the two men.

Clarke looked at John for a moment, who saw the anger clouds disappear from Clarke's eyes.

"C'mon Aussie. Save it for that bastard ashore, our Chief here is on your side as we all are, so don't lose it just yet." John added smoothly, gently ushering Clarke out of the office.

"Apologies for my men Chief, maybe a touch too long in the sun these days. See you later." John whispered diplomatically, and left the office.

"C'mon you jailbird. Time for you to bend a few figures never mind a few noses!" John joked, as they entered their own little office.

CHAPTER XXXII

Good Vibes

"**Aussie!** The brass hats want to see you in the skippers' day cabin." John called as he entered Clarke's cabin, but found nobody there.

John moved quickly over to the porthole and saw Clarke just about to climb into the back of a taxi. He noted the name of the taxi firm and its telephone number then went into the saloon to meet up with his other friends.

"Aussie has just done a bunk. Here's the details of the taxi he's just taken, I think we'd better get ashore and get hold of him before he ends up in the nick for a very long time." John announced breathlessly to his other two friends.

"Bloody hell. We'd better get after him. He'll probably make his way to his tugboat friends first before he starts to tackle the ferryboat men, but then again, it's probably what he'll do first anyway, knowing Aussie's temper." Larter said quickly.

"You two had better go on. He's supposed to meet the Captain and the Chief right now, so I'll go to try to sort something out this end. We'll meet up as planned." John said hurriedly, gulping down his offered drink.

"See you John. C'mon Andy, lets get him before they do. He's got the inquiry at 1400 so we've only a few hours until then." Larter commanded, rushing out of the saloon heading ashore.

John went to Denton's Day cabin to find he was not only in company with Hodgson, but also with the Purser, and three other gentlemen.

"This is Mr Chambers and his two aides just arrived from Sydney, who've come to see us concerning 3rd Engineer Clarke. You will explain the history of what had transpired." Denton stated, introducing the men to John.

John told the waiting men what had happened, offering a

diplomatic solution to save his wayward friend from more trouble.

Chambers and the other gentlemen shook their heads in amazement at what Clarke had done or was about to do, while Hodgson and Denton spoke up offering mitigating circumstances in defence of Clarke. John was secretly surprised and delighted his two top officers were arguing against the will of Chambers and his companions.

"It appears gentlemen, that Clarke needs our help in this matter, not a witch hunt as subscribed to this minute." John started, then went on to tell them about the predicament Clarke had found himself in at Port Stanley, of how he had been vindicated in the end by what he had done.

"Okay then 2nd. We will attend this meeting as members of the public, but should he so much as disgrace our shipping company then he will no longer be considered as employable with us. In fact, never mind his promotion, you can forget it as I am seriously thinking of making the decision right now to get rid of him." Chambers pronounced.

"With respect Chambers, Clarke was hired just for the one voyage, and only then on my own recommendation. I might add that during which time he has shown a true understanding of what was required of him throughout the performance of his duties. If you wish to develop the new Taraniti complex and have somebody within, holding shall we say, company minded policies, then Clarke is your man. You can take it from me, Clarke would be an excellent promotion choice even up to the heights of Senior Engineer to oversee your ship repair unit which I understand you also wish to develop." John said swiftly trying to stave off any counter statements from Chambers or his companions.

"You seem to be well informed 2nd, I'll give you that, but as far as man management is concerned, that is my problem not yours. He remains as I have stated." Chambers said vehemently.

John sighed and went to leave, but turning round went right up to the now seated Chambers and to almost poke his face into his.

"You sir, are an absolute imbecile. It will cost you the best part of a million pounds to get a workforce relocated and settled on Taraniti. If that's what you've got in mind then you just carry on, but just remember this, Chambers. Clarke is a Taranitian Islander whom I have had the honour of training up to his current level of expertise, who is also one of the local tribal Chiefs there with a full work force of their own. So think about that and shove it right up your pompous arse when you're spending those millions." John hissed, walking out of the cabin with Chambers stammering and coughing in his attempt to demand that John was to come back again.

John paid no attention to the shouts or pleas from Hodgson and Denton to come back instead he calmly walked over the gangway and ashore to hail a taxi to take him where he was meeting his friends.

"Where did you find him Bruce?" John asked, meeting up with his friends in the foyer of the hotel.

"Trying to drown the ferryboat skipper, down at the Holman jetty." Larter said quickly as Clarke tried to extricate himself from the wrestling hold Sinclair had him in.

"Get off me you Scotch haggis yaffling caber tosser! I'm all right I tell you! I'm bloody all right so let go before I break your bloody arms." Clarke shouted angrily but was ineffectual in breaking free from Sinclair's powerful arms.

John came up to them telling Clarke they were only trying to protect him for his own good, and if he promised to behave Andy would let him go.

After much struggling and cursing, Clarke finally succumbed and agreed to the terms of his captors.

"All right then Aussie. You are on your word not to escape nor do anything that might jeopardise your tugboat mates chances with the board of inquiry." John demanded, nodding for Sinclair to release him. Clarke almost fell to the floor as Sinclair let him go.

"All right you lot. All right!" he shouted in agreement, grabbing a beer off a tray from a passing waiter then quaffed it down in almost one gulp.

"Ruddy hell Andy! It looks as if your quaff record is on the line. Look at that!" Larter said watching as Clarke drained the glass. That swift drink seemed to have settled him down from his irate outburst.

"Now that you've wet your warbler Aussie, it might occur to you that we three are only here to see that nothing befalls you during the inquiry this afternoon. It is only an inquiry not the full-blooded murder trial you think it is, even though it might just come later. So kindly accept our help, sit down and help us drink a few schooners in the meantime." John said quietly but with meaning.

Clarke studied John's face then looked around at the other two before he finally sat down heavily into a large chair.

"Fair enough John. I'll accept what you say, with my apologies and thanks to you two for stopping me from drowning that bastard." Clarke mumbled, as Larter offered him a cigarette, with Sinclair giving him another schooner of cold beer.

The tenseness of the situation eased off until John saw that Clarke was back to his old easy going self again, and for John could finally sit down next to him.

"Now then Aussie. All 4 of us have been together in this situation before, so we know the score when it comes to tribunals, inquests and the like, especially Bruce here. He has a pretty good knowledge of maritime or other laws, which are the same throughout the old Commonwealth and the dominions. You will tell him what information you have and any other items we can put together to hand into the clerk of the inquiry." John said quietly and appeasingly.

Clarke spoke slowly to them explaining what information he had gathered, of what in his opinion, should be the proper outcome of the inquiry. John, Bruce and Andy spoke only to ascertain certain points, until Clarke had finished his monologue.

"It appears Aussie, you've come across some crucial points of maritime law which perhaps, and I must emphasise, only perhaps, might influence the outcome of any decision made by the chairman of this inquiry. Providing all the relevant facts and evidence you have spoken about has been examined in full, then as far as I can see, your shipmates are in the clear. However, it'll be down to the cunning and almost criminal display by the opposition to persuade the Judge to the contrary. All we can do now is approach the clerk of the inquiry to have your testimony and evidence accepted, so it can be taken into account.

As for the rest, it will depend on the judicial side whether or not you and your mates become the prosecutors instead of the defendants facing murder, or the lesser evil of manslaughter charges." Larter informed.

Clarke scowled telling them quite emphatically what he said was the truth, and even the physical facts would bear out what he maintained.

"That dear Aussie, might be so. As I've just said, it's all down to which side can put up the best argument to blame the other. At the end of the day the lawyers will be the only winners out of this when they collect the legal aid funds from the central legal system here. They don't give two monkeys who really is at fault, just as long as they manage to feather their own pockets beforehand." John said bitterly.

"Well it ain't going to be my mates on the tug, that's for certain. I'll see to it, even if I do have to drown that weasel of a bastard ferryboat skipper. I don't mind going to the gallows for him, that's for certain. It really was him who was at fault as I've already told you." Clarke said agitatedly.

"Okay Aussue, calm down! Softly softly catchee monkey!" Sinclair said evenly, holding Clarke's shoulder to prevent him from standing up again.

John looked at the clock on the wall and told them it was time for them to get a taxi to take them to the inquiry.

"Don't forget Aussie, once we get there you'd better be on

your best behaviour, or nobody will ever listen to what you've got to say, and maybe you could be thrown into the dungeons until its all over, without you even getting another word in edgewise." John advised, as they all climbed the stone steps up into the forbidding looking building where the inquiry was to take place.

"You are one of the tug boat crew, you will be required to sit with the others. Your friends may sit over in the public gallery." The usher said pompously.

"I have my own legal representation here, so I shall bring him along with me. His name is Mr Larter, esquire." Clarke snapped, which drew an instant agreement from the usher.

Clarke and Larter were separated from the other two only by sitting in the seats directly in front of them.

"Nice and cosy Aussie. We're right behind you. Just let Bruce do the work now." Sinclair whispered into Clarke's ear.

John sat down and immediately thought of his own predicament in Bridgetown.

'Here we bloody well go again. Let's hope that Bruce is able to speak on Aussie's behalf as Belverley did for me in Bridgetown.'

"Just like old times John!" Sinclair whispered, which seemed to affirm his own thoughts.

"All rise! Commonwealth Judge Sir Mortimer of the Brisbane Maritime Commission!" the clerk of the inquiry shouted, to silence the room full of people.

A very large bewigged man with flowing black robes sauntered into the room, followed by a retinue of men who were carrying large bundles of papers and other items which were to be produced during the inquiry.

Once they had all settled down, Mortimer started to speak in a very high almost effeminate voice, which belied his enormous stature.

"Jeez! A ruddy puff ball of a woofter!" Clarke hissed, receiving a dig in the ribs from Larter for his troubles, telling him to shut up.

"This inquiry is to find out exactly what happened on the day of the incident between the tug *'Mackenzie'* and the ferry boat the '*Brisbane Whippet*'' Mortimer stated, then went on to describe the scene of the accident.

He ordered the inquest to commence, which started with the various boxes of manuscripts containing the facts, figures, statements and cross-examinations of various people.

"This is going to be one very long day. I reckon it will take at least 2 days before we get round to actual verbals from eye witnesses." Larter whispered to Clarke and the other two.

"Just as long as everything I have told you is declared, then I don't care what happens. I know my theories are correct, but it's up to you to convince the others that they are." Clarke said softly.

The inquiry adjourned for the day, but it was two days before Clarke had the chance to put his new evidence forward, which the inquiry had not, up to that time spoken or thought about, as Clarke revealed the damning evidence against the ferryboat skipper.

Larter took up the role of representing Clarke, producing all the sketches, drawings, tidal listings and other documentation to demonstrate what Clarke was telling them.

There was a hushed silence when these facts and figures were explained, which upset the legal team who were representing the ferryboat skipper.

Larter then began his defence speech.

"It appears your honour, the ferry came out into the oncoming tug as if to beat it on the turn to get the other side. The modern phrase is 'playing chicken', which means whoever gives way first is the loser. The tug's mean draught is around the 12 foot mark, however, whereas as the ferry has only got a 3foot draught which means it can turn into waters much too shallow for the tug. The tug was showing a a long black cylinder, which means in international law, that the vessel is restricted in its movements due to its own draught. The mid-channel at that time was just over the 2 fathom mark which is the same draught of the tug. Should the tug venture into shallower water then the first thing the Engineer would know long before the Captain of the vessel, is that his propellers would be striking the river bed causing untold damage to them, let alone causing the vessel to go aground.

I re-iterate the facts as presented. The ferryboat is a much smaller vessel but with a higher speed and manoeuvrability in shallower waters, it had come out into the mid-stream area without warning, and into the waters occupied by the tug. In short, right into the path of the oncoming tug

The tug was on a well-known and timed transit down river, and she has to remain in the mid-channel to save her from coming to grief. It is apparent the ferryboat tried to outrun the tug but misjudged his timing, thus was simply run down by the tug limited to the said mid-stream waters. His ferryboat was virtually overloaded with passengers thus causing the vessel to handle sluggishly not only with her speed but also her steering capabilities. However, I can offer a like for like and a succinct comparison between the two can be made thus:-

A pedestrian steps off a pavement onto the roadway and directly into the path of an oncoming vehicle a few feet away. The driver of that vehicle would have had no chance to take avoiding action even though he had perhaps the full road to do so. The person deemed to be at fault in the resulting fatal accident, would be the pedestrian not the vehicle driver.

Having made this comparison, it is therefore my client's opinion it was the fault of the ferryboat skipper that caused the fatal collision and not the fault of the tug and her crewmen.

Finally, and not to put a finer point on these proceedings, I have another factor which I wish to mention on my clients behalf, possibly the main factor which you might wish to examine in greater detail.

The ferryboat skipper has interests in a tugboat who is in direct competition to our clients. Therefore on the news that the ship the *Repulse Bay*, currently tied up in the Deakin's ship repair yard was to be moved down stream for further repairs, the *Mackenzie* had to be delayed awhile for the rival one to reach the ship first, therefore gaining the contract. Perhaps the ferryboat skipper's action was merely to have the *Mackenzie* swerve to cause it to go aground, but did not take into account that a possible collision could happen causing the deaths of his passengers." Larter concluded.

The entire room fell completely silent for several moments before the judge cleared his throat to offer his deliberations.

"It appears all this new evidence sheds a completely different light on the events. I shall therefore call for an adjournment to enable these new facts and figures to be taken into consideration. This matter will be concluded in one months time as announced by the clerk of the inquiry." Mortimer stated, before rising to take his leave.

"All rise. Judge Mortimer is leaving this inquiry. All parties involved in it will meet here in exactly one month from now, as per calendar dates." The clerk announced in a loud booming voice.

"There you are Aussie, you had your say and yet you're still able to come with us for a few beers. Not like in Port Stanley." Sinclair said with a smile, shaking Clarke's hand followed swiftly by the other two.

Clarke gave a big grin and gave a mock salute to his three friends in turn.

"I must have been a ruddy 'goliah' back then. Mine's a full schooner of the amber nectar, not forgetting one of your glasses of Nelson's blood." he said jovially, as they left the impressive building making their way back to their hotel.

Once there, John told Clarke what had happened on the ship, but suggested he thought seriously on it let alone the seemingly obvious results of the inquiry.

"So that's what that clown Chambers thinks. I've got news for him, we, the ocean going tugboat fraternity here in Brisbane that is, have got together with a shipping baron called Hunter. We've already got the salvage contract for Taraniti including all the other nearby group of islands. But this man Hunter wants us to set up a ship repair unit based at Taraniti, as the last stop repair yard this side of the Pacific. I'm the senior Engineer within our company but am still not qualified to take on the ship repair skylark. Which is why I've been doing moonlight shifts with Deakins to get myself all clued up, and why I volunteered to team up with John on this trip, just so I could learn the best from the best." Clarke confided in his usual 'Gung Ho' attitude.

"Thank you for your vote of confidence in me Aussie, but I feel that you might be passing up a golden opportunity to get promoted up the proverbial ladder. We sail shortly for Hong Kong with you being the acting 2nd Engineer. If you did, then at least when you come back here, your papers would be marked down as a 2nd instead of a 3rd. Again and I must say, this Hunter fellow would look more favourably towards promoting a 2nd up to his Repair unit Superintendent Engineer instead of a 3rd. Maybe you should think very seriously on this matter, never mind this inquiry, for whatever the outcome it appears you have the insight of your people to draw upon to guide you." John countered.

Clarke saw a look on John's face, which told him John was speaking from the heart, but influenced by his spiritual experiences on leaving Taraniti.

"You appear to be getting a visitation experiencing the good vibes from TeLani and the rest of the tribes on Tarnaiti, John. It is good you do, because I will listen to what you have said and act upon my own visitations when they arrive. I also have got similar vibes concerning this court case. Thanks to Brucie and his clever way of putting our case to the judge, we'll be the ones let off and that piece of shit the ferryboat skipper will be jailed for a very long time." Clarke said quietly, shaking John's hand in a gesture of good will towards a kindred spirit.

"So that was why Captain Joe Tomlinson was always in the

know as to what was going to happen. Like a psychic or crystal ball gazer in the fair ground and all that." John said slowly, with a faraway look on his face.

"Yes John. Believe me, since our recent visit to Taraniti it has upped the stakes for all four of us, life will not be the same. Life must take it's own course without our interference. It's just we'll be able to make our own choices much more easily and for the better, that's all. It's why I only signed on for just the one voyage John, and why I'm staying ashore to rejoin my old tugboat mates. Lastly, that's why I had to speak my piece at the inquiry these last few days." Clarke concluded, as the friends settled down to yet another large schooner of the amber nectar.

CHAPTER XXXIII

So Long

John woke early and decided to take a shower before getting dressed for the day.

He enjoyed the early mornings when people were still in the land of the nod and the sun was just peeping over the horizon before the cool of the morning was spirited away by the smiling suns rays.

'Time for an early morning cuppa before the circus hits town again.' John mused, trying to tiptoe out of the hotel room thinking his friends were still asleep.

"Morning John. If you wait a mo, I'll come with you." Clarke whispered, appearing almost fully dressed as if from nowhere.

John merely nodded and held the door open for Clarke who was hopping on one leg, trying to pull on his shoes as he went along.

"Only going for a quiet stroll along the river before breakfast Aussie." John whispered, when Clarke finally caught up with him. They strolled along the street, down to the river before sitting on a bench overlooking a small part of the river.0

"We've got to report back today Aussie, but from what you said yesterday, it appears you'll not be returning with us. If that is so, then I'll send your belongings over to the repair yard office for you. But what will happen to you now?" John asked during an indulgent leisurely smoke.

"Must stay for this inquiry John. Me mates have had their tug impounded upstream in their own caisson basin until the verdict, but that bastard of a ferryboat skipper is still free to operate and earn his dollar a day. But before you say anything more, no I shall not be going near him. In fact I'm on my way back to Taraniti on one of the other tugs who're going to retrieve a stranded ship out there. I should be back in time for the verdict as it's only a 4 week return trip at the most."

"Sorry you're leaving Aussie, we will miss your bad manners and all your Antipodean and barmy logic, me especially. There are only two things I ask of you Aussie, one, that you earn your spurs by becoming a top-rate Engineer and be an upstanding citizen of your islands. The other one is that you keep in touch with me and let me know of TeLani and the children. I have always tried to impart as much engineering know-how to you, and teach you the proper ways of the engineering world. You do intend to improvise, which on occasion is fine, but you really must not try not to cut engineering corners just for the sake of it, or you'd become a real cropper if you do. As for me, I'm due to become a student of the International Shipbuilders College as soon as I get my next promotion, but for now, a trip up to Hong Kong to where the *Repulse Bay* was built." John said sombrely, keeping his gaze on the small flotilla of ducks swimming upstream and past them.

"John, I must confess that nearly everything I know, I learned from you. I do have my own ambitions as you know, but it will all be done on Taraniti. I shall keep in touch with you as and when the time is right, you need not worry about TeLani and everyone there. Just remember everything TeLani and her mother told you, to honour their wishes, for that's all they want off you now until you're in the deep 6." Clarke responded with equal candour, then standing up, offered his hand.

"Now I must go John Grey. I wish you and your mates well. Keep the faith with TeLani and act on what your vibes tell you, for you to live a ripe old age just like I have been promised. Tell the lads that I said 'so long' but will see them off when they leave the Deakins yard." Clarke said sadly, and shaking John's hand firmly but gently, embraced him like brother to brother.

"So long you Aussie reprobate." John whispered, watching Clarke leave him.

Clarke only went a few yards before turning round, retracing his steps.

"You will not be sailing with the ship. Don't ask me right

now how I know, but my vibes are telling me, and they're usually 100% genuine. It is very important you tell Bruce and Andy to be on the deck looking out for me when the ship leaves the yard. This is my final farewell to you John, and my final payback to you for all you have done for me over the time we've spent at sea together." Clarke breathed, then turned around to leave John non-plussed by this sudden burst of secret information.

'We'll be best shipmates for ever Aussie, just like Bruce, Andy and me are.' John finally managed to whisper at the distant figure of Clarke.

John returned to the hotel room to find the other two had just got up, getting ready for their breakfast.

"Morning you two lazy sods! Aussie is already on his walkabout." John greeted, which gave way to a good- natured banter session between three very close friends.

The three friends walked into the dining room to take their breakfast, with John explaining albeit with a lump in his throat, about Clarke, and what he had advised.

"If Aussie tells us this then that is what we shall do." Sinclair admitted.

"It appears all three of us are somehow linked with Aussie and Taraniti, although I cannot fathom out why. I understand the bond and feeling I had with Helena, also the entirely new but even more potent bond with Princess TeLani. I also know of the spiritual and human bonding Aussie has with his people on Taraniti. Maybe it's something about our close friendships and the inclusion of Aussie Clarke's existence within our, shall we say, embrace, has or is starting to affect us all. Maybe if we..." John said quietly with emotion, before he was interrupted.

"There is no need to explain how you feel John. Bruce and I share the same feeling as you, although maybe not as strong, considering you were the chosen one for those Taranitians, Aussie was an Islander anyway, and we only happened to be there at the time to get involved." Sinclair said softly.

"Yes John. This is something the three of us cannot express in words just in our feelings. Sufficient to say, we three share a special relationship above and beyond the realms of just being shipmates, with an added bonus in the shape of Aussie Clarke. Then again, let's not forget those who were with us on the *Invergarron*. Mention one mention all was the order of the day if I remember." Larter added, with equal sombreness.

The three friends discussed the possible outcome of the inquiry, of what they though of their missing friend, until Matthews, who on finding them, made his way over to them, interrupted them.

"Mr Larter, there you are. I am expecting some re-directed mail, which I need for our next voyage. Would you kindly go and bring it on board for me. I understand there is quite a backlog of mail to pick up so I suggest you take a helping hand with you." Matthews requested but seemed to be an implied order.

"Certainly Purser. I shall take 3rd officer Sinclair with me. Be kind enough to inform the Captain I have done so, just in case he's looking for him." Larter replied evenly, nodding to Sinclair to agree with him.

"On our way Purser." Sinclair said, rising up to carry out the 'request'.

"See you both later. Don't forget what we've been talking about. I shall be in the engine room with the Chief if you need me." John replied, watching his two friends leave the saloon.

CHAPTER XXXIV

Arrive Safely

John was standing inboard side of the ship, watching the ship getting ready to move down stream to where it would load up with her stores and the like for the next voyage.

He noticed that both Larter and Sinclair had managed to get on board before the gangway was taken off some ten minutes earlier, so decided to go and meet them in Matthew's office.

John saw several sacks of mail, which were being systematically opened, with the contents being allocated to the various crew's quarters where the recipients would receive their mail.

"Here're two for you John. This one must be urgent as it's a ships telegram." Larter stated, handing John a small brown envelope along with a large Hodgson one that looked very official.

John looked at the postmark of the Hodgson one before he ripped open the small brown one

'To 2nd Engineer John Grey, MS Repulse Bay. c/o Deakins Ship Repair Yard. Kangaroo Point Brisbane. Queensland. Australia.

Dad died on Tuesday morning in Lisburn hospital. The funeral's on a week Friday. Hope you can make it. Love Mam.'

John stood in shock at the news but managed to hand it over to Larter to read, which he did out aloud.

Matthews who along with the other two, offered their swift and sincere display of condolences, prompting Matthews to tell him he would get the clearance for John to take his leave to attend the funeral, joined both his friends.

"We'll get your things packed John, then escort you to the airport." Sinclair said swiftly, putting his large arm around John as if to steady him in his moment of sudden grief.

"Yes Grey. Leave the manpower to your Captain and me. I'll phone the agent for him to book you on the next flight back to the UK." Matthews advised, picking up a ship's telephone, speaking directly to the Captain on his internal phone link.

"The Captain says he's sorry to hear of your bereavement to sanction for you to leave as soon as possible. He will arrange with the management team to have you rejoin the ship again, probably in Hong Kong. In the meantime you will be required to take certain 'baggage' back with you, which you will drop off when you arrive in London. I am to arrange that as well." the Purser announced, putting the phone gently back into its cradle.

"Right then 2nd Engineer. About turn! Quick march! And get to your cabin right now." Sinclair barked, like a sergeant major on the parade ground.

The friends marched out of Matthew's office, arriving quickly into John's cabin.

"Just you get changed into your civvy clobber John. We'll pack your bags and make certain you've got enough supplies for the flight, even though you'll probably get enough duty frees whilst on board.

The Purser will arrange for your flight back to the UK probably by Quantas to Singapore. Then by BOAC via Delhi, Constantinople, maybe Zurich, before getting to London airport. That's the quickest route anyway." Larter explained, so John simply did what he was ordered to do by his friends.

"Now John. Maybe you can drop a few letters off for us in the airports local post-box when you get home, as you'll probably arrive long before the postal service can deliver it from here. Matthews will be giving you some leave pay along with your appropriate travel warrants. Make sure you come back on the day they state, or you'll be paying your own fare back." Sinclair added.

"Not only that, make sure you don't bump into any of Belverley's cronies when you have to report to this shipping agent's office, which after all, is only next door to theirs." Larter advised.

John was listening to the advice offered by his two friends, as he got dressed ready to go.

"Do you realise what Aussie told me has turned out to be true. I have a strange feeling about all this, and according to Aussie I must act upon my 'vibes' as he calls them. Promise me you both will look after yourselves, because these vibes tells me something awful might happen between now and when we all meet up again. Please don't ask me about all this, but look out for each other." John said in a still voice, almost like a whisper.

Larter and Sinclair looked at each other then at John to see he was almost in a trance-like state when he said it.

"John. We will do as you ask that is a promise, but you had better make sure you return in one piece." Larter said slowly, with Sinclair nodding his head in agreement.

"Right then 2nd Engineer Grey. Let's get you ashore by way of the Pursers office." Sinclair said abruptly, breaking the solemnity of the moment.

The friends left Matthew's office with the sacks of mail and other deliveries which were due to be made by John, then walked swiftly over the gangway to an awaiting taxi.

"Take him to the airport, but make sure he gets on his flight. Here's a 5 spot to cover the trip." Larter ordered, handing the taxi driver the money.

"No worries mate. His flight is not due out for another few hours, but thanks for the tip anyway." The taxi driver said, pocketing the money then loaded up his vehicle with all the bags of mail.

"See you in Honky Fidd, John! Don't forget to drop our letters off as soon as you land in Blighty." Larter said with a grin and shook John's hand in farewell.

"Aye John! You'll probably be in Hong Kong before us, so keep the bar seats warm for us." Sinclair said, also shaking John's hand in farewell.

"See you there, but remember what I told you and what Aussie and I spoke about. Be careful my friends." John replied, waving to them when the taxi sped away from the ship.

"They must be good mates of yours then mate!" the taxi driver stated amiably, driving along the busy streets of Brisbane.

"Yes. I'm also leaving behind another special mate, who is involved with his tug and a ferryboat incident. I hope he and his shipmates get proper justice, especially from the way I witnessed it." John started to say, before the taxi driver interrupted him.

"Well he better not be part of the tugboat crew, as me and me mates intend giving them their come- uppance. I lost my Sister and brother-in-law with their two children, thanks to those drunken killers. Me mate on the ferryboat got drowned along with his intended bride who should have been married the next day." The driver snarled, expressing his anger and disgust at the whole affair.

John listened to the man's anger but never interrupted him until it was time to get out at the air terminal.

"This is my stop driver. But I would suggest you take the time to investigate exactly what really happened that day, before you take liberties of your own. Before you do, do yourself a bloody big favour and start thinking on this. Judging by the way you drive, some day and it will be soon, a child will appear from nowhere right in front of you. Just what would the result be to the inquiry into the death of the child? I would suggest you'd be exactly in the same position as them, mater! Would you be considered to be a drunken murderer like them or what?" John stated angrily, slamming the door of the vehicle, causing the door glass panels to rattle. The taxi man gave John a blank stare before he roared off to his next hirer, leaving John with a big pile of mailbags and other luggage to gather up for him to take into the air terminal

John's flight to Singapore was arduous but not as much as his flight to London. He was thankful for the chance to stretch his legs on each stop of the flight, even though it was only within the changing scenery of the different airport lounges.

He read and reread the in-flight booklet about the planes he flew in, comparing the differences between the 4 propellers of the Bristol Britannia that QUANTAS operated, with the four powerful jet engines of the Comet Mk IV that BOAC used for his flight back home.

'This means I've now traversed the globe although in more than one aircraft. Perhaps each different aircraft has its own problems just like the different ships I've been on. The main thing is, as long as we arrive safely without using parachutes then I suppose it doesn't matter. Come to think of it, we've always got lifebelts in view everywhere, so where have they hidden the parachutes?' John mused, drifting off into yet another catnap before being rudely oaken up by an insistent stewardess telling him to belt up, ready for another landing.

His aircraft finally touched down safely onto British soil, and John left the plane for the last time.

'Now for the Heysham boat train from Euston, let's hope I can make it on time.' he mused, as he was waved through the customs barrier to board the air terminal coach that would take him to his train station.

"Mr Grey. We have a gentleman from your shipping agent who wishes to have a word with you." the pretty stewardess announced as she presented the man to him.

"2nd Engineer Grey? I'm the Belfast agent, sent to pick up your parcels." the stout man announced, showing John his security badge.

"Pleased to meet you. Yes, there are 5 brown and 2 blue bags on the wagon behind us. I've only got my own luggage with me." John responded, standing up from his seat, pointing to the lorry being loaded with the passengers' luggage and other items.

"Fair enough. Here's the receipt for them, with further instructions for you when you arrive back in Belfast. We shall meet again in five days at the address I've given you. Enjoy your holiday!" the man quipped as he turned to leave.

"I'm not on leave pal! I've come home to bury my father. Now piss off before I stick one on you." John responded angrily, the man had obviously not heard him, so he vowed to have a word with him next time he went back to the Belfast HQ..

***

John sensed there was a massive change and air of arriving home again. The house somehow looked much smaller now, the cinder path down the side of it seemed to have become overgrown, his dog was now just padding along slowly instead of racing towards him. The front door seemed to need a good lick of paint, as much as the hinges needed some oil to stop them squeaking.

"Ma I'm home!" John greeted as he entered the hallway of the spacious cottage.

His sisters and each of their children greeted him first before he finally embraced his weeping mother.

"Glad you're home son. Come in and have some breakfast." she said tearfully, and ushering him into the kitchen sat him by the roaring fire.

John had his breakfast then dished out the customary presents to his sisters and the children before he finally gave his mother hers.

He sat and talked about what had happened to his father and whatever plans were for the day of the funeral before he explained that he was due to return to his ship again.

"It was nice of them to allow you to come all this way. Your last lot wouldn't have done that anyway. You must have a good Captain or whomever." his mother stated, looking around the room at her brood of children with her grandchildren running around noisily, getting into all kinds of mischief that children usually get up to. They were not to know, as they were all too young to understand their grandfather was in his coffin in the front parlour, awaiting his burial.

The day of the funeral was a kind one for the family, as the rain held off until they were back into the safety of the cottage.

"Just as well the church is this end of the Blacks Road, not right up the top. Look at the rain coming down." John said quietly to his sisters, looking out of the kitchen window.

All the family were engrossed in the after burial event, which lasted into the evening and time for John's sisters and brothers to leave for their own homes.

"I leave in two days time dear mother. So we'll get all the legal stuff along with the other paperwork done before then." John whispered to his still weeping mother.

"You're a good son. Please stay with me. Don't go back to your ship, get another one that sails around the coast." she pleaded.

John embraced his mother, telling her that he really must finish his job on board his ship before he went onto another. He explained it was the way of things, and besides he was due to come home soon anyway. He did not have the heart to explain to her the way of things on board, nor what had happened to him whilst he was away all these months.

"I'm sure you're doing the right thing John, but isn't it time you found yourself a wee girl and settle down now. Leave the sea for her to have a family perhaps?" she asked hopefully.

John's thoughts turned swiftly to Helena, then of TeLani and her children, but shook his head slowly.

"Mam! I'm not leaving the sea until I've got my Chief Engineers promotion. Maybe when that happens I can look out for a wee girl as you put it then. In the meantime dear mother, it's about time we all got to bed. Tomorrow's another day." John said softly, before kissing her on her cheek to go upstairs to his bedroom.

"Night son!" she called as he shut the door quietly behind him, leaving her to sit quietly by the flickering embers of the log fire.

TRB

The Repulse Bay is the seventh book within the epic
Adventures of John Grey series, which comprises of:

A Fatal Encounter
The Black Rose
The Lost Legion
Fresh Water
A Beach Party
Ice Mountains
The Repulse Bay
Perfumed Dragons
Silver Oak Leaves
Future Homes

Also by the same author
Moreland and Other Stories

All published by Guaranteed Books, an imprint of
www.theguaranteedpartnership.com